THE VAMPY

RedEye

G. P. Taylor is the author of several best-selling novels, including *Shadowmancer*, *Shadowmancer: The Curse of Salamander Street*, *Wormwood* and *Tersias*, as well as the *Mariah Mundi* trilogy. A former vicar of Cloughton in Yorkshire, he has enjoyed a varied career, moving from rock music to social work to ten years in the police force before his ordination. He now lives with his family in Scarborough.

Praise for *Mariah Mundi*

'When Harry Potter hangs up his wizard's cloak, booksellers will be looking to G. P. Taylor's *Mariah Mundi: The Midas Box* to keep the cashtills ringing.' BBC News

'It really is wonderful, wonderful stuff . . . Mariah Mundi surpasses Potter on just about every level there is. Highly recommended.' *The Bookbag*

'The book that combines the big story of C. S. Lewis and the plot of an Indiana Jones movie. We could genuinely be looking at the book series that will replace Harry Potter at the top of every child's wish list.' *BuddyHollywood Review*

by the same author

Praise for *Shadowmancer*

'The biggest event in children's fiction since Harry Potter.'
The Times

'The adventure unfolds at a vivid and breathless pace.' *Observer*

'*Shadowmancer* is flying off the bookshelves as if a wizard had
incanted a charm on it.' *Herald*

'A magical tale of vicars and witches.' *Daily Telegraph*

'A compelling and dark-edged fantasy . . . highly recommended.'
Independent

Praise for *Wormwood*

'*Wormwood* is breathtaking in scope . . . an extraordinary
achievement told by a master storyteller. The book is, quite simply,
marvellous.' *Guardian*

Praise for *Tersias*

'It is, in a word, brilliant. Colourful, dramatic, relentless, accessible
to children – and more frightening for their parents.' *Scotsman*

'The plot hurtles along carrying the reader from one cliff-hanger
to the next.' *Daily Telegraph*

THE VAMPYRE LABYRINTH

RedEye

G. P. Taylor

faber and faber

First published in 2010
Faber and Faber Ltd
Bloomsbury House
74–77 Great Russell Street
London WC1B 3DA

Typeset by Faber and Faber Ltd
Printed in England by Mackays of Chatham plc, Chatham, Kent

A CIP record for this book
is available from the British Library

ISBN 978–0–571–22694–8

2 4 6 8 10 9 7 5 3

In regard to

The Vampyre Quartet

THERE WAS ONCE a time in England when no one would ever believe in a creature that stalked the streets at night, taking its pick of anyone who dare stray out after dark. Those who spoke of such a thing would be thought of as foolish and contemptible.

Eight hundred and sixty-six years ago all that changed. It was then that the first legends were spoken about a quartet of creatures that could live for ever. It was said that immortal monsters, capable of both love and murder, had chosen to live in the world of man. They were a secretive, deceptive and powerful enemy of humankind who desired one thing from us – blood.

In the dark north, even to this day the belief in four such monsters persists. Much has been written of the creatures. Sceptics have denounced the legends as poppycock and the ramblings of a flibbertigibbet. Others far wiser have spoken of what they have heard in whispers and have locked their doors and windows, never inviting a stranger to cross their threshold after dark.

This is especially so in the small coastal town of Whitby – the place where the legend began and where some would say it continues. You may have heard of the place and the beasts that prowl its streets. Some dare not give them a name, but to those who are willing they are known as the Vampyre Quartet . . .

RedEye

[1]

Brick Lane – 7th September

JAGO HARKER ran through the streets clutching the small leather bag that contained his whole world. His fingers were tightly entwined with those of the woman he pulled along. She stumbled on the broken glass that littered the pavement as they both weaved in and out of the smashed market stalls of Brick Lane.

The whole of London seemed to be fleeing, a mass of people frightened from their homes by the exploding iron caskets that fell from the sky. Far to the east they could hear the bombs begin to explode on the Isle of Dogs. Jago looked up. The sky was filled with aircraft. They were like the black shadows of a flock of small birds against the blue sky of that late afternoon. He could not believe what he saw. It was like the swirls of starlings that would winter-roost on the top of his flats in Old Nichol Street, Shoreditch.

The aircraft were soon overhead. He listened as the low hum of their engines echoed in the street. His mother clutched his hand tightly as Brick Lane began to explode behind them. A bomb landed on what was left of the market. It blasted two barrow stalls high into the air, splintering the frightened crowd with shards of wood. All was silent for the briefest moment as Jago gripped his mother close to him and pulled her instinctively into the doorway of a tobacconist's shop.

The earth shuddered. Screams rang out as a bomb blew out the front of the pub on the corner of Bethnal Green. The street was filled with thick white dust that blotted out the sun and covered the bodies in the road like a fall of snow. The crowd ran, children screamed, an old woman stood shaking as she looked around helplessly. The air-raid siren wailed a few streets away as the thud, thud, thud moved slowly to the west.

'You have to get away . . . It's all arranged,' Jago's mother said, her voice in panic as she tied the label on to his leather jacket. 'A good school – nice town. I spent some time there myself.'

'But I want to stay with you,' Jago protested as he tried to untie the string and the cardboard tag.

'It's all decided. You are being evacuated tonight. You've got to get away from the bombing. It's important.' His mother tried to smile but just looked even more concerned.

'I'm fifteen. I don't want to go. Only *children* get evacuated.'

His mother looked at him and held his face in her hands.

'I know,' she said. 'But do this for me.'

She reached to her bag that was slumped in the corner of the shop doorway. For a while she fumbled inside, looking through scraps of paper until she found what she had been searching for. Without a word, she handed Jago an old sepia photograph.

He stared at it for a while as the whir of the bombers faded away.

4

'Who is it?' he asked as he looked at the two young girls not much older than him leaning against the ruins of a stone pillar on a sunny day.

'It's me, and an old friend,' she said softly, as if the thought brought back a fond memory.

'When was it taken?' he replied, unable to believe that the woman in the photograph was his mother.

'Sixteen years ago in the town where you are going. It's a good place – now promise me that whatever happens . . . you will go there. Keep the picture and find her. She's called Maria. You must find her.'

Her voice was insistent. Jago knew it would be pointless to refuse.

'But I will come back. As soon as I hear this is over. I'll be back – understand?'

His mother nodded, smoothed back his long black hair and kissed him on the forehead. Jago was tall for his age, his angular features and olive skin a welcome sight to all who knew him.

'We better get going. It's a long walk to King's Cross.' She stopped, thought and then went on as if she had to add something important. 'Everything will work out for the good – never forget that.'

The dust in the street settled. His mother looked out from the doorway anxiously. Jago listened for enemy aircraft. They heard a distinct drone, a drawl of anger like a wounded animal. He waited before he moved.

'All clear,' he said confidently.

His mother had grown to trust his uncanny knack of seeing the future. Jago was always able to tell if an air attack was coming. He would often wake in his sleep and drag her from the bed to the shelter below their overly tidy flat in Abingdon House, Old Nichol Street. If the unseen, unheard warning came sooner, he would take her to the Underground station at Aldgate and wait for the bombing to start. He would tell her when the bombers were overhead, and even though they were deep below the city they would feel the tremble of the explosions above them.

She was always astonished that he would know the bombers were coming an hour before the siren started to wail. It was as if he had a sixth sense, that he could glimpse the future, but then again, he was so much like his father.

Jago could not make the comparison. His father had never been mentioned to him. He didn't know what he looked like or where he was from. His mother kept that a guarded secret. As far as he was aware, there had been just Jago and his mother, Martha, all his life. No family, few friends and no one who had known them longer than when his mother came to London fifteen years ago. When he had tried to talk about his father, he was met with a wall of silence, a solemn look at the floor and a tightening of the lips. Jago had learnt not to ask. His mother had learnt not to look so closely at her son and see in him the man who was his father.

Yet that was so hard for her. As he grew in age and learning, Jago looked just like the man she had met all those years ago. She had been seventeen; it was the day of the photograph that her son now gripped in his hand.

'We'll have to be going,' she said impatiently, as if she was irritated by the frequency of the bombings. 'The night train leaves at seven o'clock from Platform 9.'

She spoke as if she had to give him this vital piece of information. Then without another word, she dug in her pocket and handed him a tattered brown envelope stuffed with crisp five-pound notes. Jago had never seen so much money.

'Where did you get this?' he asked.

'You'll need it. There's fifty pounds – keep it safe,' she replied as she pushed him from the doorway and picked her way through the debris that filled the junction with Bethnal Green.

'But . . . but I never knew we had so much money,' he argued as he followed on.

'I've been saving it. Didn't want to spend until there was a good reason,' his mother said coldly as she walked ahead clutching her bag.

'But you don't earn five pounds in a month – how did you get all this?' he asked as he stuffed the wad deep inside the pocket of his leather coat.

'It was sent . . . to pay the rent. That's all you need to know.'

'Who by?' he asked as a building further down the road collapsed, sending a pall of dust high into the afternoon sky.

'Never you mind. Someone kind . . . very kind.' She scolded him with a smile.

The street hung heavy with acrid smoke. There was no wind or ounce of breeze. Jago could see the plumes of flames from the houses on Petticoat Lane. He tugged his mother by the arm of her coat and tried to hold her close so as not to be lost in the crowd of people that pushed them on like flotsam on a human tide. He looked at the worried faces of those who pressed close to him. Some stared with deep, rimmed eyes and already looked dead; others seemed to have life. It was as if those who would not make it had been marked for death and were already, in some strange way, leaving this world. They were half alive, doing all that you would do but waiting to go on, though not knowing their fate. Jago panicked and wanted to close his eyes. A woman several years younger than his mother looked at him. He shuddered as he saw what looked like wisps of her soul pouring from her eyes like a thick white vapour. She scurried ahead with a flock of children around her waist, shouting as she pushed through the crowds of people.

His mother pulled the collar of her coat even higher. Jago couldn't see her face for the hat that was pinned to the side of her head. It looked more like a brown dinner plate with two fake roses sewn on to it.

The bombing had blown out the fronts of the tall grey houses on City Road. The crowds had gone and they walked alone through the deserted streets towards King's Cross station. Jago was surprised by how silent the world was, even in war. There were no cars, buses, no rumble of the Underground. All he could hear were faint distant voices and the occasional bell of an ambulance far away. What people there were had gone north towards Hampstead. All they now passed were row on row of empty houses. Some were bombed out, some boarded, and others just left with their doors open as if waiting the imminent return of those who lived there.

His mother was intent on seeing him off. He knew it was to make sure he caught the train. His leather bag felt heavier than it had before and grew more cumbersome with each mile they walked. The man in the flat downstairs had made

8

it for his last birthday. He had known Jago since he was born. Cresco would often look after him when his mother was at work. He was always avuncular and kind, and would tell him stories about the eastern land of Garbova, somewhere near the Black Sea, and the great castle that overlooked the town.

Jago didn't mind being left with 'Uncle' Cresco – the stories he told were magical and came to life. Cresco would smile at him as he spoke, his face would wrinkle and his thick brows would rise higher with every word as Jago listened. He would tell him of the great evil that took the land and how one man with a brave heart overcame it all.

On the mantelpiece above the fire was a golden cup that Cresco had said had once belonged to the King of Garbova. It was the only thing of value that he had in the tiny apartment. The cup was polished and worn. It was edged with faded reliefs of strange animals that were almost rubbed bare.

In one story he had told Jago that to drink from the cup would give protection from any harm between two full moons. Cresco had taken the chalice, poured in a slosh of red wine and, as he told the story, sipped from the gold cup. Then he handed it to Jago. At first he hesitated, as the sweet smell of the wine seemed to fill the room. Cresco talked more and more; his words were like a magical spell that entranced Jago as he stared at the wine that shimmered in the light of the fire.

'The Cup of Garbova – the cup of crimson wonder,' Cresco had said, and in that moment he looked fifty years younger. 'Found by Krakanu, a boy like yourself, Jago. The Apsara – an evil creature had stolen the sun and the moon and the world had no light. Krakanu searched the caves underneath Castle Garbova and killed the demon. When he stabbed the beast through the heart, the cup fell from within it. Three drops of its blood smeared the side. Krakanu drank from the cup and was unbeatable in battle. Here, Jago – drink – for your own good – you never know when the battle will come to your door.'

Jago had reluctantly drunk from the cup. He felt no different. Cresco looked at him and smiled. Jago would never forget seeing the tears in the man's eyes.

The leather bag, like his coat, had taken Cresco many hours to cut out and sew together. Each was finished with elaborate stitching. His mother had told him that Cresco was once the tailor to the Tsar of Russia and that he had fled to London. Cresco himself was far too humble a man to ever mention such a fine thing.

As he walked, Jago looked at the bag. In it was everything he owned, everything he was being forced by his mother to take. Even Cresco had left him a parting gift wrapped in newspaper and stuffed in the bottom of the bag. From the smell, Jogo knew it must be wurtzl sausage or smoked fish.

If he could have had his way, Jago would have gone back to the apartment and taken his chances. He would have run with his mother to the night shelter when the bombers came, and shopped for her during the day.

Cresco had stayed.

'Nothing makes me run any more,' Cresco had said to him that morning when Jago had told him he was being evacuated. 'I have spent too much time running. Now I stand and fight. This is my country now. I am an Englishman. I will

10

stand in the park and shake my fists at those bombers – they won't kill Cresco – I have drunk too many times from the cup.'

Jago hadn't believed him. He was an old man who often wandered the landing of the apartment block in just his underpants and shirt, with remnants of his breakfast tucked in his grey beard. Cresco had escaped from a forgotten odd corner of Europe that in his mind was a fearful place of ghosts and phantoms. The war had followed him through Austria and France and only a narrow strip of water stood between him and the old enemy.

Now, Jago knew his life was changing. Cresco's stories were just words and even Krakanu couldn't save them. As they turned the corner of Cubitt Road, he shuddered.

'They're coming again,' he said in a whisper as his feet gathered pace.

'It's over, Jago. They have sounded the all clear.'

'It's from the north – they've turned back.'

'It can't be. The siren would have sounded,' his mother said, knowing she should trust him.

Jago stopped and looked up. He sniffed the air and listened like an animal awaiting the hunter.

'Run, mother!' he shouted as he grabbed her hand and pulled her on.

'What is it, Jago?' she asked as a shudder of fear rippled her spine.

'They're coming low and fast – near to the ground,' he said as he ran faster.

His mother ran with him, holding his hand as she looked to the northern sky. The bombers always came from the east, she thought as she tried to keep pace, jumping over the broken windowpanes that were scattered in the road. Together they ran towards Gray's Inn Road and Coram's Fields. Jago knew the way. It was where he had gone to school until it had been bombed.

'There's a shelter at Russell Square,' his mother said as she listened to the low hum of the approaching aircraft.

'We'll never make it – they're too close,' he said as he lost grip of her hand.

'It's not right, Jago. I don't like this.' She felt something was wrong, that this was no ordinary attack.

'Run faster!' he shouted as the planes came closer.

Like a carriage from a fairground ride, a small bomber circled overhead. Its black wings cast a serpent-like shadow on the ground as it sped closer. Jago looked up. He could see the pilot looking down at him as they ran across the field. There was a burst of machine-gun fire that ripped through the grass. It smashed into an old oak tree and sprayed shrapnel in the air.

Another small black bomber swooped in like a falling eagle. It was as if *they* were the targets. Its engine droned, whined and was then silent. It fell from the sky with its bomb doors open.

'Run, Jago, run!' his mother screamed as they hurried from the park and into Regent's Square.

Jago bolted as fast as he could. Fear seared through his veins and made him tremble.

'Keep running,' he pleaded. But his mother had slowed to a walking pace. She no longer cared and had given up the will to fight.

12

Then, taking a final look at Jago running ahead, she stopped and turned to face the bomber that was diving towards them. Martha Harker dropped her bag to the floor and let her coat slip from her shoulders. The sunlight cast shadows through her flowery silk dress as she raised her arms to the sky. Jago looked back as he grabbed the railing by the alleyway and panted for breath.

'Don't stop, Jago. Never look back,' she said as she stared into the approaching hail of bullets that were already churning up the street and coming towards them. 'Remember, I will always love you . . .'

'NO! MOTHER!' he screamed as he saw the metal casket fall from the aeroplane.

It was as if the whole world turned slowly. He watched as the bomb fell and bullets smashed into the pavement. His mother stood without fear, her palms upturned as if to receive a gift.

It was then that a hand grabbed him by the throat and pulled him down a small flight of steps to the basement of the house. Jago heard the whistle of the bomb as it fell to earth like a comet. Another hand smothered his face as the body of a man pressed him to the ground. He was held tightly in amongst sodden leaves and street rubbish that had piled up through the years. Just for a moment he saw the man's eyes staring at him. He was held in a steely blue gaze. Each eye was rimmed with silver.

There was a loud explosion. The world was consumed in a brilliant white light. It burnt brighter than the sun. The earth shuddered as the buildings all around began to fall. The sound deafened his ears. Rubble crashed around him. There was screaming in the street. He could feel the man holding him close, he could smell the scent of cologne on his shaven face.

Then came the darkness and the swirling cloud and dust as the masonry filled the open cellar. Soon there was silence, deep and impenetrable like death itself. There was no pain, no hurt, no fear. All he could feel was the man holding him, as if he was a sleeping child cuddled by his father. Then even that feeling faded and there was nothing. It was as if he slept without dreaming. It mattered not that he couldn't move as the collapsed building pressed down upon him.

In his dreaming he could hear fire engines in the street and smell the approaching flames. Someone pulled his arm from the rubble as he opened his eyes and dragged him from the dirt.

'Got one! Young lad . . . just where he said.' As the voice spoke water was splashed on his face to wash the dust from his eyes. 'And his bag. Can't believe he's alive.'

'Where's my mother?' Jago asked as rough hands helped him to his feet.

'Only found you because some bloke told us you were down there,' the fireman said.

'There's a man down there with me – he pulled me from the street and covered me when the building fell,' Jago panted.

'There was no one there but you, lad,' the fireman replied.

'My mother! She was in the street when the bomb came down.'

'She's not here now. No one survived, lad, bomb fell just there,' he said as he pointed. 'If your mother was out here she wouldn't have . . .' As he walked Jago to the ambulance the fireman saw the tag on his jacket and read his name. 'You being evacuated?'

'On the night train,' Jágo replied anxiously. 'To Whitby.'

'A strange place to be evacuated. People expecting you in Whitby?'

'Yes,' Jago replied vacantly, not knowing if anyone was expecting him or not. He knew no more than what was on the tag tied to his jacket, his name and evacuation number written on it by his mother.

'Then we better get you there. If we get news of your mother we can send it on,' the man said as he noted down the number on the tag in a small black book. 'That's all I need to find you.'

Jago looked around the street. There was no sign or trace of his mother. It was as if she had been just a vague memory. The bomb had smashed every house into small pieces of rubble. Where he had last seen her was now just a scorched piece of earth.

'But my mother – is she dead? Where is she?' he asked nervously, wanting to cry.

'There's a war. Things happen. You *have* to go to Whitby. There'll be people there who'll look after you. Understand?' the man said sharply.

He was given no time to think. The fireman insisted he get into the makeshift ambulance that had once been a grocer's van. It had old cauliflower leaves in the corners. A camping bed was pushed to the back and some old equipment strapped to the side. The van was ramshackle and looked as though it could care for no one. A woman in a nurse's dirty uniform looked pitifully at him.

'The man, the man . . .' Jago stuttered as his teeth chattered with the sudden chill that overwhelmed him. 'What was he like?'

The fireman rubbed his hands on his thick jacket, thought for a moment and then looked to the street to see if he was still there. There was something about the way Jago stared that was quite unsettling. He had never seen a boy look so frightened.

'Just an ordinary bloke. Businessman – dark suit – northerner, I would say.'

'Did he have blue eyes . . . with a silver rim . . . like a wolf?' Jago asked, remembering what he had seen.

'Never noticed,' the fireman replied as he threw in Jago's bag and closed the back of the ambulance, shutting out the light. 'He was just a man in a long black coat. Said he saw you run down the steps before the bomb went off.'

'How come he survived when no one else did?' Jago asked as he was plunged into the darkness.

[2]

Bartholomew Bradick

THERE HAD BEEN NO TIME to complain and no one to complain to. It was as if he had been imprisoned in the ambulance for his journey to King's Cross station. Jago had slumped against the wall of the van, wondering if he were still dreaming. The only thing that made him think he was awake was the distant rumbling of another wave of bombers and the smell of leaking petrol. When he had arrived at the railway station, the doors were pulled open and the same fireman who had locked him in pulled Jago from the van.

'Platform 9,' the man said sternly, as if he knew exactly where the train would be. 'You don't want to miss it. You never know what might happen to you if you stay behind.'

The words sounded like a threat. Jago stepped from the van to the pavement and looked around. The bombers had struck the Marylebone Road. A single deep crater steamed outside the St Pancras Hotel.

'Any news of my mother?' he asked, not knowing what else to say.

'She's dead. They found this just before we set off. You have no one and nothing to stay in London for now. It was all that was left of her.'

The man handed him a small silver wristwatch with a smashed face. Jago knew it well. He turned it over and looked at the back and read the words: *Martha – Whitby 1925.*

'That's all?' he asked despondently.

'Well, she didn't have time to leave a will if that's what you mean,' the man laughed. 'Get the train, boy. Get out of London before it's dark. There might be more than the bombers that are after you.'

He said no more as he slammed the door shut and got back into the van and drove off, leaving Jago by the side of the road. London felt suddenly cold and unwelcoming. He fought the desire to run back to the place where he had last seen his mother. The cardboard tag on his leather coat flapped and twisted in the stiffening breeze.

'She's dead, Jago,' he said to himself as he turned slowly towards the doors of the station. 'Can't stay here.'

An old charabanc bus rattled through the debris on the Marylebone Road. It stopped at the bomb crater and the door opened. A woman in a pleated skirt got out. She adjusted the hat on her head and pulled a young child from inside the bus. Then more came, one after the other until the pavement was full of children. Each one had a tag tied to their coat. The younger ones carried the obligatory gas mask in its brown box. In virtual silence they formed a long line and without any word from the woman they snaked their way towards the station.

'On your own?' she asked as she approached Jago. He nodded. 'Then you better come with me. I am the Evacuation Officer. You look too old to be sent away.'

The woman tried to look kind. Her brow was deeply

furrowed and her eyes were drawn into her head that looked as though it was held together by the tight knots of her hair. Jago clutched the watch in his hand and followed her step by step as the clouds blew in from the west and the sky darkened.

On Platform 9 of King's Cross station the train waited, steam hissing from the black engine. Soldiers in muddied uniforms guarded the entrance as a fat porter hurried the children along the platform. Jago looked up at the bomb-broken glass that hung from the steel girders high above the platforms. Crowds of people stood and watched as the children walked towards the train. The Evacuation Officer went ahead, holding up a furled umbrella.

'This way,' she shouted. Jago noticed a man in a long black coat watching from the shadows of the soup kitchen. 'No lagging behind,' she said as she prodded him with the tip of her umbrella. 'Have to get the train. Expecting another bombing anytime.'

'It won't be for an hour,' Jago replied without thinking. 'I can't feel them.'

The woman shrugged her shoulders.

'It leaves in five minutes and from the tag on your coat you have to be on it.'

Jago looked back at the soup kitchen, but the man was gone.

On Platform 9 three soldiers guarded a black iron gate that kept back a sea of children. Jago was by far the oldest. He felt out of place and stood awkwardly, leaning against a pile of empty mail sacks.

'Time!' shouted the porter as he waved a green flag. The

soldiers opened the gate and the Evacuation Officer counted the children as they filed by.

As each one passed she told them a carriage number. Jago waited until they had all gone ahead. A small girl gripped his hand for a moment. She looked up at him with tear-filled eyes before being dragged away by a red-haired boy.

'My sister,' he said. 'Can't stop crying.'

Jago understood.

The Evacuation Officer looked at him and checked the number on his tag.

'Jago Harker . . . Whitby?' she said, surprised. She checked her papers. 'Cattle truck . . .'

She pointed to an old wooden truck at the end of the train. It had an open wooden door that slid on metal rails, and Jago could see the floor was covered in straw. In the shadows was a wooden pen filled with bleating sheep. Chalked onto the side in tall white letters was the word WHITBY.

'Animals?' he asked. 'What about a seat? How will I know when I am there?'

'Not for you to argue with. You are being evacuated – not taken on holiday. Whitby is the end of the line.'

It was as if she had rehearsed the words already. Without argument, he got inside and made a manger of hay bales and straw. It was warm and dark and the sheep fell silent. He wondered if he was to travel alone. His answer came quickly. The door was slid shut and locked from outside. The train whistle blew and the wheels began to turn as they scraped against the rails. Jago sighed as he sat back alone in the darkness. It pressed in around him. He didn't feel scared but sobbed softly and quietly as he thought of his mother.

'I feel like that sometimes,' said the voice of a man from somewhere in the darkness.

'What?' asked Jago. 'Who is there?'

He sat up, startled. There was someone in the carriage with him.

'A traveller, just like you,' the voice said. 'Was in amongst the sheep – thought I would be alone.'

Jago could make out the shape of a man sitting against the sliding door. He was wrapped in a thick dark coat. The broken slats let in the half-light of the fading sun. It wasn't enough to see him clearly and Jago did not want to move. The man stared at him.

'You're not being evacuated?' Jago said, as he wondered if there was a way of jumping from the train.

'Too old for that,' the man replied. 'Just going home – making sure I get back, and stealing a ride is one way.'

'What happens if they catch you?' he asked.

'You going to tell on me?' the man asked with laughter in his voice. 'I don't think you'd do that, would you, Jago?'

He was frightened that the man knew his name. A sudden desire came to him to break from the carriage, scream and leap to the track.

'You know me?' Jago asked, his voice hushed.

'Longer than you think, Jago Harker,' the man said as he came towards him from the shadows.

In the darkness Jago could see the outline of two silver eyes. They burnt in the darkness like a ferocious wolf. Instantly he knew it was the man from the bombing.

'It was you. From the bombing. You saved me – covered me and then vanished.' Jago pushed himself fearfully against the bales of straw trying to distance himself from the man. 'It was you who told the fireman where I was buried. How come you weren't killed?'

'Frightened, Jago?' the man asked.

Jago swallowed hard. 'Why did you do that – what about my mother? Why didn't you save her?' he asked.

'What would be the point in that? There is a point in all our lives when we have to die. I cannot change that. With you it was different. I knew if I dragged you down the steps you could survive. I had to make a choice, Martha or you.' The man spoke softly as he came closer. 'I never got a good look at you – I have heard that you look just like . . .'

Jago looked at the man. All he could see were the bright silver-blue eyes rimmed in shimmering steel. His face was thin and shadowed. Stubble was on his cheeks and framed his thin lips. He stared and stared at Jago and then reached out and touched his face.

'How do you know my mother? Who are . . .' were the only words he could say before a hypnotic sleep gripped his body. Jago tried to force his eyes to stay open, but they closed painfully.

'Be quiet, Jago. It is best you don't know who I am,' said the man, and he pressed harder on Jago's forehead with the tip of his finger.

The night and the day went quickly. Jago felt as if he were dead. At one point, sometime in the night, he thought he heard the train stop, and from the muffled sound of the engine he guessed it was in a long tunnel, but he drifted back to sleep and it was only when the train was crossing the bleak moors that he woke.

'You there?' he asked as the train crept slowly into the station.

There was no reply. The engine stopped suddenly. Jago shuddered as the door was opened and a bright torch shone inside.

'Jago Harker?' asked a man on the platform. Jago shielded his eyes from the bright light as he nodded his head. 'You're the only one on the list. Should have been in carriage number three. Thought you had ran off.'

'I was told to get in here. The Evacuation Officer said this was the carriage for Whitby.'

'Carriage for sheep – not for people.' The man laughed. Jago could not see his face but his voice sounded warm, as if he could be trusted.

'Where are all the others?' Jago asked.

'They got dropped at Malton. Children for farms – that's what they were. Didn't no one come to let you out at all?'

Jago looked around the carriage for the man.

'No.' He hesitated. 'All alone.'

'Then we better get you something to eat,' said the man as he held out his hand and pulled Jago from the darkness of the carriage. 'I'm Bartholomew Bradick. Stationmaster.' He paused. 'Though there aren't as many trains come here since the start of the war. Five a week, that's all.'

Something in the man's voice made Jago sigh. It was as if he had instantly found a friend. He knew nothing of the man, other than that he was quite short and round, with a waistcoat tightly buttoned over his fat stomach. He wore the uniform of the North Riding Moors Railway and the teeth he had left were stained by pipe tobacco. The railway station was just like Aldgate Underground. The walls were covered in the same posters and the clear night sky was vaulted above their heads like a ceiling of stars. Jago looked up and saw the light of a comet.

'What's that?' he asked as Bradick led him into the station office.

'That?' he shrugged in reply. 'That is known in these parts as *RedEye*. Came on the same day one hundred years ago and will stay there until it vanishes back to where it is from. It's a comet – deep in space and always burns blood red.'

'I looked at the sky every night in London and never saw it,' Jago said as he was taken inside.

'That's the thing,' Bradick replied heartily, 'get further south than twenty miles and it's invisible. It's as if it just appears above the town and can be seen from nowhere else. Not a good thing, if you ask me.'

Bradick smiled as with one hand he showed Jago the expanse of the room. There, burning brightly in the black grate, was a coal fire. In the middle of the room was a neat wooden table covered in a cloth and dressed with a bowl of flowers. On the wall hung several badly painted landscape pictures with matchstick figures. In the corner on an old desk were a telephone and typewriter, with a railway timetable on the wall behind.

Jago could smell hot tea and warm toast. He noticed the man looking curiously at him, as if he was expecting Jago to comment on the room.

'It's lovely,' he said nervously, not knowing if it was the right thing to say.

'Have you been to Whitby before? You seem very familiar?' Bradick asked and then went on before Jago could reply. 'You are the first evacuee we have had. The mayor was going to come and welcome you – but . . . he's *indisposed.'*

'Not well?' Jago asked politely.

'Drunk,' Bradick replied as he wheeled in a tea trolley from a small room with a smoked-glass door. 'They found him in a hedge. Stuck in the branches. He'd fallen in headfirst and couldn't get out. It's the worry – that's what got to him. Undertaker found him – thought he was just half a man.' Bradick stopped abruptly as if he had said too much.

Jago smiled as Bradick handed him a cup of steaming tea with the sweet smell of sugar. It was something he hadn't tasted for the last year. In Shoreditch food was rationed, and sugar was traded as gold. He had once seen a man who had found a bar of chocolate. It was dark and rich and covered with mildew. Jago had saved the piece he was given for three weeks, until he could no longer resist eating it.

'Cake?' Jago asked as the man handed him a plate with a thick slice of sponge topped with cream.

'Made with ten eggs,' Bradick boasted as if it were a sign of his wealth. 'I have chickens,' he whispered.

'Am I staying with you?' Jago asked, wondering if it had been decided whom he would live with.

Bradick frowned and rubbed his wrinkled face with one hand whilst with the other he hitched up his trousers and pulled his thin, stained tie into place.

'No room here, Jago. But you can come and visit. I would like that. Don't get many visitors since Mrs . . .' Bradick looked sullen and sad. His warm, open, round face narrowed pitifully.

'Did she die?' Jago asked quietly, thinking Bradick looked like a shaved walrus.

'Went to Hull,' Bradick interrupted. 'Met a haberdasher who could offer her a never-ending supply of buttons. And you, Jago – what of your family?'

'My mother is dead,' he said, barely believing the words he spoke. 'That's what I have been told. A bomb . . .'

'And you still came to Whitby?' Bradick asked.

'I have nothing to stay for. No family,' he replied. 'The man insisted.'

'Then we shall be family together. Are you sure you have never been here before – you look so familiar?' Bradick asked again.

'Never been north of Hampstead Heath.'

'Strange, you look like someone I have met.' The small wooden clock on the wall chimed nine times. 'Ah,' he said as if he remembered a vital piece of information as he got up from his seat by the fire. 'There is a curfew at midnight. Everyone has to be within doors. I better tell you where you are staying.'

'Nearby?' Jago asked.

'Not quite. And perhaps, not so friendly. But don't let me put you off. Take as you find – that's what I say. It's a fine house on the other side of the river. A school of some importance on the top of the cliff by the church and the ruined abbey. You can't miss the place. Sadly, you'll have to walk on your own as I can't leave the station. I will give you directions and this note.'

Bradick handed Jago a long brown envelope with crisp black lettering on one side.

'A school?' Jago asked.

Bradick stood up and looked towards the door. 'More of an orphanage – bright children, invited to live there – not many,' he stuttered. 'It's called Streonshalgh Manor, an old house with old memories.'

Jago had discovered that Bradick had a habit of whispering whenever he said anything of importance. It was as if he wanted to keep it from the world. Jago looked at the envelope. On it were his name and directions from the station to the Manor. He could feel a stiff piece of paper inside.

'Can I open this?' he asked as his thumb flicked the frayed edge.

'I would keep it as it is, Jago,' Bradick explained slowly with a raised eyebrow. 'When you get to Streonshalgh Manor, ask for Mrs Macarty. You are expected.' He sighed as if he didn't want the lad to go. 'Her face can wither prunes but her heart is softer than many people would think.'

Jago smiled and walked towards the door, carrying the leather bag in one hand and the envelope in the other. Bradick smoothed the cloth of his waistcoat, straightened his tie and opened the door, and together they stepped onto the empty platform.

He looked up. The strange comet was still high above them. It had neither moved nor changed. A full moon climbed slowly towards it as if the two would soon meet.

'Never seen anything so strange,' Jago said, in awe of the heavens.

'Walk quickly and stay on the roads, Jago. This is Whitby and not as safe as London – even without the bombing.' Bradick shrugged his shoulders and curled his lip in a frowning smile. 'One thing,' he asked as Jago turned to walk away. 'When did your mother die?'

'Yesterday – in the evening before I caught the train.'

Bradick sighed loudly and held out a hand.

'I am not surprised by the fiery trials we all go through,' he said. He stepped towards Jago and hugged him tightly. 'There's always a cup of tea and good food in my office for you, remember that, Jago.'

Jago stood uncomfortably for a moment, wrapped in Bradick's arms. He could smell the sweat of the day mixed with tobacco and fire ash. He didn't mind – deep in his heart, he felt he could trust this eccentric man who stumbled over his words and said too much.

'My mother lived here once,' Jago said when Bradick had released him from his grip. 'She gave me a photograph taken by some ruins,' he continued as he fumbled in his pocket. 'This is her.'

He showed Bradick the photograph. The man took out a pair of silver pince-nez spectacles and stuck them to the bridge of his nose. He said nothing as he moved towards the open door to cast more light on the faces before him.

'*This* is your mother?' he asked urgently as he gasped.

'The one on the left. The other girl is called Maria. I was told to find her.'

'Dear Jago – what has brought you to this place?' Bradick asked as he looked anxiously up and down the platform before stepping back inside his office.

'What do you mean?' Jago asked.

'You won't find this woman and you must never mention to anyone that your mother was here – do you understand?'

'Why?' Jago asked.

'Just do what I say. Leave this picture with me – don't take it to Streonshalgh Manor. It would not be good for you if it were found.'

'It was the last thing she gave to me. I want it,' he protested.

'Then it is better kept safe with me . . . You'll be late. Go on, Jago, be off now.' Bradick suddenly slammed the door shut, plunging the platform in darkness.

Jago banged on the office door.

'I want the photograph, Mr Bradick – it's mine!' he shouted as he heard three bolts slide into their keepers and the mortise locked turned to keep him out.

'It wouldn't be a good thing. I will keep it safe and no one will know. Remember, Jago. Mention it to no one when you get to the Manor – especially Mrs Macarty.'

'But . . .' Jago protested as he saw the office light dimmed and heard the shutters pulled across the window blinds.

Inside, all was silent. He stood in the chilled night as the moon cast his shadow across the stone floor of the platform. Jago felt alone. On the far side of the town, on the clifftop, he could see the dark shadows of Streonshalgh Manor and the ruined abbey. He wondered where his mother had lived and why her face should frighten Bradick in such a way. Jago had wanted to tell him about the man in the carriage, but hadn't dared. Life did not make sense – but then, for Jago Harker it never did.

[3]

Streonshalgh Manor

JAGO TRUDGED ON, his feet tired, his mind confused and his heart weary and full of pain. His one overriding thought was for his mother. All he could see every time he closed his eyes was that final glimpse of her. She was surrounded in sunlight, her hands held up as if praying. He could picture every detail as if it were burnt into his eyes. Her coat was crumpled at her feet. The contents of her handbag had spilled across the street. She waited, knowing what was going to happen but as if she didn't care.

In life he had never felt alone, she had always been there. He remembered being lost in a London market when he was a small boy. She had found him; her hands had wiped away the tears. Even when he had been left with Mr Cresco, Jago knew she would come back and together they would sit by the fire in their flat and eat buttered toast. Now, his heart felt as if it would burst. Tightness gripped his throat as he wandered through an unknown town to the looming shadow of a dark house on a clifftop.

The road from the railway station to the town was lit by the full moon and the glow of the comet that coloured the sky deep red. The road was broad and edged with the brick walls of houses yet to be built. Their foundations were set in four rows of bricks, the work suddenly stopped and now grown over with brambles. An occasional car sped by, its lights shaded for the blackout. No one was on the street and not a house light was to be seen. He could not escape the shadows of the ruins on the far cliff on the other side of the river. The long avenue that he now walked along was straight and broad. He could see the tall chimneys of Streonshalgh Manor. As he approached the open gates to the park he looked again at the envelope in his hand.

Jago traced the line from the station with the tip of his finger. Somehow he had lost his way. The open gates led into a neat park. There was an old building with a copper roof surrounded by trees. The path dropped steeply to a ravine below, where he could see the grey slate rooftops of several large buildings. On the other side of the road was a row of high terraced houses. They swept down the hill towards what he thought must be the town. Each had a metal gate with a brass handle and a flight of steps to the door in the tall facade of brick. They reminded Jago of Belsize Park. His mother would take him there Sunday after Sunday. They would walk through Primrose Hill to the old pub at Haverstock. He would sit outside, drink shandy and listen to the music. His mother would be gone for an hour and then come back for him. She never said where she had gone and he never asked. What she had been doing never mattered. It didn't cross his mind.

If the houses were familiar, the road to the town was not. It narrowed quickly and became steeper with every step. With it came the smell of the sea. It blew in on the fresh wind

31

that now rattled the chains on the rusted gas lamps. From somewhere near, Jago could hear music and laughter. The night grew darker as with every minute a sea-mist drew in and cloud covered the town. He looked up as the moon struggled to keep light. Then it vanished, and even the bright glow of the comet could not light his way. Jago fumbled down the dark street as he made his way to the harbour and the bridge to the east side.

That is what it had said on the envelope. *Find the bridge – cross to the east side – follow Sandgate – through Arguments Yard and along to the steps.* He could remember the directions – but now as the moonlight faded, the town changed. Jago shuddered as he turned the corner of the street. On the hill was an old boarded-up café, the sign swinging back and forth in the breeze. The window had been smashed long ago and the door nailed shut. He walked down the cobbled path and could hear the ringing of a hand bell nearby.

The old bank on the corner was also empty. He looked across the road. There, built on the side of the river by the bridge, was a tall building divided into a number of small shops. A narrow alleyway led through it, spewing mist from the river like a dragon's mouth.

By the bridge was a man. He stood outside a white-painted hut and rang a brass bell that hung from the wall. Jago could hear the sound of an engine and the clattering of cogwheels. The road that crossed the bridge began to split in two and rise up. A gate swung across and was locked shut. The man looked around to see if all was clear and then rang the bell again.

Jago waited in the shadows. It was instinctive and he felt

safe. He knew the man would ask him questions. Stranger in a strange town, and in the middle of a war. Jago didn't want to explain to the man who he was or where he was going. It would only be a matter of time before the bridge was down and he could cross to the other side. He decided that when the gate was open he would wait for the man to go back into the hut and then cross quickly, head down.

There was a sudden thud that shook the ground as the bridge stood fully open. The man on the bridge flashed his torch three times upriver. Just at that moment there was a parting of the clouds above the town and the moon shone down through the fog. Slowly and silently, the conning tower of a large submarine came into view. It glided silently through the opening as it sleeked out to sea. Jago pressed himself back into the doorway of the disused bank so as not to be seen.

Three men in dark uniforms stood at the front of the black conning tower as the fin slipped silently down river. A tall silver periscope turned towards him as the submarine sailed on. Jago looked out from the shadows, knowing that it had fixed upon him and even in the moonlight could see him clearly. The green orb of light that came from the lens stared towards him like the eye of an animal. One of the men pointed towards him. Jago could do nothing. Then the submarine sailed on beyond the piers and towards the deep sea.

On the bridge, the man went back inside the hut. Jago waited as the bridge was lowered and the gate automatically opened. He could see the rim of light around the door of the cabin and a shadow move inside. All was then quiet. Jago gripped the handle of his bag, looked back and forth and then slipped out from his hiding place. He had never been frightened of the dark outside. It was only the shadows of confinement that unnerved him. Quickly he was across the bridge and before the moon could disappear again, he checked the directions on the envelope.

'Sandgate,' he said out loud as he looked up at the sign carved into the stone of the house on the corner. It was unusual to see a street name. Most had been taken down to confuse the enemy if they invaded.

Sandgate was narrow and lined with curious shops. One sold fish, another what vegetables could be found. There was a photographer's and jeweller's that sold black polished stone and the stone bones of long-dead monsters. He followed the pavement until he came to a large market square. In front of him, just like on the map, was a colonnaded building with a high clock tower. Jago turned the corner and walked towards the end of the street. It followed the line of the harbour and every five yards he could see dark alleyways that dropped to the waterside.

Behind every other door he could hear talking but no one came out into the street. He had never known such a deserted place as this. Doors were all locked, windows shuttered and barred. It was as if everyone wanted to keep out the night and stay inside until morning. Jago thought it strange that there was no sign of any bombing. Perhaps the war hadn't reached here yet – that's why he was here, he thought, as he stopped to listen at the door of a house.

He waited a moment before walking on, hearing a familiar voice on the radio. 'Here is the news and this is Alvar Lidell reading it.'

Jago smiled. The voice was familiar. Alvar Lidell spoke swiftly as he always did. Jago remembered how he would go downstairs to Mr Cresco's apartment and listen to the large wooden radio that stood in the corner of the room. The valves inside would spark and glow as the voice vibrated and crackled through the speaker.

'You always need the news, Jago,' Cresco would say as he gave him another orange that he had hidden under his sofa. 'But it is what he doesn't say that is important.'

Jago had never known what Cresco meant. A clock somewhere near chimed loudly, the sound echoing over the town. Ahead of him was a flight of steps that seemed to go up the side of a mountain. Strands of mist weaved in and out of the houses and the smell of the sea was at its strongest. Jago could hear waves breaking on a nearby beach. The alehouse at the bottom of the steps was eerily empty. Like most of the houses in the street, its windows were boarded with black shutters.

'Going far, lad?' asked a voice from the nearby shadows.

Jago turned. All he could see in the darkness was the glow of a burning tobacco pipe and the outline of a man leaning against the wall.

'Streonshalgh Manor,' Jago replied cautiously as he thought of running.

'Not far to go then,' the man said as he stepped towards him. Jago noticed he carried a digging spade. He was tall, thin, with a work-worn face and deep, penetrating eyes. He wore an old black gabardine coat with leather-patched elbows 'Not from around here, are you? I'm Jack Henson – gravedigger. Just finished.'

'Digging graves?' Jago asked.

'What else would a gravedigger do?' Henson asked with a laugh. 'What do you want at Streonshalgh Manor?'

'Living there,' Jago replied. 'Been evacuated.'

'Just arrived on that train that rattled through, disturbing everyone? Heard you were coming – our only evacuee. Londoner, some said – is that true?'

'Shoreditch,' he replied as he walked slowly towards the steps.

'*When will you pay me, say the bells of Old Bailey – When I grow rich, say the bells of Shoreditch* . . . Do you know that, lad?' Henson asked as he walked alongside. 'I knew a lass who went to London, left here years ago and never came back. Some say that in London there is a man who keeps an elephant in his house. Is that right, lad?'

'If it were, I never saw him,' Jago replied as the man kept pace with every step he took.

'One hundred and ninety-nine of these – a stairway to heaven, some say.' Henson laughed again as he chewed on his pipe. 'I'm Jack Henson – remember that name – have the cottage by the abbey. Handy for the gravedigger.'

The man stopped and held out his hand.

'Jago Harker,' Jago responded as he grasped the strong, rough palm in his fingers.

'I'll walk you up the hill – shouldn't be out alone in this place, Jago. There are legends that have a habit of coming true.' Henson puffed on his pipe without regard to the steep hill that was sapping Jago's strength and breath.

'Legends?' Jago gasped as he stopped on a wide stone landing and pretended to look out to sea. 'You mean ghosts?'

'Sometimes they are the same – sometimes not. Around here they can mean anything.' Henson strolled up the steps with the spade over his shoulder.

'Don't know if I believe in anything like that, can't be frightened by what you can't see,' Jago panted as he followed on, wondering how a man who looked so old could walk so quickly.

'They all say that. Mrs Macarty will cure you of your ignorance. A week of her cooking and you'll be believing in the devil and all his works.' Henson laughed again as he struck his spade into the earth at the side of the steps and then pointed up the hill. 'There she is,' he said earnestly, his voice stripped of all mirth. 'Streonshalgh Manor. Not the happiest place in the world, but some would call it home.'

Jago looked up. The moon was forcing its way between the wisps of high clouds. They were now above the mist that filled the estuary as it rolled in from the ocean, and in the steel-blue light he could see the rooftop of a large baronial house. A tall grey wall, breached by dark windows, reached up to a thick slate roof. To his left was an old church surrounded by a thousand gravestones. The last of the steps gave way to a path that wound its way through the tombs to a pair of iron gates.

The Manor House looked cold, empty and unlived in. It was nothing like his flat in Old Nichol Street. There was no Mr Cresco, no radio and no mother. Jago tried to stiffen his trembling lip and fight back the sudden urge to cry.

'Looks a nice place. I'm sure I will be very happy here,' he said as he nodded to the man and gave a slight bow before walking on.

37

'You're really not frightened, are you?' Henson said. He was looking at Jago as though he was measuring him for the size of his grave.

'Frightened? No,' Jago replied as he walked on, not wanting the man to know the truth.

'House by the abbey ruins. Can't miss it. Jack Henson. Gravedigger. Don't forget. Curfew at midnight – don't get caught – they'll think you're a spy. Remember my name.'

Jago looked back. The man stood defiantly at the top of the steps. His long white hair blew in the wind as he raised his hand in farewell.

'Mad as cheese,' Jago said under his breath as he clutched the cold iron gates of Streonshalgh Manor for the first time.

Four tall chimneys towered over the house and cast moon shadows on the ground. There was not one light at any of the twenty windows that Jago counted. He slowly pulled open the gate and stepped inside. His feet crunched on the cold gravel path that took him towards a tall statue that stood guard with sword and shield.

Jago ignored the look of its cold eyes as he walked up the steps and knocked on the door. The house seemed to tremble and he heard footsteps scurrying along the stone floor towards him.

'Who is it?' asked the voice from inside.

'Jago Harker. I've been evacuated from London,' he replied as he anxiously checked the tag on his leather coat.

He heard voices whispering inside as if they fought as to who would open the door.

'Evacuated?' said another voice as a small spy-hole was opened and someone stared out. 'Jago Harker?'

'From London,' Jago added, only to make the confusion and hubbub worse.

'He's from London,' said the indecisive voice.

'London?' asked another.

Then it came like the roaring of thunder at the start of a storm, shaking the nail-studded door.

'TO YOUR ROOMS!' The voice billowed angrily. 'Every one of you. What have I said about going to the door? You never know who could be there.'

Jago heard hurried footsteps running away. He stepped back from the door and gripped his case with both hands as he waited.

A bolt was slid, then another and another. The lock was turned with a great key that churned in the workings as it clicked each tumbler one after the other.

The vast brass handle moved slowly. Inch by inch the door opened and a shard of paltry candlelight flooded out.

'It's me, Jago Harker,' he said before he could see what monster was on the other side of the door.

'Mr Harker, how nice to see you,' said a prim and neatly pinnied woman of meagre height with a bright smiling face. 'You have travelled far to be with us . . . Welcome.'

Jago looked beyond her to see if someone else was hiding in the shadows, someone more gruesome than the woman who stood there now.

'Is Mrs Macarty here?' he asked.

'Yes,' she said with a smile that reminded him of a smug fat toad he had once caught at Rotherhithe.

'I have been told to ask for her and give her this,' he replied as he handed the woman the envelope.

She held up the candle and looked at the writing and then turned it over and admired the map drawn by Bradick.

'You did well to get here on such a dark night, Jago. Bartholomew Bradick is not the best at giving directions. He works in the world of train lines and feels no need for roads,' the woman said as she looked over his shoulder into the night and sniffed the air. 'Best you come in.'

'And will I meet Mrs Macarty?' Jago asked.

'You have,' she replied. She stood aside and gave him her hand in welcome to the house. 'I am Mrs Delphine Macarty.'

Jago stepped inside. The house was all he expected it to be. Every wall was panelled with oak, every fireplace stained with wood smoke. He stood in a grand entrance hall. A long staircase led off to an upper floor. A small fire burnt in a blackened grate. Dust covered most of the flagstones. Three small faces peered down from the landing above as Jago was led towards what smelt like the kitchen. Mrs Macarty was quick-footed; her long skirts polished the stone floors as she walked.

'A wonderful place,' Jago said without meaning it as he followed on.

'I am glad you think so. This will be your home until the end of the war – whatever the outcome. The War Office was insistent you came here. I can't understand why as you look far too old and are far too tall. I only hope I have a bed long enough to fit such a gangly creature,' she said. The charm she had first given him now appeared to be vanishing.

'I am six foot and fifteen years old,' Jago insisted, hoping it would make a difference.

'We are a society of orphans – one ceases to be an orphan at sixteen and, according to these papers, you at least have a mother,' she said dryly as she led him along a dark corridor.

'My mother is dead. She was killed in a bombing . . . yesterday.'

Mrs Macarty stopped and turned to face him. She looked up and sighed as she held the candle to his face.

'I am glad to see you are beyond tears. You either hated her every fibre or have mourned enough on the train from London. I do not like tears. I have never cried myself in these last forty-five years since my own parents died and will have my orphans do the same. Crying, Jago, does not make the man.'

She inspected his face again with the candle, looking for any trace of a tear stain.

'It was a long journey,' he replied as he took a breath. 'I will try to be a good example for you.'

Mrs Macarty smiled at him. It was genuine and warm.

'I am beginning to like you, Jago,' she said as she pulled at her long silver hair and twisted a lock in her fingertips. 'I think I will change your room. You are a lad who could do with a view and a window that doesn't shut so as to let in all that good sea air. I might even be able to find a few pieces of coal for your fire.'

Jago tried to look as though he appreciated her words. He could see her eyes flicking like a snake's tongue across his face, as if she looked for something that she could not see.

'It would be welcome,' he said slowly with a nod of the head. He noticed the peculiar pig-nose shoes that stuck out from under her long skirt.

'I knew you were a gentleman. I could tell it from the

41

way you knocked at the door and stood your ground. It has been a long time since we had a gentleman around here.' She shouted the last words as if she wanted all those listening upstairs to hear her. Mrs Macarty leant towards him slowly. 'There are those who may be jealous about the room you are to have, Jago. It hasn't been let for many years. Don't let them frighten you with rumours.'

'I shall only believe what you say, Mrs Macarty,' Jago replied warily.

'Good, good,' she said as she whispered close to his face. 'I wouldn't want you to get unnecessarily . . . worried. You better follow me. I will bring you some soup later before you sleep. Must be tired with all that travelling . . . and grieving.'

Jago thought he had heard her giggle as they took to the back stairs. She led on quickly, her feet skipping over the bare boards to the landing above. A long corridor led to three dark oak doors that stood side by side.

'It is a fine place, Mrs Macarty,' Jago said as he saw her take a key from her pocket and open the door farthest away.

'I haven't had time to clean. I was going to put you in with the other boys – but you are almost a man and perhaps you will need a room of your own,' she said as she twisted the tag on his coat and read his name several times under her breath. 'Very well. I will leave you to it. Soon be breakfast . . . the soup can wait until then. It would be best that you get some sleep.'

Jago had been looking forward to something to eat, but she slipped the blackened iron key into his hand and was gone from the room. 'Breakfast at seven – the smell will lead you to it,' she laughed. 'Matches in the pot by the window.'

Jago found the matches and lit the candles on the mantel and then pulled the thick red curtains. They did nothing to dampen the chill breeze that crept in through the gap under the bay window. As he did so, Jago was sure he could hear voices on the landing outside. They chattered eagerly to one another as their childlike footsteps scurried quickly over the bare boards. He quietly crossed the room and opened the door. The corridor was empty, all but for a blue Dutch plate on which were laid sweet biscuits and what looked like cheese. To the side of the plate was a matching cup filled with tea.

'Thank you,' Jago said as he looked for any trace of the giver.

There was the echo of laughter and then the slamming of a door. All was quiet.

In his room, Jago ate the cheese and looked out of the window across the churchyard to the sea below. He would have called any man a liar if a day ago they had said he would be in such a place as this.

Outside Streonshalgh Manor, the statue of the gladiator was frozen in time, his long, bronze sword pointing towards the church. The moon shadows ran quickly out to sea, the clouds blown by the fresh wind.

As Jago sipped his tea and thought of Old Nichol Street and Mr Cresco, he heard the sound of clattering hooves. On the road, in the shadows of the ruins of the old abbey, were four dark horses with funeral plumes. They regally dragged a black hearse with glass windows. Six men walked slowly behind, each one dressed in a long purple coat. The deathly cortège turned into the churchyard and there it stopped.

Jago looked on as Jack Henson appeared from behind the gate and pointed across the churchyard. The coffin was taken from the bier and carried away to the shadows of the church.

Suddenly, a bell rang in the house.

'All in bed!' shouted Mrs Delphine Macarty.

[4]

Black Strackan

H E LAY ON THE TALL four-poster bed for almost an hour. Each column of wood reached up to the ceiling like a burnt tree trunk. The chiming of the church clock kept him awake and aware of the time. The house creaked and moaned as the timbers cooled. It was a house of numerous noises, some fearful, others not. Jago counted the footsteps along the corridor that went to and fro on tippy-toe. It was as if everyone in the house came to his door and listened. He was expecting at least one of them to knock and ask to be invited in but no one did.

Mrs Macarty continued to shout instructions from far away. She captained Streonshalgh Manor from her wicker chair by the fire in the kitchen and appeared to have the ability to know when a child was out of bed. She would call each miscreant by name, then in a shrill voice command them to return immediately to their room. Eventually, the house fell silent.

Jago still could not sleep. He wrapped himself uncomfortably in the over-blanket. Propped up by the stiff pillows, he watched the candle flicker on the mantel. There were too many dark corners for him to feel welcome. In the half-light, the furniture appeared to move with each jitter of the candle flame. Shimmers of light ran back and forth against the dark, carved panels. Each was caught menacingly in the corner of his eye. The heavy curtains moved slowly from side to side like the heaving chest of a sleeping beast. It was so unlike his home and the small, neat room next to his mother's. There was nothing familiar here, nothing matter-of-fact. It was a room that conspired to frighten him, as if it wanted to tell him all that had gone on years before.

Jago did not believe in ghosts. They were just the creatures of Mr Cresco's imagination, and in all his tales of haunting they were soon and easily vanquished. Now, as Jago lay on the bed, wrapped in the blanket, he began to wonder.

According to Cresco, houses had memories. In some supernatural way, they could recall all that had gone on before.

'Some people call it being haunted, Jago,' Cresco had once said excitedly when they had finished listening to the news on his wireless radio. 'People expect the ghost to be in human form. They want a man to appear with his severed head under his arm and wail like a banshee. That is only in fairytales. But, in my old country, the ghost that could terrify you more than any other was the house itself. To see a spectre appear is one thing, but to live within it is another.'

When Jago asked Cresco if his stories were true, the man had sighed and looked to the fire and covered his mouth with his shaking hand.

'Some people run away from that which they can see, others from that which is invisible.'

Cresco never spoke again that evening.

Jago mulled the words over and over. The thought of a

46

house being a ghost had become even more real. The room felt oppressive, as if it argued with itself and didn't want him to be there. Half asleep, he thought of his mother and wondered why she had wanted him to come to this place.

Footsteps walked the landing outside his room. They were heavy and slow and he knew they were not those of the children or Mrs Macarty. As they came closer, he pulled the blanket higher to his face and feigned sleep. They stopped outside the room. Jago listened. The handle turned slowly and the door creaked. He held his breath and for a moment opened his eyes to see who was there.

Staring at him through the half-open door was a man who held a lamp in one hand and a set of keys on a large ring in the other. He cowered under the doorframe to look in. Jago had never seen anyone so tall or with such giant hands. Their eyes met as the man shone the lamp into the room.

'Sent to see if you were asleep,' the man said in a voice that bubbled in his throat.

'I was,' Jago replied with a yawn as he saw the man look about the room as if he was seeing it for the first time.

'Some might say you are lucky to be in here – others might not,' he said. He stared at Jago through sunken eyes that were set in a wolf-like skull.

'My mother wanted me to be evacuated here and this is where I shall be,' he replied, watching the man edge further into the room.

'Didn't bring much with you,' the man said as he looked at the leather bag by the window. 'Would have thought evacuees would bring all they needed. We don't have enough to keep you in clothes.'

'I have enough,' Jago replied.

The man laughed. His face broke into a smile as he tapped his dirty work boots on the floor.

'Tallow!' screamed Mrs Macarty from the room far below. 'Leave the boy to sleep.'

'Sleep – that's what she wanted me to see. But you're not . . .' he said plainly as he stooped back through the door. 'I will come back, later.'

When Tallow closed the door, Jago got from the bed and slipped the key into the lock. Then he took his bag and placed it against the door.

'Don't want him in here again,' he said under his breath as the curtains moved with a sudden gust of wind that rattled the hem weights on the floorboards.

Jago went to the window and looked out. The night was darker. The moon burst in and out of the clouds as the wind gusted against the high towers of the abbey's ruined arches. In the precinct by the churchyard, the coach and four stood just as he had last seen it. The horses held themselves stiffly against the breeze as their funeral plumes blew in the wind.

Jack Henson came from the shadows of the church. A man in a long purple coat handed him an envelope. Jago could see it flap in his hand before he quickly put it inside his jacket. Henson stood there, arms folded, and watched the men climb back into the carriage and drive away. Jago hid his face between the curtain and the wall so he could not be seen. Henson turned and looked up at the house, examining each of the twenty-one windows that covered the facade. Then, without warning, he looked straight at Jago and waved before stepping back into the shadows.

Footsteps came again along the landing. Jago could tell that it was Tallow coming to check if he was asleep. The door handle turned.

'You asleep?' Tallow whispered in his bubbling deep voice, loud enough to wake the dead.

'Asleep,' Jago replied.

'Good,' Tallow said, and to Jago's amazement he walked off, satisfied that he could tell Mrs Macarty that Jago now slept. His feet trudged as he went.

Jago sat on the bed and looked at his leather case. It was all he had of his old life. He still could not understand why Bradick had taken the photograph of his mother from him. He reached out and slipped the case from the door to his bed and began to unpack everything.

In the dim light he found two clean and neatly ironed shirts, four pairs of socks, pants and handkerchiefs. They were all pressed and starched into precise squares. The socks were ironed and folded into shape. He searched the bag for something from his mother. Deep within, under a pair of trousers, was the parcel from Cresco. Jago had forgotten it was there. Somehow it felt different, heavier than he expected for something so small. He laid it on the bed and began to unwrap it. When he had removed four layers of newspaper, he found a note. It was written by Cresco, and he could hear his words leap from the page.

'*Drink from the cup on every full moon – drink well, Jago – drink well . . .*'

Jago read the first line as he unwrapped the final layer of the parcel and there was the cup.

'The Cup of Garbova. It can't be,' Jago said as he looked

at the chalice and lifted it to the light. He knew this was the most valuable possession Cresco had.

In the crumpled wrapping Jago also saw a small silver pot. Just like the cup it was etched with ancient figures smoothed with use. It was the size of an egg, with a cap that unscrewed. Jago put down the cup and looked at the note.

'*Anoint the doors and windows where you sleep, Jago. Do this every night . . .*'

Jago read the second line of the note and then unscrewed the lid. The pot was full of a viscous balm that smelt of figs and goose grease. He dipped the tip of his finger into the lotion. It burnt like ice on his hand, following the line of his veins to the wrist. The room filled with the fragrance of lavender. The candle on the mantel flickered and sparked.

'*Do not forget my instructions, Jago – your life could depend on it. Abba Julius Cresco.*'

Jago read the final line of the note and wondered what he meant. The old man loved to be theatrical. His flat was full of strange painted icons and old bones. Jago thought he was just a lonely old storyteller who collected relics that interested him. But there was something about the note that demanded he take it seriously.

Jago did as Cresco asked. He got from the bed and smeared some of the balm above the door and window. He didn't know why, but he knew he had to. Then, taking the last of the cold tea, he put it into the chalice, swilled it around and drank. It tasted different, and some of the liquid crystallised on his lips in fragments of what tasted like salt.

'Good – you listened,' a voice like that of Cresco said behind him.

50

Jago turned and shivered. The room was empty. There was no one there.

'Cresco?' he asked, wanting a reply and to hear his voice again.

There was silence. The only sound was the wheezing of the wind as it whipped through the high chimneys of the house. Jago put the chalice and the pyx back into the bag and covered them with the trousers. He lay on the bed, wrapped himself in the blanket and closed his eyes. The room didn't seem so fearful now. The shadows did not dance the way they had, and no longer did he fear sleep. His final thoughts were of his mother. Jago again saw her standing in the street just before the bomb struck. He sniffed the air and smelt the lavender as he settled back on the pillows and slept.

The dream that came to him the moment he closed his eyes had been waiting for him, waiting to pounce from the darkness of his mind. It churned his imagination to the point of waking. It was then he heard the sound from the corridor outside. Someone or something was being dragged slowly along the floor – he was sure of it. The sound came from outside the dream and then he heard it no more.

In that instant, Jago stood outside Streonshalgh Manor. The night was dark and yet he could see clearly as if it were day. He looked up at the house and could make out his own room from the flickering of candlelight through the crack in the curtains. Jago knew that this was a dream. He could feel neither cold nor the breeze that blew. The clouds raced across the moon and high above him, every now and then, he glimpsed the red-eyed comet. The statue of the gladiator that stood on the stone pedestal was just as it was in the waking

51

world. All that was different was that Jago was translucent and ghost-like.

He looked at his hands; they shimmered like a wind-blown pond. His clothes had not changed, and more than anything he felt a deep, insatiable hunger. It was something different from anything he had ever felt before. It yearned in his guts, craving to be satisfied.

Jago thought this to be the beginning of a nightmare. He remembered such a dream from childhood. In that dream he had been locked in a cupboard that grew smaller with every minute. Somewhere within it was a rat that scurried about his feet. Jago had screamed to be released but all his mother could say was that she had no hands and could not find the key. It had started just like this. But just as quickly as it had begun it was over.

This dream went on. Jago walked into the churchyard. All around him, men, women and children were sitting on the tombs staring at him. No one spoke. They were garbed in grave clothes, sodden and ragged. Their faces were ashen, as if each was a living corpse.

A woman the same age as his mother held out her hand as she stepped towards him. Jago touched her fingers. Before his eyes she fell into a heap of dust that blew away between the tombstones.

'She had to go that way,' said the voice from the shadowed lee of the church. 'Life cannot touch death.'

'What?' asked Jago as he turned to see who had spoke.

'This is our eternity – we cannot leave this place whilst he lives,' a man said as he picked up the long tail of his sallow coat from the grave on which he sat.

'Who?' Jago asked – never having spoken like this in a dream.

'Strackan,' replied the man as he bowed his head in reverence. 'He holds us between life and death and now brings more to us each night.'

The man pointed with his long finger to a fresh grave by the side of the church. Jago took several steps towards it and then stopped. At first he was not sure, but as he looked on the newly dug earth began to move.

All he could see were the tips of three white fingers that pushed out of the soil like spring buds. Then, with each moment, more of the hand appeared. It was as if someone were digging their way out of the grave.

'What is it?' Jago asked the man who was now standing by his side, just out of his reach.

'Those who were wise would bury us face down so we could not dig our way out. They would wrap the caskets in holly whips and anoint our heads and put stones in our mouths. They have forgotten the old ways of how to keep us silent.'

'The dead are dead and cannot come to life,' Jago said.

'But we are not dead,' the man whispered in reply, as if to keep his words secret. 'We are shadows waiting for the sun to set us free – are you the one?'

Jago shook his head to escape from the dream, hoping he would soon wake.

'Why do you ask me that?' Jago said as he watched the ground open in the grave.

'Your hand – look. That is why Margot turned to dust . . . the anointing . . .'

Jago looked at his hand. Each vein burnt blood red from the tip of his finger to the cuff of his coat. His hand glowed as if coated with phosphorescent gold.

'Margot?' he asked.

'My wife – the woman you touched – it was your anointing . . .'

'So if you gave me your hand it would happen to you?' Jago asked.

'Touch me not – it is not the way.' The man stood back from Jago fearfully.

'You're a dream – you cannot die,' Jago said.

'Dream?' screamed a child in rags who was clinging to another grave, one with no name and just the etching of a skull to mark who lay there. 'I was taken from my mother and brought to this place – this is no dream. She brought flowers every day – year in, year out, and then she came no more. I am – I am no dream,' the boy said as he looked at Jago through doleful eyes that were steeped in remorse and pity.

Jago stepped quickly to one side as the body in the grave pulled itself from the earth. A woman with red hair dragged herself free from the soil and then stood up. Looking around, she gasped for air. She was different from the others and had the appearance of one who was still alive.

'And her?' Jago asked. 'Why is she so different?'

'New to the moon,' the man said. 'For thirty days she will be that way and before the next full moon she will change to be like us.'

'A ghost?' he asked as he reached out to touch the woman before him.

'She can't see us – not yet,' said the man. 'She is alive like you – perhaps she looks for you as you sleep.'

'I will wake,' Jago said as he stamped the earth with his feet. The shadows around him screamed and moaned. The child hid behind the grave in fear of what Jago would do. The man stood further away.

'Strackan will not be pleased. He lives in your world and by now will know you are here.'

'Strackan? I don't care for creatures of dreams. I sleep and you are just my imagination.' Jago stepped towards the man. 'Strackan is cheese. I know when a dream is a dream.'

'Then you know nothing,' screamed a woman with a half-eaten face who stood on a flat tomb. 'Strackan will do to you what he has done to us.'

From all around him came cries of fear at the mention of the name. The shadows howled like wolves, and it was then that Jago saw that each one was chained to its grave.

Jago ran in fear towards the steps, desperate to wake from his sleep.

'There will be a kill tonight. As one is buried in darkness – so will one be taken from life – that is the way. Whilst the red star shines, Strackan will do this to the world,' the man shouted to him.

'Imagination, that's all you are – be gone,' Jago said as he sprinted down the steps towards the town and the tiny hous-es that clung to the side of the cliff below the tall chimneys of Streonshalgh Manor.

When he reached the alleyway that led to the beach, Jago stopped running. He looked back. The corpses that had crowded around him were gone. Even though he thought

this to be a dream, he was out of breath. It was unlike anything he had known. The streets were empty, the houses dark
and shuttered. Jago was alone – or so he thought.

As he walked, he was unaware of the dark shape that followed him along Church Street towards the cobbled marketplace. It kept pace, always at a distance, following his every
move with the eyes of a cat. As he had done when waking,
he looked at the houses and listened at the doors. As before,
some rooms were quiet, others had voices within. Then came
the whispering – at first like a seeping but with every step it
got louder as he approached a cottage near to an alleyway
with a sign above that said *Arguments Yard*.

A woman stepped from the shadows of the doorway. She
didn't see him; it was as if she was not part of his dream. Jago
stepped through her before he could stop. He shuddered;
everything in her mind flooded his. He knew her name –
where she was going – who she was meeting. Jago could even
smell the beer on her breath. In that instant, he knew her
husband was a fisherman at sea. The woman was going home
– she was worried about the dark, about walking alone. Her
thoughts were a deluge on his mind, like a loud voice speaking in his head. Jago could sense everything about her.

'Sara,' he said as she walked away from him. She stopped
and looked over her shoulder. Her worst fears were being realised. Sara walked faster. Jago called her name again. 'Sara.'

The woman started to run towards the steps that led to
the church. Part of his mind seemed tied to hers. He felt her
fear and she his.

'Moses Clark!' She shouted the name of her husband in
desperation, as if he would come to her aid.

Then it struck without fear or warning. The dark shadow that had stalked Jago leapt from the blackness. It took the woman by surprise, but not before she could see its face. Jago shared the vision – he too smelt its breath.

It was a dog with the body of a man that bit her face and sank its teeth into her cheek.

'No!' Jago screamed, knowing it was already too late. The images of her mind had stopped. She thought of nothing, she was quite dead.

The creature looked at him as it dropped Sara Clark to the ground.

'A boy?' it asked as it stepped nearer. 'In this town, at this time?'

'A dream – just a dream,' Jago said, wishing he could wake.

'Lucky she is dead. I will save you for another day,' it said.

Jago stared at the creature.

'Are you Strackan?' he asked.

'You are well informed for one so young,' the creature said as it stepped back into the shadows, dragging the woman with it.

'No,' Jago shouted as Strackan stepped into the shadows. 'Leave her.' He lunged to grab Sara Clark and pull her from him. Strackan lashed out and struck him across the face. The blow knocked him back against the wall and he stumbled into the darkness of Arguments Yard.

Jago dreamt of nothing more that night. The wind stopped its picking at the roof tiles and swirling of the sea. The sun rose quickly and cleared what fog had clung to the river. He stirred in his bed to seven chimes of the church clock.

The room looked different in daylight. Gone were the shadows and fears of the night. He pulled back the thick red curtains and looked out to the churchyard, thankful that no one was there. Jago laughed to himself as he wiped the sweat from his face and poured the cold water from the jug on the washstand into the bowl. Then he looked at his hand. It was stained red with blood. Jago found the mirror on the wall by the door and stared at his reflection. It was with fear that he touched his face. What he'd thought was the sweat of the nightmare was far worse. Three talon-like cuts sliced across his cheek.

'Strackan?' he asked himself as the fear dawned that his experience of the night had been more than a dream.

[5]

Staxley

MRS MACARTY WAS RIGHT in saying that the smell of breakfast would be easy to follow. It permeated the whole house and crept upstairs like London smog. Jago was not sure, but the thick blue haze on the landing made it look as if the house was on fire. It sparkled in the sunlight that flooded in from the large rose-shaped window above the oak staircase. There was a strong smell of burning food – eggs in particular, as well as the faint odour of toast. Jago liked none of these things, he never had. Breakfast was a meal that he never usually ate – his bed, the warmest and most comfortable place in the world, saw to that. But here in Streonshalgh Manor the bed and his dreams were particularly cold and uncomfortable. He was sure he would never miss breakfast as long as he lived here.

The house didn't appear to be as threatening as on the night before. It didn't creak or moan, and sunlight had banished all the dark shadows. What he hadn't noticed the night before were the paintings that were hanging on every wall. From their appearance, the subjects of these portraits were obviously all members of the same family. From their dress, the paintings had been done over many hundreds of years.

59

What caught his eye was the similarity of one man who appeared in every generation of the gallery that stretched along the panelled corridor and down the stairs.

Jago stopped and read the inscription embedded on the gold frame of the largest painting. He brushed away the thick spider's web that covered the writing. The words shone brightly: *Baron Pippen Draigorian 1165*.

The man in the picture towered above him. He wore a golden coat with a cloak over his shoulder. His face was thin, his eyes dark and piercing. The lips were narrow and curled up at one side in an arrogant smile. It was this peculiar look that was the same in each portrait. It was either the same man again and again or the bumptious expression of the Draigorian heirs had been handed down from generation to generation.

'That's the Lord,' Tallow said. He was surprisingly close to Jago, who turned, startled. 'Saw you looking . . .'

'Tallow?' Jago asked. The man appeared even bigger in daylight than he had in the dark of his room.

'Tallow,' he replied with a nod of the head as he clanked along the corridor with a metal bucket and ragged mop. 'Going to clean – not your room.'

'Does he still live here?' Jago asked.

'Lost the Manor in a game of poker. Never stays in Whitby for long. Goes away and then the next in line comes back. Lives at Hagg House – but you'll know more of that if what Mrs Macarty says is true.'

The man sloped off and was gone in three long strides. Jago stood and looked at the picture and then sniffed the air. Something was definitely burning. Wisps of smoke spiralled up the staircase towards him. It was acrid and burnt his eyes.

'Porridge?' Jago asked himself as he took the stairs three at a time until he came to the hallway.

A woman, enveloped in a shroud of smoke, pushed open the scullery door and ran from the house with a burning pan in her hands.

'Forgot, forgot!' she cried as Mrs Macarty appeared close behind with a sweeping broom in her hands.

'You're the cook – how can you forget the porridge?' she screamed. She looked as though she would have bent the broom over the woman's back had Jago not been there. 'Jago, good to see you. Thought you would have still been in bed – first morning and all.'

Mrs Macarty seemed pleasantly surprised. Jago even noted a hint of a smile that softened her eyes and made her look as if she was squinting at him. She said nothing of the cuts to his face.

'I smelt breakfast,' he said as he stepped to one side to allow the cook to come back into the scullery.

'Didn't we all,' Mrs Macarty replied soberly.

The woman had left the pan outside and the door open. It burnt in the yard near to the statue of the gladiator.

'Still burning,' she said, pointing to the pan. 'Din't know porridge was so combustible.'

'Neither did I,' Macarty added with a raised eyebrow. 'The worst of war, Jago, is not being able to get the proper staff. This is the first post Maisie has had as a cook – isn't it, Maisie?' she asked.

The woman nodded and skulked back into the scullery,

firmly closing the door behind her as if she didn't want Mrs Macarty to follow.

'I cook,' Jago said.

'Then we will have to take you up on your offer,' she replied as she pointed to the dining room with the broom. 'Breakfast is in there. I would suggest you eat it as quickly as you can. Once it's gone, it's gone, and the other boys don't stick to any convention of politenesses.'

Jago looked inside the room. Like all the others it was clad in dark wood panels. Again, pictures of the Draigorian family bedecked the walls. There were three tables, each with three chairs. One table was full of boys the same age as Jago. When he entered the room, the eldest boy looked at him and then turned away without breaking from his loud conversation.

At another table, three younger children looked meekly at the door. Jago couldn't tell if they were boys or girls. They wore the same clothes. They all looked the same, with their hair cut in a pudding bowl around their heads, as if they were a family.

'You new?' shouted the boy at the first table as he got to his feet.

Jago understood this wasn't said in welcome. The boy looked him up and down in search of any weakness. Jago had seen it all before, in every playground of every school he had been expelled from. In ten years, he had been forced to leave all the schools in Shoreditch. It would always start with that look and Jago would never back down.

'Jago Harker. Arrived last night,' he said, staring the boy in the eye.

'I'm Staxley – this is Griffin and Lorken. You can sit with her.'

The boy pointed to a table in the corner of the room. Jago hadn't noticed the solitary girl. Her face was covered in long ringlets of red hair that hung to the table like clusters of ruby vines.

'You'd be good for each other,' Griffin added, slathering his words like a hungry dog.

Jago didn't reply. He looked at the girl, who kept her head down and face covered. He walked across the room, pulled out a chair and sat at the table.

'You get what you want from there,' Staxley said, pointing to a trolley in the corner of the room. 'This table goes first, always. Come on, boys – before there is none left.' Jago didn't move. He smiled at Staxley, watching him and the others carefully as they helped themselves, filling their plates then slumping back in their seats. 'Gladlings next,' Staxley added as he filled his mouth with bacon and chewed contentedly. 'All they eat is bread – never knew anything else so why feed them more?'

Timidly, the three smaller children got up from the table and crossed the room. Each came back holding a single crust of toasted bread. All the while they kept their eyes to the floor for fear of looking at Staxley and his companions.

'Your turn,' Lorken said, food dropping from his mouth as he spoke. 'You and her can have what's left.'

The girl never moved. She kept her face to the table, her hair curtained so she could not see or be seen.

'Breakfast?' Jago asked as he stood up. The girl nodded.

Jago went to the trolley and took what was left. There was

just enough to fill one plate with a crisp egg and burnt bacon. He picked a knife and fork from an old wooden tray and went back to the table.

'Good to see you've learnt the rules so quickly, Jago,' Staxley said as he finished his food. 'This is how it's been and how it will be. We were here first, understand?'

Jago didn't answer; he pushed the plate towards the girl and slid the knife and fork in place.

'Thought you might be hungry,' he said.

'Quite,' the girl replied in a whisper without looking at him.

'All that was left,' he said.

'More than yesterday,' she replied as she looked up. 'I'm Biatra – been here a couple of days. People call me Bia . . .'

Jago said nothing. He couldn't help look at her face. There was a distinct scar on her top lip that twisted into the base of her nose. On the side of her face, her skin was stained as red as her hair. It looked like the shape of the new moon cut with a thin cloud.

'Jago,' he finally managed to say.

'I was born this way, before you ask,' replied Bia quietly. 'They won't let me forget it.' She nodded to Staxley, who was grinning like a pig. His hair was spiked on top and shaved at the sides.

'*He* was born like that,' Jago added and then laughed.

The girl smiled and took her hand from her mouth.

Without warning, a tight fist gripped Jago by the ear and twisted it hard.

'Don't think I didn't hear what you said,' Staxley muttered as he pushed his face closer to Jago.

'You were meant to,' Jago replied. Without hesitation, he took hold of Staxley's fingers and started to squeeze tighter and tighter until he screamed. 'And tomorrow, Staxley, the Gladlings eat first, understand?' he said as he crushed Staxley's fingers to almost breaking. Lorken jumped to his feet, pushing back the chair. Griffin stood but held back as he looked to see what would happen. Jago held Staxley in his grip. 'Call off the dogs, Staxley.'

Staxley looked back to the table and the two sat down.

'Not here, not now,' he said to them. 'Stupid thing to do on your first morning, Jago. We could have been such good friends.'

'Friends, friends . . . Good to see you're all getting on so well,' Mrs Macarty said as she entered the room carrying a pot of tea. 'I expect you'll be going to work now, Stax. Go on and earn your keep. Madame Trevellas will be waiting.' She laughed as she eyed them keenly. 'And you too, my little Gladlings – schoolwork and then help Tallow with the rooms, understand?'

Bia did not look at Mrs Macarty. She ate the food and didn't speak.

'And what would you like me to do?' Jago asked her as Staxley looked back from the door.

'It's arranged for you to go with her. She'll take you to Hagg House – meet young Mr Draigorian – Biatra will tell you what to do.'

'And school?' Jago asked.

'School? Long forgotten for a lad of your age. The Gladlings are good learners, but you'll have to work. Drink your tea and then be off. Isn't that right, Biatra?'

Bia looked up and tried to smile.

'Yes, Mrs Macarty,' she said.

'Biatra is from Whitby. Lived in the town. We never usually take locals. Only those selected from other parts of the country – the needy. But Biatra had no choice but to come here since . . .'

Mrs Macarty left the words unsaid and walked away with her hands clasped.

'Since?' Jago asked.

'My mother is missing – father at war. No one left. Had an auntie once but she went away long ago and never came back. Officially classed as an orphan. Get special treatment because of this,' she said, pointing to the cleft scar on her lip. 'But don't you think I'm different or stupid. Can't help what you're born with.'

Jago looked at her eye to eye.

'Looks like the moon has touched your face,' Jago said as he gently touched the port-wine stain under her left ear.

'It causes trouble. They all think I'm a bad omen – freak of nature.'

'For that?' he asked.

'This is Whitby. Full of superstition and magic,' she replied.

'And don't you believe in all that yourself?' Jago asked as he got up from the table.

'I believe in what I can see – ghosts are for stupid people. I was told that a Vampyre had taken my mother. That's what they said when she went missing a week ago. Vampyres – how stupid.'

'What's a Vampyre?' Jago asked.

'They say around here it's a creature that hunts for people at night and takes them away. Sometimes it looks like a dog, a man or just a shadow. Last time it attacked was a hundred years ago. When that comet appeared. Now, they say it's here again, they say Strackan has come back,' Bia said as she threw back her long, red, spiralled locks of hair.

'Strackan? Is that its name?' he asked as he remembered his dream.

'One of them,' Bia replied, wondering why he had such an interest. 'My mother talked about Vampyres all the time. Now she's gone.'

He could see she was about to cry. Jago felt uncomfortable and out of place.

'My mother is dead,' Jago said as he put his hand on her shoulder. 'She was killed in a bombing two days ago.'

'My mother is still alive,' Bia snapped. 'I know it. She's not dead. I'll prove it. Vampyres don't snatch people from the street and kill them – there are no shadows that suck the life from you.'

'It's not true,' Maisie said as she stepped in the room and looked at them both. 'I've seen Strackan. I know he's real.'

'You would say that – your family always did. They made money from it,' Bia shouted.

'How?' Jago asked.

'They sell charms to ward off Vampyres – stop them reading your mind – that's what Vampyres do. Maisie has a stall in the market. Trinkets, amulets, black stones.'

'They work and if your mother had one she would still be here today,' Maisie said cuttingly as she ran from the room.

'So they really do believe in Vampyres?' he asked.

'Vampyres?' asked Mrs Macarty as she stood in the doorway. 'I heard all this noise and wondered what was going on. Thought it must be something,' she said with her arms folded.

'Is it true?' Jago asked her.

Mrs Macarty looked surprised.

'Some around here would say that Strackan was real. It started in the time of the Reverend Obadiah Demurral – but that was long ago. Lord Strackan was a name that we all feared as children. My mother said that if we weren't good he would snatch us from our cot and we would never be seen again. But then again, she could lie straight in bed.' Mrs Macarty laughed. 'This won't get you to work. You know what Draigorian thinks about lateness, Biatra.'

The girl nodded and stood up to go.

'So I take him with me?' she asked.

'He's expected,' Macarty replied lugubriously, as if she didn't want Jago to go. 'Tallow isn't what he used to be. I have a few jobs around here when you get back, Jago.' Mrs Macarty smiled and touched the cuts on his cheek. 'You been scratching in your sleep?'

'They were there when I woke. I don't know how it happened,' Jago replied.

'Does that to people, that bed. It belonged to Pippen Draigorian, the man who built this house – you can't throw out something like that.' She thought for a moment. 'I'll get you an extra pillow for tonight.' Bia left the room and Jago followed. 'Don't be late back, Biatra. Draigorian only pays for eight hours – remind him of that. And Jago, save some of your strength – don't want you too tired.'

Outside Streonshalgh Manor, the porridge pan still smouldered by the statue of the gladiator.

'Agasias the warrior,' Bia said mockingly as she pulled her coat tightly to her to keep out the chill morning breeze. 'Maisie will tell you that she's seen him come to life.'

'That's what she told you?' Jago asked as he walked quickly to keep pace.

'Maisie says all sorts of things. Told me the Manor was haunted, that Strackan took my mother – but at least she goes home every night.'

'And you don't believe her?' Jago asked.

'All superstition. My father went to war and something happened to my mother. That's all I know.'

'And Draigorian?' he asked just as they walked quickly towards the steps by the church.

'His family used to own Streonshalgh Manor and then it was lost. They're all buried behind the church. Every one of them back to Pippen Draigorian.' Bia looked up at the clock on the tower of the church. Jago could tell she was thinking. 'We had to learn all their names at school.'

'I don't want to look,' he said before she could speak.

'Come on. Then you can tell Maisie. She tries to frighten everyone with the story about how she saw Pippen Draigorian coming from the grave.'

He followed reluctantly. Bia wound her way in and out of the tombstones until she was at the far side of the church. Jago remembered it from his dream. The scene was fearfully uncanny; all was just as he had seen it the night before. There was the fresh grave. The soil was beaten down with no marker to say who was deep within.

'Who died?' he asked.

'A woman from the factory. It's by the river – there was an accident,' Bia said as she gripped a large brass handle embedded into the wall of the church. 'This is the door to the Draigorian tomb and here are the names.'

Jago looked from the grave to the wall. He hadn't seen this in his dream. The stones of the church looked as though they formed the door to the vault. It was about the same height as Tallow and wide enough for a coffin to be passed through. A double-handed brass ring was slipped through a stone sculpture of a large dog to form the handle of the door. A skirting of lead filled the entrance so it could not be opened easily and two long bolts held the stones in place.

'How do they get in?' Jago asked.

'Draigorians never seem to die in Whitby. They have a house in London. It is always by coincidence they all die there. My mother said that the last time one of them died it took two days to open the tomb. They brought him on a train and four horses carried him through the town. Look – here's his plaque.'

Bia pointed to the bottom of a neat row of brass plaques that lined the wall. The oldest was that of Pippen Draigorian, his name high above the others.

'He died in 1193 aged one hundred and two,' Jago said. He then read each of the thirteen names until he came to the final one. 'Xavier Draigorian, 1929. Age ninety-seven.'

'They all die old,' Bia replied as she rattled the handle in the dog's mouth. 'We'll be working for Crispin Draigorian and he's really ancient.'

Jago wasn't listening to what she said. Without a word he

was walking towards the grave he had seen in his dream, the grave clung to by a ragged boy. It was small and made of sandstone. The end was carved with a skull and crossbones. He bent down and looked at the carvings.

'So it really *was* here,' he said to himself, not realising that Bia had followed him.

'What was?' she asked.

'This grave – do you know anything about it?' Jago asked as the chill morning wind blew through his hair.

Bia looked confused. Her eyes flicked from the grave to the church clock.

'Only what Maisie said,' she replied reluctantly.

'More ghosts?' Jago asked.

'It's the grave of the first boy ever to be taken by Strackan. It's the oldest grave in the churchyard. The money to bury him was given by –'

'Pippen Draigorian?' he asked before she could go on.

'How did you know?' Bia asked just as the clouds parted and the churchyard was flooded with warm sunlight.

'The kind of boy whose mother would bring him flowers every day until she came no more,' Jago replied.

'Has Maisie told you?' Bia asked, unsure how he knew of the boy.

'A boy who is weeping and can be heard in the dark of night?' Jago asked, knowing what she would say.

'A ghost that cries for his mother who didn't come back,' Bia answered as the dark clouds rolled in from the sea.

[6]

Crispin Draigorian

THE ROAD FROM THE TOWN clung to the narrow strip of land between the fishermen's cottages and the far side of the harbour. It twisted towards the thick woodland on top of the hill. Jago walked with Bia. Conversation had stopped by the bridge across the river. It was as if a cowl of dread descended on her. He had tried to talk, but she never replied to any of his questions. The silence was uncomfortable; Bia walked quickly and Jago kept pace. It gave him time to think of all that had happened. His gulps of breath kept down the panic that tried to break from his chest every time he thought of his mother. Despite his fears, there was something about Whitby that made him feel at ease. The light was benevolent, the clouds high, the sun cool. It felt as if he belonged, like he was a part of the place. London was always moving; people ebbed back and forth like the tide. Here there was space and openness, while the houses were small with neatly painted doors and flowerpots at the windows.

'That's it, up there,' Bia said eventually as they started to walk up a hill towards a large white-painted house above a factory on the quayside. 'Hagg House. Home of Crispin Draigorian – and the place we'll be cleaning.'

'Cleaning?' Jago asked quite surprised.

'Mrs Macarty gets paid for our work and we get bed, board and a shilling a week,' Bia replied, as if it was quite acceptable for this to be done.

'How much does she charge Draigorian and who makes the profit?' Jago asked pointedly as he snorted his breath.

'Better than working in the factory or being on the street. That's where I would have been without my mother around. I worked there before she . . .'

Jago stopped at the entrance to a short gravel drive that led from the road to the stone-roofed factory with crumbling brickwork. The large building looked as though it was falling into the river. A high wire fence surrounded it. Two soldiers in black uniforms, unlike any he had seen before, walked with dogs around the perimeter. They gave him a cursory glance before one of them nodded and they carried on their patrol.

'What happens in there?' he asked, looking at a more modern building that covered part of the river.

'Something to do with the war,' Bia replied. 'Submarines, I think. Best not be hanging around. They don't like townies in there.'

'What?' he asked.

'They get all their workers from elsewhere. They live in the huts by the river. No one ever sees them. More like a prison than a factory,' she went on. 'When they opened the factory, that's when the noises started under the sea and the rumbling. My dad said they had tunnels going out to the bay – filled with explosive. That's what he'd heard in the pub.'

'You ever been in?' he asked inquisitively. 'Could be well worth a look.'

'They'd shoot you as a spy. They caught one. Chased him through the town and gunned him down outside the church on Baxtergate. My mother saw it. They said he was an infiltrator. She said he was screaming for them not to shoot – but they cornered him against the door and shot him dead.'

'Spies? In Whitby?' he replied.

'That's what my mother said. Must be something really secret going on in there to get spies. Draigorian owns the factory, but no one knows what it's really for.' Bia tugged his coat for him to move on.

Jago looked up to the roof of the factory. There, by the tall, blackened chimneystack, was the eye of what he knew was a periscope. Just like the one he had seen on the submarine, it glowed in a deep green as if it was illuminated from within.

'And they watch us through that thing,' he said as he pointed up to the roof.

'They have them all over the town. When the war started the first one appeared. Can't understand it. They say they are there to protect us. But they never saw where my mother went.'

'What did she do?' Jago asked.

'She mended shoes by day and was an air-raid warden at night. She left and never came back. I just can't understand it.' Bia sighed. 'On the day after she went missing a letter arrived saying that my dad had been lost in action and that he was most probably a prisoner of war.'

Jago could see the tears well in her deep blue eyes. Bia pulled her hair across her face and wiped away the tears. He wanted to cry with her, to take her in his arms and hold her close. He knew that's what his mother would do. Every

74

morning as soon as he woke from his sleep she would hold him tight and whisper in his ear. 'You're a special lad, Jago – always remember that.' She had said those words day in and day out for as long as he could remember.

Jago reached into his pocket and pressed the handkerchief into her hand.

'My mother ironed it – gave it extra starch – careful it don't cut, it's so sharp,' Jago said.

Bia looked up at him as the cleft scar on her lip twitched anxiously. 'Mine would do the same – pressed them into squares that were so stiff they wouldn't open,' she said, smiling. 'Old Draigorian will think we're not coming – better be off.' She coughed as she walked on. 'One thing. Only speak when he talks to you and watch out for Clinas the butler. He's Mrs Macarty's brother. That's how she got you the job.'

Within a minute the house loomed above them as if it had risen from the earth of the thick woodland that surrounded it. The walls were freshly painted, the brass door handles brightly polished. In the light of the morning sun that warmed the estuary, the windows shone like silver. Even the fallen leaves had been picked from the gravel drive and not a flower was out of place. It stood in stark contrast to the rows of shabby huts that Jago could see lining the riverbank at the bottom of the escarpment below the house.

'He lives here?' Jago asked as he followed Bia to the back door.

'Since the death of his father. Lived in London before then. We'd never seen him until he arrived.' Bia knocked on the door and then rubbed away the finger smudges with the hem of her coat sleeve.

The door opened. A man in every way the image of Mrs Macarty stood before them. He was dressed in dapper black trousers, white shirt and yellow waistcoat. His sleeves were covered in leather cuff aprons that were wrapped around his arms to the elbow. For a moment he stood glum-faced and curled his lip as he inspected them both with a critical eye.

'Three minutes early,' he said in a slow drawl. 'How do you explain that?'

Bia laughed. The man held his surly look for another moment and then smiled.

'This is Jago, Mr Clinas. He's our new help,' she quipped as she stepped by him and walked into the large kitchen.

'Then Jago better come in before he catches his death,' Clinas said as he held out his hand. 'I am Clinas – but I expect that she has told you all about me and you will have met my sister?'

Jago didn't know what to say. He had expected that Clinas would be like his sister. When he first saw him and his sullen face, he was sure that he was right. Now the man smiled warmly and held out his hand to be shaken.

'Jago,' was all he could reply as he gripped the man's hand. It was soft and warm and he could feel the beating of a pulse that he was not sure was his own.

'Then, Jago, you must have tea . . . and toast . . . and possibly both,' Clinas said with an effete manner. 'I have orders to introduce you to the Master at ten sharp. So we have plenty of time.' Clinas scrutinised Jago's face as if he recognised him. 'Are you sure we haven't met before? You seem familiar.'

'First time here,' Jago said quietly as he stepped into the house. 'It couldn't be possible.'

76

'Did you sleep well? My sister isn't the best of hosts and that house is the coldest in Whitby. I told Mr Draigorian the other day that it wasn't a loss when it was gambled away. Hagg House is far brighter and better, if you ask me – which I know you haven't.'

The man gabbled quickly as he suddenly took three eggs from his sleeve and began to juggle them in the air. 'The first one I drop, you can eat,' he said as he laughed. Then, with sleight of hand, the eggs vanished. 'Ta-daah,' he sang irksomely.

Bia clapped. Jago leant back against the metal counter.

'Jago got his ear twisted by Staxley. Then he saw him off and he went away red-faced,' she gossiped as she put the kettle on the range at the far end of the ornate kitchen.

'He's one to watch, Jago,' Clinas said as he walked to the pantry and took out some bread. 'Don't turn your back on him. He came here for two days and took whatever wasn't nailed to the floor. He has a libertine approach to property.'

'Said he was in charge and I would have to obey,' Jago answered.

'Not one to take on alone, but you look a big enough lad to fight for yourself,' Clinas replied as he sliced the bread and somehow managed to fry the eggs at the same time. 'By the marks on your face you already have,' he added.

'Just woke up with them,' Jago said without thinking. 'Must have scratched myself in the night.'

He saw Clinas look at Bia but the man said nothing. It was as if he needed no words for her to understand. His eyes said it all. For a moment there was an uncomfortable silence. Jago looked out of the window to the factory below. Steam spilled from the chimney, rolling down the brickwork and across the broken roof tiles.

'Tea,' Bia said as Jago turned to the long table in the middle of the room.

The fried eggs had been plated on a slice of thick bread that he dared to believe had been covered in butter. It had been so long that Jago had forgotten what butter tasted like. Clinas saw him staring at the food.

'Rationing in London, Jago?' he asked.

'Everything,' he replied. 'Never seen so many eggs in two days.'

'We have some things we can't get hold of, but the Master has many friends,' Clinas said reverently.

'What do they do at the factory?' Jago asked as he watched more steam billow from the chimney.

'Careless talk costs lives, what you don't know you can't tell and what you never ask won't get you in trouble,' he replied. 'It's all for the war effort and that's all I need to know.'

Clinas wiped his mouth and got to his feet in anticipation. A bell rang in the corner of the kitchen. Jago looked up. There on the wall was a row of small bells, each with the name of a room underneath. Steel wires disappeared into the ceiling. Clinas walked to the doorway and picked up a telephone. He glanced at the bell that was ringing and then dialed a number.

'Mr Draigorian,' Bia whispered as she ate the bread and eggs. 'He knows you're here. Been waiting to meet you.'

'But it's not ten o'clock,' he protested.

'Just do what he says,' she said under her breath.

Clinas put down the telephone and smiled.

'Show Jago the way, Biatra, and wait outside,' Clinas said as he opened the door. 'He'll tell you what he wants you to do. We have lunch at twelve-thirty. Leave what you're doing and come here,' he smiled. 'And welcome to our little family.'

It all appeared too perfect. Despite the warm welcome, Jago thought that something would go wrong. A sharp pain of trepidation twisted his stomach. He had the urge to run as a bead of sweat burst from his forehead.

'You look sick,' Bia said as she led him from the kitchen up two flights of servants' stairs and then on to a long white-painted landing.

They walked along the darkened corridor until they reached a large pair of oak doors. A sign hung from the handle, and on it were written the words KEEP OUT.

Jago looked at Bia, who knocked briskly and then stepped back before sitting down on an old chair opposite the door. She picked at the green flock wallpaper with her fingernails. Jago waited.

'Come in,' said the voice from the other side of the door.

He hesitated and looked at Bia, who nodded for him to go in. Jago turned the handle very slowly, hoping the door wouldn't open. When it did, he stepped inside.

The room was dark and lit only by a candle on a desk by the boarded windows. He could see the shadowy outline of a man. Jago closed the door and stood in the gloom. On the walls of the room he could vaguely see the outlines of picture frames. There was a sofa and table by an empty fireplace.

'I am Jago Harker,' he said, not knowing what else to say.

'I know,' replied the man. 'Mrs Macarty told me all about you. From London, aged fifteen. Sent here by your mother.'

'She's dead,' Jago said.

'Time goes so slowly, Jago,' the man said in reply as he tapped the desk with the tip of his pen. 'Step into the light so I can see your face.' Jago did as he asked. Stepping closer he glimpsed the face of the man. *Pippen Draigorian*, he thought for a moment as the man smiled. 'Crispin Draigorian,' the man said as if he could read Jago's mind. 'Pippen Draigorian died some years ago, but I admit there is a resemblance.'

'I'm sorry, I didn't realise I said . . .' Jago answered, wondering if the words had left his lips.

'Everyone who sees that portrait at Streonshalgh Manor makes the same mistake and I heard from Clinas that you were in my old room. So you would have seen the portrait of old Pippen even with your eyes closed. We are very much alike. Some people call me a throwback.'

'Your old room?' Jago asked.

'Did I say that?' he replied. 'I meant *the* old room. My family moved to Hagg House before I was born. I have visited Streonshalgh Manor several times – but bitterness at the loss of such a beautiful place makes one quite scornful. I hope one day to buy it back – but not before you have grown up and left.' Draigorian laughed quietly and then leant forward and looked him up and down. 'Have we met before?'

'I have never been here,' Jago said, wondering why it was that everyone in Whitby asked if they had seen him before.

'It's because you look familiar,' Draigorian answered the unasked question. 'Your mother – where was she from?'

Jago hesitated. He tried to keep the photograph of his mother out of his mind for fear Draigorian would see it. He quickly thought of the bombing, Cresco and Brick Lane.

'London. My mother died in London.'

'I see,' Draigorian sighed. 'London must be such a terrible place. My own son is there at the moment. I fear for him. Whitby has not yet been touched by the war and I hope it will remain that way. It is enough for us to cope with the comet. It isn't really a comet but a conflagration of several stars, an alignment beyond belief – have you seen RedEye?'

'At the station last night,' Jago replied.

'I hear the mayor was found drunk in a hedge,' Draigorian said immediately after the very same thought had crossed Jago's mind.

'Mr Bradick welcomed me to the town. I am the only evacuee.'

'Then we should make you welcome. It is a shame you have to come here to work. Can you read?' he asked excitedly. 'I have several rooms filled with books that go back hundreds of years. I am sure a lad like you would enjoy looking through them.' Draigorian stopped for a moment and looked at Jago. 'In fact,' he said, 'if you can read you can find one book that I fear is lost.'

'Yes,' muttered Jago, not really knowing what Draigorian wanted him to do.

'Good,' the man said. 'I have misplaced something that I need. A book of great price and value. Perhaps you will find it for me?'

'Of course,' Jago replied as he watched Draigorian study him intently.

'It is an old diary of a foreign king. It is called The Book of Krakanu. It is very old, the binding is blue – that is what I remember. I lost it many years ago and cannot find it.'

Jago could not believe the words he had just heard. He thought of Cresco and the tiny flat below his own in Shoreditch. In his mind he saw Cresco by the fire, and just as he was about to imagine the man start to tell him the story he looked at Draigorian.

'Krakanu?' he asked.

It was as he spoke that Jago saw the man clearly for the first time. He didn't look as old as Bia said he was. Draigorian was definitely not ancient. His eyes sparkled in the candle-light and a broad smile cut across a lined face. If anything, Jago thought, the man was not much older than his mother, but he knew that could not be.

'That is the name. I would be most obliged if you could find it for me,' Draigorian said as he studied the boy. 'I have a condition that stops me leaving this room in daylight. It comes and goes and has been the curse of my family. Some call it porphyria – it is when daylight burns the skin. If you could find the book for me, it would be work well done.'

Jago felt as if the man stared deep within his mind. He was the image of the painting of Pippen Draigorian. The eyes and the smile were just the same. For a moment he dared wonder if a man could live that long and never change.

'And that is what you would want me to do?' Jago asked.

'I am an old man, and it would be good to find the book before I *go on*,' Draigorian said softly as he moved his finger through the flame of the candlelight. 'I find it hard to see with just a candle, and all the rooms are shuttered so I can walk the house in the day. You, Jago, would have the light to guide you in what I ask.'

Jago looked at the outline of the picture above the fireplace. It was the only one he had seen in the house that was of a woman.

'Who is that?' he asked as he stared at the shadows across her face.

'A dear, old friend,' Draigorian replied as he again tapped the desk impatiently.

There was a gentle knock at the door. Clinas stepped in. He carried a tray on which were a glass of wine and a slither of cheese.

'Time for you to eat and for Jago to start his work,' Clinas said as his eyes told Jago to leave the room. 'Biatra is outside – she will tell you what to do.'

'I have given him a job, gainful employment, Clinas,' Draigorian interrupted. 'Jago is to be my librarian. The boy can read and he knows what I want him to do – don't you, Jago?'

Jago bowed his head.

'So he is not to clean?' Clinas asked sharply as his mood changed, his words tainted with slight protest.

'Far from it. Jago is to sort all my books and he has all the war to do it.'

'The library – but what if . . .?' Clinas asked, eyeing Jago warily as he left the room.

Draigorian looked as though he had suddenly remembered some vital piece of information.

'I think . . . I think he will be good for the job, Clinas – under your guidance, of course,' he replied.

[7]

Poltergeist

THE DOOR OPENED and Clinas stepped outside. He
looked perturbed, his brow was wrinkled and a flick of
long black hair trailed over his face. Jago could see that what
mirth he had was now no more. He nodded to Bia, who was
standing by the shuttered window, allowing the thin shafts of
sunlight to dance across her hand.

'Jago is going to the library,' Clinas said to her as he pushed
Jago in the back.

'The library?' Bia asked. 'He's not coming with me?'

She sounded concerned, as she stared at Clinas.

'He'll be fine – we'll get on with what we have to do. Be
back in the kitchen for midday, Biatra. I'll show Jago the library.' Clinas tried to sound convincing. He glanced at Bia as
she walked back along the corridor without a word. 'She's a
good lass – shame about her mother,' he added.

'Disappeared?' Jago asked as Clinas walked ahead of him
along the corridor, then opened a panelled door in the wall
that led to a flight of narrow wooden stairs.

'You'll hear all sorts of things about that, Jago,' Clinas said
as he went ahead and lit a small lamp with a Zippo lighter.
'Her mother hasn't been the only one who has gone miss-

ing. There's talk that only last night a woman vanished on Church Street – nothing to say she had even been there. Since the comet came back, six people have vanished. Just like before.'

'Before?' Jago asked as he trooped on behind, taking each step carefully in the shadowy gloom.

'A hundred years ago, one person vanished every day it lit up the sky,' Clinas said. He opened a small door that led on to another dark landing. 'It's expected – rumours spread and if someone goes missing they blame the comet. They say it makes people go mad – up there always looking down on them like the eye of God.'

'Do they ever find them?' Jago asked as Clinas lit another lantern that hung on the wall with a brass stand.

'Sometimes,' he said slowly. He thought how much to tell Jago. 'There's a tradition that if someone goes missing you always give them a funeral the next day – even if you can't find the body. Started with the sailors, when they were lost at sea. So many empty coffins in that churchyard, all with a headstone.'

'Why?' Jago asked.

'People need somewhere to go when they're grieving – especially for those lost at sea,' Clinas replied as he got to the library door.

'So where did they all go – these people who disappeared when the comet arrived?' Jago asked.

'I did hear that they found a boy once, but he was all messed up and could have fallen from the cliff. Could be they are still alive and just left the town. Whitby does that to some people.' Clinas pushed open the door and looked inside. A cold, icy chill rushed through the doorway and filled the corridor. Clinas shivered. 'Never come up here,' he said. He stepped inside, flicked the wheel of the lighter and held the flame above his head. 'Must be a candle somewhere?'

'What about opening the shutters?' Jago asked.

'Can't do that – never. Mr Draigorian wouldn't like that.'

'But he's not here,' Jago replied.

'Can't take the chance. The light will burn his skin. We only open the shutters at night, and now with the blackout we don't even do that.' Clinas found the candelabra on the table and lit the candles one by one. 'It is inherited. His skin blisters.'

As each light grew in brightness, Jago could see more of the vast room. It disappeared into the distant darkness and its oak-ribbed vaulted roof made him feel he was inside a whale.

Shelves of books stretched from floor to ceiling. Each was crammed with volumes and volumes of novels, journals and other books. Their leather spines were dull and dusty, as if no one had visited that place for some considerable time.

Clinas looked uncomfortable. He shuddered every now and then as he looked around to check if they were alone. It was the smell that Jago recognised more than anything – the sultry, musky odour was the same as that in Cresco's apartment. It made him feel at home.

'Where do I start?' he asked Clinas as he walked to the fireplace and looked at the smoke-stained portrait that hung on the only piece of wall not covered by books.

'He gave you the job and not me,' Clinas replied cautiously as he backed towards the door. 'You sure you know the way back to the kitchen? I'll beat the dinner gong for you to find us.'

'I should be fine,' Jago said as he looked to the highest shelf. 'One book to find in all this?'

'Mr Draigorian is not the man he once was. He becomes forgetful. The book might not even be here. Which one has he asked you to search for?' Clinas asked.

'The Book of Krakanu,' Jago answered.

Clinas shook his head as he stepped from the room. 'Never heard of it – not something I would read.' He laughed nervously. 'Better be off – jobs to do.'

Clinas said no more. He closed the door quietly as he left the room. Jago listened as his footsteps echoed along the corridor and then down the dark stairway. He was left in a cold, bleak silence with just the light from five candles in the centre of the long table that seemed to run the length of the room. Thick curtains that trailed to the floor covered the window shutters, blocking out the light. Jago did not dare open them for fear of what could happen to Draigorian. It was clear the library had not been used for some time. A fire was set in the iron grate ready and waiting to be lit. Two leather chairs stood as sentinels, their claw feet gripping a shabby and threadbare rug. It was as if the room had just been left and that someone was reluctant to return.

'Some job,' he said out loud to break the silence. He took several books from the nearest shelf and laid them on the table.

Jago had decided to clear a shelf at a time. He would examine each book before returning them to their place. He knew it would take some time, but as Draigorian had said, he had all the war to do it. Being in the library was better than cleaning and at least this way he would be alone with his thoughts.

It wasn't too long before he had cleared one shelf and neatly placed the books on the table. He checked each title as he replaced the books and searched the back of the deep shelf. After fifty books, his fingers became numb with the cold. Jago rubbed his hand over the candle flames. Then, taking a candle, he lit the tight rolls of paper beneath the wood and coal in the grate. It was something he had seen his mother do so often. Jago didn't want the memory. It was painful how an action in everyday life could lead the mind to a place it didn't want to be.

As he watched the flames he thought of his mother and wondered if she could still be alive. Jago had tried not to give way to the thought, but it flooded in and he could not resist. The fire burnt quickly; the tinder took light and flames licked the back of the grate. Shadows danced across the ceiling. Jago could see more of the room. High above were cornices of gold in the shapes of animal heads. White plaster filled the gaps between the long crooks of oak beams. He could see how this insalubrious room had once been grand and inviting – but there were no echoes of the past, now it was dust ridden and dirty. The long curtains were moth-eaten and broke away from their hems.

Jago warmed himself by the fire and when his hands could again move he filled the shelf and then started on another. It was as he pulled the third book from this upper shelf that a small picture slipped from inside the cover. It fell to the floor onto its face, leaving the bold writing for him to read.

1861 London PD.

Jago turned the frail old photograph. There was Crispin Draigorian just as he was now. He was no younger, no older. In his hands was a small chalice. It was identical to the one given to him by Cresco.

'The Cup of Garbova,' Jago said, realising what the man held. 'But how?' He looked again at the date. 'Eighty years ago? That makes him over a hundred – it can't be . . . PD – Pippen Draigorian . . . never . . .?' There was a sudden dull thud as a large volume fell from an upper shelf and landed on the floor. The book burst open and pages fluttered to the wooden boards. Jago jumped back and looked for a moment. The book then closed by itself and slowly moved towards the table, sliding across the floor. 'Who's there?' he asked, believing there was someone in the room.

The book stopped. In the light of the fire, Jago watched as the cover opened. It was as if someone invisible was casually browsing to find an item of interest. He stepped back towards the door. In his mind he knew he should run, find Clinas and tell him what he had seen. Jago didn't care if they didn't believe him. All he knew was that books did not have the power to move by themselves.

Just as he touched the brass door handle, another, smaller book fell from the highest of the upper shelves. It seemed to float like a small bird. Jago was mesmerised by the flapping flight of the book that winged its way towards him. There was another thud as a third book crashed to the floor and then the sound of laughter coming from the darkness at the far end of the room.

He tried to turn the handle. It wouldn't move.

'Who is it?' he demanded

There was another crash of a falling book and then the silver candelabra that Clinas had taken so much trouble to light began to slide away to the far end of the room. Jago watched as his breath faltered. He could feel the pulse beat in his neck and his leg tremble.

'Show yourself – come out! Bia, is that you? Clinas?'

The elaborate candlestick slid further away until it came to rest at the far end of the table. And now Jago saw what he had not seen before – a high-backed mahogany chair, and on the table was a solitary dinner setting of silver cutlery. He pulled on the door handle again, but it would not move. Jago was trapped.

The fire dimmed in the grate as a breeze of chilled air was sucked into the room. He watched helplessly as one by one the candles were blown out until all that lit his sight was the dull glow of the fire. He could not be sure, but now he thought he could see a shape in the chair. It was the outline of a man with a hollow void where the face should have been. There were no features, no contours, just blackness.

'Who is it?' he asked again, his voice cracking in his dry throat.

'Find me,' said the voice from the shadow. 'Will you find me, Jago?'

'Who are you?' Jago asked, backing away.

'Who do you want me to be – your mother – father – who?' The voice was shrill and mocking.

'Why are you doing this?' he asked.

'You came to me – you are searching for that which is not yours.'

'I'm looking for a book,' Jago replied, wondering what he was talking to.

'If only that were true,' said the voice. Then the shadow began to fade until he could see it no more.

'Where are you – what are you?' Jago demanded in the silence of the room.

Everything was still. The shadow had gone. Quickly, Jago searched the room. His hand still trembled. He took the candles and lit them from the fire. The light was warm. Holding the candelabra above his head he looked about and checked all the dark corners. He could find no one. The chill of the room began to lift as the warmth of the fire took hold again. Jago sat at the end of the long table and wondered if he was going mad and had dreamt it all. He looked at the photograph. It was Draigorian. Jago tried to make sense of all that had happened. He knew he was not dreaming and that the shadow was real.

It was then, just as he stood from his seat, that another book fell to the floor. He swallowed hard and gripped the candlestick in his hand.

'Did you think I had gone?' said the voice from behind him.

Jago could not move. He could feel the cold gasp of someone or something breathing on his neck. He stood as still as rock. In the reflection of the candelabra he could see a dark shape. It was close by, so close he could feel it touching him.

'What do you want from me?' Jago asked.

'Did you sleep well last night?' the shadow asked. 'You saw Strackan take that woman from the street and did nothing.'

'I was dreaming. There was nothing I could do.'

'You could have stopped him and saved her life,' it said in a whisper of cold breath.

'I was asleep – if I could see him, then . . .' He thought for a while. 'He was in my dream.'

'No, Jago. You were in *his* reality,' the shadow replied as he felt it come closer. 'How would you like to die?'

Jago could feel the hand tighten on his neck. Its fingers dug into his skin. He stood helplessly, not knowing what to do.

'Why kill me?' he asked.

'I can feel you shaking – is this what fear is like? Can you taste it?' the shadow asked.

Jago placed the candelabra on the table and tried to stare at the light. The hand gripped him tightly. Whatever the creature was, it had human form. He could feel it press against him. He could feel the grip of its hand. Jago felt he could not escape.

'I don't know you,' Jago said as the shadow pushed him forwards.

'Do you have to know who I am?' it answered.

'Are you Strackan?' asked Jago.

'Something far worse,' it whispered.

Jago slid his hand into his pocket. He could feel the pyx that Cresco had given to him. 'Tell me one thing,' he said as he undid the lid. 'What good will my death be?'

'You don't know who you are, do you, Jago? You don't know what you are?' the poltergeist said as Jago smeared his fingers with the thick resinous gel.

'I won't die,' he said as he took the hand from his pocket. 'Not without a fight.'

The shadow laughed. Jago turned quickly, breaking its grip, and lashed out with his hand. He ducked and struck a blow across what should have been its face. There was a loud shriek as the shadow broke into fragments of mist. Jago lashed out again at what remained, his hand slipping quickly through the air.

Again, Jago thought he was alone. Then, one by one, books began to tumble from all the shelves. They smashed to the wooden boards. Jago grabbed the door handle to get from the room. It burnt his skin.

'Going somewhere?' he heard the voice say as a book struck him in the chest.

Jago turned. Another book hit his shoulder, then another and another. It was as if the whole room was alive. Everything danced in the air as if on strings pulled by invisible hands. The long table up-ended and stood upright like a rearing horse. The chairs gathered around him and pressed in as if they were a herd of pigs biting at his legs. Even the two sentinel chairs by the fire rattled angrily.

The candelabra slid from the table, but instead of crashing to the floor it flew towards him. Before he could move, it stabbed into his chest, the candles burning against his leather coat before the flames died. The clock from the mantelpiece shot across the room and hit him in the face. Jago fell backwards, stumbling over the chairs.

Everything in the room began to clatter. He prayed that Clinas or Bia would hear the sound. No one came. The chairs stamped at him, their legs attacking him like spears. One pinned his coat to the floor whilst another chair beat him across the back. The fire burnt brightly in the grate, roaring angrily up the chimney and filling the room with acrid, choking smoke.

'No!' Jago screamed as he pushed away and got to his feet, just as a fire iron sped across the floor and impaled itself in the skirting board.

Dust billowed like smog as the wind shuddered through the floorboards beneath him. All the while he heard the laughter like that of chattering children.

'Give it up, Jago,' the voice bellowed from inside his head. 'You can't escape me.'

Jago dived and gripped the hem of a curtain. A hand grabbed his ankle to pull him back He twisted to get free as he dragged himself towards the window.

Reaching out with his hand, he gripped the bottom of the shutters.

'If only I can –' he gasped as another fire iron flew through the air, just missing his head.

Jago held on to the shutter as tightly as he could. His fingers pushed the catch upwards. He could feel himself being dragged back towards the table that was now moving up and down like the blade of a guillotine. The whole room was shaking. Jago gripped the handle as tightly as he could. He wanted to cry, wanted to give in, wished it would all end.

The tips of his fingers gripped the catch as he was lifted from the floor and pulled backwards towards the thumping table. The shutters held fast. Jago could hold on no more. The long table rose in the air as if preparing to slice down on him. His hand slipped from the catch as Jago flew backwards towards the fire, but just as the table was about to crash down upon him the shutter gave way. Sunlight flooded the room. It was blinding, bright and white. It filled every corner of darkness. The table hung in the air momentarily like an axe about to fall. Jago crashed to the floor. The table tilted and dropped on top of him, its long clawed leg smashing into the board next to his face. Everything in the room that had danced through the air suddenly fell. Chairs, books, candlesticks and pictures were strewn all around him.

He lay panting and out of breath. The sunlight bathed his face. Jago rolled from under the table and got to his feet. The room was devastated as if it had been struck by a tornado. He knew the light would keep away the shadow and that it could not come again.

Jago pulled the chair to the window and looked out. Far below the house he could see the wooden huts that lined the riverbank. A group of men in long grey coats snaked their way towards the factory as a horn sounded.

In the room all was still. Orbs of dust floated through the thick air. Every book from every shelf was thrown to the floor. Pinned to the wall by the fire iron was the photograph of Crispin Draigorian. The charred poker pierced his heart.

Jago set about the room. Within an hour he had stacked what books he could back on the shelves and straightened the table and chairs. By the far wall, in the part of the room that had been consumed by darkness, was a gilt frame. It looked as though it had fallen from the wall years before. It had been covered in a muslin cloth held in place by a stack of books. He lifted the picture and turned it to the sun before stepping back to see what it depicted.

The canvas was old and marred by smoke and dirt. Jago looked in surprise. The painting was of two men in frock coats, dressed in the fashion of a much older time. The younger held a long sword proudly at his side. Both men were smiling, their jewelled fingers clasped in friendship, and both wore the same ring on their smallest finger, a wide band of gold cut through with a woven trellis. Jago had never seen anything so beautiful before. He stared at the men. Their eyes were bright and shone from the painting as if they had discovered a wonderful secret. In the distance on a small hill was a woman holding an apple with a snake at her feet. It was a strange and eerie portrait of another land, a faraway, forgotten part of the world with mountains and forests.

Jago knew from his looks that one of the men was a Draigorian, that he was sure of. The other made his stomach turn and a cold shiver run down his spine. He hoped he was wrong but every detail, every mark on the man's face, he had seen before. Jago had studied that face for hour upon hour since he was a small boy. He had looked in those deep, bright eyes and wondered about the scar on the man's brow. There, in the painting that was done so long ago, was every detail exactly as he had last seen the man, days before. A rush of panic filled his beating heart.

'Cresco?' Jago asked as he looked at the man. 'It can't be . . .'

[8]

Supper

JAGO HAD NOT BEEN CALLED to lunch. The gong had not sounded and no one had come for him. He was thankful when at five o'clock Clinas arrived at the library and told him it was time to leave. The room was in every way just as Clinas had last seen it. There was no trace of the disturbance or the poltergeist. The shutters were back in place and the tattered curtains drawn. All the books were arranged correctly on the shelves.

'A productive day?' Clinas asked.

'Quite,' Jago replied as he rubbed the dust from his sleeves.

'You look as though you have been dragged through a hedge,' the butler remarked as they walked along the shuttered corridor and down the stairs. 'I heard some banging – everything all right?'

'Fine,' Jago replied, wondering if Clinas knew more that he would say.

Bia was waiting for him by the open kitchen door.

'Will you be watching them build the Penance Hedge?' Clinas asked Bia as they left. He looked at Jago and realised he didn't know what he meant. 'It's on the river – done at low tide – Biatra will show you.'

Bia smiled at Clinas and shrugged her shoulders.

'What did he mean?' Jago asked as they turned the tree-lined corner of the drive to Hagg House.

'Every time the comet appears they build a wicker fence in the mud of the river. It has to last three tides. When there is no comet, they build the hedge on Ascension Eve.'

'And they think it will protect them?' Jago replied as he looked down the track to the gates of the factory. 'Why do they do that?'

'There was a knight who was hunting a beast – a monster – with two companions. The animal took refuge in the house of a hermit in those woods,' she said, pointing to the tree-covered slopes of the river. 'The hermit refused to let the knight kill the creature, said it had found sanctuary. So he mortally wounded the hermit. Before the hermit died he told the knight that he would be cursed unless he built a wicker hedge in the sands of the river. He should do this as a penance for his murder or disaster would befall the town. The descendant of that knight builds the hedge – he'll be there now. It's low tide.'

Jago had often thought that the stories of Cresco were beyond madness. Now Bia spoke the same way. He felt a growing dread. Ghosts and shadows were suddenly very possible. Jago was fearful and alone. He could tell no one, and he could sense a dark and chilling numbness within. He knew his heart ached for his mother.

'Have you ever been in the library alone?' he asked, wanting to tell the girl what had happened, but knowing she wouldn't believe him.

'Why?' she replied curtly, as if she didn't want to be asked.

'Didn't like the place – and what's all that about Draigorian being in the dark all the time?'

'He's sick and there's no cure. Clinas said he's dying.' Bia coughed as she spoke. 'It's said to be a bad thing if a Draigorian dies whilst the comet is here.'

'What difference will it make? Is that why he wants me to find the book?' Jago asked.

'Clinas told me the book wasn't there and that he was just giving you something to do. It's a task without an end. Clinas said that when you had searched the library you would have to do it again and again. It's as if he wants you in that room,' she said churlishly.

'I'd rather clean,' Jago replied.

'I'd rather you cleaned too. Clinas wants everything to be done his way. Not a thing out of place, not a smudge of dirt – not even a fingerprint,' Bia said as they reached the quayside. 'Told you they would be here.'

Bia pointed to the spit of sand that stretched from the harbour wall out into the estuary.

Jago looked across the harbour. The sky was crystal blue and coloured the water that rushed to the sea. On the long and narrow finger of sand, three men stood and waited. One of them was bent double, his back weighed down with a bundle of reeds tied with thick rope. The two others carried wooden stakes and an iron hammer. A small crowd of people had gathered on the steps below the quayside.

From where he stood, Jago could see back up the river. The white walls of Hagg House stood out against the green of the woodland. Below was the factory that came out into the estuary further than he would ever have thought. It covered the deep water. Two steel doors stopped him seeing what was inside.

'So they'll build a hedge on the sand?' Jago asked.

'*He* will,' Bia said, pointing to a tall man with dark hair who carried the reeds. 'That's Hugh Morgan. It was his family that killed the hermit.'

It was as if Hugh Morgan had heard what she said. He dropped the reeds from his back and stood upright and looked at them. Bia lifted her hand but before she could wave he had turned away.

'So he'll build the hedge and Whitby won't be destroyed?' Jago asked sarcastically. 'Didn't think some sticks in the mud could do so much.'

'He does it every year. He has to do it now RedEye is back.'

'So who are the men with him?' Jago asked.

'They work for him,' she replied as she pulled on his coat. 'You'll have to come back – we can see if the hedge lasts the tide tomorrow. Mrs Macarty will be waiting. We have to be back for supper.'

Jago looked up to the sky. Even in the daylight he could see the outline of the comet high above them. He glanced back to Hugh Morgan. The man took a long stake, held it high in the air and then stabbed it into the sand, burying the carved tip a foot deep. The crowd roared and cheered as an old man with a bent back and red jacket blew a hunting horn to let the town know the hedge was being made.

Bia walked on, not caring if he followed. It was the busiest Jago had seen the streets of Whitby. Crowds of people hurried from work. There were very few men. It was just like in

London except for the smell of the sea and the constant noise of the crashing waves. Jago caught up with Bia and walked next to her. They stopped to look into the shop windows of Church Street as they made their way back to the steps. The bookshop with the gold-lettered sign was full of people, so full that a small queue trailed out of the door and into the street. Further along, just by the Town Hall, was a peculiar shop that sold all types of herbs and spices. The smell lingered in the air. A cured ham dangled in a net bag from a hook outside. It looked as though a whole pig had been sliced in two and left to cure in the sea breeze.

Jago laughed. 'Looks like Tallow,' he said, pointing to the poor creature. 'Will they eat that?'

'All but the snout,' she replied as they walked through the misty smoke that had been sucked through the alleyway from the herring house.

'Who lives there?' Jago asked as he walked by the entrance to Arguments Yard and saw a door that had been tied shut with a red ribbon.

'I did,' Bia replied. 'The ribbon is to tell people that whoever lived there is missing – no one will go in the house for a year and a day or until they come back.'

He pointed to the door of another house.

'They all have ribbons tied on them,' he said.

'Six houses – most of the row – all from the same place,' Bia said.

He could tell she wanted to walk on. She didn't look at her house and kept her eyes to the ground.

'Aren't the police looking for them? Doesn't someone tell the newspapers?' he asked.

101

'Not allowed. It's because of the war. The police think they have all run away or jumped from the cliff – that's what they tried to tell me. Said I could go back. They told me my mother would never come home.'

'Where did Sara Clark live?' Jago asked as the street took on an eerie familiarity.

'Number 16 – just up there,' Bia replied. She pointed to a house that was further up the street. It too had the familiar red ribbon tied to the door handle.

'Are you sure?' he asked as he looked back to the doorway where he had seen her come from the night before in his dream. 'She didn't live with you?'

'What?' Bia asked in a grimace of annoyance. 'She never lived with us. She hated our family – always had – what made you say that?'

'Nothing . . . Nothing made me say that, I just thought –'

'She's missing – Clinas told me. Her fella won't be back until Friday next week. He won't know until then – so we don't speak of it, understand?'

Jago knew he couldn't talk to Bia about Sara Clark. He wanted to tell her everything, the dream, the library, every detail of what had happened to him. It burst within like a contained madness.

'What if there *are* Vampyres – what if they are taking people?' he asked. 'Strackan could be real.'

'Been here a day and talking of Strackan, you have been busy,' said Jack Henson as he stepped from the doorway of the Black Boar. Bia backed away. It was clear she didn't like the man. 'Now then, Biatra,' he said in a whisper, 'what you been telling the *Algeniro*?'

'Told him nothing,' she protested. 'He's been listening to Maisie and Clinas Macarty. Talking about Vampyres – you know what they are like. The whole town believes in them.'

'Whole town believes we'll win this war – doesn't mean to say it's true,' Henson replied. He put his spade over his shoulder and followed them up the steps. 'No rest for the wicked – no rest for those who're missing,' he murmured under his breath.

'So where have all the people gone?' Jago asked him.

'Some might want you to know – others might try to stop you finding out,' he said as he watched his own feet trudge up the shallow steps. 'If I was a lad of your age I would be keeping in after dark and trying not to dream.'

He looked Jago in the face as he spoke. It was as if he was trying to tell him something. Jago looked back. Henson scowled through thin lips.

'Digging another grave?' Jago asked.

'Surprised you don't know why and who for,' Henson said as he rested and looked out to sea. 'Always best to have an empty grave – never know who you might find to fill it.'

Henson sneered, his face wrinkled and lined.

'Better be off,' Bia said, wanting to get away from the man.

'Better be,' he replied. 'You know things too well, Biatra. You be keeping this lad out of here at night. Can't be having him talking to my guests.'

'Guests?' Jago asked as they were far enough away for Henson not to hear.

Bia waited until they were in the courtyard of Streonshalgh Manor before she replied.

'It's what he calls the people who are buried in the church-yard. He looks after them. Digs the graves – keeps it all tidy. He says they are all his guests. Everyone in the town pays his wages. Penny a house – penny a grave – that's what my mother says. Jack Henson has always been a gravedigger. He used to frighten us with stories of ghosts.'

'And Vampyres?' Jago asked as the cold grey stones of the Manor loomed before them.

'What do you think?' she said in reply as they got to the nail-studded oak door of the old and ramshackle house.

Jago took hold of the handle. Before it could turn, the door opened.

'So you have decided to come back,' Mrs Macarty said with her arms folded. 'I saw Jack Henson talking to you – what did he want?'

'He was telling Jago to keep out of the churchyard,' Bia said impatiently as the smell of fried sausages wafted down the hall.

'Well,' she snorted. 'Perhaps he's right – with all that's going on, might not be a bad idea.'

'Sausages?' asked Bia as she went into the panelled dining room.

'Tallow's cooking,' Mrs Macarty said in what could only be described as a very lopsided smile of relief. 'Maisie has had to go, they have found her cousin.'

'Sara Clark?' Jago said. 'Is she well?'

'As well as can be expected for someone who is dead,' Mrs Macarty explained in a matter-of-fact way as she followed them into the dining room.

The dark room fell silent. Bia looked at Jago and wondered

why he had asked about Sara Clark. How did he know her name?

Staxley stood by his seat, waiting for them. His pack of dogs surrounded him, each glaring at Jago as he came in.

'Lasted the day then, Jago,' Lorken growled under his breath as Jago walked by.

'Sure did,' Jago whispered. He stood by his chair waiting for Mrs Macarty to tell them to be seated.

'But you might not last the night,' Lorken answered with a nudge of his elbow.

'It's only right that we just bow our heads and think of that poor family who have lost their daughter,' Mrs Macarty said. 'For those who don't know, Sara Clark went missing and they found her body at the bottom of the cliff. It looks as though she had an accident. They'll be burying her tonight.'

Jago looked about the room. Every eye was fixed on the large silver tureen on the stand by the door. The Gladlings quivered in anticipation. After a respectful pause Mrs Macarty nodded graciously.

'She was half-eaten,' Laurence Gladling, the tallest of the Gladling children, murmured to Jago as he served him a plate of sausages that defied all rationing. 'That's what I heard Tallow say to Maisie before she ran off screaming.'

Jago nodded and started to eat.

'Shame what happened to Sara Clark,' Staxley said as he leaned over to Jago. 'I heard there was not much left. Looks like she'd been eaten by a pack of dogs.'

Bia shuffled closer to Jago.

'Why tell me, Staxley? I never knew her,' Jago answered.

'You never know who will go missing next – never know

who will fall off that cliff into the sea.' Staxley looked smugly at the other boys as they troughed from their plates.

'I thought we'd settled this at breakfast,' Jago snapped back.

'You were just lucky – took me off guard. I can take you, Jago. You wait and see.'

'You don't want to fight me, Staxley. Not in this place,' Jago answered.

'Not frightened?' Lorken asked as he wiped gravy from his face with the cuff of his shirt.

'Not by you, Lorken. Why should I ever fear someone as ugly as you?' Jago said, and he laughed in the boy's face.

'It's not worth it, Jago. You have to live with them,' Bia replied quietly.

'She's right. Scar-face knows what the score is. We run Streonshalgh Manor – always have and always will. You give in to that and everything will be fine – understand, London boy?'

Jago saw Laurence Gladling staring at him, willing him not to back down. The boy looked frightened, as if Jago was his only hope. He sat at the table clutching the hands of his companions, Morris and Boris, in anticipation.

'Someone needs to teach you a lesson, Staxley,' Jago replied as he ate the sausages. 'This place would be fine if it wasn't for your bullying.'

Griffin coughed suddenly. He seemed to be choking on his food. He was bigger than all the others, with a hard scowl and broken nose. His dark hair fell over his face and his eyes widened in a breathless stare as he tried to speak.

'Stuck . . .' he gasped as his face reddened to bursting.

Staxley hit him hard on the back. 'Stop messing Griff – what's up?' he asked.

Griffin could not speak. He stood up and looked about the room as his eyes bulged. He tried to grab the back of the chair as he shook helplessly.

'He's choking,' Bia shouted, hoping to be heard by Mrs Macarty.

Jago didn't wait. With one hand he pushed Lorken out of the way. Grabbing Griffin in a bear hug, he gave a sudden and sharp tug to his chest. Griffin choked even more, and tears of fear rolled down his cheek as he gasped and gasped.

'What you doing to him?' Staxley screamed in panic.

'Get out of the way,' Jago shouted as he pulled harder.

Griffin coughed as the air exploded from his lungs. A bullet of meat shot from his mouth, followed by what looked like a gallon of water and tomato skins. Staxley didn't move. The spray hit him in the face. Griffin coughed some more as he stared at Jago.

'I was choking . . . You saved me – how did you do that?' Griffin asked as Staxley wiped the contents of Griffin's stomach from his shirt.

'I would have done that – he just got in the way,' Staxley said odiously as he stared at Jago.

'Doesn't matter who did it,' Bia butted in. 'Griff is alive, that's the point.'

'You would say that, scar-face, wouldn't you?' Staxley laughed as he turned away.

Bia lunged forward. In her mind he had insulted her for the last time. A sudden snap broke the silence. The punch hit him in the eye. Before Staxley had time to speak he was on the floor, hanging on to the table leg and wondering what had happened.

'No one ever call me that again – understand?' she screamed through her teeth as she pulled back the strands of her hair to bare her face. 'This is from birth. It's not my fault and it's not a curse. It's how I am. The next one of you that calls me scar-face will get the same as Staxley. I have had enough of you, all of you.'

Bia ran from the room. She didn't want them to see her tears.

'What is all this noise?' asked Mrs Macarty as she walked in with her arms folded.

'Griffin was choking – Jago saved him and Staxley fainted,' Laurence Gladling said quite confidently from the safety of his table.

Mrs Macarty looked at him suspiciously as his siblings nodded in agreement.

'Is that right, Griff?' she asked the boy as he pulled on his jacket.

Griffin nodded and smiled at Jago.

'I couldn't breathe and he did something that got it out, Mrs Macarty, honest,' Griffin replied quickly.

'And Staxley fainted with shock I suppose?' she said, as if to give them the answer.

'Exactly,' Jago said, wanting to go after Bia.

'Then all's well and none of you will spend the night in the attic for fighting,' Mrs Macarty replied, having obviously been listening from the corridor, as was her wont. She looked at Jago. 'Better go and see where she is, Jago.'

9

Hocus Pocus Hoc Est Corpus

THERE WAS NO SIGN of Bia anywhere in Streon-shalgh Manor. Jago searched all of the places where he thought she would be. He even asked Tallow what room she was in, but when he knocked on the door there was no reply. Turning the wooden handle, he stepped inside. The room was empty and unlived-in and smelt of mould. There was a case of clothes laid on the narrow bed. The sloped roof cut down sharply to the small windows that looked out over the harbour. A braided rug covered the bare boards by the fireside. He could hear the jackdaws roosting in the eaves as they cawed and pecked at the stones. The wind rattled the roof slates and blew clumps of matted soot down the chimney and into the blackened, empty fire grate. A small electric light burnt silently, filling the room with a meagre glimmer.

It was then that he saw her through the window. Bia stepped from the shadow of the church and picked her way through the gravestones towards the headland. She was shaking her fist and hitting out at the air in anger. He turned to open the door. As he did, he saw a simple wooden frame on the bedside table. In it was the picture of a man with his arm around a woman holding a small child. Jago picked up the frame and looked closer. He knew he had seen the woman before but didn't know where. Holding it under the light, he stared at it for a while before putting it back.

Jago left the room. He ran the length of the corridor, down the stairs and, turning on the landing, he charged past the picture of Pippen Draigorian to the front door.

'Not wise to be out when it's getting dark,' Mrs Macarty said. She appeared from the shadows as if she had been waiting for him.

'I was going –'

'After Biatra?' she asked knowingly.

'She's in the churchyard. I saw her from the window,' Jago replied.

'And who would I be to stand in the way of family?' she asked. Jago had no idea what she meant. 'You better be after her, but watch the time. The funeral will be there within the hour. They don't like snoopers at those things. Go get her – be quick about it.'

Jago nodded as Mrs Macarty opened the door. He leapt down the steps and ran across the square, past the statue and through the gates. High above, the comet had been obscured by a veil of cloud that filled the sky to the horizon. It had a ghostly glow that changed with every gust of the wind as if the sky was on fire. Far to the east, the first crescent of the moon was breaking through the sea below the clouds.

Bia was by the edge of the cliff. Jago could see her clearly. She stood on the precipice with her arms outstretched as if she was going to fly at any moment. Long ringlets of her red hair blew back as she leant into the wind. It was as if she was being held in place by the fierce vortex that blew up the cliff from the sea.

Jago stopped running and circled around to the side, hoping she would see him out of the corner of her eye and not be startled. Her toes were at the very edge of the cliff and she leant out like someone about to fall. Her eyes were firmly shut, her mouth open as she gasped the gale that blew into her face.

'I can see you, Jago. I know you're there,' she said as she leant out further, kept in place only by the force of the wind. 'I want to fly, to jump from this place and fly – do you understand that?'

'But you'd crash to the sea – you'd be killed,' he replied as he edged his way closer to her.

'What is there here for me?' she answered, still with her eyes closed.

'There's . . .' he said, unable to think of anything.

'Nothing,' she answered. 'All is lost – I have no one. Would you want to live in that house when every day you knew they laughed at you behind your back and called you scar-face and blood-head?'

'It's words,' Jago said. 'And what you did tonight really showed Staxley.'

'He won't stop. I just made it worse. He'll find a way of getting me – they always do. You never looked like this, you don't know.'

Jago slowly edged closer. He looked over the brink and his stomach churned. The cliff fell away to the sea far, far below.

'Come back, Bia. Don't lean so far out,' he said as she swayed with her arms outstretched, her hair blowing in long strands. The wind blew her back, holding her like a soaring bird.

'Does it frighten you?' she asked.

'Yes,' he said simply, his words just heard above the sound of the wind. 'Everything has frightened me since I got here. Nothing's right. You're all I've got.'

They were words he hadn't meant to say. For a moment she hesitated. He thought she would fall. Jago dived for her, grabbing Bia by the waist and pulling her towards him.

'What are you doing?' she screamed as they fell into the long grass.

'You would have fallen. I saw it happening,' he said.

Bia began to laugh. 'It's what I do – would it matter?'

'It would to me,' he said as he felt her breath on his face.

'If I could give you this – would you take it?' she said, pointing to the mark on her face. He didn't reply but just looked at her, thinking about what she had said. 'Do you know what it's like to be laughed at and scorned?'

'Weren't you the one who said you were no different and told them to get on with it?' he answered.

'It gets to you sometimes. Staxley is a pig. Everyone does as he says because they're frightened of him.'

'But not you?' he asked.

'Why should I? He can say what he wants.'

'So what were you doing?' Jago asked.

'Sky flying,' she said matter-of-factly. 'I saw the birds flying on the wind. It's so powerful just here. The wind is forced up through two gulleys in the rock. My dad said that a woman fell over the cliff just here and was blown back. You should try it.'

'I'll leave it to you,' he replied as he looked back to the dark silhouette of the church. 'Mrs Macarty said I had to get you back before the funeral. She said they didn't like snoopers.'

'Only because they don't want anyone to see how she's buried,' Bia replied.

'How would that make people want to stop us looking?' he asked.

'They'll be burying her face down. They put the coffin in upside down so she can't get out,' Bia said as she got up and leant on an old grave. She looked at Jago and realised he didn't know what she was talking about. 'They think Sara Clark will become a Vampyre, and they'll wrap her in holly wands and put a stone in her mouth. They were the old ways of how to keep a Vampyre in the grave.'

Bia raised an eye at Jago and tried to smile. It was half-hearted but spoke of what she really felt.

'Why do they think she's a Vampyre?' Jago asked, not wanting to tell her what he had seen in his dream.

'When the comet appeared before, a hundred people were found dead. The rumour was that Strackan had killed them all and they too would be Vampyres. They were all buried by the edge of the cliff. On the night the comet vanished, it is said they all broke free from their graves and ran through the town. The next day, another hundred people were dead. Some looked as though animals had eaten them. Others looked as if they had died of fright. Every one was buried face down and wrapped in holly wands, just to make sure.'

'Did *they* come back to life?' he asked.

'After they were buried, a storm came and part of the cliff

fell into the sea. The coffins were all lost, all but one – and that was empty.'

'So they were Vampyres?' he asked.

'That's what they say.'

'And now the comet's back it will all happen again?' he asked.

'Jack Henson believes it and he's the one spreading all the rumours. If he says it's true then the whole town will follow him. He's got good reason. Henson thinks a Vampyre murdered his wife.' Bia suddenly crouched into the shadow of a stone. 'They're here. The funeral. I can see the horses.'

Jago peered out from his makeshift hiding place in the long grass just as four black horses walked slowly towards the church. They pulled the sleek black carriage he had seen the night before. The horses were braided and plumed and looked as though they floated upon the veneer of mist that seeped through the gates. Jack Henson walked by their side, spade over his shoulder, lantern in his hand, followed by four men in black top hats. The hearse was now out of sight. Jago crawled closer to the grave by the wall of the church.

'Come on,' he said to Bia. 'I want to see what they are doing.'

She followed reluctantly, keeping as low to the ground as she could. Then the singing began. At first it was a low drawl of words they couldn't understand.

'It's just as my dad said – the witches' song to keep her in the grave,' Bia whispered as four men rounded the side of the church with the coffin wrapped in knotted holly wands high on their shoulders. Jack Henson followed them. He carried a lantern on a short staff. As he walked he chanted. Jago could make out only some of the words; the others were drowned by the wind.

'Holly . . . grave . . . blood . . . death . . .' Henson croaked like a crow.

The procession turned again as they lowered the coffin to the ground. There was no priest, no blessing, just Jack Henson chanting as the men tumbled the coffin into the deep grave. There was a dull thud as it sank into the earth.

'Stones,' shouted Henson as he stuck the lamp into the soft earth and watched it swing back and forth. 'Better keep her in with the stones.'

They watched as the four men began to throw rocks on top of the coffin. They thudded loudly and without respect. Then an old woman hobbled to the graveside, her arms wrapped around a bundle of herbs. They all fell silent.

'Sara Clark . . . by the power of hemlock and rue I command you to stay asleep and not to wake. By the essence of larkspur and crowfoot you shall always keep within this grave,' the old woman said as she scattered the herbs onto the coffin. 'By the light of day and the moon at night, rest until the end of time.'

'So mote it be,' ended Jack Henson as he picked up the lamp and lowered it into the grave. 'With fire and earth be made fast and not stir. Is she for staying?' he asked the woman.

'If the wands have been tied and she faces the earth, she will not stir. Strackan will have to dig her from the ground to bring her to life,' she replied. She pulled a black shawl over her head and turned against the chill breeze.

'We should have done this from the start. Pointless only doing it now – what about all the others?' he asked the woman, as if she would have the answer.

'Those that you buried we can be protected from. It's the ones that haven't been found I'll pray for,' she said as she turned to walk from him.

'What do you mean, Polly Peckentree?' Henson said. Jago watched him grip the woman by the shoulder.

'Strackan has them hidden away. Neither dead nor alive – that's what I mean. Sara Clark can be thankful she is dead. Trapped in that grave she'll be – but the others – servants, that's all they'll be . . . For ever.'

Jago slipped to the ground so he could not be seen. His last glance was of Henson following the pallbearers back to the hearse. The wind dropped as the sky cleared and the tufts of grass that surrounded each stone shimmered gold in the light of the full moon.

'See,' Bia whispered after some time. 'I told you they all believed in Vampyres.'

'What'll we do?' Jago asked.

'Wait until they've gone and then sneak off,' she said.

'But Mrs Macarty – she told me to bring you straight back.'

'Tell her you couldn't find me – tell her I was lost.'

'Tell her you're hiding behind graves in the churchyard,' Jack Henson snapped as he grabbed Jago and dragged him to his feet. 'I thought I told you to stay out of here at night for your own good?'

'It's my fault – he came looking for me,' Bia said as she stepped away.

'Always your fault, always your fault,' Henson said as he

pulled Jago to the edge of the cliff. 'What did I say could happen to you if you were caught around here?'

'You said you didn't want me talking to your guests?' Jago asked, hoping he was right.

'Funerals are private things,' Henson said, shaking Jago as hard as he could.

'So private no one comes but you and Polly Peckentree? She's a witch and you know it,' Bia said without thinking. 'You were making sure Sara Clark didn't come back. She never got a proper funeral.'

'Can't have her running free. You should know that.' Henson held Jago by the scruff of his neck. 'Precautions, that's all it is.'

'Witchcraft and superstition – frightening people to believe that the dead are Vampyres. That's all,' Bia said.

'What else do we do – let them all run free?' he asked as he held Jago closer to the edge of the cliff.

Jago looked down. The sea broke on the rocks far below. The surf crashed against the harbour wall and vast green breakers rolled in like undulating hills.

'Mrs Macarty knows we are here,' Jago said as his feet began to slip from the edge. 'She saw us go. If anything happened *you* would be asked all the questions.'

'Accidents happen – especially to inquisitive people. What's another body at the bottom of the cliff?' Henson stopped. It was as if he was caught by a conversation that only he could hear. He lifted Jago closer to him and looked into his face. 'There's something not right about you, something not right at all. You make us shiver . . .' He pulled Jago back and then pushed him towards Bia. 'Let this be a final warning to you

117

both. This place is out of bounds – awake or asleep – do you understand?' he said as he looked at Jago.

'Asleep?' Bia asked.

'Awake or asleep – he knows what I mean,' Henson muttered as he walked back towards the grave through the wind-beaten stones. Henson stopped by Sara's grave and looked in. He turned and pointed to Jago. 'It's not by chance you have come back. Don't think you can kid me. I know who you are – we all do.'

'What?' Bia said as she looked at Jago. 'Asleep?'

Jago shrugged his shoulders.

'He's a mad old fool,' he said.

'A seer – knows when things will happen, or so they say. What did he mean when he spoke to you?'

It was the moment that Jago wanted, the moment he had been waiting for. He wanted to tell Bia what he had seen in his dream. But he thought and then let it pass, never to come again. He looked up. The comet looked down on the earth like the eye of an all-seeing god. He mourned for London, mourned for his mother and mourned for Cresco. It was as if they had never been and his old life was a dream that he had mistakenly glimpsed.

'If it were true, all that Henson said – what would you think?' he asked her.

Bia looked about the churchyard. The night had crept about them quite silently. It had stolen the light without them seeing. They stood surrounded by markers of lives long lost. Each was a cold stone monolith that reduced life to a name on stone.

'That's where we end up, Jago. There's nothing else. Sometimes I think there is, but when I really think I know there can't be,' Bia said, pointing to the grave. 'Someone is taking people, or else they are just running away – but it's not a Vampyre.'

They listened for a moment to the sound of Jack Henson shovelling earth into Sara Clark's grave.

'Mrs Macarty will be wondering where we are,' Jago said.

'All she cares for is her money. What did Henson mean when he said awake or asleep? I saw the look in your eyes and you knew what he meant.'

'Perhaps his guests had told him I was in the churchyard last night whilst I was dreaming. They could have seen me and chased me from here.' Jago tried to laugh but a shiver-finger ran down his spine.

Bia looked at him. 'I know a truthful face,' she said as they walked through the mist that hugged the graves, 'and to believe you would be madness.'

Henson worked on. He was but a dark shadow against the lee of the old church. He paid no attention to them as they walked on. Henson muttered and gnarled and moaned as he argued with himself in a half-heard, echoing conversation. He looked up as their shadows danced across the low mist and caught his eye.

'Don't you be coming back, Jago Harker. Not tonight, not any night,' he shouted.

Jago raised his hand as if to agree.

'Why should he think you will be back?' Bia asked.

'He doesn't like me – that's all. I don't know why,' he answered. Then he saw Polly Peckentree on the seat by the iron gate. She sat in the moonlight with the low mist swirling

119

about her feet, huddled in her shawl and waiting for Jack Henson.

'Don't speak,' Bia whispered as they drew near.

'Biatra Barnes – I pray they will find your mother,' the old woman said.

'She'll be back,' Bia answered firmly as a moon shadow crossed her face.

'Who is this?' the woman asked as she stood to look at Jago.

'He's from London and an evacuee,' Bia said.

The old woman gasped in surprise. 'Can't be,' she said slowly. 'It just can't be.'

'I'm Jago,' he said as he held out his hand.

'Don't touch me – never touch me – I know who you are,' she said, stepping back from him. 'I wouldn't walk out with him – not this boy, Biatra. This lad is trouble and you know it – don't you, boy?'

[10]

The Lost Griffin

THEY CROSSED the large cobbled square in front of
Streonshalgh Manor in silence. Jago glanced to the statue
of the gladiator. It cast its moon shadow across the stones like
a giant bird about to swoop down. The house towered over
them, its cold grey stones dark and foreboding. Mrs Macarty
stood at the door and held back the long blackout curtain as
she tapped impatiently with her foot.

'Longer than I thought,' she said with a note of irritation
in her voice.

'I couldn't find her,' Jago tried to say, but he suddenly
realised by the look in her eyes that he had been caught in
the lie.

'You were by the graves – near the cliff edge, Jago – hiding
and watching. It's not only you who can look out of the attic windows and see what's happening,' she said with a curl
of the lip that he quickly understood. 'Both of you, to your
rooms before I have Jack Henson at my door complaining
you were snooping.'

'He caught us, told us to stay away,' Bia said as they stepped
through the doorway.

'I saw it all. What business did Polly Peckentree have

121

with you?' she asked, closing the large studded door behind them.

'Just said hello. She's never met Jago before,' Bia lied.

'Well, enough is enough.' Mrs Macarty sighed. 'Tallow has left a drink in your rooms. Hope it is still hot. Best you both be off to sleep. Rid your minds of what you've seen.'

Jago was thankful that it was all she had said. Delphine Macarty was so unlike his mother and yet there was something about her that warmed his heart.

'I'm sorry,' Jago said. 'I shouldn't have lied to you.'

'Sorry? A strange word to be used by a lad of your age. Don't say it too much around here. I can't be having everyone thinking I'm going soft.' She smiled as she watched him walk up the stairs. 'Just need a word with you, Biatra – if you don't mind.'

Jago knew he was meant to go. Bia looked up at him just as he turned out of sight around the corner of the landing. There, as usual was the smirking face of Pippen Draigorian. He looked down from the picture with eyes that seemed to know what Jago had seen.

'Goodnight, old man,' Jago said to the painting as he walked along the dark landing towards his room.

It was then that Jago noticed the door was open a slither and a slit of light came through the crack. He felt in his pocket and found the key. He was sure he had locked the room when he left.

Jago walked slowly, the floorboards squeaking beneath his feet. A shadow moved in the room that was lit by a small fire burning in the grate. Jago got to the door and listened. He tried to peer inside without being seen. Someone was in the room. He could hear them placing coals on to the fire one by one.

He gripped the key in his hand, knowing that it would strengthen his fist if he had to fight. He slowly pushed against the door, hoping it wouldn't make a sound. The door opened, Jago looked inside the room. There, hunched over the fire-place was the figure of a man.

'Mrs Macarty told me you could do with a fire – being out in the mist for so long,' Tallow said as he turned around

'How did you know it was me?' Jago asked.

'Shoes,' tallow replied as if Jago should know what he meant. 'Shoes tell everything about the man,' he continued. 'You have leather soles, twice mended and double stitched.'

'And you can tell that by the way I walk?' he asked.

'The way a man walks says more about him than the look on his face. You've an honest gait, big strides, even when you're trying to keep quiet.'

'Then I shall have to watch my step,' Jago laughed.

'Is that what Henson told you?' Tallow asked with an unusual clarity in his voice. 'Did he tell you to watch your step?'

'Told me to keep out of the churchyard,' Jago answered. He sat on the bed and reached out for the steaming cup of milk on the bedside table. 'Did you bring this?' he asked as he gulped the drink.

Tallow stared at him through his dark, deep-set eyes. 'Mrs Macarty told me you'd be wanting something. Milk and ver-vain, it will help you to sleep. Not a room I'd like to be in, if I was to be honest,' he said reluctantly.

'I have nowhere else, Tallow,' Jago replied. He leant back

against the pillows and looked around the room to see if everything was as he had left it. 'Do you live here?'

'Used to, long time ago. Came here just like you. Work here sometimes and sometimes for Hugh Morgan. That's where I live,' he said as he stacked the last piece of coal from the bucket on to the fire. 'It's a far walk. Will stay here tonight and then head for Hawks Moor tomorrow.'

'Hugh Morgan?' Jago asked. 'The man who has to build the wicker fence?'

'Not to be joked about. That fence can save us all,' Tallow answered as he got from his knees, picked up the coal bucket and turned to go. 'Penance Hedge is an important thing.'

'Like wrapping holly sticks around coffins?'

'As powerful as that – if not more. Hugh Morgan will never be free from what his family has done. Killing that hermit will be with them for ever.'

'Does everyone believe in all this superstition just like you?' Jago asked.

'Never heard of any of it until I came here. It's all true. I've seen things on that moor that would frighten any man.' Tallow towered over Jago, his head higher than the corner post of the grand oak bed. 'Not talk for night-time. Even with that vervain you would never sleep. That's why I never walk back to Hawks Moor once it's dark. Hugh Morgan told me that.'

'And he believes in it all too?' Jago asked.

'As much as most and more than many,' he said as he bent to walk though the door. 'Drink and sleep – that's what Mrs Macarty said I had to tell you.'

Tallow closed the door. A candle on the mantelpiece lit the room, and the flames took hold of the coals and flickered

124

shadows over the ceiling. Jago listened to the seagulls as they came in to roost on the ruins of the abbey. The waves crashed against the pier walls and the church clock chimed the quarter hour. He looked about the room and hoped it could be different. Jago had expected something other than this. All he could feel was that somewhere in a cold London street, his mother was trapped under the rubble just like he was. He hoped that she would be found and come for him.

Jago sipped at the milk. It tasted of bitter herbs that burnt his tongue. In a strange way, it was pleasant. Soon, he felt sleepy. He looked at the jug and bowl on the stand but could not bother to wash away the dirt of the day. His body felt heavy as his mind drifted and thoughts of London filled the empty silence. The house was still, and for the first time since he had arrived he could not hear the wind.

Then, just as he knew he was about to sleep, he heard the sound. It danced along the floorboards of the corridor and then clattered against the door to his room. It was the sound of rolling glass. It came again, a familiar childhood sound – a glass marble rolled on the wooden floor and clunked against a door.

Jago sat up and listened. The clattering noise came for a third and then a fourth time. He went to the door. When it was opened, he found four glass orbs like bull's eyes in a neat row.

'Marbles?' he said out loud. The corridor was dark and empty; Jago could see no one. Then he heard the clunk, clunk, clunk of another glass sphere falling down each of the wooden attic steps. The marble rolled across each tread, dropped down a step at a time, turned and then slowly came towards him. It stopped at his feet. Jago picked up the glass ball. 'Very funny,' he said, hoping whoever was doing this could hear him. The sound came again, this time faster. The new orb rolled urgently from the other end of the corridor. It clattered across the boards and when it got to his door stopped. 'Who is it?' he whispered, not wanting to be heard by Tallow or Mrs Macarty.

No one answered. The passageway was silent. Jago was sure he could see someone in the shadows by the large aspidistra that bushed out from the alcove by the far window. He stepped from his room and quietly walked towards the window.

There were three doors in the passageway. Two looked as though they could be bedrooms, the other was chipped around the frame and could be a store cupboard. He edged along the wall, listening hard with each small step. Another marble rolled from the dark alcove. It meandered slowly along the polished wooden floor as if pushed by an invisible hand. Jago stamped on it with his foot, stopping it dead.

There was a dull click as the door to the storeroom opened. Jago waited, wondering who was playing this game. He wanted to run and lock himself in his room.

'Jago, Jago,' came the voice of Laurence Gladling from deep within the darkness of the storeroom. 'Help me get out of here,' he said with a grunt.

Jago hesitated. In the clearing darkness he could see the faint and shadowy outline of Laurence Gladling. It looked as though he was strapped to a chair.

'What have they done to you?' he asked as he stepped into the room.

'Don't . . .' murmured Gladling in muffled protest.

A hand shot from the dark and grabbed Jago by the arm. An old flower sack was thrust on his head and he was grappled to the floor. He tried to fight. There were too many hands holding him down.

'Just thought we would have a word,' Lorken said as he tied Jago's hands with a thin rope. 'You have to know what we can do, understand?'

'Takes two of you to do it,' Jago snarled.

'You hold him. I'll search his room,' Lorken said.

Jago couldn't see who held him down. He bit at the sack on his head as he tried to shake it free.

'Wouldn't be doing that,' Griffin said. 'Just stay where you are and he'll be back.'

'If he takes anything from my room, it will be the last thing he ever does,' Jago answered. 'Thought you'd be different, Griffin. You're not as stupid as they are.'

'My mates, Jago. Look after each other,' Griffin answered as he pushed his knee into Jago's back.

'Nothing there,' Lorken said as he came back. 'Just a bag full of rubbish, some clothes and an old tin mug. Do you have anything worth stealing?'

'Not that you would ever dare,' Jago replied, hugely relieved that Lorken had been too stupid to discover the money that his mother had given him. He tried to work out where Lorken was standing so he could kick him as hard as he could.

'Get out of here, Gladling. You've served us well. Remember – not a word or else it will happen to you,' Griffin said. Jago heard Gladling scurry from the room.

'They made me, Jago, made me . . .' he said in a whisper.

'Had to get you in here somehow. I knew you wouldn't come on your own,' Staxley said from the shadows. 'You need to be taught a lesson.'

'What you going to do to him, Staxley?' Lorken asked excitedly.

'Tie him up and leave him in here for the night,' he replied. 'That should teach him a lesson.'

'Is that all?' Lorken asked. 'Let me just have a minute with him.'

'That's all I would need to sort him out,' Jago answered before Staxley could reply.

'If that's what you want, Jago. I'm sure Griff can truss you so it won't be too hard for Lorken to finish you off. And if you breathe a word to Macarty – we'll get you again and again.'

'And scar-face – both of you,' Lorken growled. 'Tie him tight, Griff.'

'You watch me,' Griffin said. He twisted the rope until Jago screamed. 'Feel that, London boy?'

Jago felt the rope tighten until it burnt. The pain went away as Griffin pushed him back against the floor. He wasn't sure, but he thought he could feel the cords sag and loosen.

'Not too tight,' Lorken laughed. 'Got to give him a chance.'

'He'll have a chance all right,' Griffin said. 'Just stay where you are and take the beating, Jago. Best to learn who is in charge of this place.'

'Come on, Griff, let's leave them to get *friendly*,' Staxley said as he stepped over Jago.

The door shut. The room was plunged into total darkness.

He could hear Lorken breathing. He gasped and sighed excitedly as he moved about the darkened room.

'Didn't like you from the first day I saw you, Jago. Been waiting for this,' Lorken gulped feverishly.

'Get on with it, Lorken,' Jago answered as he realised his hands were free.

'Then have some of this,' Lorken grunted as he kicked out in the dark.

Jago spun round and pulled the hessian sack from his head just as the kick hit him in the chest. He gasped in pain. The blow came again. This time he caught the boot, twisted the leg and sent Lorken crashing to the floor. He dived on the boy, pressing him to the coarse wooden planks. Lorken growled like a dog as Jago picked up the strand of cord and tied his hands.

'Things different now, Lorken?' Jago asked as he pulled the rope tight and then covered the boy's head with the hessian sack. 'Shall I do to you what you were going to do to me?'

'No, no!' Lorken pleaded.

'Different now Staxley has gone – not wanting to fight?' Jago asked.

'You don't understand. I had to do it. It's the way it is. Staxley says he knows who the Vampyre is and if we don't do what he says then it will come and get us.' Lorken spoke in a hissing whisper.

'Am I supposed to believe that?' Jago asked as he pulled the rope even tighter.

'It's true. He always says if we don't help him, then he will feed us to Strackan.' Lorken groaned in pain.

'Staxley says he knows who Strackan is?' Jago said quietly.

'He knows his name. That it's someone we all know but would never guess.'

Jago thought for a moment.

'You're lying, Lorken,' Jago said as he twisted the rope even harder.

'It's true. Staxley says he has met him,' Lorken answered through gritted teeth.

'Very well,' Jago said as he loosened the rope. 'You say that if Staxley thinks you chickened out you'll end up being fed to Strackan?'

'Yes,' Lorken replied earnestly.

'Then you can go,' Jago answered as he pulled the sack from Lorken's head.

'What?' he asked, surprised by his sudden freedom.

'Go – tell him what you want. I won't say anything,' Jago answered.

'But why would you do that?' Lorken asked disbelievingly.

'Do you want to get eaten by a Vampyre?' he asked.

Lorken shook his head as the bindings fell from his wrist. All he could see was the dark shadow of Jago looming over him. He tried to speak.

'Thanks,' Lorken gasped suspiciously as he gulped tears and rubbed the dew from his pug nose. 'And you won't say a thing?'

'Promise,' Jago said simply as he opened the door.

'I better go first. Stay here for a while. They could be waiting by the stairs,' Lorken said as he got to his feet. 'You're weird, Jago. I would have beat you if I had the chance and wouldn't have cared.'

'I know,' Jago said. 'So would I until I came here.'

Lorken didn't understand. He left quickly. Jago heard his footsteps go down the empty corridor and then up the stairs to the attic rooms where they all slept. He waited in the dark and wondered if what Staxley had said was true. The door to the attic room slammed and was followed by laughter that echoed through the house.

Jago went to his room. Everything he owned was scattered on the bed. His leather case had been tipped out and rifled. There by the pillow was the Cup of Garbova. It sparkled just like it always had.

'He must have seen this,' he said to himself. 'Why didn't he take it?'

'Some people are too dull even to see gold,' Jago heard a voice say from behind him.

He didn't dare to turn for fear of what he might see.

'Cresco?' he asked, remembering the voice from before.

'No . . .' it said.

'Then who are you – why are you haunting me?' Jago answered.

The fire glinted and crackled in the hearth and cast his long shadow against the dark wood panels. A single candle on the mantelpiece flickered and danced. The mirror above the fireplace in its lustreless gilt frame was dimmed and misted and covered with a coating of dust. Jago could feel the presence near to him as it swept across the room like a chill breeze.

It then appeared. Slowly, vaguely and without a sound, a finger marked out a single word:

VAMPYRE . . .

[11]

Yassassin

JAGO STARED AT THE WORD etched into the mirror for almost an hour. He waited to see if the ghostly writer would return. It was a surprising thought to him that he felt so calm. He began to believe that he too had been killed in the bombing and that this was a strange afterworld. What he had experienced in the last days was beyond belief. All that he loved was gone and now he found himself in a dark room of Streonshalgh Manor where a candle flickered and the fire faded into dull embers. Jago sat on the bed and waited, wrapped in his leather coat. Sleep was the last thing he wanted – despite the jumble of his thoughts, he knew that any dream would not be peaceful. Yet something deep within him urged him to close his eyes, just for a moment.

'No,' he said to wake himself as he felt sleep take him. Then, getting up from the bed, he went to the window and sat on the long ledge next to the cold glass. 'If I just stay here for another hour . . .'

Jago pressed his face against the icy window. It was marked with an early frost which melted to the contours of his cheek. All he wanted was to wait for the brief night to pass. When dawn came he could sleep – it would then be safe. With an ever-growing numbness, he closed his eyes. The mist of sleep had come. In drudgeful slumber, he leant against the window and felt himself falling.

'Thought we wouldn't see you here again,' said a sudden voice. Jago opened his eyes. He was surrounded by fog. A man swished the tail of his dusty and matted frock coat from side to side, the same man he had seen in his dream the night before. 'Your kind of people never learn.'

Jago stood back and looked at him. He was just the same as he was before. His thin and flaking face was covered with a short stubble of spindly grey hairs. As he spoke, Jago noticed he only had three teeth in the whole of his mouth.

'Why shouldn't I be back? It's just a dream,' Jago said.

'Another night, another dream. Another night, another death?' the man said. 'If you listen you can hear Jack Henson digging the graves. Is that just a dream?' Jago looked around him. The mist began to clear. He was in the churchyard. It felt like he was asleep and all this was in his head. To his right was the door of Draigorian's tomb that was built within the wall of the church. On his left was the grave of Sara Clark. It was now filled with soil and covered in holly leaves. The man noticed him looking at the grave. 'They did what I said. Buried her in holly to keep her in. Listen – listen . . .'

Jago listened intently. From deep within the earth he could hear someone screaming. 'What is it?' he asked.

'She wants to be out. Strackan will be calling her. Always on the first night of their death,' the man said in a meagre whisper as if he didn't want to be overheard. 'It is only then they are useful to him.'

As the mist cleared further, Jago could see more of the

dead. Just like before they sat on their graves in tattered clothes, waiting endlessly. A young child huddled by the slab of stone that marked his short life. He looked up at Jago and tried to smile. The church looked stark, grim and bare. Ivy crept around the stones as if to pull it down piece by piece.

'It's Sara Clark – she's screaming,' Jago said as he listened to the dull cry that came up from the grave.

'She can't get out. Not buried face down,' the man replied as the small boy crawled towards Jago. 'He's never seen life so close before,' he went on, pointing to the boy.

'Did Strackan bring him here?' Jago asked.

'Brought us all. One by one and night by night. We are but broken jars waiting for what is to come.'

'And what is that?' Jago asked.

'To be set free. We are of no more use to Strackan. We are the remnants of the rage that burns within him.'

'You're ghosts?'

'We live long and never leave this place.'

'So how can you be free?'

'If Strackan is killed then we too will die with him. We are a memory of what we once were. In life I was a tailor, a maker of fine clothes, and now look at me – a man of rags.' The man held out his hands to Jago. They were covered in blisters and worn to the bone.

'How can you kill a shadow?' Jago asked

'Strackan is a man like you – a man of long life – a Vampyre,' the ghost said. 'He told us he saw you – scratched your face with his fingers.'

'Who is he?' Jago asked just as he saw Jack Henson turn

the corner of the churchyard and walk towards him. 'No – Jack Henson.'

'He can't see you,' the man said, 'but be careful what you say. He listens to us all the time.'

'What? What?' Henson asked. 'Who is it you are speaking to, Ebenezer Goode?'

'The one you buried screams to be free,' the ghost of Ebenezer Goode said.

'She can stay where she is. I told you before. I'm not having Strackan taking what he likes from the town – do you hear me?'

Henson looked about him, trying to see where the words were coming from. Jago could see him clearly. There was a brightness to his face that he had never noticed before. The wisps of his beard swirled about his long chin

'He speaks not to us,' the ghost replied.

'Who is with you?' Henson asked. 'I sense someone listening to me.'

'Can he see me?' Jago asked in a whisper.

The ghost shook his head. 'You are quite invisible.'

'Invisible?' Henson ranted. 'Who is it with you?' He reached out with his open hand as if to sense the temperature of the air. 'Tell me, Ebenezer.'

'Go, boy,' Ebenezer said. He waved with his bony fingers for Jago to leave him. 'Stay to your world. It is not safe for you here.'

'Boy – what boy? World – what world?' Henson muttered as he peered into the darkness that surrounded the high stone walls of the church. Jago watched as Henson then closed his eyes and reached out with his hands. 'Jago Harker

135

– I know you are meddling. Do as Ebenezer says – get away from here.'

Jago looked on as the ghost of Ebenezer Goode held up his hand and smiled.

'Go now, boy,' the ghost whispered as he crossed his thin lips with his finger to bid Jago to be silent.

'It's him, I know it,' Henson screamed as he smashed his spade into the mired dirt and holly leaves that covered the grave. 'I will find you, Jago, and so will Strackan. Do not meddle with this boy, Ebenezer – do not meddle.'

'But he could be the one?' asked Ebenezer Goode.

'You pin your hopes on such as that?' Henson shouted, his words echoing in the night. 'Just because he can see you?'

Jago waited no longer. He ran from the churchyard, winding his way in and out of the graves until he reached the steps. Stopping, he looked out over the dark roofs of the cottages that clung to the cliff. In the estuary below, he saw the conning tower of a submarine making its way out to sea. All was quiet. Jack Henson continued to dig a grave. Jago could hear the chiselling of the metal spade as it cut through the hard earth. He looked back to Streonshalgh Manor. Moonlight shone on the layer of frost that clung to every slate on its vast roof. The town was silent and in his dreaming he felt a breeze cut across his face.

Taking the steps two at a time, he was soon in Church Street. The narrow cobbled road fell away in a slight hill towards the marketplace. The houses were tall, thin and crammed together, some of them converted into shops with bowed windows. He remembered each one from his walk back from Hagg House. The street appeared darker than before and even in his dream the comet still hung in the sky. Hiding under the portico of the town hall was a man – Jago could see his shadow cast by the moon. It was as if he was waiting for him to arrive. Jago too waited.

The door to the bookshop opened. Jago heard the bell chime as a young woman in a short coat stepped into the street. He saw her stop and look towards him, staring as if she could see him.

The young woman turned suddenly and walked away. Her footsteps echoed on the cobbles and then, as if this was an encore of the night before, the shadow of a man stepped from his hiding place and followed her.

Jago knew instantly that it was Strackan. The figure skulked in its long black coat, the collar turned against the wind, fedora hat tilted across the brow. The man walked faster, keeping pace with the woman, and Jago followed.

It was then that Strackan looked back. He saw Jago and started to run.

'Come on, boy – catch me before I get to her,' he taunted in a voice that only Jago could hear.

Jago hesitated and then without knowing why began to run. It felt as if this was what he was meant to do. Stride by stride he chased after Strackan, who by now was just behind the woman. She turned and before she could scream, Strackan had taken hold of her throat.

Jago ran even faster, his feet hardly touching the stones. It was not like any other dream he had ever had.

'Never!' he screamed at Strackan as he gained ground and then, when close by, Jago leapt at him as he dragged the woman towards an alleyway.

Strackan looked up as Jago landed, knocking him to the floor. The woman started to scream as Strackan's hand was freed from her face.

'Get off me!' she cried tearfully. She lashed out at Jago, snatching the button from his leather coat.

As Strackan lunged for the woman's throat Jago saw him properly for the first time. The black fedora hat fell to the floor in the struggle, and Jago stepped back in horror. Strackan had the face of a man. It was old, wrinkled with gnarled features as if made of oak. The bark-like skin was stretched over the thick bone, the lips were cankerous and pulled tightly back over the teeth of a dog. The woman tried to scream but before the sound could leave her throat she collapsed back, unable to move.

'What did you expect?' Strackan said remorselessly, staring at Jago with burning red eyes. 'Died of fright, what use is she to me now?'

'Why take her?' Jago asked.

'What else am I supposed to do? It is my life,' Strackan snarled as he sniffed the air. 'I had been waiting for her and waiting for you. I had to teach you what is to be done.'

'I would never do that, never,' Jago said.

'One day you will – one day not too far from now. When the comet has gone. You will seek people, just like me,' Strackan answered, smiling at him.

'You're mad. Mad as hell,' Jago shouted.

'You will come to know hell better than most, Jago Harker. I have waited all these years for you to come back to this town. Why do you think you are here?' Strackan's breath wheezed and groaned as if he could barely breathe.

'I am an evacuee, from London . . . My mother sent me here,' he answered.

'Your mother always knew that your fate lay in this place. She didn't dare bring you back. Is she dead? It is your nature and your future, and . . . Jago Harker, born of Martha, one day you will be just like me.'

'Never!' Jago shouted as Strackan got to his feet and picked the fedora from the ground.

'Your fate and mine are entwined. We are the same root. Did she not tell you?' he asked as he walked back into the shadow of the alleyway.

'I know nothing of what you say – you are a dream, Strackan.'

'Then explain the marks on your face – how did they get here?'

'I did them whilst I slept.'

'And the mirror – who wrote upon it?' Strackan asked. 'Ask yourself why I haven't killed you.'

'Because you don't exist,' Jago replied.

Strackan laughed. With a swirl of his coat he disappeared into the dark shadows.

Jago followed, wanting to know more. 'Who are you? What are you?' he screamed, but the shadow was gone.

There was a murmuring from the entrance to the alleyway. Jago turned. The woman moved slightly. He ran back to her and lifted her head from the floor, cradling it in his arms.

'Vampyre?' the woman muttered, her lipstick smeared across her face in a gruesome smile.

'I am not a Vampyre,' Jago answered as the woman opened her eyes. 'Where are you from? I will take you home.'

The woman didn't speak; she slumped back in his arms and groaned. It was then that Jago saw the three razor-like cuts to the base of her neck. They were the same as those on his face. She gripped the sleeve of his jacket and then looked at him.

'Vampyre?' she asked again, She gasped for breath and then sighed.

Jago laid her down against the side of the alleyway as carefully as he could. Strackan could not just disappear, he thought. The woman didn't move. He was sure she was dead. He didn't notice her hand gripping tightly to the button from his coat or the slight, faint pulse of life that beat erratically beneath the porcelain-white skin of her neck.

Following the alleyway, Jago ran from the street until the cobbles narrowed to no wider than his shoulders. The path twisted and turned through a labyrinth of houses and yards that were cut into the cliff. With each stride he went higher and higher, until he was on an old donkey path that led out of the town. Looking back, he could see Whitby. The harbour was just as it always was. Several fishing boats were tied against the quayside. The streets were empty as they always were just before the curfew and the church clock chimed midnight.

Soon the low walls gave way to slight hedges and then open fields. The path wound its way down and then up the side of a narrow valley. Far below, Jago could see Hagg House. It cast its moon shadow towards the estuary and nearby, surrounded by trees, the chimney of the factory bellowed out gusts of acrid black smoke.

Like a wise dog chasing its prey, Jago knew in his heart

that this was the way he should go. There were no tracks or any sign of Strackan, just a feeling that the man had been on the pathway moments before. He could sense that the essence of the air had been cut through. The atoms had been disturbed and swirled about him like the orbs he had seen in the library.

The path soon opened out into a small lane that led across the top of the moor. Jago could see the ruins of the abbey on the cliff top, its stone ribs breaking from the ground like the carcass of a gigantic dead whale washed up on the shore. An old window at the peak of a tall facade of ruined stones caught the full moon. Just for the briefest glimpse it held it like the eye of the leviathan.

Jago's feet trudged in a worldly pace, not like a dream. The hedged lane rose up and up to the brow of a hill. On each side was a copse of trees that looked to be purposefully planted as a boundary to a great estate. A wall of neatly mortared stones ran from east to west as far as he could see. The air here was crisp and still. The dark of night was fading as clouds moved across the sky and the blood-red light of the comet fought against the moonlight.

Climbing the stone wall, Jago looked across a land far different from that through which the track had led him. On the far side, where the hill fell away steeply, small trees laden with fruit covered the ground. In the midst of this vast orchard was a tall spire, and beneath it the roof of a large house with a stone turret at each corner. Jago could clearly see the tall green hedges of a vast maze or labyrinth. In the garden below, the shadow of someone was moving through the trees.

'Strackan,' he whispered to himself, knowing that in his dream this was the place of the creature.

'Jago! Jago!' He heard Bia calling him.

Opening his eyes, he looked up. Bia stood above him, in her hand a tall candlestick. The flame flickered against the ceiling of his room and cast her shadow against the wall.

'What are you doing here?' he asked.

'Looking for you. Henson has been at the door demanding to see you. He told Mrs Macarty you were in the churchyard talking to Ebenezer Goode – he's been dead for years. He gave her this, said he found it and it belongs to you.' Bia unfurled her hand to show him the button from his leather coat.

'But I've been asleep,' Jago answered. Bia looked confused; her brow was furrowed as she looked away. 'What is it?'

'When I came in the room the bed was empty. You weren't here, Jago. I called your name and looked in the cupboards, thinking you could be hiding from me. When I turned around you were on the bed. You just appeared. You weren't here . . . And look – the button – it is missing from your coat.'

'But I was asleep. I dreamt of Strackan. He attacked a woman from the bookshop. I was here.'

Bia looked sullen and anxious. Her hand cupped the side of her face.

'That's the other thing he told Mrs Macarty. He found a woman in an alleyway. She'd been attacked. Henson had heard her screaming. She was from the bookshop.'

Jago shuddered visibly.

'It can't be . . . Is he still here?' he said.

142

'Henson has gone. Jago, you haven't been dreaming – what you saw was real.'

'Say nothing, Bia. Tell Mrs Macarty I am in my room asleep. Please.'

[12]

The Thirteenth Step

JAGO NEVER SLEPT at all that night. The room appeared to move with his every breath. Thankfully the candle on the mantelpiece lasted until the sunrise. Bia had gone down stairs and told Mrs Macarty that he had been asleep and couldn't have left the house. Jago had heard the woman stomping about and cursing and shouting that he would have to explain everything in the morning – that had been one cause of his sleeplessness.

The other was far more painful. As he fought sleep, everything began to bubble and burst inside his mind. In a heated rush of thoughts, every word, every memory replayed, as if they were happening again and again. It was something that Jago could not control. He could see the face of his mother bathed in sunshine, moments before she was killed, and then that of Strackan edged in darkness. The voice of the man in the carriage on the train whispered to him constantly. He waited out the hours, counting each one by the chimes of the church clock as the waking nightmare went on. The spell was only broken when he rose from his bed as the sun touched his window and bathed his face in the cold water from the bowl on the washstand.

He took a deep breath and looked at his reflection in the mirror. The word on the glass, which had been so plain the night before, had gone. Jago hid the Cup of Garbova under the thick mattress of the bed and in it he placed all the money given to him by his mother. He smoothed the sheets and folded everything neatly. He pictured Mrs Macarty searching his room and knew this was a warning, just like when he could see the bombers long before they arrived.

With the needle and thread his mother had left him in his bag, he took the spare button and sewed it on his leather coat. Opening the door, he clutched the other button in his hand, expecting Mrs Macarty to be waiting for him at the bottom of the stairs.

As he turned the landing he could see her shadow by the door to the refectory. She waited impatiently as Staxley and Griffin pushed by him and ran on without speaking.

'Did Biatra give you something last night?' she asked. He saw she was inspecting the front of his coat to see if anything was out of place.

'This?' he asked as he handed her the button. 'She said that Mister Henson thought it was mine.'

'And was it?' she asked, not convinced by the newly sewn button on his coat.

'Must have dropped it in the churchyard when I went to find Biatra,' Jago said with a forced smile.

'Must have,' she echoed as she looked into the dining room. 'I have bagged you some food to eat on the way. Biatra thought you might prefer that. The word is that you did not have a very good night last night. The cleaning cupboard is not a place I would advise you to explore. There are some

145

things I know it is best to leave for others to sort out, Jago. Lorken is one of them.'

Jago nodded as Bia came from the kitchen clutching a brown bag. Mrs Macarty obviously knew some of what had gone on, even though Lorken would never have told the true story. As he followed Bia through the door he cast a glance to Staxley. He sat by the fire, flanked by his eager hounds. Jago nodded to Griffin and Lorken, then without thinking smiled at Staxley. He didn't reply, but before Jago walked on, Staxley slowly drew his hand across his throat. The sign needed no explanation.

'Come on, Jago,' Bia said as she sprung out of the door. 'If we walk quickly I know a place where we can eat.'

Jago said nothing until they had got to the statue. Agasias the bronze warrior stared down at them and cast his shadow across the cobblestones. Bia seemed excited; she walked nervously ahead of him, turning back every now and then to see if he still followed.

'I had a cat like you once,' Bia said as they reached the gates of the churchyard. 'He followed me down the street and I would look back to see how far he would go. He always stopped when I got to the river. Then he turned back and when I got home he would be sitting on the doorstep.'

'What happened to him?' Jago asked.

'Disappeared,' she said as she hitched the bag higher on her shoulder.

'Why am I like the cat?' Jago asked.

'No . . . I was just wondering when you will vanish and not come back,' she replied.

Jago didn't know what she meant. He followed because

146

he could smell the hot meat and bread in the hessian bag.

'So where shall we eat?' he asked. 'Did you cook?'

'It was Tallow. He said you needed something to fill your boots. Just down the steps and along the harbour. Won't matter if we're late. It's Tuesday, Clinas won't be there today. Well, not until later.' Bia saw Jago shrug his shoulders, 'Servants' day off – even in the war they get a day off.'

'Why wasn't he called up to fight?' Jago asked. 'He's not too old.'

'Draigorian fixed it with the Ministry of War. It's because he owns the factory. He can get whatever he wants. If the war goes on, he'd do the same for you.'

'I want to fight. I want to get the pilot of the plane that killed my mother,' Jago shouted as he looked up to the clear and peaceful sky. 'Doesn't the war ever come here?'

'Not a bomb or a plane, not since they opened the factory,' Bia answered as she turned the corner of an alleyway between two alehouses. It was narrow, cold and smelt of fish. A trickle of water led from a pipe sticking out of a cottage wall and meandered around the pebbles that littered the ground. 'It's like they don't come here for a reason. Not allowed to talk about it. Careless talk – you could be a spy.'

Bia found a ledge of rock just below the sea wall out of the wind. She opened up the bag and handed Jago some of the food. The breakers rolled in through the jaws of the harbour mouth and up onto the small beach beneath the houses. Looking up, he could see where the cliff had given way years before. Tufts of grass clung to fragile spurs of dark earth supported on broken pillars of rock. A gravestone perched on the edge as if it was soon to fall.

He looked at her. She seemed uncomfortable, despite her smile.

'You haven't asked about last night,' Jago said as he chewed on the bread and sipped the tea she had poured from the flask.

'What can I say? Jago Harker is a ghost boy? Not everyday someone appears in an empty room,' Bia answered abruptly. 'Then you tell me you were dreaming and Henson gives Mrs Macarty a button from your coat that had been in the hand of a woman attacked outside the bookshop . . .'

Bia gabbled her words hurriedly and looked out to sea.

'I *was* dreaming,' Jago answered as he watched a woman walking along the strand of the beach. She was picking sea coal and putting it into the sack she dragged behind her.

'You weren't there, Jago. The sheets on the bed were ruffled, but it was empty. When I turned around you had just appeared.'

He looked on as the woman picked up more coals.

'Then I don't know what to say. I thought it was a dream.'

'Dreams don't scream, dreams don't make people vanish. What are you, Jago?' Bia asked.

It was a question he couldn't answer. The woman picking sea coal smiled at him as she walked by. She dragged the sack effortlessly even though it was half full of wet black rocks.

'If it wasn't a dream, then Henson can speak to the dead and Strackan is real,' Jago replied.

'Ebenezer Goode?' Bia asked.

'That was the man. I could see him.'

'He was the first one to go missing when the comet came

148

a hundred years ago. People say he walks in the graveyard. Haunts the place night after night. The legend was that he can't get down any further than the thirteenth step. He'll always have to stay to the churchyard and will never be free.'

'Thirteenth step?' Jago asked. 'From the top or the bottom?'

'Thirteen from the street. Each one is marked with a brass plate.' Bia pointed to the steps. 'But you should know that. You met him last night – that's what Henson told Mrs Macarty.'

Jago looked away from her eyes. They seemed to peer inside him.

'I wish it were a dream, but since my mother died, I have been hearing voices and seeing things. Now I think the dreaming is real.'

'If you can see Ebenezer, you could find out where my mother is,' Bia said hopefully.

'You think she's alive?' Jago answered.

'If the spirits say she is then all's well. They should know if she's dead.' Bia got up and faced him as spirals of sand blew about her feet.

'I don't think I can trust what they say. They are all shadows, not like real people,' Jago said as he turned to go.

'*Did* you see Strackan? Is he real?' Bia asked.

'Yes,' Jago said quickly.

'Trouble is, Jago . . . I believe you,' Bia answered as she followed him up the dark alleyway back to the street. 'Changed my mind about many things since meeting you.'

'I'm trouble, Bia. That's what everyone in London always

said about me. Think it must be true,' Jago said. They turned the corner of the alley and joined the crowd that now filled Church Street.

'What happened between you and Lorken?' Bia asked as they pushed their way through the people.

'Did he tell you?' he asked. A knife grinder on the corner of the market square sang as he sparked blades against the stone.

'I heard him talking to Staxley when I was making breakfast. He said he gave you a good hiding.' Bia punched the air with her fist.

'He can say what he likes,' Jago was about to go on.

'Trouble is, I heard him in his room last night. It's the one next to mine. He was crying and moaning in his sleep. Not right for someone who has just won a fight.'

Jago shrugged his shoulders. It was enough to tell Bia he didn't want to talk about Lorken any more.

'I heard that Staxley knows who the Vampyre is,' Jago said quietly as they huddled together by a shop window, waiting for a bread cart to squeeze by them.

'That's what he says. Told me that he would set the Vampyre on me and to watch my neck,' she replied.

'Do you think he does?' Jago asked.

'He's a liar and a thief. Mrs Macarty can't get him to do a job for longer than a day. Every time she sends him anywhere he always gets sacked – well, every time other than when he went to . . .' She stopped talking – in the reflection of the shop window she saw Staxley, Lorken and Griffin standing behind them. Their images in the glass looked like three fading ghosts.

'Heard you mention my name, scar-face,' Staxley said as he prodded her with his stiff little finger.

'Don't, Staxley,' Jago said as he stood between them, shielding her from Staxley's narrow-eyed glare.

'Thought you'd had enough and were going to obey now?' Staxley asked.

Jago looked casually at the sky and then all around him before he replied.

'Don't think I will,' he slowly mused as he stared Lorken eye to eye.

'Do it, Lorken,' Staxley muttered under his breath.

'Not here, Stax – not now – too many people,' Lorken stuttered.

'Griff?' Staxley asked, wanting him to attack.

'Lorken is right – too many people,' Griffin answered as he stepped back.

'Do it yourself, Staxley,' Jago answered keenly, his hand clenched and ready to fight.

Staxley looked at each of his companions and saw their reluctance to fight.

'Griff's right – you'd only go running to Mrs Macarty and wailing. Lorken will sort you like he did last night.' Staxley shrugged his shoulders like a trembling dog as he tried to keep his face steely thin.

'Is that right, Lorken?' Jago asked with a smile. 'Just like last night?'

Lorken looked away and said nothing. Staxley knew what the gawping stare on his face really meant.

'There's more than one way to get you, Jago,' Staxley said as he stepped back, pushing Lorken out of the way. 'You will do what I say – just like everyone else. If not you are no use to me at all.'

Jago stood as tall as he could and stared at Staxley as he walked away.

'You make it worse for yourself,' Bia said as she stepped from his shadow. 'If you just went with him it would be so easy for you.'

'I wouldn't do what he says, never. I don't care what he does to me,' Jago answered, never taking his eyes from the three as they walked into the crowd of people gathered around the market stalls.

'Do you care what he will do to me?' Bia asked softly, covering the scar on her lip with her hand.

'I won't let him,' Jago answered. Without thinking he took hold of her hand and pulled it away from her face. 'Friends don't let that happen.'

'Is that what we are, Jago Harker – friends?' Bia asked, hoping there might be something more between them than simple friendship.

'Friends,' he said as he squeezed her hand.

Jago looked down the crowded street. Horses clattered over the cobbles and women at market stalls shouted out their wares. He had seen this so many times before in Brick Lane in London. It was both familiar and unfamiliar, the same and yet so different. Everyone went on as if the war was a memory or took place in a different world. Life had not changed; all was as it always had been. From somewhere nearby he could distinctly smell the aroma of cooked eggs.

Then, without warning, his stomach suddenly churned and he shuddered and convulsed. He gripped the window ledge of the shop to stop himself falling over. A searing, burning pain shot through his spine. A woman passing by stopped and looked at him, then another and another until a tightly knit group pressed in on them both.

'What is it?' Bia asked as she held him.

'We have to run,' Jago muttered. 'Get out of here.'

'Why?' she asked, her voice tinged with fear as she gripped his hand.

'They're coming – enemy bombers,' Jago said as he stumbled over the words that stuck in his throat.

'How?' she asked.

'I just know, I can feel them.' For a moment she did nothing. Jago tried to stand as the pain subsided. 'They're coming from over the sea – flying low – two of them. I can see them in my head.'

'They don't come here – never have – why should they now?' she asked. All around them the crowd stared at Jago as he shook uncontrollably.

'What's wrong with him?' asked a woman with a pushchair and screaming child.

'Said the bombers were coming and that he could see them in his head,' laughed the man sharpening knives on a gritstone.

'It's true – you've got to take cover, now!' Jago shouted, knowing they didn't believe him.

'Don't be stupid, lad – why should they come this far north when all the rich pickings are in London?' the knife grinder asked mockingly as he tested the blade across his green and blistered tongue and then wiped the steel on the scarf around his neck.

'I tell you, they're coming. Two of them – here – now!' Jago shouted to the crowd as the vision of two aeroplanes burnt painfully in his mind. 'Run – hide – take cover.'

'Are you stupid?' the woman asked as she lifted her child from the pram and held him close.

'It's true,' Jago said. He pulled Bia and began to run, pushing his way through the people. 'They're going to bomb the square – I can see it happening . . .'

'Stupid boy,' shouted the knife grinder as he spun the gritstone with the long iron pedal tied to his shoe with raffia straps.

Far out to sea, shielded by the sun, two dark shapes sped low and fast across the water. With every passing second they got nearer the coast like dark avenging angels approaching with wings outstretched.

It was only when they were a mile out that the sound of their engines echoed against the cliffs. Everyone in the streets stopped and looked up to the sky. Bullets from the forward guns hit the harbour wall, cut across the bridge and then smashed into the town hall clock.

Bia stood at the street corner and looked up. The bomber banked to the north and as it did, the spinning casket fell from within it.

'Bia, no!' Jago shouted as he pulled her into the shop doorway.

The first bomb fell silently towards the marketplace as the other aircraft opened fire and smashed the grey slate tiles from the roof above their heads. Shards of stone fell all around them like splintered glass. They clattered against the cobbles, making the sound of a badly tuned piano played by a petulant child. Jago looked to the knife grinder – he had jumped from the grinding stool but could not get free from the bindings that held him to the machine.

The first explosion tore through the row of cottages that crowded against the quayside. People screamed as black acrid smoke billowed from the burning houses and the ground shook. The woman with the child pressed herself against the stone wall of the shop, holding her baby close as she sobbed.

'How did you know?' Bia asked. She shielded her face as a crescendo of bullets smashed the windows along the street.

'I could see it – feel it – burning in my head,' Jago answered as he covered her with his coat.

There was another explosion, then another and another. The town shook and the screams of the people echoed through the narrow streets of the quayside. Smoke hung in the air and swirled in the morning breeze. The last aircraft banked steeply over the town and then turned back out to sea, the faint hum and drone of its baleful engines slowly fading.

Jago looked across the marketplace. The gritstone wheel of the knife grinder turned and turned. The foot pedal went back and forth. The leather shoe was still strapped in its place, but the man was gone.

'Is it over?' Bia asked as she looked up to the cloudless sky.

'It has just started,' Jago answered, looking around at the chaos of burning houses and blown-out windows, his heart telling him what was to come.

[13]

The Labyrinth

THEY RAN AS HARD as they could, until their lungs felt as if they would burst. Bia never looked back to the town as they followed the road along the side of the estuary until it came to the factory and Hagg House above it. Jago had taken her by the hand and was urging her along. She tried to keep pace with him, knowing he wouldn't stop until they were far away from the bombing.

It was only when they got to the narrow dirt road that led to the factory gates that Jago stopped running. He let go of her hand and slumped by the side of the road.

'They'll come back again,' he said as he looked back to the town. 'Not today, but they will be back. I can't understand why they didn't want to bomb the factory.'

Bia shrugged her shoulders. It was all she could do to stop herself from crying.

'Never seen a bomber before, didn't know they were so big,' she said. She was lumbering up the hill, leaving Jago behind. 'I just want to get inside, don't feel safe with all that sky above me.'

'I know when they are coming – I can see it in my head,' Jago answered, trying to calm her fear.

156

'Doesn't stop them bombing. That knife grinder just disappeared. It was as if he had never been.' Bia waited for him to follow on.

Jago knew what she meant. His heart was burning for his mother – like the man in the marketplace, she too had just vanished.

'Do you know Bradick – the man at the train station?' Jago asked.

'Why?' she answered.

'He seemed to know me. When I showed him a picture of my mother, he took it from me. It was as if it would do me no good if people found out who I was.' Jago stood on the grass bank and looked back at the column of smoke that spewed from the bombed cottages on the quayside.

'I know him, he was a friend of my father's before the war,' Bia answered as she stood in the shade of a tall chestnut tree and kicked the spiked fruit with her feet. 'They were at school together.'

'I wish I could show you the picture of my mother. It was taken here in Whitby. She lived here for a time,' Jago said, trying to picture her living in such a place.

'Lived here, in Whitby? Is it where she met your father?' she asked, astonished that he had never mentioned this before.

'I don't know. I don't know who he is. I was born in London. That's where she went to when she left. She never spoke of anything and never of my father.'

Bia looked at him and tried to smile. 'It's a small place. Someone should know something about him.'

'I don't want to know,' he replied. 'What good is it now?'

Bia would have answered, but for a sharp voice coming from the garden.

'Quickly! Quickly!' a man screamed.

'Draigorian – he's outside – in daylight.' Bia ran towards the clumps of ornamental bamboo, where she had heard the voice coming from.

Jago gave chase and in three strides had caught her.

'Thought he couldn't stand the daylight?' Jago asked as they jumped the steps to the ornamental Japanese garden that enclosed the lily pond.

'He can't. I have never known him to come out of the house, not in daylight,' Bia said as she turned instinctively through a small archway made of cut stone.

'Where is he?' Jago asked as the garden returned to its silence once more.

'There's a place through here,' Bia said, slowing to a walking pace. 'It's hard to find. He shouldn't be outside.'

The dark path dropped through a slight ravine made of ornamental stones piled on top of one another. They were covered in thick moss with bursts of large, jagged ferns spilling in between.

'Mr Draigorian!' Jago shouted, hoping to hear the man's voice.

'This way, this way!' came the reply from the far side of a tall stand of spiked dead flowers. They had dried on the stem to form a barricade of seeds pods and stalks in the overhang of a willow tree that stopped the light. 'I can't see, I can't find my way back . . .'

It was then that Jago saw him in the shadow of a tall tree. Draigorian leant against a standing stone that had been placed in the ground. It looked as if it had been there for many years.

'You all right?' Bia asked as she saw him.

Draigorian nodded. His hat was tilted across his face to shade him from the light, and his eyes were covered by a thick black scarf. For a moment Jago thought of the night before.

'Strackan . . .' he whispered to himself.

'Just a man, Jago. An ordinary man who came outside when he heard the bombing,' he answered as if he had heard what Jago had whispered. 'I thought I would be safe here, but I have lost the glasses that protect my eyes.' Draigorian gestured with his gloved hand to the ground near his feet. 'When they fell from my face, the light was so bright that I was blinded. I cannot see where they are.'

'They're here,' Bia said. She picked up a pair of thick-lensed dark spectacles from the gravel path near to where he stood.

'At last,' Draigorian answered as he allowed the scarf to drop from his face. 'Will you help me back to the house? It is the day that Clinas takes off. I am here quite alone.'

As Draigorian took hold of the spectacles, Jago saw his eyes. They burnt like dark stones set within two pools of blood. If he was not mistaken, they were the same eyes he had seen the night before.

Draigorian held out his arm for Jago to take hold and steady him.

'Will the light hurt you?' Jago asked as he helped the man.

'Not as much as your thoughts,' he whispered in reply so

only Jago could hear. 'I will be fine in such company, Jago,' Draigorian went on. 'If you hadn't come I would have been there until night. It is really quite difficult with this condition of the skin.'

Jago guarded his thoughts. It was as if Draigorian could understand all that went on in his mind.

'They bombed the cottages by the quayside,' Bia said as they helped him up the steps back to the house.

'I heard them, thought they were coming to destroy my factory. That is why I came outside.' He stopped walking, as if short of breath. 'Do you know, I have not stood under a tree for many years. I have watched them leaf and bud and then fade away from my window at night, but have never stood beneath one.' Draigorian coughed and with his free hand pulled a handkerchief from his pocket and wiped his mouth. 'I think the experience could even be worth what will happen to my skin. What do you think, Jago?'

'I don't know,' Jago answered.

'Just what I expected from one so young. It is only when you get to my age that you think such things.' Draigorian pointed up to the branches of an oak tree above him. 'What do you see?'

'A tree?' Jago replied not knowing how to answer.

'A tree indeed,' Draigorian blustered merrily. 'But I see a struggle between earth and sky. Gravity pulls at the branches to bring them to the ground and the strength of the tree is shooting them to the stars. It is a battle between life and death and every year death will come to the tree. It will lose its leaves and cast its fruit. Passers-by will think it is no more. What kind of tree are you, Jago?'

160

'He's a plum tree, Mr Draigorian,' Bia answered before he could speak.

'A plum indeed, Biatra,' Draigorian replied eagerly. 'And, you are a willow – a willow with long red hair – thoughtful as it stands by the water.' Draigorian touched the side of her face gently. 'And I, a gnarled old oak with bark for skin stretched over the thick bone.'

Jago swallowed hard as he heard his thoughts spoken by Draigorian. The man said no more until they got him to the house. Bia went ahead and opened the kitchen door. The fire was set in the grate ready to be lit in the afternoon.

All was clean with nothing out of place. The white tiles had been polished; the brass around the fire glowed brightly. Clinas Macarty always made sure it was that way on his day off. He would prepare all that Draigorian would need and then would go to the town and drink tea. Bia had watched him many times. She knew he would never take all the hours he was due and by lunchtime he would be back at the house.

'Do you need anything?' she asked him as Draigorian slipped his long black coat from his shoulders and rested it on the back of a chair.

Draigorian looked up at the clock on the wall and made his calculations as to the time it would take for the task he would set.

'Perhaps you would do me one thing?' he asked cautiously. 'Something that I would not like dear Clinas to find out?'

Bia looked at Jago and then nodded.

'I have an item that needs to go to a friend of the family, quite locally of course – nothing too far. I don't think that Clinas would approve of this as it is seen as an heirloom and

Clinas always likes to keep what is mine within the house. Do you understand?'

'Keep it secret?' Bia asked.

'Precisely,' Draigorian replied. 'There is something in my study that I would like to show you. Bring me some tea in five minutes and I will set your work for the day. You can go together. It is a long walk, but I am sure it will be easy for you both.'

Draigorian sighed and sounded relieved as he went through the door and up the stairs to his room. Jago watched the way he walked and tried not to think anything that the man would sense. Bia took out a tray from the cupboard and set the tea. Everything was placed neatly – napkin, silver spoon, china cup. The kettle gurgled on the stove where it had been warming since Clinas had left.

'What do you think he wants?' Jago asked.

'It's an errand, wants us to take something without Clinas finding out,' she answered.

'Why should that be kept from Clinas?'

'He thinks Draigorian is selling things off to pay his debts. Since the war, money has been tight. Clinas keeps a track on things. I heard the government doesn't pay on time for the work at the factory.'

'So he sells things from the house?' Jago asked.

'If you look in the hallway upstairs you can see the marks on the walls where the pictures have gone. Clinas told me they were in storage in case we were invaded. I think he sold them,' Bia said as she placed the small decorated teapot on the tray. 'That's why Clinas never takes the whole day off. I was here once when a man came to see Draigorian. They argued and Clinas threw the man out. I think it was all over money.'

Bia picked up the tray and nodded for Jago to open the door. She went ahead until they came to the study. The house seemed to wheeze with every step they took – like a living creature, listening and waiting for them. Jago looked back down the long candlelit passageway with its shuttered windows. It was just as Bia had said. On both walls were the marks of old picture frames and in some places the hooks on thick wires hung empty from the high rail.

'Tea!' shouted Bia as she pushed against the study door. It opened slowly and they stepped inside.

'Good,' Draigorian said happily. 'Now what you are about to do for me will always be a secret. Yes?' he asked as he looked directly at Jago.

They both nodded. Draigorian pushed the darkened spectacles further up his long nose to fully cover his eyes.

'We won't speak of it,' Bia answered loudly, her words echoing in the room.

'Speak of it, Biatra? Don't even think of it.' He laughed as he lifted a leather case from the floor and put it on the desk in front of him next to the skull in which he kept his pencils, poked through each eye socket. 'I will show you this before your journey as I know that you will not be able to walk all that way without your curiosity opening the case.' Jago looked uneasily at Bia. 'I was once a child and would have looked inside as soon as I had got from the house. I would rather show you now in the secrecy of this room than you look when on the road.'

'Where are we to go?' Bia asked.

'I will come to that, Biatra. In this box is something that my family has protected for many, many years. A friend requires it on loan and you are to take it to them.' He slowly opened the black case, flicking the two latches one after the other and lifting back the snakeskin lid. 'I don't think you will have seen anything like it before. It is very old, older than me.' He laughed as he spoke, his words filling the dark, high-vaulted room.

Draigorian slipped his gloved hands into the case and from within pulled a silk bag. Something looked familiar to Jago. He felt as though what he was about to be shown would not be a surprise. As the black bag was opened, Jago could see the rim of a gold chalice. Like the Cup of Garbova, it had worn writing around the edge, and as Draigorian peeled back the cloth Jago could see it was identical to the cup given to him by Cresco.

'It's beautiful,' Bia said as the candlelight shimmered in the gold reflection.

'You don't seemed surprised, Jago – have you seen something like this before?' Draigorian asked.

Jago wished he had bought one of Maisie's talismans for stopping a Vampyre reading his mind. He tried to look surprised and admire its beauty.

'It's amazing,' he said softly, not daring to wonder how there was another cup just like his own.

'Truly amazing,' Draigorian said, 'and beautiful. Before my family came to this country we had two such cups. One was taken from us and has never been recovered. They were very, very old. Hugh Morgan would like to examine it more closely. He is a fine artist and this is going to be a part of one of his paintings. I would like you to take it to him at Hawks Moor. Do you know the house, Biatra?'

'Take the dale road and up to the moor and before the bay, there is the house,' she answered.

'Precisely,' Draigorian replied. 'And now you have seen the chalice there is no need for you to stop on the way and look at it – is there?'

'Do you trust us to take it?' Jago asked. 'It must be worth hundreds of pounds.'

'Its value is not in its worth but in what it represents. We live in dangerous times and to have it preserved for ever in art would be a fine thing,' said Draigorian as he covered the cup in the silk bag.

'So we just take it to Hugh Morgan and then come back?' Bia asked.

'Hugh Morgan and no one else. It is a secret for which you will be rewarded. Show the cup to no one on the road – no one at all,' Draigorian insisted eagerly as he placed the cup back in the case and snapped the clasps tightly shut.

'You said there was another such cup – where is it now?' Jago asked.

'If only I knew,' Draigorian answered. 'It was a long time ago and in another land when it disappeared. There is a legend that when the two cups come together any enemy can be defeated and even death itself conquered. But then again, it is just a legend and any legend is a glorified lie.' Draigorian laughed gently and smiled at them both. 'Whitby is awash with rumours of Vampyres and yet I have lived in the dark for many years and never seen one.'

Jago hesitated. The room was silent. No one spoke. Bia

looked at the case and then at Jago. For some reason she didn't want to touch the cup and was glad it was imprisoned within its bag. The pendulum of the long-case clock swung back and forth in time with her heartbeat.

'Better be off, Jago,' Bia said to break the silence. 'Hawks Moor is a fair walk.'

'I have a bag, take it and hide the case within. Take some food from the kitchen and I will see you in the morning and give you your reward. I will telephone Hugh and tell him to watch out for you.' Draigorian offered the case to Jago.

'Are you sure?' Jago asked.

'I think I can trust you, Jago,' Draigorian answered as he handed him the case and then gave an old fishing bag to Bia. 'Keep it in this and tell no one what you have, understand?'

'What about Mrs Macarty – what if she asks where we have been?' Bia said as she walked to the door.

'I will tell her you went on an errand. She doesn't need to know the details of your adventure,' Draigorian said as he peered over his spectacles. 'If you leave within the hour, I am sure Hugh Morgan may even feed you.' Draigorian picked up the heavy Bakelite telephone and waited for the exchange to answer. 'Hawks Moor, please,' he said. He waved them away with his gloved hand as the telephonist connected his call. 'Hugh . . . Crispin Draigorian . . .'

The door closed as Jago stepped into the hallway and he could hear no more.

'What shall we do?' Bia asked.

'Go, it's all we can do. We can't refuse,' Jago answered. He put the snakeskin case into the old fishing bag. 'In my dream last night I followed Strackan and I saw a place that might be

Hawks Moor – I saw a house and a labyrinth in the garden and the shadow that attacked the woman. I have seen this cup before. There is a photograph of Crispin Draigorian – I found it in the library. On the back it said *PD, London 1861*. Pippen Draigorian –'

'It couldn't be him,' Bia said. 'He'd be too old and he's dead.'

'PD, that's what it said. Pippen Draigorian, it has to be him,' Jago insisted.

[14]

Hawks Moor

THE ROAD FROM HAGG HOUSE was dusty and steep. The edges were overgrown with high banks of stinging nettles and hogweed that stood in clumps like dried-out sentinels. Bia carried the fishing bag over her shoulder. She wanted to look back at the town and Jago, who lagged behind, talking to himself and throwing stones into the undergrowth.

'When do you want to eat?' she asked, thinking of the hastily made sandwiches that she had so carefully wrapped in greaseproof paper and stacked neatly on top of the case.

'Cheese?' he asked in reply, having not eaten any since the outbreak of war.

'Home-made. Not like the real thing. Strange taste – but it's still cheese,' Bia answered as she stopped at the crossroads of the lane and looked at the sign that pointed to Hawks Moor. 'Think it has something to do with a sheep. Clinas gets it from a farmer, but not quite sure what it's made of.'

Bia pulled a face and laughed but Jago wasn't listening. His mind was held captive by the pillar of smoke that hovered over the town.

'Still can't understand why they didn't bomb the factory. I

saw a submarine leaving the harbour on the first night I was here. They must know what goes on down there,' he said as he turned to Bia.

'I don't ask. The less I know the better. My mother said that they had found some bodies in the estuary and they were all workers from the factory and none of them had any blood left in them.' Bia held out a thick crust of bread folded over a slice of cheese that defied any attempt at rationing.

'Can't help thinking it wasn't right. Where was the air force to stop them?' Jago asked as he took a bite from the bread.

'We don't have one near here. Nearest airbase is miles away. I saw a Spitfire once, came down the valley and then out to sea. The harbour isn't defended. They never expected anyone to come this far north.'

'Just not right,' Jago said again. 'I can feel it.'

'Which way do you want to go?' Bia asked pointing at the sign and not wanting to talk of war. 'We have a choice. They were supposed to take all the road signs down in case we were invaded, but they left this one. Two ways to the same place.'

'What's the difference?' he asked, not bothered which way they went, only wanting to get the cup to Hugh Morgan as soon as he could.

'One cuts across the land, the other goes by the coast,' she answered as she walked ahead, having already made her decision.

'Guess I'll just follow you,' he answered. He finished the stale crust of bread and hoped she had brought something to drink to wash away the taste of the cheese.

'Staxley will be that way,' she said, pointing to the coast. 'He and Griffin are working at the lighthouse on the clifftop. Didn't think you'd want to get near them.'

Jago thought for a moment as he followed her along the lane and watched the swathes of lush green undergrowth move in the breeze. Suddenly he realised how alone he was – and as he allowed the thought room in his heart it took away his breath.

'You have no one?' he asked Bia.

'All depends what you mean,' she replied as she switched the bag from one shoulder to the other.

'Your parents are both missing,' Jago went on. 'Possibly dead.'

'Possibly alive,' she answered. 'Can't give any space in my head to death. Bad enough having you appearing and telling me Strackan is real.'

'Do you believe me?' Jago asked.

'There's something not right about you, Jago. Something weird,' she said.

'Thanks,' he answered. 'Never been called weird.'

For some reason, he linked arms with Bia as they walked. It was something he had only ever done with his mother. All he knew was that he wanted to feel close to someone and not be alone.

'I have a friend in London called Mr Cresco. A man who my mother would leave me with whilst she went to work,' Jago said as they walked. 'I think he might have something to do with all that's going on.'

'How?' Bia asked, not minding that they walked so close together.

'You'll think I am really mad,' he said.

'I already do,' she replied as the hill slowed their pace.

'Trouble is,' he said hesitantly, 'trouble is, I have a cup exactly the same as the one in that case.'

'Draigorian said that it was missing,' Bia answered, not believing what he said.

'It was given to me by Mr Cresco. He hid it in my bag before I was sent here. He called it the Cup of Garbova.'

'So where is it?' she asked.

'Hidden in my room so Staxley won't find it.'

'Are you sure it's the same cup?' Bia asked.

'Quite sure. There was also another man in the painting of Draigorian I found in the library. He was with Mr Cresco. I am sure of it,' Jago continued, hoping she would understand.

'You saying they know each other?'

'They must do. It looked as though they were friends,' Jago replied.

'Is that why he gave you the cup – to give it back to Draigorian?' Bia asked.

'Cresco never said. He just hid it in my bag wrapped in paper. I didn't know it was there until I found it when I unpacked,' Jago said.

'So why give it to you?'

Jago was about to reply when he heard the sound of a car engine coming up the lane from the town. He turned and saw a black Daimler car. In the driver's seat was a man in a chauffeur's uniform, grey hat and jacket with brass buttons. The car slowed as it got near. Jago and Bia stood back into the verge, unable to get out of its way for the thick hedge of brambles. The driver edged closer as he tried to pass them.

Jago saw the rear window of the car lower as it drew alongside.

'Going far?' asked the man inside as the car stopped, blocking their escape.

'Hawks Moor,' Bia replied. She tried to smile and push the fishing bag out of sight.

'Such a coincidence,' the man said. 'So am I.'

Bia looked at Jago, hers eyes asking what they should do.

'We have to walk,' Jago said. He looked into the car but could not see the man's face.

'Walk? Walk? I wouldn't hear of it,' the man said as the black car door opened automatically with a sudden click. 'I insist that I give you a lift.'

'Mr Draigorian told us to walk,' Bia said as she tried to step back, only to become tangled in the hedge of spike strands from the brambles.

'Draigorian would say that. I know him well enough and he would not mind if I took you there. Hugh Morgan is my son. You have nothing to fear.'

Jago peered into the darkness of the car. There on the leather seat was an old man. His face was thin and framed with long overgrown white eyebrows. His skin was sun-darkened and wrinkled.

'You know Draigorian?' Jago asked as the man smiled at him.

'Longer than you could ever imagine,' he replied, his bright blue eyes staring at Jago as if he were trying to peer inside his head. 'Old friends, old, dear friends,' he sighed.

'I suppose . . .' Jago said as Bia untangled herself from the thorns.

'Of course. There shall be no suppose. Whilst I have petrol for this car it shall be used to the best of its ability and what finer thing than to give you both a lift to my son's house.' Morgan held out a welcoming hand. Without them seeing, the chauffeur had got from his seat and was now pushing them both towards the open door. 'Quickly, quickly, Rathbone,' Morgan said. 'We are blocking the road.'

Jago looked back just as he was pushed into the car. The road was empty, desolate and overgrown. It didn't look like the kind of lane that many cars would use.

'Are you sure it's all right?' Bia asked as she was pushed onto the leather seat next to the old man, whilst Jago slumped on a fold-down shelf that came out of the partition dividing the car.

'Comfortable?' the man asked as the car sped off. 'I always love it when a journey is so wonderfully interrupted. I am Ezra Morgan – and you?' he asked, staring at Jago.

'Jago Harker, and this is –'

'Biatra,' Morgan answered. 'You look so much like your mother. I do believe she was a friend of my son when they were younger. A shame how promising friendships can go the way of winter wisps.'

Ezra Morgan raised an eyebrow and laughed. The sunburnt creases of his face wrinkled deeply with his smile. Bia sighed and sank back into the leather seat and looked out of the window of the car. It was the first time she had ever been carried in such a machine. Once, when she was smaller, her father had taken her on a steam Sentinel autobus. It had drudged over the moors out of Whitby, its coal engine hissing and filling the road with steam. Bia had leant out of the open window of the Old Glory and smelt the smoke. It had faithfully taken them all the way to a nearby town, where her father had bought presents for Christmas, secret gifts for her mother. As the steam bus returned, the stoker had served hot chestnuts in paper bags that had been cooked in the firebox. Until the war, life had been that way for Bia. Memory on happy memory had filled her time with joy.

The thought of that day went as quickly as it had arrived.

'Did you know my mother?' she found herself saying.

'I did,' Morgan replied. 'She would often come to the house with her sister. It was at that time when I went away. The war has forced me to return.' Morgan coughed and pulled a starched handkerchief from his pocket and wiped a tear from the corner of his eye. 'I never thought I would have to come back. Some places have just too many memories.' Morgan steadied himself. 'And you, Jago, where are you from?'

'London,' Jago said as he noticed the driver looking at him through the rear-view mirror. 'Just arrived, an evacuee.'

'His mother –' Bia started to say.

'Is dead,' Jago continued, knowing what Bia would have said and wanting to keep this a secret. 'She died on the day I came here.'

'Poor lad,' Morgan muttered as if he were talking to himself. 'For some, death is so final. Strange, you remind me of someone I know, but cannot think who. It is your voice, it has a *familiarity*.'

'My mother said I sounded like Alvar Lidell reading the news,' Jago replied as he looked at Bia and bade her be silent with a nudge of his foot.

'London born and bred?' Morgan asked as in his mind he

examined Jago's voice for the familiar tone he was sure he recognised.

'Yes,' Jago lied, and he kicked Bia again.

'First time in Whitby?' Morgan asked. Jago nodded. 'No connection with the town?'

'Not one,' Jago answered. He could see from Bia's look that she could not understand why he didn't tell the man the truth.

Ezra Morgan scrutinised Jago and Bia before he replied. Jago was caught for a moment in his stare.

'If I were to see you both in the street, I would say that you could be related. Strange thing is that in some way we all are. Our common ancestors must all have come from the same place. Here we are, travelling to Hawks Moor, brought together by circumstance and Crispin Draigorian sending you on an errant errand.' Morgan settled back in his seat and looked as if he had found the answer to his question.

The road climbed further and, just as Jago had seen in the dream, the hedges gave way to open moor. Ezra Morgan said little else other than to point out several landmarks on the way. Jago wondered why he hadn't asked the nature of the errand. Then car dipped into a small ravine as the road clung to the side of the slope, and a canopy of trees soon shut out the sky.

Jago heard the sound of the tyres change as the Daimler left the stone road and entered the drive towards the house. As he looked out of the window he felt a churning start in his stomach. The place seemed familiar, as if he had seen it many times before. It did not seem to be his own memory, but one he had shared with someone else. Jago did not know if the house had been described to him in a childhood story. When he saw the arched doorway and climbing wisteria, he was sure that he had seen Hawks Moor before.

'Beautiful,' Bia said as the car slowed to a halt outside the house.

'Windswept, eerie and far to cold to live in,' added Ezra Morgan. 'If only the war had not forced me home from the land beyond the forest.'

Jago sat rigidly in his seat, unwilling to move.

'Are you sick, Jago?' Morgan asked.

'No,' he stammered. 'I'll be fine.'

'Stay where you are and I will go for Hugh and your errand will be complete,' Morgan said, and he stepped from the car as Rathbone held the door open.

'What's wrong?' Bia asked, wondering why Jago suddenly looked so white and bloodless.

'I don't know. I had the same feeling from before, just when the bomber attacked,' he said. He shivered and rubbed his face with his hands to rid himself of the dizziness. 'I know this house. It sounds stupid but I know every inch of the place.'

'From your dream?' Bia asked.

'More than that. It is as if I have lived here,' he answered.

The door to the house opened. Standing in the frame, tall and gaunt, was Hugh Morgan. He stepped quickly towards the car.

'I hear you are sick. Rathbone, take the lad to my study and I will bring something from the kitchen,' Hugh Morgan said as he leant forward and looked at Jago closely. 'Better carry him – doesn't look too well.'

Jago didn't know what happened next. The last thing he saw was Hugh Morgan staring at him, and then darkness fell and he could hear faint, urgent voices, footsteps on wooden boards and the closing of doors.

When Jago opened his eyes, he was in an upstairs room. He knew exactly where he was. It all seemed so familiar. The fireplace, the tall vaulted ceiling, the wooden panelled walls were just as some memory had told him. Nothing differed from his expectation. This was not the studio, as Hugh Morgan had said, but the library. The one thing that was different to how he thought it would be was that there were no books. Where he somehow knew the shelves had once been were now paintings. At the far end of the room, where the most light streamed in, was a small array of wooden stands, a table littered with paint pots and several unfinished canvases.

Rathbone had propped him by the fire on a chaise longue. Jago felt the soft pile of the red velvet sofa with his fingers. He looked to the mullioned window with its thousand panes of lead-lined glass. A long table covered in a purple cloth sprawled in front like an altar; on it rested candlesticks and a book.

Rathbone fussed with a plaid cover by his feet as he stared at Jago.

'Better keep still until Master Hugh arrives,' he said. He stacked two more logs onto the fire and bedded them into the embers with the toe of his boot.

'Is this the library?' Jago asked as his head cleared and the churning in his stomach ebbed away.

'Library? Hasn't been a library for many years – what made you think that? Been here before?'

The door to the room opened and Hugh Morgan walked in carrying a wooden tray stacked with cups, plates and curiously shaped pieces of bread. Bia followed sheepishly, her eyes looking quickly about the room, the fishing bag still over her shoulder.

'You must have fainted. They can't be feeding you enough – and with the shock of your mother being killed . . .'

Jago looked at Bia and wondered what she had told him.

'Hugh knows my mother,' Bia said excitedly. 'They were friends, it's true.'

Morgan looked at Jago before he spoke.

'Don't look so worried. You can call me Hugh,' he said as he brushed back the long strands of his hair with his fingers. 'Bia has told me all about you. Feeling better?'

Jago nodded as Hugh Morgan put the tray on the floor by the fire and pulled up a chair for Bia. He leant against the stone fireplace and looked at Jago. 'She says you had something similar this morning before the bombing.'

'Could be something I have eaten,' Jago replied.

'Tallow's cooking may be many things, but dangerous it is certainly not.' Morgan smiled at Bia and handed her a cup of tea. 'Weren't you at the Penance Hedge the other day?'

'You were the man with the bundle of sticks,' Jago said.

'It's what Morgans have to do. That *bundle of sticks* is a curse to this family but thankfully the hedge lasted the tides and so we will all be safe.'

'What would happen if it didn't?' Jago asked.

'Then the fury of the curse would fall upon the town. When my ancestor killed the hermit, it darkened all of our hearts.'

'It was just a man in a shack,' Jago answered.

'If only that were the case, Jago,' Hugh Morgan answered. 'What happened was more than a legend and it would not be worth our while to fail in our task. As a Morgan, I cannot risk the consequences. The hermit cursed us with more than having to build a Penance Hedge. Anyway, enough of this,' he said as his voice wavered. 'Crispin Draigorian telephoned to say you had something for me?'

Bia handed him the fisherman's bag.

'It's in there,' she said, suddenly remembering the remnants of the sandwiches.

'Cheese?' Morgan asked as he lifted the snakeskin case from the bag and brushed the crumbs away.

'Mr Draigorian showed us what was inside,' she blurted. 'We never looked. He told us all about it.'

'Did he indeed?' asked Morgan as he laughed. 'Then it saves me an explanation.'

[15]

Blood

TEA LASTED AN HOUR. Hugh Morgan built up the fire and as they talked they drank two more pots brought eagerly by Rathbone, who was always reluctant to leave and listened to much of what they said. The hour slipped easily into another hour and then another. Morgan finally looked at his watched and sighed.

'I had forgotten what it was like to be your age,' he said mournfully. 'Your mother and I would talk this same way and Martha would listen – just like you, Jago.'

'Martha?' Jago asked, saying the first word in over an hour. 'Did you say she was called Martha?'

'Maria's sister. Martha was the quiet one, a year younger and just as pretty,' Morgan said as he looked inquisitively at Jago.

'And they both came here?' he asked.

'Often,' Morgan said.

Jago looked at Bia. It all suddenly made sense. He remembered what his mother had said. Find Maria . . . Without the picture, he had no proof. Then he realised why Bradick had taken it from him. His mother would have been recognised – everyone would know who Jago was.

'Why did her sister leave Whitby?' Jago asked.

'How did you know?' Morgan said, not knowing why the lad should ask such a question.

'I told him,' Bia said as she chewed on a piece of cold toast and supped the last of her tea from the china cup.

'Does it matter?' Morgan enquired reluctantly.

'I would like to know,' Bia said. 'If she's alive then she is my family, Aunt Martha – there's a peaceful sound to the name.'

Jago said nothing. This was not the time; coincidences did not happen.

'If you had ever met her, you would know how peaceful she really was,' Morgan said as he got up from the fireside and walked to the window and looked out across the moor to the sea. 'No one knew why she left. Martha said nothing, gave no indication she would leave. One day she was here and the next she had gone.' The man shrugged his wide shoulders and slung his hands in the pockets of his tweed trousers. 'Funny how lives change. I went to university and when I had returned your mother had married and Martha had not come back. I am so glad that old Draigorian sent you here today. I had heard there was an evacuee in town but never thought our paths would cross.' Morgan thought for a moment as he looked at the thick, black clouds coming in from the sea. Jago could see his reflection in the window glass and thought how handsome the man was. 'Let me show you the house before you return to Whitby. I am sure Mrs Macarty won't mind.'

Bia looked at Jago and begged him with her eyes not to refuse. 'I'm sure you could manage it, Jago,' she said, willing him to get up from the sofa.

'It doesn't have to be for long,' Morgan added. 'I get so few visitors, fewer since Father has returned. There is a labyrinth, an ancient maze of hedges with a statue at the centre.' Morgan stopped suddenly, as if he had said too much.

'We'd love to,' Bia replied as she took hold of Jago by the hand. 'You can rest later. Let's walk?'

Jago stood reluctantly. The pain in his stomach had long since gone. He had stayed on the couch to listen to the stories that Morgan had told, thinking that if he moved or interrupted in any way they would stop. There was something about Morgan that he liked. In so many ways he was just like Mr Cresco. He could suspend disbelief and speak in such a way as to take your mind to the place of which he spoke and through your inner eye see what he saw in his imagination.

'Mr Draigorian said you were an artist,' Jago said as he pulled the plaid cover from his legs and got to his feet.

'I studied fine art at Hatfield College – Durham University,' Morgan replied. 'I try to be the best I can.'

'Why haven't you gone to war?' Jago asked.

Bia looked at him as if it was something he should not have said. Morgan saw her face.

'I don't mind, Biatra,' he answered. 'I have a rare blood disorder that will come upon me as I grow older. It started when I was about your age, Jago. I am not allowed to fight; it's as simple as that. Anyway, there are more ways of overcoming an enemy than by throwing bombs at them.' His sharp words ended the conversation. Jago knew not to ask again. 'Let me show you the house.'

Morgan strode from the window and opened the door. He didn't looked at Jago until they were in the long corridor that led from the studio down the dark stairway and into the grand hall below. Just like at Streonshalgh Manor, the walls of Hawks Moor were covered in paintings. It was as if every space had to be filled. But here, unlike at the Manor, Jago did not feel the eyes of every man and woman following him as he walked behind Bia and Hugh Morgan.

'Are these pictures of your family?' Jago asked, already knowing the answer.

'A tradition made by men – always have a painting of everyone who has ever lived. I prefer to take photographs and then paint over them or bring them into my art in some other way.' He pointed to the largest painting on the wall – the portrait of a man in a ruff collar stared down. 'It was all his fault. That is the man who killed the hermit – he and two of his friends.'

'Why does he have blood on the back of his hand?' Bia asked as she looked at the trickle of faded cinnabar threads that snaked to his fingers.

'That, Biatra, is the true cost of killing the hermit. What the popular legend does not say was that Tristan Morgan was attacked by something in the shack. Something that he tried to kill and that the hermit was protecting.'

'They didn't tell us that at school,' she replied.

'It does not make a good story. My family have been paint-ed as murderers and thieves when in reality they were hunt-ing a creature that the world believed did not exist,' Morgan answered quietly.

'A Vampyre?' Jago asked. The word had come to his mind as if he could read the mind of Hugh Morgan.

'That is one name for the creature. Whatever it may be

called, it attacked Tristan and his companions. All of them gave their blood that night and the curse has been with us ever since. Did they tell you that at school, Biatra?' Morgan asked as he turned from the portrait and walked to the staircase.

'And this?' Jago asked as he stared at a painting of a boy about his own age.

'That's me,' Morgan said cheerily. 'It was done before I went to university by a friend of my father.'

'Looks like you, Jago,' Bia said as she pushed him to one side. 'It *does* look like you.'

Hugh Morgan took another look at the painting and then at Jago. 'How strange. I would never have noticed until now. You look like I once did.' He stared closely at Jago.

'Who painted it?' Bia asked. She tried to make out the scrawled signature at the bottom of the picture.

'I don't know his name. He was a friend of my father; he did the painting from photographs that were taken of me on holiday. I never met the man. All I can remember is he lived in a village in Wallachia. The painting arrived in a wooden box on my seventeenth birthday.'

'You have a good memory for such things,' Bia said as she again tried to read the inscription.

'I should be able to remember it quite clearly. It was the day my father left this house without telling me where he was going,' Morgan replied. 'It rained that morning and I watched him put on his gabardine and hat and step outside. He never even said goodbye.'

'You mean he just left and didn't come back?' Jago asked.

'He arrived home at Hawks Moor eighteen years later,

three days before war broke out. Father caught the last train from Paris and arrived on the doorstep as if he had never been away.' Morgan paused and looked at them both. 'I don't know why I am telling you this,' he said as he tried to smile. 'There is so much to show you and the storm clouds are coming in from the sea.'

Jago could not be sure, but he wondered if Morgan was trying not to cry. The man turned away and took a sighing breath. Then he sped off down the staircase towards the front door and waved for them to follow.

The house was brighter here; the stair walls were painted white with pictures of landscapes in golden frames. In each was a different view of the same castle. It was tall, spired and set on a wooded hill above a lake. The land was thick with forests and in some of the pictures the moon came up from the earth in its fullness. Jago stopped at the nearest painting. He read the gold plaque pinned to the frame: *1815. The Land of the Forest.*

'Do you think it was true?' Bia asked when she was sure Morgan couldn't hear her. 'About his father just leaving?'

'What do you think?' Jago asked. 'He told us he had recently come back – of course it's true.'

As they spoke, Rathbone stepped through the heavy curtain inside the front door. He straightened his chauffeur's hat and looked up at them as they walked slowly down the stairs. Then he whispered to Hugh Morgan, who nodded and turned to them, a look of disappointment etched on his face.

'I am afraid my father insists on seeing me,' he said, the regret clear in his drawn voice. 'Perhaps . . . perhaps you could look about the house until I return. I will show you the labyrinth when I come back – it is not a place for you to go on your own.'

Hugh Morgan stepped towards the door and pulled the thick green curtain away from the entrance.

'So we can look around?' Bia asked.

'Of course,' Morgan replied as Rathbone waited for him to step outside.

'But don't touch anything,' Rathbone said before he followed on.

The door slammed shut and the air shook. Jago listened and there was silence.

'I've been here before,' he said as he stepped from the staircase onto the tiled floor of the hallway and looked across the expanse to the fireplace.

'In your dream when you followed Strackan?' Bia asked.

'No. I mean I have been in this house before. I remember it but can't think when it was. It must have been when I was a child.' Jago looked up at the wooden stars embedded in the ceiling and etched with gold paint.

'I thought you lived in London all your life?' Bia asked.

'I did, but I can remember coming here. It must have been a long time ago – when I was a small child. It's the smell of the place – it hasn't changed. We went to the studio, but then it was a library with lots of books.'

'Why should you have come here? It can't be true. You're imagining it,' Bia answered.

Jago thought harder. He looked as though he was racking his brain to find the memories he needed to make sense of it all.

'My mother brought me here,' he said slowly as he thought.

186

'We stayed one night.' He ran his fingers along the rough stone of the fireplace and hoped it would speak to him.

'I'll ask Hugh Morgan when he comes back. He'll be able to remember,' Bia said excitedly, knowing that if Jago were lying it would call his bluff.

'No – don't say anything. It's too complicated,' Jago answered quickly.

'Then it's not true,' she snapped. 'You're lying –'

'It's not a lie, Bia. Honest,' Jago said as he looked about the hallway. 'It's best he doesn't find out – not yet.'

'Why not?' she asked. 'If you had been here before that means your mother knew Hugh.' Bia stopped speaking and looked at him. For some time, she studied his face. 'What was your mother's name?'

There was silence as they looked at each other.

'Martha,' Jago said solemnly. A thunderous crash lit the black sky, casting shadows of the mullioned windows across the floor.

'Aunt Martha?' she asked, hardly able to say the words.

'I think so. The picture that Bradick has will prove it. It was taken in the ruins of the abbey,' he answered slowly. 'Maria and Martha together. Maria has to be Mary – your mother.'

The thought of Biatra being his cousin made him smile. Before he could say anything else, she had wrapped her arms around him. Her face was pressed against his as she kissed him on the cheek. Jago felt a sudden need to push her away but then, when he heard her sobbing gently, he held her close.

He could feel her body shaking. She felt soft and warm, just like his mother. Jago hugged her tightly as she tried to speak. They spent the time greedily trying to absorb the years they had missed of each other's lives

'Don't leave me, Jago. You're all I have left,' she said. She was admitting to herself that her parents were dead.

Jago let go of his embrace and pulled back the long strands of red hair from her face.

'It has to be a secret. No one can know – not yet,' he said as he leant against the wood-panelled wall that stretched the length of the room along either side of the hall fireplace.

There was another crash of thunder. The sky sparked with lightning as the panel he leant against gave a dull click.

'The wall's opened!' Bia said. She slid her fingers into a narrow slat that had come away from the other boards of limed oak. 'It's a door.'

Jago stepped aside as she opened it further to reveal a small room set into the wall next to the large stone fireplace. A candle burnt on a table by the far wall. A cladding of dripped wax covered the holder until it could not be seen. On the wall, high above everything else, was an old painting of four men. It was set in a gilded frame that looked as new as the day it had been made. The men's faces were unfinished, as if the artist had been called away and never returned. Everything else about the image was perfect. Just like the painting of Tristan Morgan, each figure had the stain of blood across the back of a hand. It ran from the wrist and followed the course of the veins to the longest finger.

'Who are they?' Jago asked as he took Bia by the hand and stepped inside the room.

'They look old. What are they wearing?' She pointed to the figure of one man who stood in front of the others as if he deemed himself more worthy. The man wore a suit of armour over a vest of chain mail.

Jago shivered as he looked at the hand of the man in the armour. On the smallest finger of his left hand he wore a wide band of gold cut through with a woven trellis.

'Cresco . . .' Jago whispered the word, barely louder than a breath.

'What?' Bia asked as she closed the panelled door.

'Nothing . . . I thought – but it can't be,' he said, stumbling over his words.

The storm rumbled outside. In the secret room all was still. The candle was as steady as a watchman at a shrine. It reflected on Bia's face and softly lit her scar like an autumn moon.

'We shouldn't be here,' Bia said as a sudden draught flickered the solitary light. 'What if Hugh Morgan comes back?'

'IF?' shouted a voice – it was Morgan himself, and he seized her by the arm and pulled her from the room. '*If?*'

'It was an accident,' she blurted quickly as she saw the resentment and anger in his sallow face.

'Accident?' he shouted as he bared his teeth like a dog.

'My fault,' Jago said as he stepped between the two and squared up to Hugh Morgan. 'I leant against the wall and the door opened. You can't blame Biatra.'

'I told you to look around the house, not burgle the place,' Morgan protested as he shook his head.

'We didn't know it was there. It was my fault,' Jago said again, standing his ground.

Morgan breathed heavily and pushed back his rain-sodden hair.

'This makes it all the more difficult. You have complicated

a matter that was already very complicated,' Morgan said. He stepped towards the fireplace and gripped the stone with his hand.

'We'll go. We won't tell anyone,' Bia said as she stepped away from him, keeping Jago between them.

'You can't. The storm is too dangerous. By the time it passes it will be dark and you cannot leave the house and walk across the moor,' Morgan answered. 'Not alone and not tonight.'

'But we have to get back. Mrs Macarty will be expecting us,' Bia said as she moved towards the door. Morgan followed her every step with his steel-blue eyes.

'I will call her. It will all be arranged for you both to stay here,' Morgan snapped angrily.

'What if we don't want to?' Jago asked.

'Rathbone!' Morgan shouted. 'Biatra and Jago will be staying the night.'

The man stepped from behind the curtain, the heels of his long riding boots clicking against the tiled floor like the ticking of a clock. It was obvious from the smug look on his face that he had been listening to all Morgan had said.

'Where will they sleep?' he asked as he stroked the stubble on his chin.

'The turret room. Light them a fire and bring them some supper. And Rathbone?'

'Yes, Master Hugh?'

'Lock the door.'

[16]

The Vampyre Quartet

TOGETHER THEY WATCHED the raindrops cascading down the window of the room. Dark clouds moved slowly in from the sea, each lined with lightning effulgence. The silver blades of bright light crackled and danced like angels tiptoeing across the black water. With each rumble of thunder, a knife-bolt hit the land, searing the sodden cliffs above the bay. Hawks Moor stood defiantly as it had done for eight hundred years. The wind beat against its ancient stones and ripped long strands of wisteria from the walls. The labyrinth below the window shook its green hedges like a bristling dog. The storm drew closer and pounded the earth as if dragon wings beat above the house.

'Will he let us go?' Bia asked as she moved away from the window to be far from the storm.

'He'll have to. I think he wants us to stay the night, that's all,' Jago answered. He stood like a captain on the bridge of a stricken ship. 'He just didn't want us going back over the moor.'

'They could have taken us in the car,' Bia said as she warmed herself by the meagre fire that Rathbone had prepared when he locked them in the room.

'The roads will be flooded, he wouldn't risk it,' Jago said.

'Then we stay here?' Bia asked as she looked at the two beds on either side of the vast room surrounded by windows. 'It feels . . .'

'It's just a room,' Jago answered quickly before she could go on. 'And Hugh Morgan is just a man.'

'But if you sleep you might leave, just like you did at the Manor.'

Jago didn't look at her. He stared out of the window as he thought what to say. Perhaps she was right and for some reason he had no control over his mind.

'You sleep and I will stay awake,' he answered just as the rain began to ebb away and the thunder stilled its breath. 'I'll watch over you.'

Bia looked at the bed by the window. It was propped against a narrow section of panelled wall.

'Do you think there is another room hidden in here?' she asked.

'Looks old enough,' he replied as he looked at the walls. Unlike every other part of the house, this room had no pictures – here, on each side of the turret a long window stretched along the wall. 'Can't be in the walls, though,' he said after much thought. 'If there is a secret way out of here then it would have to be through the floor.'

'Then I'll look for it. I don't like it here. I want to go home.'

'Home or Streonshalgh Manor with Staxley and the others?' Jago asked.

She sighed. Bia could not go home. Her house on Church Street was empty, its door marked by a missing-ribbon.

'We could go somewhere else,' she said suddenly. 'We could run away, start a new life.'

'In a war? They would never allow it,' Jago replied.

'We are all the family we have. No one could stop us. We could get work – go to London, stay with your friend in his flat – live at your flat – find work,' Bia spoke quickly, the words tumbling over one another.

'How would we get there – walk?' he asked.

'If we had to. There's a boat leaves for London every week, and the train. We don't have to stay here, not any more. We only have a few months and then we'll be too old for Streonshalgh Manor – they always move people on, especially the older ones.'

'But how do we prove we are family?' Jago asked. 'We just have our own word for it.'

'The picture that Bradick took from you. If we got it back then we would have the proof,' Bia said just as the door lock clicked.

'Thought you might need food,' said Hugh Morgan as he stepped into the room. 'The views from here are quite spectacular. My grandfather had it built so that he could see the ships sailing to Whitby.' Morgan looked at their silent, glum faces and then went on. 'You are not prisoners, you can go whenever you would like,' he said.

'Then why lock the door to the room?' Bia asked.

'It was to dissuade you from leaving. It is dangerous on the moor – especially in the storms,'

'Frit we'd been got by Vampyres?' she asked belligerently.

'I knew your mother, Biatra. It is to her that I owe a debt of making sure nothing happens to you,' Morgan snapped sharply. He placed the tray on the narrow table at the end of a bed. 'Vampyres do not come into the equation.'

'So when can we go?' Jago asked.

'In the morning,' Morgan said calmly. 'I have telephoned Mrs Macarty and Draigorian and told them of your predicament. You can go straight from here to Hagg House. I will get Rathbone to drive you.'

Jago leant against the stone mullion of the window

'And you won't lock us in?' he asked.

'As long as you don't go prying into rooms where you should never be,' Morgan replied as he took the four paces to the window and looked out.

The storm cleared slowly. To the far south an edge of brightness cut across the clouds. The last barrage of rain crashed against the leaded windows as icy droplets rolled across the roof to the iron drains. The rain washed the feet of the three hideous stone gargoyles that stood guard on the lintel caps.

'Promise,' Bia shouted from the fireside.

'Is that a question or your answer?' Morgan asked as he pulled his jacket tighter to keep out the chill of the room.

'We promise not to go looking about the house,' Jago said as he looked down on to the green-hedged labyrinth.

'And not go outside?' Morgan asked.

'No,' Jago said. 'We'll stay here.'

Morgan eyed them both warily and then smiled at Bia.

'Just like your mother,' he said. 'I could never trust a thing she said – but will take you at your word.'

'Why did they plant the hedges so close to the house?' Jago asked before Morgan could walk away.

'That started with the Penance. Every year they would take what was left of the Hedge from the shore. The story is that each stalk pushed into the earth sprouted and grew. As they built the hedge year on year so the labyrinth was formed.'

'Can we go in? I heard of a maze where you have to search for the centre and find your way out again,' Bia said as she came to the window and looked out.

'I have never been in. Tallow cuts the hedges and picks the weeds. It's a place I have never had the urge to explore,' Morgan said. Bia watched him closely as he walked to the door without looking back. 'We serve breakfast in the kitchen. I'll tell Rathbone to wake you.'

Morgan stopped and looked at Jago. 'I would lock the door if I were you,' he said as he took the key from his pocket and threw it on the bed.

The door closed and they listened to his footsteps clatter down the corridor and then fade away.

'Are we staying?' Bia asked.

'Do you really want to run away?' Jago asked.

'I don't want to stay in Whitby any more,' she replied.

'But what if your mother comes back?' he asked.

'I've thought about that. She won't. I know it. I just didn't want to dare believe she was . . .' Bia couldn't say the word. It was as if it was still forbidden.

'Then we'll get away. I have fifty pounds hidden in my room. We could use that and get to London. It would pay the rent on the flat – as long as you don't mind the bombing,' Jago said excitedly as the thought of escaping from Streonshalgh Manor filled his mind. 'There's one thing I have to do before we go.'

'What?' Bia asked.

'Staxley. I have to fix him good so he won't hurt anyone again,' Jago panted.

'Tomorrow night – we could wait until he fell asleep,' Bia answered. 'His room door doesn't lock.'

'And then we'll get the train to London?' Jago asked.

'To London,' Bia echoed. She smiled at him, wondering if it would ever happen.

Jago looked out of the window. The storm had passed and the night closed in as the sun set above the wild hills. The water in the bay shone silver as it reflected the moon. Where it met the sea, the land was edged with the purple of the moor and the dark alum stains of the far cliffs.

It was then that he saw Tallow. The man walked across the gravel drive holding a tall lantern. He wore the same clothes he'd worn the day before. They clung to his skin as the rainwater dripped from his brow.

Tallow took long deliberate steps, as if counting his paces or playing a game in his mind. The lantern rocked back and forth above his head and its faint light shone down on him. Step by step, he made his way to the entrance of the labyrinth. As he approached the entrance, Jago could just make out the shadows of two men beneath the large oak tree that covered the driveway.

'Bia,' he whispered as he pressed himself close to the stone mullion so as not to be seen. 'It's Tallow. He's gone into the labyrinth.'

Bia came to the window and looked down. Tallow had gone. She could vaguely follow the path of the light as it sparkled through the top of the hedges.

'I can see him,' she said. She pointed to the maze beneath them.

'What are they doing?' Jago asked as Tallow reappeared. 'It's Draigorian.'

There was Draigorian in his black hat and white gloves and holding a long cane. He was talking to Ezra Morgan as if they were old friends. The old man laughed and looked up as if he expected to see them at the window.

'Look out,' Bia said as she ducked from view. 'Did he see us?'

Jago crawled under the window to the far side of the room. He peered over the ledge but could see no one.

'They've gone,' he said as he got to his feet and looked down.

His eye traced the passage of a light through the avenues of the intricate maze. It strayed neither to the left nor the right and did not double back on itself. All the while he watched, the light got closer to the centre of the labyrinth.

'What are they doing?' Bia asked. 'Why should Draigorian be here with Ezra Morgan?'

'They are old friends – that's what he said in the car.'

'And who else was with them, besides Tallow – there were three men,' Bia said.

'Three?' Jago asked.

'I saw two and the shadow of another behind them,' Bia replied as she looked down and traced the final steps of the lamp until it stopped in the centre of the maze. She looked at Jago, who smirked elfishly. 'No, Jago – we promised Hugh Morgan we would stay here.'

'How would he know?'

'If he checked the room?' she replied.

'And what will he do to us? He was in love with your mother, you can tell,' Jago said as he walked to the door and picked up his jacket from the chair by the fire. 'Coming?'

He didn't wait for her to reply. He slung on his coat as fast as he could, carefully opened the door and stepped in to the passageway. Bia followed, took the key from his hand and locked the door.

Hawks Moor was empty of life. Jago sensed it as he walked along the dark corridor with Bia close by. He felt like an animal. Every sinew in his body tingled and shook with anticipation. Bia held on to the hem of his coat. Soon they found the back stairs. They were narrow, neatly swept and smelt of cooked chicken.

'Kitchen?' Bia said as they took the first step together.

'Must be,' Jago replied as he nudged ahead. 'Don't speak.'

The stairs spiralled down to the kitchen. The door opened next to the shutter of the small lift that would take food to the upper floors. Jago had seen one before in a London hotel where his mother had worked. He waited a moment and then looked around the room. It was empty. An old oven gurgled in the fireplace. A large pot full of chicken bones and water rattled on the stove top. The lid shook with the bubbling liquid and clattered on the pan.

Across from the stove was the doorway to the outside. It was guarded by a thick curtain. Jago looked at Bia.

'Could be locked,' she said, knowing what he was about to ask.

'Don't know until we try,' he said as he slipped behind the curtain.

A cruel draught that blew back the drape and the dark of the night seeped into the room. Jago looked up at the sky. It seemed different, darker than he had known before. The bright glow of the comet had gone; in its place was a mantle of stars that prickled against the dark velvet sky.

'RedEye,' Bia said instantly, her voice just above a hush. 'It's gone. It can't be, they said it would be here for days, just like before.'

Jago again checked the sky. There was no sign of the comet. From horizon to azimuth, the sky was dark and crystal clear. The thunderstorm had blown away all the clouds; a fresh breeze came in from the sea and rattled the autumn branches all around them.

'Is that why Draigorian is here?' Jago asked.

'What?'

'The comet has gone and Draigorian sent the cup to Morgan,' Jago answered.

'Doesn't make sense, what difference would an old chalice make?' Bia replied as they hid under the dark canopy of a tall yew tree.

'It's not just any old cup,' Jago said. 'It can change your life when you drink from it.'

'How?' Bia asked.

Footsteps came from the far side of the house, crunching on the shingle. Like before, they were measured, equal and counted.

'Tallow,' Bia whispered as they retreated further into the darkness of the canopy.

The footsteps came closer. Tallow walked towards their hiding place, his hands tucked into the top of his trousers, his lips counting each step for no purpose. He passed by without noticing them staring at him.

'Why does he do that?' Jago asked when he was out of sight.

'Tallow counts all the time. Footsteps, teaspoons, plates, beans in a jar. He can't stop it. I heard that was why Mrs Macarty sent him here. It drove her mad,' Bia answered as they left the darkness and sloped closer to the labyrinth.

The black of night came down quickly. Without the comet, soon every tree was outlined in just the silver of the moon. Somehow, even that seemed fainter and more distant than it had. At the entrance to the labyrinth, Jago stopped. He hesitated for a moment before crossing the long stone that marked the threshold. The air seemed thicker and held him back, as if it wasn't his place to be there.

'Don't speak,' he whispered to Bia, his lips close to her face. 'You can stay and look out for Tallow.'

Bia kept hold of his coat. She didn't want to be alone, not at night and in the dark. They could both hear Tallow coming around the corner of the house. His footsteps were ordered, each stride the same length, taking the same time to cover the ground. 'Inside . . . quickly.'

It was a step that Bia took with apprehension. The entrance to the maze was made of dense privet and holly leaves. To one side was a sudden turn and then an alcove of topiary.

Jago put a finger to his lips; his eyes were wide as his hair blew across his face. At the corner of the avenue was a candle lamp. It was in the hand of a statue of a creature half man, half dog, set on top of a marble plinth.

'That way,' Jago whispered pointing to the statue.

'But what if . . .?'

Tallow's footsteps didn't turn at the house as they had expected. They were soon at the mouth of the labyrinth. Jago held his breath and pulled Bia into the alcove, smothering her mouth with his hand.

'Who is it?' Tallow asked in the darkness, just a yard from them. 'I can hear you there.'

The man waited a moment and peered around him. He stepped back from the threshold and out of the maze.

'Quickly,' Jago said.

'No. I'll stay here,' Bia insisted.

He could feel her hand tremble slightly and knew she was afraid.

'I'll just go and see what they are doing. They won't hear me. You hide here. Don't move until I come back.'

Bia stared at Jago wide-eyed. He knew she didn't want him to go. 'I won't be long,' he whispered.

In three steps he had vanished. Jago followed the glimmer of the lanterns and turned at every corner where there was a stone sentinel. The hedges towered above him, blotting out the light of the moon. They twisted and turned, folding back on themselves and taking him deeper and deeper into the labyrinth. Soon he could hear voices. One he knew well – Crispin Draigorian.

'Are you sure it could be him?' Ezra Morgan asked from the other side of the thick hedge that divided him from Jago's hiding place.

'Positive. I could feel it in his mind,' Draigorian said eagerly. 'I set him on finding the book in my library, but I could tell he already knew of it.'

'Then what shall we do with him?' asked the one voice that Jago had never heard before. It sounded younger, softer – the voice of a woman.

'He has to be stopped, stopped before he brings destruction,' Draigorian said. 'If he has the cup in his possession then it will be difficult for us all.'

'I told you never to trust that fool. You said he would look after the boy until he was of the age when he would be useful to us. All he has done is sent him back here,' Morgan growled angrily. 'He knew what would happen and he cares not.'

'But he could have been killed in the bombing and then where would we be?' Draigorian answered sharply. 'It is time – the Lyrid of Saturn.'

'Bloodless,' cackled the woman. 'We need the blood for the cup – we need the Cup of Garbova.'

'It's a difficult decision,' Morgan said. 'He is nearly flesh and blood.'

'Who would you wish to use? It has to be the descendant of one of the Quartet. When your son was of age you went away. You knew he would have to be spared. You cheated us.' The woman snarled. Jago could hear the rustling of her skirts against the stone floor at the centre of the maze.

'And you said the boy would be looked after and what happened?' Morgan shouted, his voice hot with frenzy.

'She is right, Ezra. This could have been completed years ago,' Draigorian added feebly.

'Very well. So mote it be. We cannot do anything until the moon of Friday – the Lyrid of Saturn. I will try to keep him here. But my son must never know,' Morgan said.

'And the girl?' the woman asked, her voice excited.

'Blood for blood . . . You may keep her like you have the rest,' said Ezra Morgan as he slapped his hands together. 'One more missing child will not matter. If she satisfies your appetite, then so be it.'

'It has to stop, Ezra. Eight hundred years is enough for any man,' Draigorian snapped. 'I am tired of this life. I will drink no more blood.'

[17]

Molech

IT WAS THE RAPID BEATING of his heart that first alerted him to the rising sense of fear twisting in his guts. Just like before, the world began to spin as a vision came to mind. Jago gripped the hedge and held on for his life. In his mind, he could hear the calling of a morning crow. Trees hemmed him in from all sides and his feet slipped on a shaded path. Bia was screaming – she was close by. He breathed hard as he tried to stop himself from falling over. His heartbeat thumped in his throat and made it hard for him to swallow. Then, as quickly as it had come, the vision was gone.

'Then it is decided. Friday . . . the thirteenth . . . the Lyrid of Saturn,' he heard Morgan say as the world stopped spinning and he regained his breath.

'But what of *him*?' Draigorian asked. 'Shall we call him from London? The Quartet?'

'It matters not. Three will be enough for what we seek to do,' Morgan answered.

Jago realised their meeting was coming to an end. Half drunk with fear and the aftermath of the vision, Jago staggered to the entrance of the labyrinth.

Bia was gone. There was a faint impression of her against

the leaves of the hedge where they had hid, but nothing more. Jago knew he could not call out. Already he could hear the footsteps of Morgan and the others coming from the inner circle of the maze.

Peering around the hedge, Jago could see Tallow by the front door. It looked as though he was counting the stones that made up the archway. Slowly, he moved from his hiding place and made his way to the back of the house.

As Jago took hold of the door handle, he became suddenly aware of someone looking at him intently. His hand froze to the wooden ball as he thought of running.

'What kept you?' Bia asked. 'I had to move – Tallow came looking. I'm sure he thought someone was there.'

'We have to get out of here,' Jago said as he opened the kitchen door and he and Bia stepped inside. 'That is what this is all about: a trap to get us here – in this house. It's to do with blood.'

'Blood?' Bia asked.

'My blood, your blood . . . We're both going to be dead. I heard them.' Jago panted. 'It's planned for Friday. Ezra Morgan will try to keep us here. We can't do anything to make him suspicious.'

'So what –?' Bia asked as she tried to take in the words.

'Let's get back to the room,' he whispered.

Taking the same back staircase, they were soon on the upper landing and at the doorway to the turret room. Jago took the key, opened the door and walked to the window. In the driveway below he could see Draigorian walking to his car. Rathbone was with Ezra Morgan. Tallow stood anxiously by the oak tree and tapped the back of his hand.

'I wish I could hear what they were saying,' Jago said as he felt Bia close by.

'We should get away tonight,' Bia answered. 'I don't want to stay here.'

'Trust me, Bia. If we left now they would come after us. We have to make it look like it is all normal. Whatever happens we should wait until the morning.'

'But there's no one looking for us now. If we disappeared then it wouldn't matter to anyone.'

Below, the car drove off and Morgan stomped back to the house, followed obediently by Tallow and Rathbone.

'Where is Hugh Morgan?' Jago asked. 'He wasn't there.'

'Is he involved?' Bia asked.

'I can't be sure. I could only hear their voices. It was Draigorian, Ezra Morgan and a woman.'

There was the familiar sound of footsteps on the stairs to the room. Jago ran to the bed, leapt upon it, wrapped himself in the blanket and pretended to be asleep. Bia slumped in the chair by the fire and closed her eyes.

Four distinctive raps beat slowly against the wood.

'Jago? Biatra?' the voice whispered. 'Do you sleep?'

'Who is it?' Bia asked as she got up from the chair and unlocked the door.

'Ezra Morgan,' the man said. He pushed the door open and peered inside with a tormented smile on his face. 'I am the harbinger of some bad news,' he said as he stepped inside, the floorboards creaking beneath his leather boots.

'What?' asked Jago as he slipped his hand into the pocket of his coat and gripped the silver pyx in his fist.

'Things have changed and Whitby is no longer a safe place

for you to live. I have just had a phone call from Mrs Macarty. The bombing, the dreadful bombing . . . The Ministry have asked for you to be moved here. Both of you.'

Bia looked at Jago in disbelief. It was just as he had said. She looked down to the floor and tried to hide what she felt.

'Here?' Jago asked. 'Hawks Moor?'

'Yes,' Morgan said discreetly as if he didn't want anyone else to hear. 'I will tell Hugh in the morning. He is not due back from Whitby until later tonight – urgent business.' Ezra Morgan smiled at them both. 'Hawks Moor is a nice place – your mother liked it here, Biatra.'

'What do you think, Bia?' Jago asked. His eye was caught by the ring on Morgan's finger, a wide band of gold cut through with a woven trellis. 'It is certainly nicer than Streonshalgh Manor and Staxley isn't here and the room is so clean and warm.'

'If you wouldn't mind,' Bia said to Morgan as she smiled. 'How long would it be for?'

'Until the end of the war or until you are old enough to find a place of your own. You are very welcome.' He spoke quite humbly and stroked his long chin eagerly. 'Sadly, it is not open to negotiation, but I am glad that you agree with the decision made.'

'Agree?' Jago said. 'It's the best thing that has ever happened to us.'

'So glad, so glad,' Ezra said as he backed out of the room like a housemaid. 'One more thing,' he said. He straightened up and clasped his hands tightly. 'Rathbone will take you to Whitby. I have arranged for Mrs Macarty to pack all your things and for you both to go shopping – on my account, of course.'

'This place feels just like home,' Jago answered.

'Home? Interesting,' he muttered slowly.

Morgan closed the door. His heavy footsteps trudged along the landing and then down the stairs.

'Just as you said,' Bia whispered as she wondered how they would escape.

'What do you know about Vampyres?' Jago asked as he walked towards her and then pulled the wooden shutters across the window to keep out the chill of the night. 'Draigorian said he had had enough of life and it had to stop after eight hundred years.'

'My mother told me they lived for ever,' Bia answered.

'Can they be killed?' he asked.

'I don't know. I never believed in them – thought they were make-believe.'

'I think Draigorian and Morgan are Vampyres,' he said quickly. He went back to the fire and poked the embers to gain more light. 'Draigorian is dying because he won't take any more blood. He's killing himself.'

'There's just one Vampyre – Strackan,' Bia answered as she too drew closer, not wanting the shadows of the room to press in on her. 'That's what the legend said. Strackan is the only Vampyre.'

'*Was* the only Vampyre. Hugh Morgan said it when he was showing us the painting and talking of the Penance Hedge. Just think, if Ezra has lived as long as Draigorian then he too is eight hundred years old. He is really Tristan Morgan. He was the one who chased the creature to the hermit. They

were hunting a Vampyre and the curse was that they too became Vampyres and that is why they have lived so long.'

'It's stupid . . . I don't like it,' Bia argued as she buried
her face in the American quilt that straddled the back of the
chair. 'It's a fairytale to frighten children.'

'Before I came to Whitby I would have said the same as
you. But now I know differently. They have to be stopped.'

'Kill them?' Bia asked

'If we have to,' Jago answered.

'We can't – they're people,' she whispered, as if just speaking her thoughts would bring condemnation upon her.

'They're Vampyres – who should have died long ago. They
have no right to be alive and they are killing people every
night.'

'I can't believe it, I can't,' Bia said, struggling to hold on
to her mind. 'Let's just get away from here. When Rathbone
takes us into Whitby, we could get our things from Mrs
Macarty and run away. Please, Jago, please?'

Jago looked at the glowing red embers and then at Bia. His
face glowed bright red from the heat of the fire.

'If we wait until morning we can leave here before anyone
is awake. If we leave at first light we can be at Streonshalgh
Manor before Ezra Morgan can telephone Mrs Macarty.' Jago
spoke as he thought, regretting the day he had listened to
his mother and agreed to be evacuated. 'Get some sleep. I'll
keep watch.'

'Don't leave me, Jago,' Bia said as she slumped into her
chair and pulled the quilt around her. 'Don't disappear.' She
curled her legs beneath her and pulled the quilt even tighter. She looked at Jago and could see the worry on his face.

'Cousin?' she whispered to herself as she dozed and thought how they would escape.

Jago put some elm wood on the fire and watched it start to blaze. There was something protective about the radiance that pushed away the darkness and made all things well. He stared at the flames and then at Biatra. Her head leant against the wing of the leather chair; her long red hair fell over her face. She was the only family he had. Jago wished that his mother could have seen her.

The fire crackled and embered as the hours passed. Jago watched the flames change and slowly die. He sighed, his breath as heavy as his eyelids. Sleep slipped in quietly and quite unnoticed.

'Biatra . . . Biatra,' came a voice from the window, followed by a tap-tap-tap on the glass. 'Biatra . . . I am here,' said the voice from outside.

The tapping came again. Bia stirred in her sleep as the sound broke into her dream of her mother.

'Mother?' Bia asked as her thoughts raced.

'Biatra, down here,' the voice came again from the garden.

Jago was asleep, wrapped in his leather coat as if he was waiting to leave. Bia went to the window and pulled back the shutter, still sure she had heard her mother calling. Looking down into the garden she could see the faint outline of a woman. The night sky grew brighter in the east. It was cloudless and filled with fading stars. The woman waved, her red hair curled about her shoulders.

'Mother?' Bia whispered, still thinking it was a dream as the woman below began to walk to the high-hedged entrance of the maze.

'Come with me . . . . Leave Jago, let him sleep . . . I haven't long.' It was as if the woman sang the words and only she could hear them.

Bia picked up her coat from the bed and without making a sound unlocked the door. She took a last look at Jago as he slept soundly and she pulled the door shut.

The house was dark and whispered as she walked. A breeze blew through the gaps in the floorboards and tickled her feet.

Soon she was at the maids' stairway, which twisted down to the kitchen in complete darkness. Bia listened at the door and, when she was sure there was no one on the other side, slid it gently open. In ten steps she was out of the kitchen and into the garden. Hawks Moor cast its long black shadow as it loomed above her. She gave no thought for Jago or Vampyres; all she wanted was her mother.

Beneath the soles of her feet she could feel the sharp gravel stones as she ran. Turning the corner of the house she caught a fleeting glimpse of her mother as she stepped into the labyrinth.

'Mother!' she shouted as she gave chase.

'Biatra,' said the voice as it led her on.

'Wait . . . Mother!' Bia said as she ran on.

As she turned the corner of the entrance Bia saw her mother. She was waiting at the end of the avenue by the statue.

'Biatra . . . Biatra, it is really you,' the woman said as she held out her hands towards her.

'How did you know I was here?' Bia cried out as she ran faster.

'They told me. I didn't believe them.' Her mother smiled. 'I have something to show, it's here.'

'But where have you been?' Bia demanded as she gripped her mother tightly and felt the warmth of her skin against her own.

'It was the war. A secret. No one could know. I'm back now.' She stopped and brushed the hair from Bia's face. 'I have something that will take the mark from you. It will give you skin just like mine.'

'How?' Bia asked as her heart leapt in her mouth. 'And Jago, how do you know Jago?'

'I've always known. That's why Martha left Whitby. She was having a baby. We couldn't tell anyone,' she said as she walked deeper into the maze. 'It was a secret.'

'Mother,' Bia said with a sigh as she held her hand tightly in her own.

'We're together now – that's all that matters. We have to be quick. The light is coming and I need the shadows of the night.' Bia looked confused and was about to speak. 'It's a spell. A healing spell, I bought it from Maisie's cousin.'

Her mother held out a small glass jar. The vial was filled with green liquid.

'It looks disgusting,' Bia said.

'You don't drink it,' her mother laughed.

Bia had no idea how far into the maze she had walked. The hedges were high above them, almost to the height of small trees. The privet and larch were intertwined to form a thick hedge. The darkness grew thicker, more viscous and heavy. A shallow mist filled each of the countless avenues that led here and there.

'Where are we going?' Bia asked as a shudder of cold ran the length of her spine.

'To the centre of the universe and the Lyrid of Saturn . . .'

In the house, Jago woke from his sleep. The scent of smoke filled his head. It was acrid and black, a mixture of brimstone and treacle. He coughed and looked to the chair. The dream of Bia lost in the labyrinth was still in his mind's eye.

'Bia . . . Bia?' he asked as he looked around the room. Seeing the shutter open, he ran to the window. There below he could see the fresh footprints on the dew-stained grass by the entrance to the maze.

'Bia, no!' he said as he ran to the door of the room. Soon he was down the stairs and through the kitchen. Inside his head he knew which way to run. It was an instinct that he didn't know he had. The dream in his head went on – he could see Bia with a hag of a woman. 'Biatra!' Jago shouted as he turned into the maze.

'Jago . . . Jago,' Bia said.

'Run. He can't find us. The spell won't work if he finds us. We have to be alone.'

'But?'

The woman dragged Bia along another avenue and then another until they neared the centre of the labyrinth.

'Soon be there. Then you'll be cured. How good will that be?' her mother said as they ran. 'Got to do it before the boy finds us. Can't be found, can't be found . . .'

The voice changed to a low dog-like growl. Bia could hear Jago running back and forth along the avenues near to her.

The hedges were too thick for her to see, and the hand on her wrist grew painfully tight.

'Mother, it's hurting,' she tried to say as she was dragged around the final corner of the avenue.

'It will soon be over,' her mother replied. 'Soon . . . so soon.'

The maze opened into a square formal garden. Small box hedges surrounded neat lawns. Each was trimmed precisely. In the centre of the garden on a small triangle of shingle was a long black stone resting on two similar lintels of jet.

'What is this place?' Bia asked as her mother dragged her to the stone.

'Don't worry,' her mother said as she brushed away the hair from Bia's smooth white neck and pulled her closer as if to embrace.

'What are you doing?' Bia asked as she pushed her away. 'I don't like it.'

'Biatra!' shouted Jago. 'Get away from her!'

The girl turned as the woman pulled her viciously towards her and grabbed her by the hair.

'On the tomb,' the woman growled, and she opened her mouth that was filled with dog-like teeth.

'JAGO!' Bia screamed as the women bit at her throat.

'Leave her!' Jago said as he pushed his way through the final hedge of the maze and into the garden. 'She belongs to me.'

The woman laughed, her mouth covered in blood.

'Too late, Jago Harker, son of Martha,' she howled as she dropped Bia to the ground. 'She is dead. One of us for thirty days and thirty nights and you cannot stop me.'

Jago leapt towards the woman, jumping to where she stood. The Vampyre stepped back as Jago landed on her and fell against the holly hedge, a long splinter of living wood piercing her shoulder. She screamed as she tried to pull herself from the spike.

'Holy wood,' the woman muttered. Jago saw blood trickle across her shoulder. 'Get it from me and I will give you anything you want,' she demanded.

'Tell me – are you Strackan?' Jago asked.

'No. Get me from this stake,' she pleaded. She slumped to the ground, unable to move.

'I will set you free if you tell me one thing,' he said as he lifted Bia from the ground and realised with joy that she was still breathing.

'Anything,' she wheezed.

'Biatra is still alive. Is there a cure for your bite or is she cursed?'

'Only one thing can save her. Get the dew of the grass from holy ground. Before the dawn breaks wash the wound, and then anoint her with myrrh balm. But Jago, you will not find that in this country.' The woman laughed. 'Let her die. I will take care of her for you.'

Jago felt the silver pyx in his jacket pocket.

'Myrrh balm?' he asked as he unscrewed the lid and held out the ointment. 'Just like this?'

'No – it can't be,' the woman said as she sniffed the air. 'Where did you get it?'

'From my uncle Cresco – where else?'

'Jago, I can see you,' Bia said as she sat up against him. 'My mother was here.'

215

'Is that your mother?' Jago asked as he pointed to the woman impaled on the holly stump.

'Who is she?' Bia asked, as she looked at the figure in a crimson dress with long black hair that trailed across her hag face.

'I was your salvation,' the Vampyre said. 'I would have cured your scar, given you the looks of a lady, taken away your disfigurement of birth.'

'That is a Vampyre as old as Crispin Draigorian and Ezra Morgan,' Jago said.

'You forget one other name – Julius Cresco, your avuncular *uncle*. More of a nanny, to make sure the blood was protected until this time. We have watched you all of your life. Paid for you and waited. This is your inheritance. Soon you will be one with us.'

'Tell me one more thing before I set you free. If I were to become a Vampyre how could I be killed?' Jago asked as the woman writhed in pain.

'A silver knife will take your life, a branch of holy wood will hold you fast. Myrrh balm will stop your breath. Fire, drowning . . . Most of us die through starvation. We lose the will to take life. However, that has been something I have always enjoyed,' the woman said as she licked the side of her bloodstained mouth. 'We can survive most things. I even like eating garlic, and don't believe anything you are told about charms and medallions. They don't work against us. You will be quite safe.'

Jago lifted Bia to the stone, tomb-like table and walked towards the Vampyre. He held the silver pyx in his hand.

'Set me free, Jago. What are you going to do?'

216

'What someone should have done long ago,' he said coldly as he smoothed his fingers into the balm and then broke off a long spike of holly hedge and smeared it with myrrh.

'Jago, you promised – you said you would set me free if I told you how to cure the girl,' the woman screamed, unable to move.

'Don't look,' Jago said as he turned to Bia.

Bia closed her eyes as she heard the woman grunt and then take several short, sharp, jagged breaths. Then she breathed no more.

[18]

Villains

THE SMALL SPIRE OF THE CHURCH broke over the horizon a mile away from Hawks Moor. Jago could see it clearly as he walked Bia to the road through the fields that surrounded the house. The sun had not yet broken the edge of the sea. Its amber glow coloured the sky to the east and made the ocean look like a distant land. In the plateau above the bay, a low mist filled the pockets of the hedges and snaked along the riverbed that melted into the sea at Boggle Bay.

Bia walked as fast as she could. Her heart raced as the venom seethed through her veins. It was as if she had been bitten by a snake. Her lips were numb and full of blood. The lining of her jaw ached as the skin was stretched tighter and tighter.

'Just a mile,' Jago said as he steadied her over the fence and onto the empty road. 'I can see the church.'

'Do you believe her?' Bia asked, squinting in the growing light. 'Do you think it will work?'

'I saw what the myrrh did to the Vampyre. If it can stop the transformation, that is all that matters,' Jago answered as he held her close.

'And if I become a Vampyre, you must kill me like you did her. Drive a holly stake through my heart,' Bia said as the hill grew steeper.

'It won't come to that. I will get you to the church and bathe the wound in dew and myrrh. It will have no power over you,' he answered as she slowed in her pace.

Jago could see her face slowly changing. The skin across her lips grew tighter still and her eyes filled with blood.

'I can taste the air,' she said in low voice different from her own. 'There is no time, Jago. Find the holly and kill me now.'

Bia groaned and slumped to the ground. Jago could hear the cracking of the bones in her face as a transformation began to take place.

'It won't happen to you,' he said as he picked her up and slumped her across his broad shoulders. 'I can see the church. I will do just as she said and you will be healed.'

'Jago . . . Jago, kill me now. Please. I don't want to be like . . .' Bia stopped speaking as her voice caught in her throat.

As he tried to run, Jago could not see her jaw breaking open and long white teeth cutting through the flesh. Ahead, Jago fixed his eyes on the gate to the church. It was covered in ivy and there was a wooden lychgate with a leaded roof.

'Don't talk of it,' he said, as he got closer. 'The sun has not yet risen. I will have time.'

'NO!' Bia growled angrily, and she suddenly sunk her fingers in his back and ripped at his leather coat. 'Don't take me in there, never, not in that place.'

With a sudden kick, Bia twisted from his grip and slumped to the ground in front of him.

219

'Bia, don't stop me,' he said as he reached out to her.

'Kill me, Jago. Before I kill you. Please,' she begged as she shuddered on the ground.

Jago could see she had changed. In the growing light the shadows of her face were darker than they had ever been. The moon scar burnt blood red, and her eyes had turned steely blue like a young wolf's. Cowering on the ground, she looked at Jago not as a friend but as walking, breathing meat.

'I can heal you. Take this all away. Just stand for me and walk through the gate,' Jago said as he pointed to the entrance of the church. 'The sun is rising – we need to go now.'

'No,' Bia panted as Jago saw her pointed, dog-like fangs for the first time. 'I can't stop how I feel. Please, Jago.'

The girl crawled backwards through the dense autumn grass at the side of the road. Jago followed, watching her every move. Bia backed against the high stone wall of the churchyard and could go no further.

'It has to be this way,' he said as he reached out for her.

'You don't understand, Jago . . . No!' Bia screamed as she leapt towards him.

Instantly Jago jumped out of the way. She landed cat-like and turned on her heels to face him. All that was Biatra had been morphed into another creature. She circled him slowly, looking for some weakness and a point to strike. In turn, Jago stepped closer and closer to the gate of the church. Bia didn't realise how close she was to the lychgate – her eyes were fixed on his luscious white skin and the beads of sweat that trickled down his neck. Bliss filled her throat as she sniffed the air made sweet with his fear.

'I'm here, Bia. I won't fight you. Take me if you want. We

can be together,' Jago said. He dropped his hands to his side and leant against the oak post.

'You are beautiful,' Bia said, her smile red against the bright white of the dog-teeth. 'I thought that when I first saw you. It will be so right – so good – we can be together.'

Jago watched as she came closer. Her eyes burnt blood red with a centre of steel that was cold, harsh and lifeless.

'Whatever you want to do with me,' Jago answered, his voice soft and fateful. 'Perhaps this is the best way. The night is past – the day is before us.'

Bia came closer and touched him tentatively with an out-stretched hand. She smoothed his shirt from the skin of his neck and tilted her head to one side. Jago steadied himself and waited for the moment as his hand gripped the latch of the gate.

'Just us,' Bia said. 'Finally, together . . .'

'Quickly, Bia. Don't wait,' Jago said as he saw the sun rising and felt the cold acid breath against his throat.

Bia tasted his skin with the tip of her tongue and felt the pulse throb. She pulled him closer until she could not breathe, savouring each second of being near to him. All around the long grass and hawthorn hedges rattled in the morning breeze. It was as if they were the only people alive and to her that was all that mattered. As they embraced the sun broke the horizon.

'It's easier than I ever thought it would be,' she said.

He felt the fangs press gently against his skin as she pre-pared to bite.

There was a dull click of the latch. Suddenly Jago lurched purposefully backwards into the churchyard as his hand gripped tightly to Bia's waist. With all his might he pulled her closer as he rolled back in the long, dew-stained grass.

Grabbing her by the wrists, he fought against her as she tried to get up. Bia bit at his hands and snarled and spat, hissing like a snake.

'It's for your own good,' Jago said as he pinned her to the ground with his knees.

With his hand, he scooped the fresh dew from the grass all around him. Bia screamed with burning pain as Jago smeared the pearls of water on the wound in her neck. Instantly she convulsed as if struck by lightning. Her hands gripped the tufts of grass, her fingers white to the knuckle.

Jago took the balm and dipped his fingers, plunging them into the two holes. Like hot pokers in beer, they blistered to the touch. Bia screamed, her voice so loud that it shook the air. A murder of crows lifted from a copse of gnarled oak trees as Jago fell forward, pinning her to the ground.

He lay there until he felt the first finger of the morning sun reach across the horizon. It cast a shadow of an old stone cross that marked a nearby grave. Jago reached out and touched the shadow as Bia lay panting for breath.

'Is it gone?' she asked, as if Jago had expelled some monster from within her.

He looked at the wound on her neck. All that was there were two small scars as if she had been stung by a wasp.

'Do you feel the madness?' he asked as he lay next to her in the grass and stroked her face.

'I think it has gone,' she answered. She searched for his hand and gripped it tightly.

Jago brushed back the mass of red curls and looked at her

face. Her eyes were as they had always been. He could see she wanted to cry.

'Then it worked,' he answered.

'The woman you killed, was she my mother?' Bia asked as she lay with him and looked up at the sky.

'No,' Jago said. 'I think that a Vampyre can change its appearance in your eyes. It is as if it has hypnotised you to see what it wants you to believe.'

'What did it feel like – when you killed her?' she said in a hush.

'I didn't think anything of it. It had to be done. I saw what she did to you. That was all that mattered,' Jago said. 'She had to die.'

'You know that they will come for us, don't you?' Bia replied as she thought of Ezra Morgan and Draigorian. 'There could be more of them and we will never know who they are.'

'They are a Vampyre Quartet, brought to life by a curse,' he answered.

'So what of Strackan – is he one of them?'

'When I saw him he was different from the others.' Jago thought for a moment. 'I need to find him and track him down. It's as if my life is part of a game and he is the master of it all.'

'But I thought we were going to leave – go to London?' Bia asked.

'When I went into the labyrinth I heard them speaking,' Jago said. 'They were talking about me – I am sure of it. When my mother was taking me to the train I was saved from the bombing by a man. He disappeared and then, on the train, he was there again. I couldn't see him, but he spoke to me. I need to find him.'

'Why?' Bia asked. 'Morgan will be coming after us as soon as he has found out what you've done.'

'I think the man who saved me could be my father. I have to know,' Jago answered.

'Then we do leave?' Bia asked.

'London,' he said in reply.

Bia turned and, without saying a word, kissed him on his cheek.

'I lost my parents and found you,' she said. 'London will be a good place to hide.'

They lay in the long grass that surrounded each grave and waited until the sun touched the old church. Then, setting off along the cliff path, they made their way towards the abbey.

Jago looked back as they reached the top of the hill. The church, Hawks Moor and the abbey formed an invisible line that stretched to the pinnacle of a hill far to the south. Ahead, the old stones of the crumbling arches rose up from the earth. Already he could see the glistening water of the fishpond and the herd of cattle that gathered close to it as they swished their shaggy red tails.

Within an hour they were on the empty dirt road that cut by the abandoned school with its broken bell under the eaves. Soon the slate roof of Streonshalgh Manor came into view. Seagulls squawked as they circled high in the air. An old man on a rusted bicycle rode by and then looked at his watch as he eyed them warily.

'When we get there, just say that we have come to collect

some things and are going to stay with Ezra Morgan – tell Mrs Macarty it's the orders of the Ministry,' Jago said.

'Will she believe us?' she asked.

'I think it has all been arranged by Ezra Morgan – she'll be expecting us to come with Rathbone. I'll tell her he has gone for fuel for the car and that we're meeting him in the town.'

'She won't believe you. She can always tell when I lie,' Bia said.

'We'll have to try. It's the only way. I have to get the chalice and the money,' Jago answered.

Bia felt her hands tremble. In her mind she could hear Mrs Macarty waking the children and see Boris Gladling running along the corridor and down the stairs in his oversized pyjamas.

'It'll soon be breakfast,' she said as they turned the corner by the ruined abbey and walked towards the statue of the gladiator.

The door to Streonshalgh Manor loomed menacingly. Each nail stared at them like an iron eye. The curtained windows reflected back the light and made the stone edifice look as though it contained no life.

Jago reached out to turn the door handle as Bia tried to cover the marks on her neck with the collar of her coat. The door opened immediately. Mrs Macarty jammed it with her foot and peered out.

'Thought you were going to live with Mr high-and-mighty Morgan?' she asked belligerently. 'Not good enough at Streonshalgh Manor?'

'He said we had to go and we had no choice,' Jago said as honestly as he could.

'He said it wasn't safe for us in Whitby and that the Ministry had sorted it all out,' Bia added, her frown reflecting the expression on Mrs Macarty's face.

'So, we are left to be blown to pieces in a hail of bombs and for some reason you two have been picked to live the life of Riley in a country house?' she snorted. 'Better come in and get your things and then you can be off.' Mrs Macarty folded her arms indignantly. 'I thought Rathbone was going to fetch you?'

'Dropped us at the top of the road, gone for petrol,' Bia said.

Mrs Macarty looked at the girl, examining her face closely. 'You don't look well, Biatra, you're all wet. What you been doing?' she asked.

'Fell over . . .'

'She fainted,' Jago interrupted quickly. 'Didn't have much breakfast.'

'I'll put that right. You get packed and I'll do you some food. Not having people think I don't feed you, even if there is a war,' she said as she unexpectedly hugged Bia and stroked her hair. 'Sometimes, we all have to make sacrifices – some more than others.' She looked at Jago. It was a knowing, cunning stare as if his fate was already written on his face. 'I sent the boys to pack your things this morning – hope you don't mind, Jago.'

Jago's heart raced.

'I'll go and see.' He tried to speak calmly, but all he wanted to do was run to his room.

By the time he was on the landing by the painting of Pippen Draigorian, he could hear Staxley laughing in his room.

Jago ran the length of the passageway and burst through the door.

'Didn't take you long to get your feet under the table with Ezra Morgan, did it, Jago?' Staxley asked as he sat in the chair by the window clutching Jago's leather bag.

'I'd rather be here – even with you, Staxley,' he answered as Griffin and Lorken appeared from under the other side of the four-poster bed. 'Lost something?'

'On the contrary, Jago. We have found something very precious, very precious indeed. You must have had it well hidden when we searched your room,' Staxley said as he rummaged in the case. 'This cup must be worth a few quid – and talking of quids, what's a lad like you doing with all these five-pound notes?'

Staxley produced the cup and the wad of notes as if he were a cheap circus conjurer. Griffin and Lorken cackled like monkeys, and Lorken smoothed his quiff of greased hair with the palm of his hand.'

'They're mine, all of them,' Jago said as calmly as he could as he wondered when he would get the beating that was bound to follow.

'Not any more,' Staxley answered. He folded the notes the best he could and slipped them into his pocket.

'I wouldn't do that if I were you,' Jago said as he stepped forward.

'Three of us and one of you?' Staxley asked. He stood and dropped the leather case to the floor.

'It's my money – my mother gave it to me,' Jago said, taking a tentative step and watching for the dogs to pounce.

'Then she is generous woman.' Staxley laughed as he took

the money from his pocket and waved it in his face. 'And where she is, I don't think she'll care.'

Jago's eyes clouded with a cold, bloody mist. Enraged by Staxley's words, he clenched his fists. A low, echoing groan left his throat as he let out a deep gust of breath. He could feel the twisting knot in his stomach stretch and stretch until it suddenly snapped. Without another word, Jago took a long step towards Staxley. He swung his arm blindly. His hand jabbed and jabbed again.

Staxley stood for a moment, the money held out in limp fingers that could no longer grasp it. He was completely breathless, so winded by the blows that he could not speak. Jago snatched the money from his hand, making ready to fight Griffin and Lorken. He turned to look at them as Staxley slumped back in the chair.

'You next?' Jago asked.

Griffin looked at Staxley, who gasped for breath.

'Not my money,' he said hesitantly, hoping that Staxley wouldn't hear his words.

'Do what you want,' Lorken added in a whisper.

'I'm taking my things – thanks for packing them so neatly,' Jago said as he placed the silver chalice in the bag and slipped the money in his pocket. 'When he's feeling better, tell him never to come after me or I'll do it again, understand?'

Lorken nodded as Jago left the room. For the first time he was vaguely aware of a telephone ringing in the house. It was a sound that was out of place and out of time. It echoed through the wood-panelled corridors and then suddenly stopped.

Turning the landing under the picture of Pippen Draigorian,

Jago looked down the stairs. Bia sat in the large chair by the door, her head in her hands, her long red hair covering her face. Urgent footsteps came down the corridor. They were snappy and clicked against the tiled floors. Jago knew something was wrong. Inside he knew he had been betrayed.

'Staxley! Griffin!' Mrs Macarty shouted as she entered the hallway. Her voice stopped suddenly as she saw Jago on the stairs. 'I trusted you, Jago,' she said as she made towards Bia.

'Run, Bia – get out!' Jago shouted as he heard the footsteps clattering on the landing above them.

'No – you're a thief, Jago Harker – stealing from Draigorian,' Mrs Macarty said as she tried to grab him.

'I've stolen nothing,' he said. He pushed her away and chased after Bia, who was struggling to open the door.

'A gold cup – priceless – that's what Morgan said,' Mrs Macarty uttered as she lashed out again, catching Jago by the scruff of his shirt. Footsteps stampeded along the corridor and turned the landing. Jago knew they had to get away.

'Thieves! Villains!' she shouted.

'I can't open the door,' Bia said, trying to turn the handle that just spun in her hand.

'Out the back,' Jago said as he twisted from Mrs Macarty's tight grip.

As he turned, Staxley, Griffin and a reluctant Lorken ran down the final flight of dark stairs. Their feet clattered on the old wood.

'He's stolen a gold cup from Draigorian,' shouted Mrs Macarty.

'It's in the bag,' Lorken said. 'I've seen it.'

'Get her, Griff,' Staxley shouted as he eyed Bia.

Griffin leapt the banister to block their escape as the sound of a car's tyres screeched on the gravel outside the house.

'Rathbone!' shouted Mrs Macarty as she ran to the door.

Jago ran at Griffin, his head down, still clutching the bag with the cup and dragging Bia along. Griffin dived out of the way as Staxley screamed in disapproval.

'Stop him!' he shouted as he chased them towards the kitchen and the back door that led to the alleyway and the old abbey.

Jago felt the breeze as the front door opened. Swirls of thick dust blew up from the cracks in the floorboards.

'Where's the boy?' Rathbone shouted as he gave chase through the house.

Suddenly, out of nowhere, the Gladlings appeared. It was as if they had been listening. Without fear, they grabbed Staxley. Morris and Boris each fastened on a leg whilst Laurence pushed him to the floor. Staxley fell back, knocking Rathbone to one side, as Griffin and Lorken stumbled over the wrinkled carpet that covered a hole in the floorboards.

'Run!' Laurence Gladling said bravely as he held fast to Staxley's head so he couldn't see and Mrs Macarty lashed out at him with a besom brush.

Jago looked back and saw Gladling's eyes asking if his debt was now repaid.

'We'll come for you,' Jago shouted as they ran out of the kitchen door and into the covered alleyway.

'We can't leave them,' Bia said, knowing their fate.

'Have to get away. They will kill you,' Jago answered as he slammed the door and they ran through the twisting corridor of high walls and dripping stone.

'Jack Henson lives up here,' Bia screamed.

They had reached a small cottage cut out of the stone of the abbey wall. The door was inset into the rough-hewn stones and half covered in a shroud of bracken and hanging grass. From far behind they heard Staxley shouting to the others as if he were a hound following their scent. 'We'll not get away from them,' Bia said as they ran by Henson's sombre cottage with its narrow windows and its door with peeling paint.

'Got ya!' a voice said as a fist snapped from an unseen passageway. Bia was dragged from the alleyway by a large hand that loomed out of the dark hole. 'You too, Jago . . .'

Before he could make a sound, five strong, grimy, mud-stained fingers had grabbed him by the coat and pulled him from the pathway and gripped his mouth so he couldn't utter a sound. Jago could smell the dirt on the hand as it pulled tightly against the three-scar wound on his cheek. They had been captured.

[19]

Gravedigger

WATER DRIPPED FROM THE ROOF of the cave without ceasing. Jago rested on a large stone whilst Bia tried to open the lock on the wooden door that Henson had bolted on the outside. A solitary candle lit the cold room cut out of the rock under the ruins of the abbey. It cast long, dark shadows and willowed back and forth in the chill breeze that came from the dark recess of the cave.

Jago had tried to see how far back the void went, but had returned to the light when the roof of the cave dipped down so he could no longer see. Bia had spent the time trying to open the door. It held fast like a castle keep. Time dragged slowly. Hours passed and more hours and still Henson did not come back.

'What's he going to do with us?' Bia asked finally as she broke her fingernails on the door.

'Give us over to Morgan, that's what I think,' Jago answered, still trying to think of a way of escape.

He had heard muffled voices, people talking angrily in another room. Henson had shouted, but Jago couldn't make out what he had said. Then, there had been hours of silence only broken by the drip-drip-drip of water from the sodden roof.

'Why so long?' she asked as she turned to look at the candle and try to judge how much light they had left.

Jago knew what she thought.

'About an hour left in that,' he said, having already made the calculation. 'What about the door?'

'Three bolts on the outside and no chance of moving them. I think we're stuck,' Bia answered sarcastically, resigned to what was to come.

'We could jump him when he comes back. I could blow out the light and –'

'You could go to the pier and have an ice cream?' Henson asked from the shadows behind him.

Jago turned. Henson stood taller than ever, his shadow cast up the wall of the cave in the dim light.

'How?' Bia asked as she pushed at the locked door.

'If Jago had gone a little further or used the candle he would have seen that this is just a hallway.' Henson laughed as he spoke.

'But I looked – the cave went down to nothing,' Jago answered.

'Didn't look hard enough. Follow me,' Henson said as he turned and disappeared into the darkness.

They followed quickly. After turning to the right and then right again, there was a narrow door cut from the rock. In the dim light it looked as though it was part of the wall, the shadow tricking the eye. Henson stepped through and was gone from their sight. Jago and Bia went after him. They walked for three paces in complete darkness. The floor beneath their feet was littered in old bones that crunched with each step.

'Sometimes the ground gives way and they fall through. I

pick them up the best I can – but my eyesight isn't what it was,' he said as he went further along the tunnel.

'They?' Bia asked.

'Dead people. All these were so poor they couldn't afford a coffin,' Henson answered as the tunnel began to fill with the soft amber light of a warm fire. 'If you'd had your wits about you, you could have spent your time in here and kept warm. Even put some food out for you.'

Jago was first to step into the room as he followed Henson. It was like a grand cavern with a chiselled roof that bore the marks and cuts of many hands. In a hundred hewn holes, candles burnt brightly. In one corner was a hearth with a log fire and an old blackened kettle that steamed and faintly whistled. Above it were bundles of herbs in tight bunches and strange talismans that dangled from pieces of thread. The fire smoke was sucked through a chimney cut from the solid stone. Before the fire was a small table carved from a single piece of wood, and on it was a covered plate of food.

'So we could have come in here?' Jago asked.

'If you had been wise enough not to have thought you were trapped by the darkness,' Henson said. 'Had to keep you out of the way of Rathbone and the others. They came looking for you, but I sent them off.'

'I heard you shouting – thought you were going to hand us over,' Jago answered as Henson offered them each a chair.

'Ha . . . That's the last thing I would do,' he said sharply, as if offended by the thought. 'Always knew there was something about you that would attract a lot of interest. See you've found your cousin, then?' he asked.

'You knew?' Bia asked.

'It was obvious from the moment I set eyes on you both together. I wondered when the boy would be back. Heard all about you from the *whisperers*.'

'Whisperers?' Bia asked.

'Ghosts, spirits – whatever you want to call them. Talk all the time – but they never come in here. Only place where I get peace from them.'

'Why's that?' Jago insisted.

'Beneath the chancel of the church. Nothing can get close to that place – too much power,' Henson said quite glibly.

'Beneath the church? That's by the edge of the cliff,' Bia said.

'Through that door are the steps into the crypt and back-a-ways is my cottage. I can come and go as I please. That tunnel comes out in my bedroom – through a panel in the wall.' Henson seemed pleased with himself and smoothed the front of his long coat. 'Anyways – the thing is, what to do with you? If Rathbone is after you, then so is Ezra Morgan and the others.'

'The Vampyre Quartet?' Jago asked.

'Didn't take you long to discover that. What else do you know?' he asked.

Jago looked at Bia, his eyes asking if he should go on.

'There are four Vampyres,' Jago said.

'Makes sense being *four* of them – after all, they are a quartet.' Henson laughed, his head thrown back as his body shook. It seemed a strange thing for him to do. Jago thought Henson had always seemed so sombre. 'So you know about the Vampyres and they know about *you*.' His voice dropped to a whisper as he leant closer to Jago and picked a piece of bracken from the cuff of his leather coat. 'I knew about you from the moment you stepped off the train. They have known about you since before you were born.'

'How could they?' Jago asked. 'My mother left here long before –'

He never got time to finish his words.

'Who do you think paid all your bills and who sent you to London in the first place? Even your name is their joke. Harker was the name of the first woman their master killed. They gave it to your mother to make her respectable so no one would think you were a . . .' Henson stopped and then went on. 'You are a Morgan – it's written on your face. Didn't they tell you that?' Henson asked.

'It must be true,' Bia said. 'Just look at that painting we saw – you were the spitting image of Hugh Morgan.'

'Is Ezra Morgan my father?' Jago asked as his stomach churned.

'He is no more your father than Ebenezer Goode is my sister,' Henson said, laughing again. 'Your mother was in love with Hugh Morgan. I would see them all the time in the ruins walking together. Hugh Morgan is your father. You have Morgan blood in your veins and you too carry the curse.'

'A Vampyre?' Bia asked. She instinctively felt her neck and the two small wounds that burnt in her skin.

'I remember when Hugh Morgan was born. The first child of that family to be born at Hawks Moor for hundreds of years. Then Ezra went away and left him alone just after your mother went to London.' Henson thought for a while. 'Do you know what they want you for?' he asked.

'They want me to be a Vampyre. The woman said that

this morning. Told me it was my inheritance. So did Strack-an when I saw him by the bookshop when he attacked the woman. He said I would be like him.'

'Woman?' Henson asked as his eyebrow curled over his forehead.

'A Vampyre. She looked like my mother and then she . . .' Bia said, unable to tell him what happened.

'Bit you?' Henson asked.

'Jago stabbed her with a holly wand. I heard her die,' Bia answered.

'Holly won't kill her. As soon as the wand is taken from her she will be back to life just as she was before.'

'I used myrrh balm,' Jago said softly, unsure if he should speak.

'Myrrh balm – where did you get such a thing?' Henson enquired.

'A man in London gave it to me before I was sent here,' Jago answered quietly. 'Hid it in my bag.'

'Your *guardian*. I thought you wouldn't have grown up alone,' Henson replied. 'He must have liked you. Myrrh balm is the only thing that will repel Vampyres. It stops them breathing and they can't drink blood. Won't kill them, though.'

'How do you know so much about Vampyres?' Bia asked.

'Let me see your neck,' Henson asked, ignoring her question. Bia showed him the wound. He grunted to himself as he twisted her head to one side. 'Typical. Well healed . . . Myrrh balm, eh?'

'Will Bia be well?' Jago asked.

'All depends on the venom. Vampyres are like snakes. You

237

can get some of the venom out, but never all of it. If you keep it covered in myrrh she will stay well – for the time being.'

'What about the woman from the bookshop that Strackan attacked?' Jago asked.

'So you knew about that?' he asked.

'I did,' Jago declared as he wondered if he could trust Henson. 'I didn't dare say anything – thought you worked for him.'

'Strackan?' Henson cursed. 'He is the cause of all this.'

'You going to hand us over to Morgan?' Bia asked him.

'Rathbone said you had stolen a cup from Morgan and that you were thieves. They are looking for you. I told them I had never seen you. Did your friend in London give you the cup that I found in your leather bag?'

'How did you know?' Jago asked.

'Was he dark-haired – a foreign man, a storyteller?'

'Do you know him?'

'Julius Cresco?' Henson said.

'Yes,' Jago answered simply as he looked at Bia and wondered what thoughts were veiled behind her worried face.

'We can't talk here – not any longer. It'll be night soon and these caves aren't the safest place to be when it's dark. If you want to truly save your friend and end all this then the answer lies in a book.' Henson stopped and looked about the room as if he had heard someone.

'The Book of Krakanu?' Jago asked.

'You know of this?' said Henson as he moved away from the fire.

'Cresco told me about the book and Draigorian set me on trying to find it in his library,' Jago answered.

'Draigorian has the book?' Henson asked as his eyes glowed and shimmered with deep consideration.

'Said he had lost it in his library – asked me to search for it.'

'Wanted you to find it . . . For some strange reason I think Draigorian was trying to help you,' Henson interrupted eagerly. He looked about the room as if distracted by something he could hear.

'I thought it was just a book of stories,' Jago said.

'I have never seen the book. But I have heard from the whisperers that it contains every scrap of knowledge to rid this world of Vampyres.'

'So we could stop them all?' Bia asked.

'But it comes at a price,' Henson said. 'The book is guarded by a poltergeist – a troublesome spirit that will try to stop you from finding it.'

'Is that something that can lift a table and throw you across a room?' Jago asked.

Henson laughed.

'I take it that the poltergeist made itself known to you?' he asked.

'It lifted the table and smashed it into the floor when I was searching the shelf. I thought it was Strackan,' Jago answered.

'Then you were close to the book. If you want to be free from the Morgan curse then you will have to find it and follow what it says.' Henson spoke quickly. 'The poltergeist can read your mind and will know your weakness.'

'So is Hugh Morgan a Vampyre?' Bia asked.

'He has shown no signs. Hugh Morgan is a throwback, a

man on his own and different from his father. Yet I cannot be sure. He keeps himself to himself and has no friends other than his paintbrush and that camera he always carries with him.'

Henson looked at Jago and signalled for them to be silent. Raising his head, he appeared to be listening to someone speaking far away.

'Who is it?' Bia asked.

'The whisperers are talking far away. I should go and listen. There has been another attack,' Henson said as he walked from the cave, snatching a candle from the rock and beckoning them to follow.

The winding tunnel went back and forth under the graveyard. An occasional foot or other bones broke through the roof where the ground had given way. Henson carried on as if this was quite normal. Jago and Bia followed in his shadow, picking their way through the bones that littered the floor.

'Where are we going?' Bia asked Jago as the passageway turned back on itself.

'I am setting you free,' Henson whispered in reply as they came to a short flight of steps that led up to a stone slab in the roof. 'This was made by the smugglers. The whisperers frightened them off. It is an incredible contraption, quite a remarkable piece of engineering,' Henson went on as he stooped down and pulled the lever. 'I can help you no more. Find the book and you will find freedom.'

Henson pulled the short iron handle that was embedded in the rock. The flat stone above their heads lifted quickly, and billows of night-mist rolled down the steps and into the tunnel.

'It was you all the time,' Bia said in sudden realisation. 'All the stories of the hauntings – people coming from the graves – noises under the earth – it was you.'

'A legend is always a good way to keep people from a place like this. Can't have everyone knowing my secret,' Henson said.

'But what about us?' Bia asked. 'We know about you and the caves.'

'There is little prospect of your living past Friday the thirteenth. It's a chance I will have to take,' he muttered quickly. 'Anyway, it's not often you meet the one who could put an end to the curse once and for all time.'

'Why does it bother you so?' Jago asked him as he stood on the first step and peered into the night.

'A Vampyre took my wife and my child forty years ago. The town said they had fallen from the cliff. I knew she had been lured to this place. Since that time I have tried to find who killed her. The woman who poisoned Biatra is called Trevellas, Sibilia Trevellas. Watch her, she is the most dangerous of the Quartet and a favourite of their master, Strackan. Find her and he will not be too far away. Some of the whisperers even say they are lovers.' Henson pointed to the night. 'This is something you'll have to do on your own. I'll keep that cup of yours for when you need it.' He looked at Jago as if he could tell what he was thinking and see the hesitation in his heart. 'You can either run from this place or stay and fight. It's your choice.'

'They'd only come looking for us,' Bia said as she held Jago's hand. 'I thought it would be good for us to get away. But if we can stop them . . .'

'We'll stay,' Jago answered. 'Friday the thirteenth?'

'That's a powerful night for them. The anniversary of when this all started all those years ago. Live beyond that night and you will have won,' Henson answered as he rubbed soil from his finger.

'Then it doesn't give us long,' Bia said as Jago strode up the steps and into the mist-filled graveyard.

Henson took her by the hand and pulled her close to him.

'Your mother would be proud of you, Biatra,' he said.

'I know,' she replied as the memory of her mother's face came to mind.

'You can still feel the venom?' he asked in a whisper as he saw her darkened, bloodshot eyes in the light of the candle.

'Yes,' she answered.

'It will get stronger. Fight it, girl – fight the desire to be like them.'

'Will it kill me?' she asked.

'Within the week if Jago doesn't find that book and destroy Strackan.' Henson stepped back from the stairs and watched as Bia walked away from him. 'Shhh . . . Can't you see I have guests?' Henson said to a voice that only he could hear.

[20]

The Book of Krakanu

THE LANE ECHOED to their footsteps as they ran through the mist towards Hagg House. On either side, the high walls of the donkey path kept out the sound of the sea as it broke on the harbour below. Bia tried to keep pace. Breathing got harder with every step as the venom brewed deep within. She remembered how her mother would break a fever when she was a small child and wrap her in a linen shawl. Her mother would bathe her head in a cold compress of nettle leaves and vinegar. Then she would be wrapped like a parcel in brown paper and smeared in goose grease. Bia would feel the heat seep from her and all would be well. Now, as she ran through the curfew streets, her hands began to shake. When she looked at the moon, every vein trembled.

'Seems different without the comet,' she said as they got to the path high above the estuary. 'The sky looks empty.'

Jago looked up. 'Feels better – don't think I'm being watched,' he said as they stopped on the corner of the lane and looked out across the town. 'Fog reminds me of London, never seen it so thick.'

From where they stood, it looked as though they could step from the cliff and walk across the estuary on the dark slither of mist that forced its way in from the sea. It filled the bottom of the town by the harbour side and hid the ships beneath its hand.

'My mother said that when it was like this, the Devil could never catch you.' Bia shivered as she spoke. 'I've never liked the fog, always makes me feel sick.'

'If we get caught after curfew we will be arrested for sure,' Jago said. He had a sudden feeling they were not alone. 'Can you feel anything?' he asked.

'What?'

'Don't know – it's like someone is near to you that you can't see.' Jago looked around nervously and held her hand. Bia felt cold. 'You all right?' he asked.

'Fine. Just feel sick. Haven't eaten, that's all,' she replied as she thought of the food her mother would make and the sweet smell of baked bread that would always be in her kitchen. There was the sound of a shrill·siren coming from the factory. 'Changing shifts,' Bia said. 'Not a good time to be near Hagg House.'

'Does Clinas sleep at the house?' Jago asked.

'Sometimes, if Draigorian is really unwell. Other than that he has a cottage on Scoresby Terrace. He lives alone – well, alone with three cats and a parrot.'

Bia smiled. She remembered the parrot clearly. It was blue and gold with a club foot. She had been to the house with a message from her father before he went away. The parrot had repeated everything she had said as if it could speak English. Bia had laughed at the bird. Then it had stared at her, snapped its perch in half with its beak and told her to go before it ate her fingers. Clinas had laughed, said the bird was incorrigible, and then pushed her out of the door. Bia would never go back; she was convinced the bird understood everything she said.

'We'll give it an hour and then we'll break in,' Jago said as he pulled up the collar of his coat and looked about for some shelter.

'It's best to hide in the woods. No one will look for us there,' Bia answered. 'No need to break in, there is always a key hidden behind the drainpipe.'

They took refuge in the woods, and the hour passed quickly and silently. Bia grew colder as the venom seeped through her veins like ice. She shuddered as her fingers began to turn blue, the tips numb and lifeless. Jago stared from the small copse of trees to the back door of the house.

From far across the fog-filled town, the church clock struck midnight. Clinas left the house. He locked the door from the outside and hid the key deep in his pocket. Before he got on his large black bicycle, he looked around and then instinctively checked the door again to make sure all was well. Then he stopped, turned and scanned the line of trees that edged the garden. It was as if he knew they were there. His moon shadow crossed the yard, and then he whistled as he disappeared.

Jago stepped from behind the tree.

'Wait,' Bia said, as if she knew what would happen.

Clinas reappeared, scurrying around the side of Hagg House like a rat. He again checked the back door and the windows. Then he walked towards the copse of trees at the bottom of the garden and, taking a torch from the pocket of his coat, scanned the wood.

Jago hid in the long grass as Bia kept the man in view. Then, like before, Clinas turned and walked away.

'Do you think he knows?' Jago asked as Bia moved from her hiding place.

'He's suspicious. We'll have to give him time,' she said.

They waited until the clock of the church struck the half hour. Bia could feel the venom numbing her feet. Her body tingled as if being warmed from a cold winter's day. The dull ache in her mouth had grown more intense. Every sense was heightened. She could see the colour of the trees in a different way. The world shimmered and glowed as if everything was alive.

'Where is the key?' Jago asked as he stepped from the copse and began to walk towards the house.

'Jago, do you have any myrrh balm?' Bia asked. 'I feel . . .'

Jago looked at her. He could see she had changed.

'Trevellas said it would cure you. Holy dew and myrrh balm . . . She lied,' he snapped.

'I need some now. I can feel it in me. It's getting worse,' Bia said softly as she reached out to him.

Jago felt the silver pyx in his pocket. Reluctantly he took it out and held the palm-sized tin towards her.

'Here,' he said as he unscrewed the ammonite lid. 'Let me put some on the wound.' Bia tilted her soft white neck so he could see the two precise puncture wounds. In the moonlight, they looked brighter, harsher, and each oozed a single drop of blood. Taking the balm he anointed her neck. The bite marks sizzled like burning meat. Bia squealed in pain.

'Sorry, I never thought,' Jago said.

'It's fine,' she said as she panted her breaths and waited

for the pain to ebb away. 'Happens every day,' she tried to laugh. 'If I ever – if I ever become a Vampyre, you will kill me, won't you?'

'It won't come to that,' Jago answered sharply. We're going to get out of this place and go to London just as we said.'

'But if I do?' Bia pressed the question, wanting to know the answer.

'The night doesn't last for ever.'

Jago turned and walked away, putting the pyx back in his pocket.

'But will you kill me?' she said to herself, as if she didn't need an answer.

Bia stood alone at the edge of the copse of trees. The breeze soughed in the branches that rustled all around her. The dying nettles, shrouded in a purple hue, swayed back and forth as if one. She twisted the dew-damp locks of hair in her fingers but could feel nothing. Her hands trembled as the venom was subdued yet again.

By the back door, Jago stood in the shadows. He waited for her to cross the yard before he looked for the key. He found it quickly. It was dangling from a sharp nail hidden behind the drainpipe and covered by the twisted stems of a climbing rose.

The door opened quietly. There was a strong smell of cooked chicken that seeped from the kitchen. Unusually, everything was out of place. Pots were stacked in the sink; knives and scraps of food were left out on the wooden cutting board.

Soon they were on the stairs and quickly made their way up to the library. Jago knew he had to find the book – it was his only chance to cure Bia of the venom, his only chance to kill Strackan. The door of Draigorian's room was tightly shut, the sign still on the handle: KEEP OUT. Jago listened at the door. He could hear the soft and gentle sound of Draigorian snoring in his sleep.

Bia stayed close to Jago. She wondered what a poltergeist was and if it really did protect the book. They turned the corner of the passageway. The door to the library was just ahead. There was not a sound in that part of the house. Jago turned the key in the door and pulled the handle. It opened slowly. He looked inside. The smell of damp paper and fungus was overpowering.

The windows were shuttered.

'Let in as much light as you can,' he whispered to Bia as they stepped stealthily into the room. 'Open the shutters.'

Bia crossed the room and took hold of the brass handles and folded back the slatted wooden panels that covered one of the windows. A shaft of moonlight was suddenly cast onto the long table that the poltergeist had brought to life.

Jago stiffened as he looked into the dark shadows. In the corner of the room, facing against the wall, was the painting he had found of Cresco and Draigorian.

'Look at this,' he whispered as he pulled back the frame and twisted the painting towards the moonlight.

Bia could see the canvas was old and marred by smoke and dirt. The painting was of two men she had never seen before, dressed in the fashion of a much older time. Both wore frock coats and the younger held a long sword proudly at his side. Both men were smiling, their jewelled fingers clasped in friendship.

'Who are they?' she asked, thinking one looked like Draigorian.

'It is Crispin Draigorian and Julius Cresco,' Jago answered. 'They both wear the same ring on their smallest finger. Look, a wide band of gold cut through with a woven trellis. Cresco looked after me as a child.'

'He'd be too old,' Bia answered.

'He's a Vampyre, my guardian, sent by Morgan and the others to look after me.' He stared at the image of Cresco and their eyes met as if they were together in the room.

Bia looked closely at the picture. In the distance on a small hill was a woman holding an apple, with a snake at her feet.

'That's her – Trevellas,' she said, knowing she would never forget the face of the woman who had tried to kill her. 'How can they be so old and yet still alive?'

'Quite simple,' said the voice of Draigorian, whose shadow filled the doorway behind them. 'When Strackan savaged us when we killed the Hermit, he gave us the curse. We would be Vampyres and would live for ever as long as at every equinox of the sun we drank human blood.'

'You were asleep,' Jago said as he stepped back.

'But not so deep that I couldn't hear the footsteps of intruders,' he replied as he took off his calfskin gloves and placed them on the table. Then, quite meticulously, he rolled back the sleeves of his dressing gown until the cuffs of his striped shirt and the gold links were clearly visible.

As Draigorian stepped into the thick quill of moonlight, they could see that his face had changed. He was younger, handsome, his skin soft and smooth. All the ravages of the disease had gone. Draigorian had been completely transformed.

'We came for the Book of Krakanu,' Jago said.

'I know. I had Clinas bring it to me before he went. I sent him home. Somehow I had a feeling you would come tonight. That is the way with Vampyres.' Draigorian spoke quickly, his voice no longer laboured or pained by the porphyria that had ravaged his body. 'Did Cresco tell you about the book?'

'So you do know Cresco?' Jago asked.

'An old friend, and the only one we thought able to look after your mother following her *accident* . . .' Draigorian said. 'He preferred to live in London. Cresco said it was anonymous. A place where you didn't always have to pretend to die and then appear again as your long-lost son.'

'You said accident – what accident?' Bia asked.

'What? The accident of birth – the accident of falling in love with the son of a Vampyre . . . The accident of having a child by him. We all knew and have waited eagerly for your return.' Draigorian stepped closer to the table and pulled out the high-backed chair and took a seat. Bia thought that his hair looked like the feathers of a glorious bird. Their eyes met and he looked deep within her. His transformation was complete. Draigorian was everything he had been in his youth.

He sighed as he looked at them both and undid the collar button of his shirt.

'If you already had the book why did you ask me to look for it?' Jago asked.

'To see if you were really the *one*. Only a descendant of a Vampyre could outwit a poltergeist and still live,' he replied as he tapped his fingers on the oak table. 'And you even tidied the room after it attacked you. I was quite impressed.'

'It could have killed me,' Jago said.

'In some ways, Jago, that might have been an answer to your prayers. Your future will be very different from that which you expected,' he said.

'Trevellas said I was to be a sacrifice. I heard you talking in the labyrinth. The Lyrid of Saturn. Friday the thirteenth. That's what Ezra Morgan said.'

'Blood for blood. Friday the thirteenth is the day that you will inherit all we have had to carry for the last age of ages. Do you know how boring eternal life can be?' Draigorian scoffed. 'The sacrifice you will make will be the same we did all those years ago. You will stop being human, that is all. We have to do it for Strackan to bring peace. Isn't that what everyone wants? It started with Strackan and ends with him. He is the one who must drink your blood and you his. That is your fate.' He smashed his hand onto the table so that the whole room shuddered. 'Is that such a bad thing?'

'You said you were sick of being a Vampyre. I heard you telling Morgan you would have no more blood. Look at you. I know what you have done and why you look so well. All those people who have gone missing – you have been killing them, you, Strackan, Morgan and Trevellas.' Jago shouted and spat his words.

'I have killed no one for many years. Clinas gives me his blood. Four cups a year. Four red cups . . . of wonder. That is how much he has cared for me. What Strackan and the others have done is no concern of mine. At the equinox of every moon, Clinas gives me what is his so I have no need to kill. I starved myself for a whole year and the only reason I have drunk blood tonight was to help you.'

'Help us,' Bia asked. 'Why?'

251

'In simple truth, Biatra, I am sick of all the lies, killing and murder that this life brings. I am tired of never sleeping. Everyone I have ever known has died before me,' he said as he reached out his hand towards Jago. 'You are the one person who can set me free and break the curse.'

'How?' Bia asked. 'How can he break something like that?'

'In Hawks Moor there is a painting of the Vampyre Quartet. To the human eye it looks as though it was never finished –'

'We know, we found it,' Bia said.

'Then you will have seen the faceless people. When one of the Quartet is truly killed, their face will appear on the painting. When the others are dead then Strackan will be at his weakest and he too can be destroyed. The world has to be rid of such a creature.'

'And I have to kill each of you?' Jago asked.

'What Morgan will never speak of is that only *you* have the power to kill us or bring us life. The curse should have rested on the shoulders of Hugh Morgan, but his father purposefully went away so it could not happen. That is how selfish the man was. It has to happen at a certain time. The Lyrid of Saturn, just as the stars fall from the sky. Hugh Morgan lost his innocence. When your mother became with child we knew we had a true heir and we gave him the name Jago Harker. That is you.' Draigorian stood quickly and plucked a box of matches from his pocket and lit the candelabra on the table.

'So what if I killed myself? It would all be in vain for you,' Jago answered.

'Did you drink from the Cup of Garbova?' Draigorian asked. 'Can you hear the voices that whisper?'

'Yes,' Jago answered.

'Then it would be futile. Cresco has tricked you, as simple as that,' Draigorian said smugly, his eyes widening as he smiled.

Jago could feel the anger rising in his stomach. He wanted nothing of this. In just a few short days his life had changed and his mother was dead. The man he thought was a friend had become a traitor.

'How old are you?' Bia asked as she looked at Draigorian's face.

'Hundreds of years – I have forgot exactly,' he replied.

'And you are a Vampyre?'

'That is what the world calls us,' Draigorian said.

'Then what is to be done?' Jago asked as Draigorian walked to the large cabinet by the window.

'I have taken the liberty of luring the poltergeist into this jug,' he said. He opened the wooden doors and lifted down a pot jug with a cork stopper and placed it carefully on the table. 'Vampyres are adept at such things. All the power, all the malevolence of the creature is contained within this flagon. The Book of Krakanu is safe for you to take.'

Jago and Bia stared at the pot jug. It looked ordinary, lifeless and empty, as if it contained nothing but air.

'The poltergeist is in there?' Bia asked as she looked at the jug.

'There it shall stay, and what is more,' Draigorian said excitedly, 'I have this for you.' The man reached back into the bureau and took out a wooden box. It was old, plain and without carving or any decorative work. Iron hinges held the lid in place. Draigorian took it in both hands and just as he placed it on the table next to the flagon he hesitated. 'Biatra, would you mind if I spoke to Jago alone. I will bring him no harm, I promise you that.'

Bia looked at Jago. He nodded and tried to smile.

'I'll wait outside,' she said as she walked by Draigorian, keeping out of arm's reach until she got to the door.

Draigorian waited until he heard the click of the latch and then looked at Jago. He slipped the catch and then lifted the lid of the box. There, on a green velvet cushion, was a silver knife. The handle was encrusted with jet and emeralds. The blade was that of a sharpened stiletto.

'I heard of your handiwork with Madame Trevellas. Sadly, the holly could only bind her fast and the myrrh balm stop her from breathing for a short while,' he said as he lifted out the knife. 'She is now quite well and wanting to see Biatra again.'

'This will kill her?' Jago asked.

'It is yours to take and stop all of this. Take it, Jago.' Draigorian handed him the knife. 'If you stab a Vampyre with this knife then it will kill them, instantly. They cannot come back to life. All you need to know is in the Book of Krakanu. It is by my bed. I shall get it for you.'

'But I will be a murderer,' he answered.

'I hear you had no hesitation when you tried to kill Trevellas. With this knife there will be no evidence,' he said feverishly. 'Vampyres show no marks of the knife. It will look as if they have just died naturally. They will be no more. Dust to dust. Dead . . .'

'Why are you giving this to me?' Jago asked.

Draigorian looked about the room as if he wanted to take

in all he could see and keep it forever as a memory. He walked slowly to the fireplace and pushed a small tin car along the mantelpiece as if he were a child.

'I am one of the Quartet,' he said in a voice so low it could not be heard outside. 'And I beg of you a favour – that you kill me before you leave this house. I will give you the book and you can bring an end to the curse.'

'Kill you?' Jago asked. 'Tonight?'

'I would prefer to say that I was being released from chains that have held me for too long. I have always been a reluctant demon.' Draigorian laughed.

Jago held the knife in his hand, then slipped it into the pocket of his coat. Suddenly the thought of killing Draigorian was as much abhorrent as it was necessary.

'I don't know that I can do this,' Jago said.

'Then consider it as we walk to my room. I am sure we can come to some suitable arrangement.' Draigorian opened the door to the room and looked back as if for the last time. The flickering candles cast long shadows across the bookshelves. Speckled particles of dust sparkled like tiny silver orbs floating through the air. He sighed. 'I have left everything to Clinas. That man is more than a friend.'

'Did he always know you were a Vampyre?' Jago asked as they stepped from the room to where Bia was waiting outside.

'Clinas guessed quite quickly. He offered to help me in whatever way he could. It is only right that he inherits all of this. Finally, Whitby shall be rid of a Draigorian forever.'

'And you'll be buried with all the others?' Jago asked.

'I shall be laid with all the empty coffins and ridiculous

255

names that fill that tomb.' Draigorian laughed. 'I am Pippen Draigorian,' he giggled. 'You will never know how good it was for me to say that name again.'

He walked ahead of them down the stairs and along the landing until he came to his bedroom. Draigorian went in and closed the door, returning moments later with a small leather-bound book.

'The Book of Krakanu?' Jago asked.

'The only one,' he replied as he handed Jago the book.

It was plain and ordinary, covered in a leather binding with just one word on the cover: KRAKANU.

'We will go,' Jago said as he turned to walk away.

'Are you not forgetting something?' Draigorian asked, his eyes sparkling as blue as his long silk dressing gown with its velvet collar. 'I will shake your hands and bid you both well,' he said.

Bia held out her hand and gripped Draigorian. It was as if he could feel her sickness. Jago steadied her with a hand on the shoulder.

'We should go,' he said as he eased her away.

'Lock the door on your way out,' said Draigorian. 'I would hate to be burgled.' He laughed, knowing how little such things would matter after the dagger was used against him.

'You are very sweet, Mr Draigorian,' Bia said.

'You may call me Pippen,' he answered as he stepped inside his room and closed the door.

When they reached the kitchen, Jago stopped.

'I'll have to go back,' he said. 'I've forgotten the knife that Draigorian gave to me.'

'But I thought . . .' Bia protested.

'Wait here. I won't be long.'

There was something in his voice that made her suspicious. She stood in the kitchen and counted the ticking of the clock over the tiled fireplace. The short pendulum beat back and forth, clicking in annoyance. It was eleven minutes before Jago returned.

'Where have you been?' she asked.

'I said goodbye to Draigorian. He wished you well,' Jago said as he felt the warm handle of the dagger in his pocket.

[21]

Scoresby Terrace

IN THE HIDDEN ROOM at Hawks Moor lit only by a shrine candle in front of the painting of the faceless Vampyres, Ezra Morgan wept. He sobbed, holding his face in his hands, and shook his head in disbelief. There in the painting was something he never expected to see. Appearing inch by inch in what had been a dark void of swirled paint was the face of Pippen Draigorian.

As he had looked at the painting, the deep blue eyes appeared and stared at him as they had done hundreds of years before. Slowly, very slowly, the face of his dear friend came to life in the portrait as if it had found its place in eternity. Draigorian smiled at his old friend and then, as if the spell had finally been broken, saw his face set in the perpetual stillness of paint on canvas.

'He's dead,' Morgan said. 'Dead . . .'

The panelled door opened. Rathbone stepped in and took Morgan by the hand.

'It can't be, Master. Impossible,' Rathbone said. 'How could it happen? He's –'

'Immortal?' asked Ezra Morgan. 'Immortality comes at a price. Someone has the Book of Krakanu. I can feel it. Pippen has been the first victim. I have known the man for hundreds of years. He was my best friend. The only one brave enough to even think about the crusade to kill Strackan. That creature had plagued this land. When we heard the hermit was keeping it safe, it was Draigorian who said we should hunt it down. When the monster struck, it was Draigorian who tried to protect me. When we realised we were Vampyres he wanted to end it all. He tried and tried but couldn't find a way . . .' Morgan wept. 'He has his wish at last.'

'Father?' said Hugh Morgan as he opened the door.

'No, Mr Morgan. Your father needs to be alone,' Rathbone said as he barred his way.

'Let him come, Rathbone. He has to see.'

Hugh Morgan stepped into the room. It was cold, and the air was thick with incense. The smoked gripped the gilt frame like the talons of a large bird. In front of the painting the candle flickered brightly.

'The painting,' said Hugh Morgan as he looked at the face of Draigorian. 'It has finally come to pass.'

'There can be only one person who could have done this,' Ezra Morgan said.

'Jago?' Hugh Morgan asked.

'Your son – who do you think?' came the stern and hapless reply. 'I saved you from this curse and now my actions have come back to haunt me. If it was you, then I know you would have taken Strackan's blood and that would have been the end of it. Now we will have to catch the boy and force him.'

'I loved her,' Hugh Morgan answered as his father sobbed.

'Spend hundreds of years in someone's company and then

tell me about love,' his father cried as Rathbone held him in his arms.

'You sent her away, we could have married, lived here, and all would have been well. But you did not like the fact she came from the old town, bottom end, not good enough. You tricked her and stole Martha from me, gave her a new name, a new life.'

'We had to guard him from the world so that *you* would be safe,' Ezra Morgan answered coldly.

'Once she was with child, I would be safe – that's what you said. I was no longer innocent. You never mentioned that the boy would take my place,' answered Hugh Morgan.

'What would you have understood? This is the Lyrid of Saturn – the comet marked his arrival – everything was in place and now this,' said his father.

'Then you should have killed Strackan long ago,' Hugh Morgan said as he stepped from the room.

'Dangerous words, Hugh. Words that would see you dead,' his father answered.

'Then let me kill Strackan, burn down his labyrinth and dig him from the ground where he hides from the light,' said Hugh Morgan as his footsteps echoed across the cold floor of the hallway.

'Rathbone, get the car ready. I need to speak to Clinas . . .'

'So,' Bia asked as she and Jago took the path through the woods towards the bank of the estuary far below Hagg House, 'where to?'

Jago looked at her and then pulled a strand of hair from

her face. 'We get to the station and buy a ticket to London,' he answered as he felt the wad of notes in his pocket and thought how he would see Cresco and confront him with all that had happened. 'I want to see Julius Cresco, the man who lives in the flat. He has some answers to give me.'

'But he's a Vampyre,' Bia said as she picked her way along a narrow path that led to the river through a field of stinging nettles. 'He could –'

'Kill us?' Jago asked stolidly. 'I'll take my chances with Cresco.'

'But we'll never get to the station at this time of night. There will be guards and the curfew. You get arrested if they find you outside and we don't have identity cards,' Bia argued, wondering where she was being taken. 'We have to use the bridge and this isn't the way.'

'Trust me. Draigorian told me of a way to get to the station without being seen,' Jago answered.

'Draigorian?' Bia asked.

'In his room when I said goodbye. He made me promise to take a letter to Clinas and post it through his door. He said I should do it tonight and that Clinas would understand. There is a boathouse by the water and a rowing boat. Draigorian told me to take it across the river and then cut up through the alleys.'

'But –' Bia tried to argue.

'There aren't any guards. Draigorian said . . .' Jago insisted. His eyes were wide, his voice strained.

'Is he dead?' Bia asked. 'Did you kill him?'

'He's dead. It was what he wanted,' Jago said coldly as he fought the urge to be sick. 'Draigorian said he would help us if I did one thing for him. I had to release him from the curse.'

'You stabbed him with the knife,' Bia sniffed. 'You had it with you all the time. You went back on that excuse and you killed him.'

'It was right. He didn't want the life any more.'

'So you killed him?' she asked. 'Just like that?'

'Yes. I had to.'

'We could have just left him and gone away,' Bia said as the sound of the river grew louder.

'But you don't understand,' Jago said. 'Strackan wants to drink my blood and make me like them. I am Hugh Morgan's son. I have a father and a family. I have to kill Strackan. You have to understand.'

It was the first time that the reality of all he had learnt had struck his heart. Jago knew his fate pursued him like a hound from hell. 'It all started in these woods. This is where the hermit lived. He was an unholy man, caring for Strackan. Draigorian said to me that he was a demon that they had to destroy. It was their quest, a pilgrimage, a crusade. And the demon won.'

'And we could have just left it all in Whitby and started again,' Bia said.

'I can't run away, not from this. I will take you to London and I will see Cresco. Draigorian told me that all I needed was in the book. In hundreds of years I am only the second child to be born of a Vampyre. That's why Strackan needs my blood.'

In the shadows of the wood, by the edge of the water, was an old boathouse. It looked as though the water was about to carry it away as it listed awkwardly to one side, its black timbers creaking and groaning with the ebb tide.

Jago opened the door and there, as if prepared for them was a long rowing boat. It bobbed in the water, held in place by a thin rope tied to a brass ring.

'I saw Draigorian in this three years ago. He was with Clinas inspecting the Penance Hedge,' Bia said as Jago quickly untied the craft and stepped inside, not waiting for her. 'Wait . . .'

'Let me do this alone. Wait here and I'll come back for you,' Jago said as he tried to push the boat from the side with the long oar.

'No. I'm coming with you,' Bia said as she leapt from the decking into the boat and stumbled.

The rowing boat rocked back and forth as Jago pushed at the side of the boathouse.

'Bia, stay here,' he insisted.

'I'm coming with you, whatever happens,' she answered. 'I don't want to be away from you. You're all I have. Live or die, we do it together.'

Jago slumped to the seat and instinctively felt the three wounds on his cheek. They burnt intensely.

'Just let me go alone,' he argued in a whisper as he folded his arms to show he wasn't going to move.

The boat moved slowly, taken by the tide towards the open doors of the boathouse. Bia wasted no time. She sat next to Jago, took the oars and pulled hard.

'You can either sit there or work, but I am not getting out,' she scolded as she pulled harder.

'Done this before?' Jago asked.

'More than you would ever know.' She smiled.

Jago slipped from the seat to the back of the boat as it left the cover of the ramshackle shed. Deep pools of dark water swirled around them over hidden stones. The moon cast its pathway to the other side of the estuary. The ruins of the abbey loomed over the town like ghostly fingers of stone. There was no light other than the stars. The sky appeared empty. Where the comet had been was just a black hole.

'Draigorian said that he knew I was coming,' Jago whispered as the boat beat steadily towards the other side of the water. 'He said as soon as the comet appeared he knew I would be back.'

'People put too much faith in the stars, that's what my father would say. Why follow the stars when you can believe in the one who made them?' Bia laughed to herself as she thought of her father lost in France. 'He went missing at Dunkirk, rode a motorbike. Never believed in any of the things my mother did. He said it was just superstition.'

'What was he like?' Jago asked as the shadow of the factory loomed nearer.

'I saw him every day of my life until he went to war. Strange how something can change you so. Father gone, mother gone, Vampyres, poltergeist, orphanage. Never expected life to be like that,' she said.

'My mother said you had to believe in something or life wasn't worth living. I can't understand why she didn't tell me –'

'What? That your grandfather is hundreds of years old and he's a Vampyre?'

Jago smiled.

'I knew there was something different. It always felt that way. Just little things, like knowing when the bombers were coming or what was inside a Christmas present before I unwrapped it.'

'Loved Christmas,' she said tearfully. 'First one I'll spend alone.'

'Alone?' Jago asked. 'You forgetting me?'

Bia rowed until the boat stuck on a spit of sand on the far side of the estuary way upstream from the town. Jago looked back at the shadow of the factory and wondered what went on inside. Even in the dead of night there was a low groaning noise that every now and then would tremble the water.

'Do you think the factory has something to do with all this?'

'Wouldn't be surprised,' Bia answered as she stepped from the boat and took the rope, wrapping it around a large stone. 'This town changed when that place opened. All the fish disappeared and there were noises from under the sea.'

Without warning a bright searchlight was cast across the water as if it searched for the voices.

'Down!' Jago said as he ducked into the boat and hid from sight.

The light scanned back and forth across the riverbank. It rested on the boat as if eyes in the factory searched the gloom. Jago waited. He couldn't see Bia and didn't know if she had been seen in the searchlight. Then, as quickly as it had come, the light was gone.

Jago crawled from the boat and scurried across the sand and into a clump of thick reeds.

'Jago?' whispered a voice near to him as a hand took hold of his sleeve. 'This is the way.'

Bia pulled him through the reeds until they came to the road that ran the length of the far side of the estuary. It was fronted by a row of high Victorian houses with bright painted doors and sculleries below stairs. They looked deserted, void of life, barren. On the corner of the terrace was a lookout made of sandbags and barbed wire. It too was empty. Just as Draigorian had told Jago, there were no guards. Soon they had made their way through the empty streets, ginnels and alleys until they had reached Scoresby Terrace.

The crowded houses hunched on the brow of a hill like the arched back of an armadillo. Each window was blacked out and criss-cross taped. Some had grimy hessian sandbags piled by the doors, and bicycles leant against the window ledges. The bags were rained-soaked and seeped grains of sand across the pavement in golden trickles.

At the end of the street, on a patch of open ground, was an air-raid shelter that looked as though it had been hastily built. A spiral of smoke filtered into the night air from the metal chimney that came from underground.

'Number 103,' Jago said as he took the envelope from his pocket and looked at the number written in bold letters.

'Do you know what it is?' Bia asked.

'His last will and testament,' Jago answered quietly. 'He showed me before . . .' Jago stopped and considered his words. 'He's left everything to Clinas, everything.'

He folded the envelope and looked on every door until he found the house. Number 103 was brightly painted and the pavement outside the terrace was swept clean. Several plants grew in neat pots on the window ledge and even the blackout curtains had been edged with ribbon. In the corner of the window facing the street was a small poster advertising that the Ziegfeld Follies were coming to Whitby.

'It'll change his life,' Bia said as Jago soundlessly slipped the will through the brightly polished letterbox. 'He was always with him, it will break his heart.'

Jago hoped that Clinas would understand. When he had left the bedroom, Draigorian looked peaceful, a shallow smile on his young face as if he had just fallen asleep.

'Draigorian said it would look like he had just died naturally,' Jago answered, hoping his words would take away the rising guilt that made his hand tremble as the envelope fell to the floor.

'Clinas loved him,' Bia said as the parrot called inside the house. 'That's what Mrs Macarty said to my mother.'

Jago listened to the squawking bird that seemed to be muttering hell and damnation. The sound of a car engine echoed through the streets. It was familiar in the way it growled and purred as it came closer.

'Morgan?' Jago asked as he took Bia by the hand then started to run. 'It's him, I know it.'

'Where to?' Bia panted as they crossed the waste ground by the air-raid shelter and headed towards the railway line.

'Bradick. We'll buy a ticket to London and get the first train out of here,' Jago answered just as the lights of the car turned in to the streets. They were muffled by a slit-like fender that covered the lens and cast the light to the ground.

Jago and Bia hid by the fence on top of the embankment and looked back. The familiar frame of Rathbone stepped from the Daimler car. He banged on the door of Number 103 and waited. A shaft of light flooded into the dark street. Rathbone opened the car door as Ezra Morgan got out and walked to the house.

'They know he's dead,' Jago said.

'How?' she whispered as they heard the sound of the factory siren across the estuary.

'The painting at Hawks Moor . . . It will have been just as Draigorian said. When one of the Vampyre Quartet dies then their face appears in the painting.'

'So why are they here?' she asked as they crept down the embankment to the railway line below.

'They'll want to go to Hagg House and take Clinas with them,' Jago answered as they walked along the gravel track towards the railway station. 'It's only a matter of time before they come for us.'

'But how will they know where to find us?' Bia asked.

'With any luck they won't, not until we are in London.'

Bia said nothing; she could feel the cold tremble in her hand as the venom surged again through her blood. This time it was all she could do to stay on her feet as the world began to change around her.

[22]

The Theosophist

THEY WALKED THE LAST MILE in silence. Bia could feel the venom taking hold of her and she held her stomach as she trudged wearily, one step at a time. She hoped Jago wouldn't see the pain on her face. The venom seared through her veins and burnt her skin. It was as if her jaws were being pushed forward as the teeth grew. She wondered if it could be controlled. Draigorian didn't look like a monster. When she had last seen him, she thought he was quite beautiful. Regardless of the myrrh balm, Bia knew that with each hour, the venom took over more of her body. Soon, she felt, she too would be a Vampyre.

'Do you have the balm?' she asked when the pain got too much for her to walk without stumbling.

Jago looked at her. He had been in another world, thinking of Cresco and why the man had been so kind to him.

'Is it the venom?' he asked, seeing her ashen face.

'I don't think it's working, it takes away the pain for a while and then it comes back.'

'There has to be an answer in the book. When we get to the station I will find out,' Jago said as he put his hand on the book wedged in his coat.

'I don't think I can get that far,' she said. She dropped her hands to her side and wanted to cry. 'I can feel it inside me – I can feel it changing me.'

Jago brushed the hair away from her neck to expose the wound. It looked as though a snake had bitten her. The punctures were precise, burnt red, and were raised from the skin like small volcanoes. He took the balm and anointed the wound. They bubbled as the balm cauterised the flesh. Bia gasped.

'It's all right,' Jago said. 'It's all right to be frightened.'

He held her hand softly in his. She could feel the warmth of his skin and momentarily wondered what it would be like to bite his neck and taste his blood.

'There is a way,' she said as her breath faltered. 'There is a way we could stay together if I am never healed. You could give yourself to them and we could be Vampyres together. Then we would never be apart. We could live for ever.'

Jago smiled as the soft breeze blew the trees around them. It was something he had thought of and then disregarded. In the time just before he had released Draigorian from life, the Vampyre had told him what would happen to him. He had said that only those who had exchanged blood with Strackan could live for ever. Those who were victims of a Vampyre would live on for the life of the moon and then die. Their souls would walk the earth and haunt the land three chains from where their bodies were interred.

'You have to get well. It's the only way. It wouldn't be right. It's not the way life was intended to be,' Jago said. 'We have to get to London and find Cresco. I know he will help us.'

'And then you'll kill him like you did Draigorian?' she asked.

It was a question Jago did not want to answer.

'It is not right that a man can live without death,' he said as he pulled her by the hand. 'I can see the station. It's a short walk. We can rest there.'

In the distance Bia could see the dark outline of the platform and the house and waiting room of Westcliffe Station. The roof was framed by white beams that shone blue in the bright moonlight. It reminded her of Christmas and taking the Boxing Day train down the coast with her mother. Bradick would stand on the platform as the train filled with people and wave his green flag as the steam whistle blew. Bia would grip the open window excitedly and breathe the cold air as the train crawled to Baytown.

The steps from the line to the platform had been recently washed. Damp patches and small puddles filled the crevices of the stone like the lakes of a small island beneath their feet. The station clock ticked silently as the hands drew towards the second hour beyond midnight. Several large wicker baskets were stacked by the entrance to the ticket office. An empty milk churn waited to be exchanged on the early-morning train. By the edge of the platform was a crate of chickens. Their white, feathered heads poked through the slats of the wooden box as they warily eyed Bia.

'I'm hungry,' she sighed, looking at the birds.

'I'll ask Bradick if he has anything for us to eat,' Jago answered.

'Shouldn't we just wait until it's light and then buy the ticket before the train arrives?' Bia asked.

'He said I could come back at any time,' Jago answered as he knocked on the door. 'He has the photograph of my mother – I want to know why he kept it.'

The door opened instantly as if whoever was inside had been expecting them. Bradick stood in full uniform; even his stationmaster's cap was in place.

'Jago Harker,' Bradick said excitedly. 'I am so glad you have come back.' The man looked beyond Jago and saw Bia standing in the moon shadow of the eaves. He tried not to sound anxious. 'And look – a face I know well . . . Biatra Barnes, what a pleasure.' Bradick smiled and then his face fell sullen and jowly. 'The curfew – what are you doing out in the curfew?'

'We want a train to London. I have the money,' Jago said as he produced the crisp five-pound notes.

'But you have only just arrived – why should you be going back?' Bradick asked.

'The photograph was of my mother with Mary Barnes. Bia and I are cousins. I have family,' Jago answered. 'If you give me the photograph we will buy a ticket and catch the train.'

'And family can stay in Whitby,' Bradick replied. His eyes flicked back and forth as he wondered what to do. 'You both better come inside. It is a dark night and now that the comet has gone I am not sure if it is a safe place.'

They stepped into the room. Burning brightly in the black grate was a coal fire – it looked as though the same coals burnt on the fire as on the night Jago had arrived. In the middle of the room the neat wooden table still had the same bowl of flowers. In front of a chair were a knife and fork, plate and cup. It was as if Bradick was about to eat.

'How much is the ticket?' Bia asked expectantly.

'I can give you a discounted rate,' Bradick answered. 'But there is likely to be much disruption. The line was bombed outside Kings Cross. You will have to walk the last five miles.'

'Five miles?' Jago asked.

'At least,' Bradick said. 'It was a direct hit on the track. You are lucky there are any trains at all. I was told to limit passengers leaving for London.'

He appeared to be uneasy with his words. Jago thought he looked tired and flustered. Bradick looked at Bia as if she shouldn't be there but he did not want to say. On the table by the typewriter and telephone was the picture of Jago's mother.

'You put it in a frame,' Jago said as he reached across and picked up the photograph.

'Yes.' Bradick tried to laugh as if this was all quite normal. 'I omitted that I knew her well. Didn't really have time to tell you the other night. She was an old and very dear friend.' His words were tinged with regret and obvious sadness. 'She never seemed to notice me.' Bradick's mood changed as he again found his smile. 'Perhaps I could cook you some breakfast? Was just about to eat myself.'

Bia nodded.

'Anything, quite starving, long night,' she said eagerly as she thought of eggs and bread. 'Could we eat a chicken? It doesn't have to be cooked.'

'Such a sense of humour,' Bradick answered, wondering if she was serious.

Bia realised how her words had sounded.

'Just a joke, toast would be fine,' she said as she wondered what eating raw meat would be like.

Bradick pointed to the table with his stubby finger and then took off his jacket and put it on the back of the chair. He quickly undid his cufflinks and rolled back his sleeves until his arms could be seen.

'Can't be messing up the uniform,' he said when he saw Jago staring at him. 'Look smart – feel good. That should be on a war poster. Never mind *Dig for Victory* and *Keep Calm, Carry On* . . . I say that we should all dress well. Very proud of the North Riding Moors Railway. We may only have five trains a week, but they shall be the best five trains that ever cruise this line.'

Jago wanted to laugh. Bradick looked like a turkey ready for the oven. His neck bulged over the collar of his tight shirt, the braces dug into his skin and several layers of stomach hung over the rim of his trousers. 'Eggs? Bacon? Sausage?' he enquired. 'I have had the great fortune that yesterday's train ran over a pig at Boggle Hole.'

'Yes!' they said together as Bradick spun on his heels and disappeared into the kitchen.

Jago held out the photograph for Bia to see.

'Proof,' he said. 'We are family.'

At any other time, she would have appreciated his words. But there, in the warmth and coziness of the Station Master's house, they seemed empty and vague.

'Family,' she echoed, as from the next room she heard a dull but distinct click.

The fire crackled warmly in the hearth, but she could feel no heat. Inside was a damp coldness, as if her heart had been taken from her. Even the smell of cooking turned her stomach, and yet the insatiable hunger ate her insides.

'You okay?' Jago asked after she had stared into the flames for several minutes.

'Fine,' she whispered just as Bradick came back into the room with a large breakfast tray stacked with toast and fried eggs and rashers of crisp bacon.

'What a blessing food is,' he snorted as he set the tray on the table and placed three plates in front of them. 'And when we have finished we shall have toast and tea.' He put a large white handkerchief down the front of his shirt to absorb the dribbles of the runniest egg anyone had ever cooked.

Jago began to eat hungrily.

'So how did you know Mary and Martha?'

'Schoolfriends, always together,' Bradick said. Bia heard other words. They were whispered in the same voice at the same time, as if two people spoke at once. 'They'll be here soon, just keep them talking – that's all I have to do.'

She looked at Jago, surprised he said nothing.

'Who's coming?' Bia asked.

'No one, dear lady. The only thing to arrive here will be the five-to-five for York via Scarborough.'

'But I thought you said . . .'

'She must have heard me,' the whisper said. 'Five minutes, that's what they said.'

'Five minutes?' Bia asked. 'What about five minutes?'

'What are you talking about, Bia?' Jago asked as he took her hand to break her staring at Bradick.

'He just said that they were coming in five minutes and all he had to do was keep us talking.'

'Ridiculous,' Bradick snorted. 'I can only speak with my tongue and then only one thing at a time.'

'It wasn't what you said. It was what you thought,' Bia answered, suddenly realising what was happening. She looked inside his mind. She could see everything. 'You work for Ezra Morgan – you called him by telephone. You rang Hagg House and Morgan answered. They had asked you to look out for us and keep us here. That's why you were ready and dressed. You have permission to break the curfew. You're the stationmaster.'

Jago looked at Bradick.

'Is this true?' he asked as he pulled the silver dagger from his pocket and held it towards him.

'Don't lie to me – don't even think of it,' Bia said as she snarled like a wolf.

'You have the mark. You're a Vampyre. I should have known, I have helped them for long enough.' Bradick laughed scornfully.

'And you tricked us?' Jago asked.

'They are coming for us, Jago. He has drugged the tea,' Bia said.

'And you would have drunk it and slept and all this would have been over and the Lyrid of Saturn completed,' Bradick said. 'Give yourself up, Jago. It is your destiny.'

'But you were so kind. I felt you were my friend,' Jago said.

'This is Whitby, Jago. The laws of the world matter little in this place,' Bradick said as he ran to the door and turned the key. 'Now you are going nowhere.'

'There's another door and it's not locked – through the

kitchen and into the ticket office. That's the way he has arranged for them to come,' Bia said as Bradick thought the
words.

'I will stop you leaving, Jago. You *have* to stay.' Bradick
lunged for Jago and grabbed his wrist and tried to twist the
knife from his grip.

'NO!' Bia screamed as rage boiled her blood.

She leapt to her feet and grabbed Bradick by the throat
and, with the strength of many men, she threw him to the
floor.

'Bia – how?' Jago said as he watched the stationmaster try
to get to his feet.

'Run, Jago!' she said as she picked the man up by his wrist
and swung him against the wall like a rag doll.

'Bia – no! Leave him,' Jago shouted as he tried to pull her
away.

'We have two minutes. I can hear their thoughts, they are
close by.'

Bradick struggled to break free from her grip. 'Kill her, Jago
– use the knife. It's the only thing that will stop her. *Please*,'
Bradick pleaded as Bia pushed him higher up the wall until
his feet dangled like those of a hanged man.

'LEAVE!' she growled as she opened her mouth and sunk
two sharp white fangs into Bradick's arm.

The man screamed. Jago ran through the kitchen and out
of the ticket office door just as the Daimler turned the corner
and sped towards the station. From inside the house, Jago
could hear Bradick screaming as he was crashed about the
room. The balm had been of little use. Biatra was transformed
into a Vampyre in search of blood.

He hesitated, wondering if he should go back for her. Bradick screamed in terror. He could hear Bia laugh as she picked him from the floor again. She smashed him against the platform door and, when it gave way, threw him onto the track.

'Jago,' she said as she saw his eyes stare in disbelief. 'It *is* me – Biatra . . .'

Bia wiped the blood from her mouth with the sleeve of her coat. Her red hair hung loosely across her shoulders. She looked like another woman.

'Bia,' was all he could say as he heard the door of the Daimler slam shut.

'Go! I will stop them from coming after you. Quickly!'

She watched as he ran off into the night, following the track to the south of the town and the bridge over the estuary.

'Biatra,' said Ezra Morgan as he stepped into the room from the front entrance of the ticket office. 'What have you been doing?'

'Stay back. I'll do the same to you,' she said as she tensed every muscle in her body.

'It'll do you no good. I too am just like you – even more so,' Morgan said. He walked towards her, followed by Rathbone. 'What have you done to Bradick?'

'He's outside,' she growled.

'I can still remember my first taste of blood. It is something you will never forget.' Morgan laughed. 'I did expect something more . . . *romantic* from you. I thought your first victim would have been Jago or Griffin or even Staxley. Not some fat old man.'

'You won't stop him. He'll track you down and kill you,' Bia snarled.

'Just like he did to my old friend, Draigorian?' Morgan asked. He wiped his hand on the lapel of his tweed suit and brushed back the long strand of hair that had fallen across his face.

'He asked him to kill him – said it would be a release,' Bia said.

'I can imagine he did. That is where Pippen and I differ. I quite like eternal life. It means I can delay facing the Creator and having to answer for everything I have ever done wrong.' Morgan gloated.

'Shall we go after the boy?' Rathbone asked.

'He has nowhere to go,' Morgan said as he stepped by Bia and looked outside at the body of Bradick that lay sprawled on the track. 'Bring me the spirit keeper from the Daimler. I know of another way of finding him.'

'Jago will come back and kill you,' Bia said as she stepped back away from Morgan.

'Here,' he said as he cast her a pair of woven bracelets. 'Wear these. They will control your urges. They are made of holly and willow wands. Take them off when you desire to eat.'

'Why?' Bia asked.

'You are now part of a family – there are thousands of us living secretly across the world. Some of the greatest people in history have belonged to our creed. I will ensure that you too will become one with us. And when we have Jago, you will be together again.'

'You would promise me that if I help you?' Bia asked. The thought of eternal life raced in her mind.

'Would you rather grow old and lose your beauty or stay just as you are now? It will soon be the Lyrid of Saturn. Be one with us, Biatra . . . You have such a beautiful name for a Vampyre.'

Bia thought for a moment and then slipped the wand bracelets onto her wrists. She shuddered as the venom instantly subsided.

'It's gone,' she said.

'And so it will,' Morgan answered slowly. 'Only until you take them from your wrist. Now, tell me one thing. Are you with us?'

He stared at Bia through eyes that had seen every dawn of the last eight hundred years. He looked neither worn nor weary. His chiselled face was tanned and weathered.

'Yes,' she answered. 'I am one with you. I know it is all I can be.'

'Very wise, very wise,' Morgan answered.

'Will Bradick become a Vampyre?' she asked.

'When you bite someone you have the choice to poison them or kill them. Looks like Bradick is dead to me,' Rathbone said as he came into the room carrying the pot jug with cork stopper that Bia had last seen at Hagg House.

'That's the poltergeist,' Bia said.

'Correct,' Morgan replied with an earnest look. 'When I release it from the spirit keeper, the poltergeist will find Jago and tell us where he is. As long as he carries the Book of Krakanu then we shall find him.'

Morgan slowly pulled the cork stopper from the jug until it popped open. A foul stench filled the room as dark vapours spewed from within.

Bia looked on as a small sylph-like creature crawled from within. It fell to the table like a wingless dragonfly. For the whole of a minute it trembled and shook as it looked around the room with its grotesque, gigantic eyes.

'Find the book,' Morgan ordered the creature, which suddenly exploded into minute orbs of light that blasted through the open door and into the dark of night. 'Find the book . . .'

[23]

The Grave of Tobias Grayling

IN THE HALF-LIGHT of the setting moon Jago ran as fast as he could along the railway line to the viaduct that crossed the estuary. He could see the red-brick walls loom out of the darkness and the silver lines of the steel track snake their way across the water. He slowed to a walk as he got closer. Sweat trickled down his back as he kept turning round to see if he was being followed. There was a nagging ache in his mind that he should not have left Bia at the station. Jago wanted to be with her, by her side, whatever the consequences. Now he knew she was captured, taken, and at the will of Ezra Morgan. For the first time he had no one to turn to, and he was struck by the penury and privation of his short life.

Jago turned and crossed the fields, keeping to the shadow of the hedges and making his way back to the town. All he could think of was finding Jack Henson and giving himself and the Cup of Garbova to Ezra Morgan in exchange for Bia's life. As he walked through the long autumn grass, Jago could hear a procession of military trucks heading towards the factory on the far side of the river.

He was soon at the junction of the main road into the

town. The street was empty, the curfew keeping all but a few to their beds. Jago knew that Morgan could travel when he desired; Draigorian must have seen to that. He began to wonder if there were other Vampyres in other towns. The idea came to him that they could have invaded every echelon of society. People were always going missing, especially in London. Nameless people who walked the streets with their belongings in old suitcases and slept under sacks in rat-filled doorways. No one cared if they disappeared.

He held the thought as he ran across the road to a small copse of trees next to a park. The long iron railings stretched around the corner and down the hill. Inside was what looked like a museum with a slanted lead roof and brick walls edged in white stone.

Without thinking, he climbed the fence and jumped into the undergrowth. Jago ignored the sign that said in bold red letters: *Whitby Literary and Philosophical Society – Keep Out*.

He wondered why a museum wouldn't want visitors. As he walked up the steps that ran under the trees he could hear voices by the large wooden doors under a stone portico. In the darkness he could see the red tip of a cigarette and make out the shape of two men guarding the door.

'Stand still,' came a voice from just a few feet behind him. 'Hands in the air.'

Jago did as the man said as he felt the muzzle of a rifle press in his back.

'I'm going home. I live at Streonshalgh Manor – the orphanage, Mrs Macarty,' he tried to say just before he was pushed forward.

'Didn't you read the signs?' the man asked in a brackish northern accent that Jago could hardly understand. 'Gates are locked so you must have jumped the fence.'

'Took a short cut, that's all,' he tried to protest as again he was pushed forward.

'Got one here,' the man shouted to the shadowy figures under the portico. 'Found him in the trees.'

Torchlight was shone in his face. Is brightness dazzled his eyes. Another man spoke.

'From the factory, lad?' he asked.

'Says he's one of Mrs Macarty's from Streonshalgh Manor,' the man behind him said as he jabbed the gun deeper into his back.

'Too old for that – just look at him.' The man's voice faded as he thought. 'Could be a spy,' he said, just above a whisper. 'You a spy?'

'I'm from London, an evacuee,' Jago argued.

'Better take you inside. Johnson?' He called to the man with the cigarette. 'Fancy getting the truth from this lad before we hand him over to the police?'

Johnson threw the cigarette to the floor and swaggered down the short flight of steps towards Jago. He unslung the rifle from his shoulder and cocked the bolt.

'Did anyone see you catch him?' he asked the man behind Jago.

'Why?' Jago asked as he saw the man's expression change and his eyes narrow. 'What are you going to do?'

The blow came swiftly and unseen. The rifle butt hit Jago in the stomach. He fell to the floor as the toecap of an army boot struck his shoulder and rolled him backwards.

'That's for talking,' the man said. 'Speak when spoken to or not at all. This is war and you could be a spy.'

'He's just a lad,' one of the others said.

'You've gone soft. Keep it shut or you'll get the same.' Jago felt the other man back away out of striking distance. The rifleman prodded Jago again. 'You a spy or what?'

'I'm an evacuee,' Jago insisted as he tried to get to his feet, only to be knocked down again.

'Who told you to get up?' the man asked. 'Better search him. Take him inside.'

Two hands gripped Jago by the scruff of his leather coat. He was lifted quickly from the floor. A hand smoothed against the pockets of his coat and felt the handle of the knife.

'What's this?' asked the man.

Jago knew they would take the knife. It was silver, precious and worthy of being stolen. He had to keep it at all costs. It was the only thing the voice in his head kept on saying.

The soldier with the rifle turned.

'Hiding something?' Johnson asked.

There was a sudden flurry of blue sparkling lights across the sky, then a rattling in the trees loud enough for everyone to hear. Jago looked up as the lights came together just in front of him. They seemed to settle on an empty flower urn that was set on a pillar by the steps to the museum.

'Johnson!' the man holding him said as he let go of Jago and pointed to the steps. 'What is . . .?'

Johnson turned as the other two men stepped away from Jago. On the ornamental urn sat a creature. It hung on to the side as if it were a gargoyle on a roof. Long bony fingers tipped with thick claws grew from stubby black hands.

'It's a g-g-ghost . . .' Johnson said as he took aim with the rifle. 'Look at it!'

Jago did not need to look. The creature was staring at him as he stood his ground whilst the two soldiers fled. It was half the size of a man, with a narrow face and large eyes like a gigantic insect's. It looked human in every way apart from its skin, which was stretched drum-tight across its bones. It rubbed the flesh on its white, etiolated face and looked about as if it had come from a world of darkness.

Johnson took a step back as he aimed his rifle. The shot rang out, breaking the silence of the night. Jago saw the creature wince, and then its face changed as if it were smiling. Johnson fired again and again until the rifle clicked and clicked.

'I have come for the book,' the creature said. 'Give it to me.'

Johnson staggered back as he heard the creature speak. Jago had heard its voice before, in the library of Hagg House. He knew this was the face of the poltergeist.

'I was given it by Draigorian. It is mine to keep,' Jago answered as he clutched the knife in his coat pocket.

'I decide who keeps the Book of Krakanu. It is in my gift,' said the poltergeist, bragging of its authority as it slid from the urn to the ground and straightened its lizard-like body.

Jago could hear Johnson choking and holding his throat. His rifle fell to the floor as he staggered down the steps, away from the beast. The man tried to scream but his voice was crushed to a whisper. In the distance Jago could hear police whistles and the frantic bell of a patrol car.

'This place will be full of people. They will see you,' Jago said.

286

'I don't care. You have the book.' The demon prowled around him like a roaring lion as if it looked for a chink in his defences.

'Take it from me,' Jago insisted as he looked at the poltergeist and wondered what world it had come from.

'Better if you just give it up,' it said.

Jago heard the patrol car coming closer, its brakes squealing as it took the narrow corners by the harbourside. He reached into his coat pocket. 'Very well,' he said as he stepped closer to the beast. 'If it is the book you want . . .'

Without warning he stabbed the poltergeist with the silver knife. The creature leapt back and squealed – the blade had caused it harm.

Jago ran towards the iron gate. Turning back he saw the poltergeist giving chase. But its legs were slow and sluggardly and could not keep pace with him. In a stride he had jumped as high as he could and with ease had vaulted the gate and was now on the street.

Across from the entrance to the park was a long terrace of fine Victorian houses. Jago crossed the road and ran in the shadow of their high garden walls overhung with ivy. He looked back to see the poltergeist slowly climbing the gate, the creature's bony fingers gripping the metal bars. Then it leapt to the ground and gained speed, sniffing the road like a dog to see where Jago had run.

Jago heard the patrol car racing towards the museum, and from an adjacent street came the clatter of running footsteps. A police whistle blew from an alleyway that entered the street ahead of Jago and two men in uniforms spilled onto the road. Their heavy torches lit the footpath.

The poltergeist didn't seem to be perturbed by their arrival. It hunched its shoulders and shuddered. Its large, insect-like eyes scanned the night. Jago knew it was looking for him. Then, it fixed its stare directly towards him where he hid, crouching under a long cover of ivy.

'This way,' shouted the copper as he pulled his companion by the shoulder and pointed down the street towards the harbour. 'It came from down there.'

The two men ran off, their hobnailed boots sparking on the cobbles. Jago took his eyes from the poltergeist. When he looked back, it was gone. All around the dark of night pressed in. He didn't want to run – the cover of the ivy protected him, surrounding him with its branches so he could not be seen.

Then Jago heard a rustling in the bushes above his head. It was as if a cat were hunting through the ivy branches in search of a lost bird. Jago held his breath and pressed himself against the cold wall.

The ivy strands hung down like the hair of a medusa as whatever was above Jago picked its way down through the brackish foliage. Then he could hear the wheezing of the creature. Instinctively Jago knew it was the poltergeist. He could feel its presence getting closer and closer. As he looked through the curtain of leaves, he became aware of two red eyes staring at him. The creature was hanging from the ivy, its head upside-down. Its wide, bug-like glare shone on his face and its tongue flickered snake-like as it tasted the air.

'Thought you'd get away? Quite a trick to stab me with a silver knife. Did Draigorian give that to you as well?' it asked as it stared at him, its parchment-skinned hands gripping to the ivy. 'I want the Book of Krakanu. Draigorian should never have let a breather take it.'

Jago felt the spine of the book, hidden in his jacket.

'You'll have to pull the book from my dead hands,' he said, wondering why such words had fallen from his lips.

The poltergeist gave a shy laugh.

'Pleasure beyond pleasure,' it said as it dropped to the ground and huddled like a small monkey by the side of the road. 'You are sought after by creatures far worse than me.'

'Vampyres?' Jago asked as he slid his hand onto the handle of the knife and made ready to strike.

'Demanding to know where you are,' it said. It stepped closer so it too was hidden in the overhang of the wall. 'Sent me – commanded me to find you. They will expect me to tell them where you are hiding.' The poltergeist changed its expression and tried to smile. It was something it had never done before. Somehow it could not quite make the correct face and all Jago could see was a grimacing, lopsided mouth full of teeth. The poltergeist hesitated as it tried to see if he still had the knife.

'Then you will have to do what they ask you,' Jago said as he stepped away from the beast.

'I thought a barter – a haggle or exchange – could be in order,' it answered glibly.

'What?' Jago asked.

'The book for your life,' replied the poltergeist. 'I am sure that it would be a fair exchange.'

'It has all I need to kill Strackan and heal my friend,' Jago said as he eyed the creature warily.

'The girl? She will be a Vampyre. They always do that.

Give her one night and she will never want to be human again. It is a life they cherish. Beauty and eternal life is hard to give up. As for killing Strackan, many have tried and failed. How do you think the Quartet came into being? They hunted Strackan and he took sanctuary. He lured them to that place, made out he was weak, dying, at his last. When they came for him he attacked and before they could even think, blood had been exchanged.'

'How do you know? Were you there?' Jago asked.

'I was once the hermit,' the poltergeist said proudly. 'I was a man more in service to Strackan than you could ever imagine. Now look at me. A demon, a poltergeist – a djinn without a lamp who guards the book that I wrote.'

'How?' Jago asked in a whisper as he looked for a way of escape.

'Every Vampyre always has a human assistant. I gave my life readily to Strackan. It was an easy thing for me to do. He would talk in his sleep and I would write down everything he said. At first I thought the stories of Krakanu were just his imaginings, but then I realised that they had a power and mystery of their own.' The poltergeist watched as Jago backed away from him. 'You can run, but I will find you. I have to have the book. I have given you a chance – now give it to me.'

The creature held out its hand pathetically as if it waited for charity. Its voice whined as it spoke, tired of the ages it had walked the world.

'Give it to you?' Jago asked as he clutched the knife. 'Give it to you?'

'Yes, yes,' it panted like a dog.

'Very well,' Jago answered as he snapped the knife from his pocket and stabbed the creature through its hand, pinning it to a large root of ivy that climbed the wall.

A burning scream went out through the night, shaking the branches of their hiding place.

'Again?' it squealed. It looked at its hand as Jago pulled the knife from the bone.

'When Strackan is dead and Biatra healed, then you can have the book. Until then it is mine.'

'Fool,' said the Poltergeist as it shook with anger, its skin flaking into tiny orbs of light as it slowly disintegrated. 'Don't make me . . .'

Gripping the knife, Jago ran from the cover of the ivy and into the street. Head down, he ran faster and faster towards the harbour. The place where he had been hiding exploded in a ball of fire. The flames chased him down the street like dragon tongues.

'He's there,' shouted one of the soldiers who had been searching for him. 'Stop!'

Three shots went above his head and ricocheted from the buildings beyond.

The poltergeist exploded into a bright ball of fire that sucked in all the light until there was not even a shadow of the red moon. Then, like a falling star, it was gone, leaving no trace but for the burning ivy bush that was now nothing more than a hundred charred branches and snarled roots.

Jago sped down the hill and soon he had reached the harbour. The swing bridge that crossed the narrowest part of the river was just closing. A group of workers, breaking the last hour of the curfew, stood impatiently by the gates, their eyes fixed at the large cloud of smoke that billowed up in to the air. A bell rang as the gates opened. More shots were fired in the park by the museum. No one appeared to care. The men walked across the bridge, heads down and staring at the ground. It was as if they were all too frightened to get involved or dare to ask what was happening in case they gave away a common secret.

Jago pulled up the collar of his coat and tagged along. One of the workers gave him a cursory glance but said nothing. On the steps of the marketplace, a man sat weaving a wicker fence. His gnarled fingers were as knotted as the willow in his hands as he sat in amongst the wood shavings from his whittling knife.

Jago walked on, his head down, as the town suddenly came to life around him. Doors opened or were slammed by the wind. Curtains were pulled to one side, careless of the diminishing black-out.

When he reached the 199 steps that led up from the town to the old church, Jago wanted to sleep. All he could think of was the night before. The face of Draigorian was uppermost in his mind. He could see the smile on the man's face as he had rested back in his bed and sighed. Jago had pulled the silver knife from his chest and put it back in his pocket without even looking at the blood.

'Three more . . . three more . . . and you weren't here to save them.' The ghost of Ebenezer Goode cackled from his prison by the thirteenth step. 'Taken last night from just by the gates to Streonshalgh House. I heard all about it from Jack Henson and saw it myself.'

Jago looked up. Ebenezer stood against the brightening sky

in his frock coat and tattered boots. His fingers were protruding from the torn gloves that hardly covered his bones.

'Three?' Jago asked. 'Who?'

'The boys – you must know them. Lined up, they were . . . as if they were waiting for it. Strackan came and took them one by one – him and the woman, Madame Trevellas.'

'Three boys? From the orphanage?' Jago said as he feared for Laurence and his brothers. 'Old or young?'

'Rough, if you ask me. Coarse-mannered, language of a navvie.' Ebenezer cackled. 'Willing, though. It was as if they wanted to be taken.'

'They allowed it to happen – for Strackan to bite them?' Jago said.

'Swapped blood – not just a bite. Hands fastened with cords and willow. Magic, if you ask me.'

Jago was beginning to understand why, but never saw the gathering of orbic lights. They clustered high on the church tower, coming together one by one, until they took the shape of the poltergeist.

'I need to find Jack Henson,' Jago told Ebenezer, who was by now following him along the path made of gravestones that ran the length of the churchyard.

'Tobias Grayling – that's who you need to see,' Ebenezer replied with a grunt. 'Get under him and mad Jack won't be far away.'

'Tobias Grayling – where does he live?' asked Jago with a shudder, as if the sudden cold chill of the air was a warning.

'Live? Live? Tobias Grayling doesn't live. He's deader than me.'

The whisperer pointed with his bony finger to a gravestone in the midst of a hundred other stones. 'There he be. Just like the rest. Dead . . .'

'But –' Jago tried to say before Ebenezer Goode snapped his finger.

'Find the stone and beneath is a stairway. That's where Jack Henson will be – down there – in the grave. He has a visitor.'

[24]

Dreams Long Dead

THE GRAVE OPENED EASILY. Ebenezer Goode had told Jago exactly how to trip the catch and stand back whilst the cantilever put in by the smugglers lifted the granite tomb slab. A row of wet stone steps covered in thick moss went down into the earth.

'Henson only used this one once,' Ebenezer said brightly as the stone slid back into place. 'It'll take you closer to him.'

'Thank you for helping me,' Jago answered the ghost as he reached the bottom step and turned the corner of the passageway.

'*You* have helped *me*, Jago Harker. When Strackan is dead I and my companions will be free to complete our lives and go on to death,' Ebenezer answered gladly as he walked up through the gravestone, his body disappearing. 'I look forward to slumber and the hope of paradise.'

When the ghost had gone Jago was alone in the candlelit corridor. 'But what am I supposed to do now?' he said to himself.

The passageway led on. Jago knew that Jack Henson would be somewhere in the narrow arched tunnels cut by the smugglers over hundreds of years. He walked deeper underground, holding out his hands and shuffling his feet in the pitch darkness. At the turn of every corner was a thick wax candle. As he went on, he could smell the peat fire and knew he was getting close to where Jack Henson would be.

Coming from the darkness, he could hear a voice. Jack Henson gabbled quickly as if he spoke to himself. Jago couldn't make out what was being said. Each sentence was short and crisp, ending with the inflection of a question. As he got to the end of the tunnel, he could see the light of the fire. To his right was the tunnel through which he and Bia had escaped. On the left was the doorway to the large room. He knew that Henson would be there, waiting.

Jago hesitated as he heard another voice.

'I have to find them. I need to explain,' Hugh Morgan said.

'I think he knows already. But believes you are just like your father,' Henson answered. 'I have been tracking them down all these years, waiting for a time such as this. They need to be stopped.'

'But it's my father, flesh and blood,' Hugh Morgan said quickly. 'I can't see him dead even if –'

'Even if he is a murderer, even if he would risk the life of your own son and turn him into a monster?' Henson asked.

There was a long silence as Hugh Morgan thought about the consequences of his answer.

Jago hid in the shadows of the doorway.

'I saved him from the bombing. I went to London to warn Martha, but didn't get there in time. I snatched the boy from the explosion and saved him from the blast,' Morgan said as Jago edged nearer the entrance.

'Then he doesn't know that it was you?' Henson asked as

he got from the chair, screeching the wooden legs across the floor.

Jago heard the clatter of a kettle as it was swung across the fire to boil.

'I couldn't resist seeing him. I had to know what he was like. My father had forbidden me to meet him. I couldn't believe he was just like me. I followed him to Whitby and even managed to speak to him in the carriage of the train.'

'Then you are in a dangerous dilemma, Hugh,' Henson said seriously. 'You have to decide between the life of your son or loyalty to your father.'

There was again a long silence. The tunnel blew a chill wind as if a grave had turned.

'Then it will have to end,' Morgan said.

'Your father plans to use the boy for an evil purpose. Strackan needs the blood of the line in order to live. It should have been your blood as the only heir. That is why your father allowed you to be with Martha Barnes. Once she was having your child then your blood was of no use. The Lyrid of Saturn is with us again. The comet has come and gone. On Friday night the sky will come alive with meteors and three stars will be in conjunction. At midnight Strackan will come to Hawks Moor and demand blood for blood.'

'How can we stop him?' Morgan asked.

'We can't. It can only be Jago. He is the heir of the blood line,' Henson said.

'But there is no time to prepare him – surely my father knows that?'

'He has been prepared. Julius Cresco saw to that. He had him drink from the Cup of Garbova on the night he came here – I am sure of that. I could see it in the lad's face,' Henson answered slowly.

'Cresco?'

'I remember hearing that he had been appointed as guardian to the boy. It was just after they had taken Martha to London,' Henson said. 'The Lyrid of Saturn has been planned for all this time. The boy grew up surrounded by Vampyres and he wasn't even aware.'

Listening to what the man said, Jago felt betrayed and angry. The one person he had loved in the whole world nearly as much as his mother had been Cresco. His face had smiled at him, he had looked after him whilst his mother worked. Now he knew the man was a cheat and a liar. He was a Vampyre just like Morgan and even Strackan. The love was nothing more than a trick to bring him to this place and this time.

'Madame Trevellas told my father that she had poisoned the girl,' Morgan answered.

'Biatra is fighting the venom. I saw her last night. But I think it will soon take her over. If she is bitten again then there will be no turning back for the girl. Are you sure Draigorian is dead?'

'I heard my father crying. When I went to the shrine, there he was with Rathbone. The painting of the Vampyre Quartet had changed. The face of Pippen Draigorian had appeared. My father said he had to be dead.'

'Then Jago found the book and the knife and was brave enough to kill him,' Henson answered.

'But Jago is too young to do such a thing. A boy of innocence,' Morgan said as he looked at the kettle steaming over the flames.

'Killing a Vampyre that wants to die is quite simple. Destroying Strackan will take cunning,' Henson replied as he pulled the kettle from the flames and poured the brew into the two cups on the table.

'I would kill him myself for what he has done to my family. Burn down his labyrinth and dig him from the ground where he hides from the light,' said Hugh Morgan.

'Then you have changed your mind? Your words have to be more than a shibboleth, a meaningless pronunciation. They have to have the resolve of your actions. You may even have to kill your father,' Henson said, and then spoke again: 'Have you heard enough, Jago? Lurking in darkness is not a good thing to do.'

Morgan sat up in his chair and turned. He looked nervous and uncomfortable.

'He's here?' he asked.

'Has been for some time. I felt the draught when the grave opened. I had Ebenezer Goode keep guard for him. 'Step into the light, Jago. Meet your father.'

Reluctantly, Jago left the darkness. He crossed the threshold of the room and stared at Hugh Morgan.

'Jago . . .' Morgan said nervously.

'So you knew all the time?' Jago asked. 'When you saw me on the riverbank, you knew it was me? It was you in the street when mother died? You were the man in the train?'

'Yes,' Morgan said as he looked to the floor.

'But you didn't tell me and let me wonder all this time and I thought you were a Vampyre like your father.'

'It is what we both are, Jago. It is our inheritance,' Morgan said. 'Thankfully we will live normal lives and not have to drink blood. Yet we are different from people. We know things.'

'What he's trying to say is that you have the senses of a Vampyre but not their need to kill,' Henson said.

'See things? Know things?' Jago asked.

'Speak to dead people,' Henson answered with a bemused shrug of his shoulders.

'And there are Vampyres everywhere?' Jago asked.

'In all walks of life, in all towns . . . and in every aspect of society. Some are quite benign and live their lives sapping the energy of those around them like a leech. Others have a lust for blood,' Henson answered. 'But,' he went on, 'the Vampyre Quartet are different. They were seeded by Strackan himself. The oldest creature from hell. That is why they have to be stopped.'

Jago looked at Morgan.

'And you – what are you?' he asked.

'I am your father and I loved your mother. If I had my way we would have been married. But I was too weak to stand up to them. They insisted she go away and I agreed. It was the worst decision of my life,' Morgan answered.

'Did I come to Hawks Moor when I was a child?' Jago asked, knowing he had seen the place before.

'Your mother ran away from London and brought you to me. Cresco soon found her and took you back. It was good to see you,' he said with regret, unable to look at Jago.

'This is all very good, but happy families will not rid us of the problem,' Henson said. 'Where is Biatra?'

'She was captured by Ezra Morgan and Rathbone. Before that, she had changed. She killed Bartholomew Bradick,'

Jago said reluctantly as he gripped his hands into tight fists. 'I should have stayed. I left her behind.'

'What could you have done? If the transformation is complete it would have done no good. Did you anoint her wounds with the balm?'

'Just as you said,' Jago answered 'But the venom was too strong.'

'There is more bad news,' Henson said as he went to the mantelpiece and took down a dried crow's claw and put it in his pocket. 'Things have taken a curious turn.'

'Staxley – Griffin – Lorken?' Jago asked.

'You know?' replied Henson.

'Only what Ebenezer Goode said when he saw me. He said that they had given themselves to Strackan at the gates of Streonshalgh Manor.'

'That is what it looked like. They made no fuss and offered their necks quite readily. But that is what I warned you of. Mrs Macarty is not to be trusted.'

'Was Madame Trevellas there also?' he asked.

'That is true,' Henson replied as he saw Morgan shiver with anger. 'Her name is not welcome in this place. She was the one who took my wife and my son forty years ago. I have a dream long dead that I shall stare into her face and have her repent.'

Jago saw Henson slip his hand back to his pocket. The man eyed him wildly as he stared and stared. Jago didn't know what was happening. He looked at Morgan, who by now had got up from the chair and was standing against the fireplace. His hand reached out for the metal poker that stood in the dusty rack.

301

'What do you want from me?' Jago asked as he wondered what they were going to do.

'Stay where you are, Jago – don't move!' Morgan said as he tightened his grip on the iron poker.

'But why?' Jago asked – and then he felt a cold, dry hand slip around his neck and grip it tightly.

'Thought you would get away with my book, did you?' the poltergeist asked as it squeezed his neck even harder with its iron-like fingers.

'This is not a place for you, Sagacious the Hermit,' Henson said.

'Nice to be known by my real name. I see we have a Morgan with us?' the creature asked. 'Just like all those years ago in my dwelling when your father came looking for Strackan with his foolish friends.'

'Leave the boy,' Morgan said as the poltergeist felt the pulse running through Jago's neck.

'Plenty of blood for the feast,' he said as he felt Jago's skin with his clawed finger. 'Just like your father.'

'He has nothing to do with this,' Morgan answered.

'So why did your father tell me to find him? He has my book. Killed Draigorian to get it. This lad is dangerous – out of control – he will kill us all . . .'

'Let him go!' Morgan said as he held tightly to the fire iron.

'Get the book from him and put it on the table,' the poltergeist said. 'When you have done that I will set him free. I will tell your father of what you have done – he shall not be pleased.'

Morgan cast a glance to Jack Henson, who gripped the

crow's claw in his hands. He had heard of the protector of the book and the legend that it was the hermit transfigured, but never expected it to be like this.

'I think we should do as Sagacious requests,' Henson said as he stepped towards them. 'We don't need the Book of Krakanu. It was written by a fool.'

'Fool? Fool?' Sagacious shouted. His body quivered relentlessly as if he were about to explode. 'I am no fool. The Book of Krakanu has every secret that is needed to destroy Vampyres.'

'But what about poltergeists – how can they be controlled?' Morgan asked.

Sagacious laughed.

'Do you think I can be tricked? This lad stabbed me twice and I should have known. Never thought he had it in him. A brave fool . . .'

'Who needs Sagacious to tell us how to control him? That magic is quite simple.' Henson went to the fire. 'Get the book from Jago and give it to the creature. We don't need his rambling words.'

Morgan held his grip tight on the iron fire rod as he heated the tip in the hot embers.

'Jago,' he said calmly. 'Put the book on the table.'

Jago slid his hand into the front of his leather coat and gripped the book. He hesitated before he threw it to the table in front of the fire.

'There,' he said. 'He can have it.'

He felt the grip of the creature loosen from his neck as it slithered by and took hold of the book. Jago wondered what evil could transform a man to this. How could the goodness of a life be corrupted beyond belief? He watched the serpentine spine of the poltergeist tremble in obvious delight.

'And you will tell Ezra Morgan where we are?' Henson asked the creature as it reached for the book.

'Of course,' it said as its hand touched the cover, the scar of the knife still visible in its tight skin.

Suddenly Morgan jumped forward. With one hand he thrust the burning poker into the table, piercing the creature's hand. The poltergeist was unable to move, frozen with pain. 'Who told you?' it screamed as the flesh bubbled and blistered.

'Burning iron holds a demon fast,' Henson said as Jago wondered what was happening. 'It can't move or change shape. It will stay just as it is.'

'Only until the iron is cold,' Sagacious gasped. 'That shall not be long . . .'

'You are so forgetful of the way in which you were transformed,' Henson answered as he took the crow's claw from his pocket and dropped it in the cup of hot liquid. 'You shall stay here until we say it is time for you to leave.'

'You can't keep me here. Strackan will search for me.'

'You are beneath the chancel of the church. Strackan does not have the power to enter such a place as this,' Morgan said as Jack Henson took the claw and tied it to a piece of red cord and looped it around the neck of the demon.

'Take it from me . . . take it from me,' Sagacious protested with shouts and screams as the claw suddenly gripped his parchment-like flesh. As he wailed in pain, the claw buried its talons into his skin as if the crow were still alive. It held him tightly, refusing to release its grip. The claw held the demon. It was as if an invisible bird gripped him so he could not move.

'How did you do that?' Jago asked as Sagacious slumped to the floor, unable to speak.

'Sagacious was once a monk at the abbey. He dabbled in the dark arts and found favour with Strackan and became his guardian. Anyone who deserts the path he once followed is a fool. He has reaped his reward. In this life there are secrets not even a demon such as he would understand.'

'And what of you? Are you man or Vampyre?' Jago asked Henson.

'He is a man who seeks to avenge the death of his family,' Morgan answered for him. He took a coil of holly rope from a meat hook by the fire and trussed the creature. 'Jack Henson brought me here and told me what my father had done to you. He is a friend.'

'Friend?' Jago asked. 'Am I supposed to trust you now?'

'I can't ask you to trust me. I know what you must feel.'

'You let my mother die in the street and you could have warned her,' Jago shouted.

'It would have been worse if she had come back here. That's what Cresco wanted her to do and that is why she sent you alone. I came to warn her – but was too late. Didn't you see her? She put her hands in the air and gave herself to death. It had to be that way. It had to be.'

'You saved me – but you could have saved her too. She loved you,' Jago screamed, his voice breaking with tears.

'The Lyrid of Saturn could not come if the mother of the child is still alive. Ask him what Trevellas did to his mother,' Henson said as he stood between them.

Jago turned. He was panting, out of breath, weary of the world and in need of sleep.

'What . . .?'

'She killed her. Lured her to the edge of the cliff and killed her. I saw it all but my father wouldn't believe me. He said she just fell and I had imagined it.' Morgan sobbed as he spoke.

'Lies, lies, to make me feel better,' Jago shouted as he ran at him, arms flailing and punching.

Morgan grabbed the boy and pulled him to his chest.

'No, Jago . . .no,' he said as they held each other in tears.

[25]

Possession

SAGACIOUS THE HERMIT struggled in a furious temper when Hugh Morgan dragged him across the floor and hung him from his wrists on the meat hook by the smouldering fire. The demon dangled like a long black ham. His feet were just inches from the stone tiles and the thick, wolf-like claws had chattered back and forth. Jago stared at the creature, unsure if it was looking more like a man and less like a demon. Something about his face appeared to be changing. The tight, parchment-like skin seemed to be smoother. The protruding bones had dulled and shrunk back in his face and the insect eyes had diminished in size. As he hung from the hook, his hands tightly tied by the willow wands, he moaned and complained bitterly.

'You go against nature. Let me out of this place. It is no good for me. Can't you feel it? Can't you feel it?' Sagacious asked over and over as he shuddered and slowly spun around and around, trying to break free of the bindings.

Hugh Morgan laughed and then looked at Jago as Jack Henson took an old box from a cupboard near to the fireplace.

'He can stay there.' Henson smirked. 'Hates it because of

307

the seeping power from the chancel. Place has been prayed in for over a thousand years. Bound to have an effect on such a thing as Sagacious.'

'You are a wicked man, Jack Henson. Evil and wicked,' Sagacious groaned through a spit-filled throat. 'When I get down from here I will make your life hell.'

'If what I have in mind works, Sagacious, that will be your future,' Henson replied as he put the box on the table and opened the stiff wooden lid. 'I think this may be of some use.'

Jago stood back as Henson lifted a small glass bottle from the box and placed it carefully on the table.

'What is it?' Jago asked as Henson took out the stopper from the silver-braced rim and cupped it in his hand as if it were very precious.

'This, Jago, is the sacrament bottle from the chancel. It is a thousand years old and was buried by Brother Caedmon just before he died. I found it only last year when the roof of a tunnel collapsed. Fortuitous that it is what is needed to rid us of Sagacious for ever.'

'What are you going to do to me? Magic? Sorcery?' Sagacious squealed as he stared at the bottle that glowed red in the light of the fire.

'I am going to leave you to the elements of this place. There is no magic more powerful than that which comes from above our heads. What will be the death of you shall be goodness and light – I don't need an abracadabra or any other meaningless incantation.'

'What will you do?' Jago asked as Hugh Morgan stepped to the door.

Henson picked the bottle from the table and crossed the dark room. He poured three drops of the liquid onto the creature's forehead and then placed the bottle beneath Sagacious. Then without saying a word, he stuffed the stopper in the creature's mouth.

'Wait and see,' Henson replied as Sagacious coughed and choked. 'It has started already.

Jago looked at the demon. The whole of the beast had changed. No longer was it a night creature with bulbous eyes and parchment skin. There before him was a man dressed in the robe of a monk. Strands of tonsured grey hair covered his face. Meek eyes, bewildered and confused, stared meagrely at Jago, pleading for mercy.

'It's a man,' Jago said without thinking, as the transformation was completed.

Sagacious mumbled, the top of the decanter stuck in his mouth.

'He was once a man who gave up all he had and now he shall be judged for his transgressions,' Henson said solemnly as he took Jago by the hand and led him to the door. 'This is not for us to witness. If I am correct, what shall take place is not for human eyes.'

Jago wanted to stay. He felt something deeply fascinating about the demise of the creature. It had tried to kill him, had been frightened away only by the light. Now it hung helplessly. A small man of slender frame with long, pointed fingers and beard-wisped chin. He looked pathetic and weak, human and helpless. Jago could see that in the process of transformation, Sagacious had begun to crumble as his flesh turned to sand. Like a broken hourglass, each particle began to drip, drip, drip into the bottle at his feet. Soon there was nothing left below his knees.

From all around a shimmering gold dust fell from the vaulted roof. The room brightened with an other-worldly light. It was then, for the first time, that Jago could see names carved into the rock: *Mashiyach – Shadday – Tsebaah – Elohiym*.

Each word was etched meticulously in the stone. They were repeated again and again until they formed intricate patterns that intertwined with each other, repeating the letters over the roof of the cave and going so high they could not be read. Around each word was a cartouche that, when they all came together, formed what looked like the shell of some large animal.

Henson tugged Jago again. 'We have to go – some things are not for the eyes of humankind,' Henson said as he looked at the words. 'You have seen something I have tried to keep secret for many years.'

Hugh Morgan disappeared into the shadow of the passageway.

'The light – the gold . . .' Jago said as he held out his hand and let the dust fall in his palm.

'Strange place – strange times,' Henson answered as he turned from him.

'What is it?' Jago asked.

'If I were to tell you, you would not believe me. The world has stared into its face for an eternity but refuses to believe.'

'What will happen to him?' Jago asked as he turned back to look at the pleading eyes of Sagacious.

'He was a wise man who took the way of a fool – a lesson to us all to stay away from the powers of hell, Jago,' Henson muttered as he walked away. Then he stopped and turned back to Jago, his mind changed. 'Perhaps you should see the consequences for yourself. We will be in the parlour of the cottage drinking tea. When you have seen enough, come and join us.'

Jago stepped back to the wall of the cavernous room and pressed himself against the cold rock. Before him, Sagacious squirmed as he hung from the meat hook. Inch by inch he disintegrated. Flesh turned to sand that was sucked by a swirling vortex into the glass decanter. With all his might, Jago had to stop himself from laughing. A fearful, cold sensation ran up his spine and stood up the hairs on the back of his neck. It was not out of humour that Jago shuddered, but out of fear at the sight of Sagacious disappearing. The hermit began to scream. The sound was muffled by the stopper wedged in his mouth.

Jago didn't hesitate. As the wasting of the hermit's body rose higher, he dashed to him and pulled the silver spigot from his mouth.

'Tell me,' Jago asked breathlessly, voicing the question that had tormented his mind through the night. 'What will happen to Biatra? The truth – before you die.'

The hermit gasped a breath of air. It was the first time in hundreds of years that he had felt the need and desire to breathe. He looked at Jago, his eyes sympathetic, his voice urgent.

'She will die, Jago. I have seen it so many times. They will promise her the world and then in thirty days she will be nothing but rotting bones.'

'How can I help her?' Jago asked.

311

'There is a place. A spring of water that falls over holy rocks. It is spoken of in the Book of Krakanu. Take her there, it is not far,' the hermit said as the wasting crept higher and higher until only his head and shoulders hung from the hook. 'Push her deep within the pool and hold her down until she cannot breathe. Make a penance for me. I once believed and in my grief it was snatched from me. Take my ashes and cast them into the pool that I may cross to the sun. Promise?'

'The pool – where is it?' Jago asked as the hermit broke into pieces and crumbled before him until all that hung from the hook were the willow wands.

'Follow the path to the wood, Jago,' the voice said as the last beads of dried flesh vanished into the decanter.

All was still. The light gave way to darkness. The carved words sank back into the stone so they could no longer be seen. Jago placed the spigot into the bottle. He lifted the decanter from the ground and placed it on the table. The glass had darkened and lost its sheen. It stood dull and opaque, as if it would never again be opened.

'Dust to dust,' Jack Henson said as he put a hand on Jago's shoulder. 'Did he tell you what you wanted to know?'

'It made no sense. I feel all is lost,' Jago answered as he held back the tears. 'I don't think I can do it. I have to find the pool by the waterfall.'

There came a sudden and dark realisation of what the future would bring. In his mind, Jago saw bombers flying low over the sea. A dark cloud swallowed them up as if they were sucked into the belly of a whale. The sky was on fire with a thousand falling stars. The whole town ran in panic as black vapours oozed from the factory and the siren wailed. Bia stood on the pinnacle of the abbey ruins, looking out to sea. Jago reached out for her and as their hands touched she fell to the field below.

'What can you see?' Henson asked. 'I can sense something.'

'It is beyond belief. Something to do with the factory,' he answered as the dream changed.

In the front his mind, Jago looked upon the labyrinth at Hawks Moor. The white gravel was bright under the verdant hedges. Bia stood in the centre. She was alone. He knew she was waiting. Henson shook him gently to wake him from the dream.

'Is there more?' he asked.

'It's Bia. She is in the labyrinth at Hawks Moor – she is waiting for someone to come,' Jago said as the dream left him. 'How can I see these things?'

'It is part of the curse,' Morgan said as he took his hand. 'Born of a Vampyre, and that is what we can see. We have to be rid of it, Jago. It is not how our lives should be.'

Jago looked at Henson.

'He is right. These are gifts we should not have. They are not for a mortal world,' Henson answered the unasked question.

'Then how?' he said simply.

'If you kill Strackan all this shall end,' Morgan said.

'Why me?'

'It has to be you. True blood follows true blood. That is what it is all about. There was once a man who gave himself in sacrifice. He shed his blood for others. Strackan has perverted that to his own ends.'

'I can't stop it. I have always had these dreams, known things before they happen,' Jago said.

'That is the way of those with Vampyre blood. But it is not how we should be,' Morgan answered. 'Strackan has to die and only one person can do that – you.'

'He is right, Jago,' Henson said. 'We all live and die by this night. I have been waiting for you since I heard the rumours of your life. I know you can do it.'

Jago looked at the gravedigger. It was just a quick glance, but it was all he needed.

'I am here to seek revenge for the death of your wife and child?' Jago asked as Henson looked uncomfortably to the floor. 'That is what this is for you?'

'I would be a liar if I said it was not so,' Henson replied as he rubbed his hands together. 'When something precious is taken from you, nothing will stop your revenge.'

'That is being human, Jago,' Morgan added. 'You can stop all this – only you. Biatra can be saved and no more people have to die. The Vampyre Quartet has to end.'

'Think of it, Jago. You could save the girl and avenge the death of so many people. You have all you need,' Henson said as he tapped the book with a long, dirt-stained finger.

Jago looked at the bottle of dust on the table. 'He wants his ashes scattering at the pool in the wood. I want to do that for him,' he said.

'It would be a good thing to do,' Morgan answered impatiently as he looked at his watch. 'Now I have to go back to Hawks Moor or my father will become suspicious.'

'I will bring Jago there tonight,' Henson answered. 'We shall stay here until it is time.'

314

'What shall I do?' Jago asked.

'We will study the Book of Krakanu and find out the secrets of how to kill Strackan,' Henson answered.

Morgan stood for a moment, looking at Jago. 'I have waited for this day for so long. Martha was the only person I have ever loved. I hope that you can find it in your heart to love me.'

Morgan turned and walked from the room. Jago listened to his footsteps as they echoed down the passageway towards the cottage.

'He has never been able to speak such words before. You have always been a distant hope in his heart,' Henson said. He lifted the bottle of ash from the table. 'A Vampyre thinks more in colours and feelings than in words. They sense the condition of the heart but cannot convey what they feel. That is why some of the world's greatest musicians and artists have been cursed in such a way.'

'So if he is half Vampyre, then I am one quarter?' Jago asked as Henson slipped the decanter back into the wooden box and ceremoniously closed the lid.

'That is why you have the precognition. A Vampyre always knows what the future will bring. That is what will make your task even more difficult. Ezra Morgan and even Strackan himself will know you are coming for them.'

'Then how shall I get near to them?' Jago asked. 'If they are expecting me then it will be impossible.'

Henson opened the Book of Krakanu and read the words. He flicked irritably through the pages as if he knew something was there that he couldn't find.

'Here – this is it,' he said after a while. 'That is all I need to know.' Henson closed the book. 'It would appear Sagacious has laughed at us from beyond the grave.'

'How?' Jago asked.

Henson opened the Book of Krakanu and showed Jago the blank pages. Each leaf was now empty of words; all the old parchment was bare.

'He *was* the book,' Henson said. 'When he died, the words died with him. All that kept them on the page was the life in his veins.'

'Then we don't know how to kill Strackan,' Jago said.

'Instinct, instinct . . .' Henson gabbled as he held the book up to the light and examined every page as if the writing were somehow hidden. 'It is all you have. It will have to be used wisely.'

'Instinct?' said Jago.

'Vampyres are hunters. They enjoy the chase more than the kill. Like a cat with a mouse, they play with their victims until they get bored; it is only then that they kill. It is as if they love fear more than the blood.' Henson looked at Jago and knew that he understood. 'You have *instinct* and so far it has served you well. Use it, boy, use it.'

Several minutes later, Jago stood outside the front door of Henson's cottage, a gas-mask bag slung over his shoulder. The day had misted. A sea fret had covered the land and chilled the sky. The low cloud hung to the stones until they dripped as if rain-washed. In his pocket he had the silver knife that he had used to kill Draigorian. Clutched in his hand was the pyx of myrrh balm.

'You have all you need,' Henson said as he held him tightly and then slowly let go. 'I will spread the rumour of your escape. They need you to be alive until tomorrow. This is the eve of the Lyrid of Saturn. Friday the thirteenth will soon be upon us. You know what to do.'

Jago looked at him for a moment and then checked the alley-way. Far away he could hear the morning noises of the town below. From the factory came a low-pitched hum, and in the harbour the steam cranes dragged fish boxes from the boats, their engines clattering with every lift. All was as it should be.

'Are you sure it will work?' Jago asked Henson, who slipped into the doorway of the cottage so he could not be seen.

'Just one telephone call and Delphine Macarty will do the rest,' Henson said as he patted Jago on the shoulder. 'All you have to do is use your instinct. Remember, Vampyres can read your mind and know what you are thinking.'

'And the Cup of Garbova?' Jago said as he looked at the hessian bag.

'They *must* have the Cup, make sure of it. Go to Hawks Moor on the Sentinel omnibus. It leaves in a quarter of an hour – should be plenty of time for you to get to the bridge. Once you are at the house do what they say. I will be there by nightfall. The Vampyre Quartet will do nothing until the night of Friday the thirteenth. That is when the Lyrid of Saturn will take place.'

Jago didn't look back. He heard the door slam and three bolts slide into place. All he could think of was Bia. His mind held the memory of her killing Bradick, throwing him through the door of the station house and onto the tracks. Now that it was daylight, it all seemed far away, in another place, another life.

Then he heard the sound. It echoed through the narrow brick walls of the alleyway that led from the cottage to the town. Footsteps, hard and brash, skipped along the cobbles like running dogs.

An incisive thought struck his mind like lightning as he listened to the pounding feet.

'STAXLEY – GRIFFIN – LORKEN,' Jago said, his voice a hiss.

[26]

Sarcophilus

JAGO KNEW HE HAD TO RUN. The voice in his head screamed for him to go as the footsteps pounded ever closer. They clattered on wet cobbles as they ran through the swirling mist that filled the empty alleyway like a flowing river.

Jago knew it was Staxley, he could sense his presence. There was something different, something even more menacing about the boy. It was tangible, palpable and present. It filled his mind as if Staxley knew where Jago was and what he was thinking. There was a sudden clattering of locks as bolts were slid and the door of the cottage opened quickly.

'Run, Jago, run!' Henson shouted as he leapt into the alleyway and held the ground so that no one would pass. 'They are on to you – they have been waiting.'

Jago turned. Henson stood in his long coat with a wooden staff in his hand. He stared into the mist. The footsteps came closer, echoing faster and faster like a stampede of horses. He saw the first boy turn the corner. It was Lorken. His hair was pushed back by the wind. Just behind was Griffin, his deep-set eyes cupped with dark rings. Staxley came last. He cantered at an arrogant pace as if he knew what was to come.

319

'Out of the way, Henson,' he shouted as Lorken drew near the man. 'This is business you will not understand.'

'Run, Jago!' Henson shouted again as he lifted his staff in readiness.

'Kill him!' Staxley screamed angrily as Lorken ran even faster with Griffin in pursuit.

Henson stood firm. Jago was frozen in his place. He wanted to fight.

'Get out of here – leave them to me,' Henson screamed as he raised the staff to strike at Lorken, who was now just feet away.

The blow was quick, decisive, like a crack of air. The staff snapped across Lorken's shoulder. Griffin leapt like a dog and smashed Henson to the ground.

'Get Jago,' Staxley hollered as they leapt the body of the old man, leaving him for dead.

Henson lay on the ground. His arm was twisted awkwardly. Lorken staggered a few steps as he recovered from the blow.

'He's mine,' Lorken screamed. 'My blood – for me . . .'

Jago knew what he meant. They were Vampyres.

He felt the knife in his pocket. It was strangely warm and stuck to his fingers as if it knew what it had to do. Jago ran. His heart pounded as he twisted in and out of the narrow lanes, each no wider than a shoulder's width and rising high above him. They stank of pot-slop and ran like a sewer. Far behind he could hear his pursuers braying like dogs as they cackled and mocked.

Staxley laughed as they gave chase. Griffin screamed, overcome with joy. Lorken kept his head down and teeth bared, ready to strike. Jago was far ahead. Lorken could see him clearly. His eyes had changed – they were dark rimmed, louche, and saw the world in a different way. He could taste Jago, smell the fear.

'Give in,' he shouted. 'I'll make it quick.'

Jago ran faster. His heart leapt in his throat as if it were about to explode. He knew he could not outpace them. Their feet hardly touched the stones; they ran as one, each knowing the mind of the others. Jago raced on. All he could think was to get to the street below.

Leaping down the flight of steps that turned from the alleyway to the donkey path, he stumbled. As he looked up at the high wall above him, he saw Griffin jump across to the low roof of a terraced house. The boy was now ahead of him. He clung to the shadows as he ran across the tiles. Several fell to the ground with a shattering clatter. Griffin laughed as he stared down at him.

'Give in, Jago. Be one with us. Think what we could do,' he said as he held tightly to a chimney pot.

'You've been tricked. In thirty days you will be dead,' Jago answered as he got up from the ground and ran.

'Ezra Morgan wants you – that is all – but we want you even more,' Griffin shouted as Jago disappeared through the covered archway under a house.

'The other side,' Staxley shouted as he leapt the steps and landed just a few feet behind Jago. 'I have him . . .'

Staxley sprinted, half running, half flying. Jago could feel him close on his heels. Ahead he could hear people in the street. It was fifteen yards to the marketplace. There on the steps of the town hall was the wise man who made wicker fences. As Jago ran towards him, he looked up.

Staxley reached out a hand. It touched the leather collar of Jago's coat. He snarled, his fanged teeth ready to bite.

'No!' said the man as he jumped to his feet and pushed the woven fence away from him.

Jago thought he was going to strike as the weaver came towards him, willow wisp in hand. He ducked as the blow swung over his head. It struck Staxley across the face. He fell, stunned.

The man looked at Jago as a woman screamed. 'Get away, get away!' he said to him as if he too could see inside Jago's mind. 'I will keep him here as long as I can.'

Staxley turned on the man and growled like a wild dog. The crowd around them fell silent.

'The boy, the boy,' shouted a woman as she saw his dog-like teeth and then gripped her child close to her. 'He's a Vampyre!'

Jago ran on. He could hear the steam bus as it stoked and boiled by the swing bridge. The street was crowded with screaming people. Looking back, he saw Staxley was surrounded, cornered against the doorway of a shop selling herbs and spices that hung in bags from a row of hooks. Market stalls littered the square under the clock tower. The noise of the harbour rose through the yards of the houses perched by the water.

The crowd surged forward. Jago pushed his way through, vanishing into their midst. He could hear Staxley growling as he snarled at his tormentors.

'Bind him,' shouted the weaver as people snatched the amulets from a stall. 'It's the only way.'

Jago hid in the entrance to an alley and looked at the crowd

322

that packed in, close and tight. No one approached Staxley. They kept him at arm's length and stopped him from running. He stared wildly, looking for a way to escape.

'I told you it was true,' shouted the man with the amulets. 'You never believed me – now look, a Vampyre here in the market!'

Staxley panted heavily, sweat dripping from his forehead. He looked each man eye to eye, face to face, as he searched for their weakness. Jago waited, hearing the steam bus gather pace up the short hill from the bridge to the corner of the street.

More people pressed towards the marketplace. Screams and shouts dragged them closer to the commotion. Jago looked up. Griffin stared down from the rooftop above him. Across the street, on the corner by the chip shop with the shuttered windows, stood Lorken. Jago was trapped.

'Vampyre!' Jago shouted as he leapt from the alley and pointed up to the roof. Griffin stood like a black crow on the pantiles.

The crowd of men surged back. It was as if every fist was raised towards Griffin. They screamed, shouted, threw cobbles at the rooftop. Lorken slipped into the shadows of a broken, bombed doorway as Griffin ran across the roof towards the cliff.

'Stop him!' shouted a man in a fawn suit and thick-rimmed glasses. 'To the church . . .'

Staxley seized the moment of discontent amongst the crowd. He leapt towards a lad of his own age and with one hand slashed him across the face. The boy screamed in agony as the crowd parted, no one willing to stop him. Staxley ran

323

back the way he had come and quickly vanished into the shadows. Five men gave chase. A man in sea-boots was just yards behind. The crowd split in two. Some pursued Staxley through the alleyway, the others skirted the rooftops towards the church steps in the hope of finding Griffin before he too escaped.

The steam bus slowed as it took the corner of the road and headed towards the factory. Jago could see the bright red eyes of Lorken glowing in the darkness of the deserted chip shop. By now the street had emptied, the crowds giving chase. Jago stepped closer to the broken doorway and looked inside. The floor was strewn with shattered plaster and broken glass. Lorken hid in the dark shadow out of sight.

'What do you want from me?' Jago asked the shadows. 'You working for Ezra Morgan?'

'That old fool?' Lorken asked. 'Staxley has been in his service, keeping an eye on things and waiting for you,' he whispered from the shadows. 'His kind will soon be long gone. Strackan wants a new servant. We are not here today, gone tomorrow. We exchanged blood – immortal, invisible . . .'

'You are still bonded to him,' Jago said.

'We will do what *we* want. There is a whole world out there. We'll be rich – famous – have what we desire, live for ever.' Lorken spewed the words excitedly. 'Be with us, Jago. You're special – that's why Strackan wants you for himself. Staxley got mad with that, but he can live with it.'

Jago could see Lorken shiver with anticipation. 'You going out on your own?' he asked.

'That's what Staxley has planned. He's not for following

anybody and certainly not that old creep Ezra Morgan. Soon as we have you, we'll be off. Staxley wants you dead. But I can talk him round. How about it?' Lorken asked through chattering teeth.

'What's wrong? You sick?' Jago said as Lorken began to shake.

'Can't control it,' he answered. 'Everything's changed. What you see – how it feels – everything.' Lorken shrugged. 'Colours are different. The whole world stinks and . . . and I can smell blood.'

Lorken stepped forward from the dark corner where he was hiding. His black gabardine was covered in plaster dust. The wet strands of his hair matted with the fine white powder. He looked different, older, other-worldly, grown up.

'Why did you do it?' Jago asked as Lorken shivered.

'Staxley has been going on about knowing a Vampyre. Griff said he didn't believe him and then when you went missing, this woman came to Streonshalgh Manor. Mrs Macarty took us to the gate and told us to do what she said. She sniffed our necks – all weird like, and then that was it. This old bloke came out of nowhere and smeared blood on our throats – told us we would live for ever and that we were Vampyres.'

'And Mrs Macarty knew?' he asked.

'She was to be our guardian. The old man arranged it all. Staxley wants to clear off. Go to London. After you're dead.'

'How did you know where I was?' Jago pressed him.

'That's where the old man said you would be. Told us to catch you and take you to Hawks Moor. Give you to Ezra Morgan. Then in the night, Staxley started to be different.

Said he could see into our heads. I thought of what you did for me. How I lied when you beat me. Stax saw it – knew the truth. Said it was worth killing you for.'

'So why should you see me live?' Jago replied as he stayed in the light.

'The Quartet, just what the old man said. There had to be four Vampyres – a Vampyre Quartet. He went on about Friday the thirteenth. It's our time now . . .'

'And he wants me to be one of them?' Jago asked.

'Sure . . . Thinks you are special, like. Said there was a curse on you and that he'd been waiting. I didn't listen; too busy looking at that woman. She told me her name. Said I could take care of her. Sibilia Trevellas – that's what she said.'

Lorken laughed to himself and then sighed. Jago had seen the look before, when Bia was in need of blood.

'You hungry?' Jago asked in a hushed voice.

'Starving,' he replied in a sigh. 'Never known a pain like it – bursts your guts.'

'Half the town's looking for Stax and the other half looking for Griffin and you're still hungry?' Jago asked as he stepped across the threshold.

'Never got the chance. Didn't want to bite Mrs Macarty. Thought of doing one of the Gladlings. Mrs M said that we should leave the kids for later and she had plans for them. Spoken for – that's what she said.' Lorken laughed as he looked at Jago and wondered if he dare ask. 'Any chance?'

Jago looked at him for a moment and then smiled. 'Blood?' he asked.

'Just enough – a drop – won't take an armful . . . Got to have something. Town will be looking out for me – they'll have recognised Griff and Staxley, they caused so much trouble. Too well known.'

Lorken nodded as he rubbed his hands expectantly and then ran his finger along the line of white teeth that filled his broad mouth. His lips reddened as they filled with blood.

Jago could see the fangs on either side. He stepped into the room. 'I suppose it would be all right,' he said as he undid his coat to the waist and then loosened his shirt.

Lorken stepped closer. Jago could hear him breathing excitedly. Clumsily, the boy reached out and touched Jago on the neck. His hand was cold. He stood in the place between life and death.

'Never done this before – are you sure?' he asked as he ran his fingers deeper into Jago's shirt, pushing back the cloth to reveal his skin.

'You need to be closer, Lorken. I need you near to me,' Jago said as he gripped Lorken by the arm to steady him in the embrace. Lorken pressed against him. Jago could feel the breath on his skin. He could smell the damp plaster of the bombed-out shop and looked at the debris scattered on the floor. 'Just do it,' he said softly as he felt the tip of Lorken's tongue touch his skin.

'Beautiful,' Lorken whispered as he allowed his new-formed fanged teeth to touch the flesh. 'Never thought it would be you. Better than Laurence Glad–'

His words stopped as he fell against Jago. It took all Jago's strength to hold Lorken on his feet as his body sagged. Jago wrapped his arms around the lad and cradled him slowly to the ground. He laid Lorken amongst the broken rafters that had fallen from the ceiling and the shattered pieces of glass

327

smashed from the mirror. Lorken looked up, his eyes flickering around the bombed-out room, and tried to speak.

'Sorry,' Jago muttered as he pulled the knife from Lorken's chest. 'It's the only way.'

'Please . . . please,' Lorken said as his eyes filled with tears. 'Don't leave me alone, it's dark, I'm frightened.'

Jago held his hand as an issue of blood trickled across the Vampyre's mouth.

'I'm here, Lorken. I will stay with you.'

'Don't want to die alone, not here,' he answered slowly, each word spoken on the wave of a fading breath. 'Thought it would be so easy. Did everything Stax ever said.'

'Forgive me . . . I had to,' Jago answered as he wiped the tears from his cheek.

'You helped me before and you've helped me now,' Lorken said softly. 'I know why.' Lorken stared at the smashed ceiling. He tried to smile. 'You're there,' he said as his eyes brightened. 'You never went away.'

As Jago turned, Lorken reached out a trembling hand as if to take hold of someone near to him.

'What can you see?' Jago asked.

Lorken said nothing. His eyes closed as he sighed a final breath. Jago slowly let go of him. Jago slid his fingers across Lorken's cheek and wiped away the blood. Looking down, he cleaned the blade before he slid the knife back into the pocket of his leather coat. 'It had to be this way,' Jago said as he took the silver jar from his pocket and anointed Lorken on the forehead with the balm. 'Go peacefully,' Jago said, not knowing why.

Suddenly, without warning, a hand grabbed Jago by the

wrist so he couldn't move. It squeezed the flesh until the bones began to break. Lorken opened his eyes. Jago looked deep within. He could see Staxley staring back at him.

'You killed him,' Staxley said as Lorken's mouth moved to the words.

'He had to die – he was a Vampyre,' Jago answered, wrestling to get the hand from him.

'We were like brothers,' Staxley said as Lorken grabbed Jago by the throat and squeezed until he started to choke.

Jago gasped for breath. The hands were stuck fast and could not be moved. One gripped his wrist and the other clung to his neck like the jaws of a wild animal.

'Let me go,' Jago coughed. The room began to fade as the blood drained from his face. 'Let me . . .'

The hand crushed his throat until he could not speak. Jago struggled for breath as the room grew black. A shadow darkened the entrance to the building. As he closed his eyes, Jago was aware of someone stepping through the door. Then he saw nothing as he slumped to the ground beside the writhing body of Lorken.

[27]

The Bookshop

A S HE AWOKE, Jago was aware of a man standing over him. The hem of a long wet coat brushed against his face.

'Lucky I found you. Two more minutes and you would have been dead.'

Jago looked up. It was Jack Henson. The body of Lorken was at his feet, the shaft of Henson's broken staff plunged through the gabardine and into his chest.

'What did he do?' Jago asked.

'That's the thing with Vampyres. It's as if they can see into each other's minds – especially if they were taken at the same time or had a connection in life. I heard the commotion. Whole town is looking for Staxley. Knowing him, he will be long gone.'

'How did you find me?'

'By chance, intuition . . . and then I heard the shouting from in here. That holly staff will hold him.' Henson looked at the twisted body that lay amongst the dirt. 'You're becoming quite an expert in all this,' he laughed. 'You were well chosen.'

'I want to go home,' Jago protested as he felt the swelling to his neck.

'Home? No such place for the likes of you. A fox may have its lair and a bird its resting place – but the Son of Man has nowhere to lay his head. That's what I was told and you better get used to it.'

Henson seemed cold, distant, uncaring. His face was ashen and lined, and his eyes flickered around the room.

'I would rather die.'

'And die you might,' Henson answered. 'Your life is unlike that of any man who has lived before. There is something in your blood that combines two worlds. You have to decide which road you will follow. Think of it, Jago. Ezra Morgan used your mother as a brood mare. He didn't want his own son to have your fate. That man interfered in the love of his son. He has to be stopped. One thing shared by every Vampyre is their obsession with themselves. That is their undoing – their weakest link.'

'And you want me to stop them?' Jago asked.

'This town has always feared the Vampyres. They snatched our children and women for hundreds of years. Not just in the time of the comet, but secretly, victim after victim. You, Jago, can stop all that.'

'Why didn't you do it?' he asked. 'It's you who really wants revenge.'

'I could have gone after them. Perhaps killed them one by one. But I could never come against Strackan. Finding him is one thing. Killing him another. It has to be you and only you. It started with a Morgan and will end with one. Finish the crusade. Sagacious is dead. Now kill the lord of them all.'

Jago got to his feet. The street outside was deserted.

'Everyone has gone,' he said as the sea fret rolled along the street like a grey carpet of mist.

'Chasing Staxley and Griffin. Vampyre-mad, and now they have them to chase. Trouble is, they wouldn't know what to do if they caught them.' Henson took hold of Lorken's feet and began to drag the body across the bombed-out shop to a back room. 'Poor lad, lamb to the slaughter. Never knew Lorken had it in him.'

'What will we do with the body?' Jago asked.

'I will come back when it's dark. Give him a proper burial. Wrap him in willow wands and bind him with holly.' Henson coughed as he wheezed his breath.

'You're not well,' Jago said.

'Took a beating trying to stop them. Not as young as I used to be.' Henson tried to laugh as he hid the body under a broken door. 'I remember your mother well. She was a bright girl – always had a sparkle in her eye. She'd be proud of you.'

'She'll never know,' Jago said sternly.

'If there's one thing all this should have taught you, it's that death is not the end of life – but just the beginning. We see through a dim glass as we stand on the earth. Have hope, Jago.'

Jago looked at Lorken. His frail body was covered in dirt, his hair smeared across his face. 'Hope?' he asked.

Henson shrugged and avoided an answer. He looked out of the broken doorway as the sky darkened.

'Don't like the look of that,' he said as thick black clouds rolled in from the sea. 'Just like night.'

Jago could sense the man was unsure what to do. 'Shall I still go to Hawks Moor?' he asked.

'Hawks Moor?' His mind had settled on a faraway thought. 'I fear our journey may end in this place.'

Then came a click of a pistol hammer as the chamber of a revolver turned, lifting the bullet into place.

Rathbone stepped in through the door. He was holding the revolver in one hand as he pushed Jago further inside.

'You are a hard man to find, Jack Henson,' said the woman who followed behind Rathbone. 'Thankfully you are so well known in this town that even the street sweeper knows where you are.'

'Sibilia Trevellas,' Henson answered. 'In all these years I have never seen your face.'

'That is the secret of a long life. Jago and I have already met.' The woman turned to him and held out her hand. 'It was a lucky blow, Jago. Your friend tasted so sweet and I hear from Rathbone that the venom did its job and she is now one of us.'

Trevellas looked at the body of Lorken.

'I killed him,' Henson said before she could speak.

'He was quite promising. I would have taken him as my own and trained him well. Death is death and there are plenty more boys – aren't there, Jago?' she said as she stroked the back of his hand. 'I hear, Mr Henson, that you are still angry after all these years about my taking your wife and child?'

'You murdered them,' Henson said as Rathbone pointed the gun at his head.

'The trouble is,' she said as she looked at him wearily, 'you have both become quite tiresome to us. Jago murdered Draigorian and you are a superstitious meddler.'

'Draigorian asked me to kill him,' Jago said.

'The only reason I didn't rip the veins from your neck is that Strackan insists on you being alive. Understand?' she snapped angrily. Trevellas looked at Rathbone. 'Can we take them to the car?'

'Not the boy. Not until it is safe,' he answered. 'I will take Henson to Hawks Moor and come back later.'

'Very well,' Trevellas mused. 'It will have to be the sanctuary. I take it that the Cup of Garbova is in that stupid bag? I have always known when it is near.'

Rathbone smiled and gestured with the gun for Henson to take the bag from Jago and step to the door.

'Where are you taking him?' Henson asked.

'The bookshop. I rent a room above. Have done for years. I thought you would have known that,' Trevellas answered as if she enjoyed the game. 'I watched you so often from the window that overlooked the street. I saw your anger and frustration. I even watched them lower the coffin into the grave.' She gave a short sigh as she smoothed her tight tweed jacket. 'What gave me the greatest pleasure was watching you suffer.'

'I will kill you,' Henson said. His simmering anger could be seen in his face.

'Don't think of running, Henson,' Rathbone said as he snapped iron cuffs onto his wrists. 'Just walk with me to the car. Madame Trevellas will look after Jago and bring him with her. Understand?'

Henson nodded and looked at Jago as if to tell him all would be well.

'They won't harm you, Jago. Not until the Lyrid of Saturn.'

'How amusing,' Trevellas scoffed as Henson was pushed

from the shop and into the street. 'That man has made it his life's work to destroy me and now his life is in my hands.'

'What will you do with him?' Jago asked.

'It is more, what will *we* do with him,' she answered. 'After tonight, Jago, you will be with us. It is what you were born for.'

Sibilia Trevellas said no more. Gripping Jago tightly by his arm, she led him from the bombed-out shop and into the empty street. He glanced as the Daimler car drove away. Henson looked out of the rear window and raised his cuffed hands to the glass. Trevellas scowled, her face like a wind-swept tundra.

'Why can't I go with him?' Jago asked as she pulled him close to her as if he were her companion.

'*Preparations*,' she replied, keeping her lips over her teeth.

The bell on the door of the bookshop jangled urgently as the door opened and Jago was pushed unobtrusively inside.

It smelt of coffee and was cosily warm. Jago had never seen such a place. High shelves were stacked with neat rows of books and by the counter a woman with corn-weaved hair smiled and knew not to speak to Trevellas. Jago hesitated; he looked up at the long, curved Georgian staircase that swept upwards under the high dome of the ceiling and circled a magnificent grand piano that looked out of place.

'Another student,' Trevellas muttered with a rustle of breath as if Jago was a labour to be endured. 'The desire to learn French is quite appealing.' She prodded Jago in the back as the woman by the counter looked the other way. 'Up the stairs and then we can start on your pronunciation.'

The woman at the counter smirked as she looked out of

the window. Jago climbed the staircase until he reached the landing and then turned towards a cream-painted door. To one side was a brass plaque and on it the words: *Madame Bryony – Teacher of French*.

He stopped at the door and waited for Trevellas to turn the handle. Once inside, he could see that the room was sparsely furnished. It had curtained windows and brightly polished floorboards. There was a chair by the open sash window. Silk netting blew gently and rustled on the floor. At one side of the room, by an iron grate, was a long sofa. There was nothing to say who used the room. It was, as she had said herself, a place to look through the glass and gloat upon those passing by whose life she had made a misery.

'I want to go,' Jago said like a demanding child. He leant against the thin wall and pressed his fingers into the damp plaster.

'You still don't understand, do you?' she asked him as she turned the key to the door and slid the brass bolt. Jago felt the wall move slightly. 'This is not a game that can be finished when you want it, Jago. It has to be completed. We have waited a lifetime for this moment and it is finally here.'

'What were you like before? Before Strackan bit you?'

Sibilia Trevellas leant against the door and eyed him from head to foot. 'Weak,' she answered. 'Weak and frail – just like you.'

'That woman knew you don't speak French or teach it,' Jago said. 'You could see it in her face.'

'She most probably does. I have never felt the need to look inside her mind. Probably not much going on other than the price of bread and what man she will seek out to ruin his life. Yet she has the good sense never to mention it to anyone.' Trevellas crossed the room to the bay window and sat on a fine Italian upholstered chair. 'Ezra Morgan has told me to prepare you for tonight, the Lyrid of Saturn.'

'Tonight?' he asked.

'Just after midnight,' she said, surprised that he didn't know. 'That's when your work will begin. It is the dawn of a new Quartet. Mrs Macarty has done a good job in selecting you all.'

'Lorken is dead,' Jago said.

'There is always Griffin and Staxley and of course your friend Biatra,' Trevellas answered as she looked at the gathering crowd in the marketplace. 'I can see that they must have escaped. Their heads are not dangling on poles.' She laughed, amused by her own joke. 'I remember in the time of the Napoleonic war, when a French ship was wrecked on the beach at Hartlepool. The only survivor was a gorilla that was found on the beach dressed in the uniform of an officer. The magistrate, being a superstitious sort of man, ordered it hanged as a spy.' Trevellas laughed again. 'Think what they would do if they knew who *you* really were . . .'

'Or you,' Jago said as he contemplated jumping through the glass of the window to the street below.

'I wouldn't do that if I were you,' Trevellas answered, knowing his mind. 'It would make such a mess and I would have to say that you were a spy. If you survived the fall, they would shoot you.'

'And all would be lost?' Jago added as he tried to rid his mind of any thoughts of escape. 'How long must we wait?'

'Until the breathers get bored of their sport and go home as night falls. The two boys should be far away. They were told that if they didn't find you they should go to Hawks Moor. Staxley knows the way. He is a fine young man. Shame it was not he who was born from that strumpet of a woman who was your mother. Is it true she is dead?'

Jago didn't reply. He looked out of the window at the thick dark cloud that covered the sky and the sea mist that began to fill the street to the rooftops of the houses.

'I can imagine she would have been hard to live with,' Trevellas went on. 'Anyone in love with Hugh Morgan must be quite difficult.'

'Why does he allow all this to happen?' Jago asked the question that had troubled him for so long.

'He is like you. Hugh is a man with a mind in two worlds. There is the knowledge that what he does is wrong and then the excitement that life can be different.'

'Is he immortal?'

'That is the curse of being born from a brood of Vampyres. Unless he takes Strackan's blood he will die very slowly and painfully. The same will happen to you. Sadly, Hugh Morgan had his chance.' Trevellas sat cold-faced and stared at him. It was as if she looked deep beneath his skin to what lay beneath.

'Did you kill his mother?' he asked.

'Of course I did – what a stupid thing to ask. She had served her purpose and Ezra wanted rid of her but didn't want to do it himself. He sent a postcard to me in Edinburgh asking me to return. I was quite surprised that she even tried to fight. Shame she had to die, I really liked her.'

Madame Trevellas smoothed the tweed of her long skirt and tapped the heels of her brown boots against the wooden floorboards. It looked as if she had done this a thousand times before as she perched in the chair by the window and looked at the crowds of people who were now shadows in the fog.

'Do Vampyres betray everyone they meet?' Jago asked.

'Jago, you have been betrayed by *everyone* in your life. Julius Cresco, your mother, Hugh Morgan, and I hear that even Bradick pretended to befriend you. Life is betrayal at the best of times. It is something not to worry yourself about. Tonight, everything shall change.'

Jago walked towards her and smiled. 'If I give in to Strackan, what will happen?'

Trevellas rested against the open window, her arms on the ledge as she stared at the street below. 'You will have a life that you could never imagine. Kings and princes will fall at your feet. You shall have time to study, create music and do great things.'

'How often will I have to kill?' Jago fought to hide his thoughts and filled his mind with words.

'We take blood at every solstice, equinox and full moon. I know Draigorian drank only that which Clinas gave to him. He never had a heart for it.' She smiled. 'I am glad to see you have changed your mind.'

'Look,' he said pointing into the fog and the vague shadow of a man walking by. 'That is what I wanted in life. Just to be . . .'

Sibilia Trevellas laughed. At last, she thought, Jago was thinking like a Vampyre.

'Like him?' she asked as she pointed out of the window.

The woman had no time to react. Jago slammed down the wooden sash as hard as he could. It fell like a guillotine and crushed her bones against the wood, trapping her wrists. Trevellas screamed as she was pinned by the window. It shook the glass. Jago kicked the chair from beneath her, and as she fell to the floor he ran.

In an instant she was free and with one hand she gripped his leg. Jago turned and lashed out. He ran again, only to be caught. Jago searched for the knife.

'Get back,' he shouted, holding out the dagger as Trevellas dragged him back.

At once she let go and cowered like a dog. Jago took the key from her, slid the bolt on the door and turned the lock.

'You'll never get away,' she said as she stamped on the floor. Jago locked the door, keeping Trevellas inside the room.

At the sound of running footsteps on the stairs, Jago turned. There, coming towards him, was the bookseller. He realised it was the girl he had seen before, the one attacked by Strackan. In her hand was a short sword.

'Don't be stupid,' he said as she drew back her arm to strike.

The woman lashed at him. Jago jumped back. The sword pierced the door and she rammed it in to the hilt.

Taking a book from the shelf he hit the woman as hard as he could. She fell back. Jago ran towards her just as she got to her feet, hissing like a cat. He pushed her out of the way but she grabbed his coat. Jago twisted and turned as she scratched at his face, pulling him closer and closer towards her.

Then the woman reached for the sword and began to pull

it from the door. The blade juddered the wood, just as the door was being forced from the inside. Jago hit her again and again. The woman fell to the floor. He leant against the wall, out of breath, blood trickling down his cheek.

Plaster smashed around him as two hands burst through the wall and gripped his face.

'Get him!' shouted Trevellas to the bookseller, who was now getting to her feet.

Jago took the silver knife and with all his strength he slashed at her hands. Trevellas screamed and he broke free from her grip. The bookseller backed off and he held her at bay with the knife.

'Stay back – don't follow me,' Jago said as she stared at him red-eyed. 'Just stay back.'

Madame Trevellas punched holes in the lath and plaster wall. Dust and spits of debris shot into the air. They followed him along the corridor as Jago edged towards the stairs. He could see her looking through the jagged gaps in the plaster, screaming as he got away.

'Don't let him go, stop him!' the Vampyre screeched as she reached through the wall in a vain attempt to catch him.

Jago got to the stairs, the bookseller woman stepping closer with every pace. He could see the three cuts upon her neck where Strackan had tried to kill her.

'Stay back!' Jago shouted. He edged down the steps, keeping her in view as she came at him with the sword.

'Stop him, Cressida,' Trevellas shouted from the locked room. 'Do what you have to – but keep him alive.'

The woman lunged at Jago. He grabbed her hand and twisted the sword from her grip. It slid between the rails and slammed into the lid of the piano. She stumbled and fell over the wooden banister to the floor below. Jago looked down at the crumpled, lifeless body that lay broken-backed over the grand piano pierced by the sword.

The Brig

IN THE MARKETPLACE, all was dark. The morning light had gone; thick fog and black cloud covered the sun. It was like a winter night. Dark shadows clung to the walls and the strange shapes of buildings loomed up from the cobbles.

Jago kept his head down and stooped as he walked. He crept between the stone arches of the portico under the town hall and crossed the square. A gathering of men circled the stall that sold amulets. He could hear the vendor shouting for trade and pontificating over the efficacy of each stone and wooden cross.

'Seen it – we've seen it with our own eyes, Vampyres here in Whitby,' the man said again and again. 'All of you need to be protected, to sleep safely in your beds, my amulets and pieces of the true cross will do that for you and at a price you can afford.'

No one seemed to doubt what he said. The crowd surrounded him with frantic hands, holding out brown ten-bob notes. Every hope was to exchange them for some relic or stone that would ward off the Vampyres that others said they had seen marauding through the town. It was as if no one had seen them with their own eyes – they had just heard from a friend, neighbour or passer-by. One thing was the same in all the stories – the Vampyres were from Streonshalgh Manor, and that was without doubt.

Jago listened to the moaning as he walked by, hoping they would give him no attention.

'Saw it myself, saw it I did,' said one old woman in a shawl and sea-boots. 'Teeth like a dog, skin the colour of death. If that wasn't a Vampyre then I will eat my own foot.'

She eyed Jago warily as he walked by. He was covered in plaster dust and blood trickled down the side of his head. It was hard for him to keep his eyes staring at the cobbles. He wanted to turn and see her superstition for himself.

'Last chance! Last chance before nightfall,' the man on the stall shouted as he exchanged the talismans for crumpled notes that he gripped in his fingers. 'Amulets – potions – Vampyre protection . . .'

Jago walked towards the entrance to the street that led along the harbour side from the marketplace. He knew the woman was still watching him; it was as if she knew who and what he was.

'Boy!' she shouted just as he reached the corner and the dark shadow of the narrow street. 'You one of them from the Manor?'

Jago didn't turn. He swallowed hard and kept his head down as he looked to the ground and tried to increase his pace without her seeing.

'You, boy! You one of them from Streonshalgh?' she asked again, with more accusation than question. Jago ran. 'There's one!' she shouted and raised the alarm. 'Streonshalgh boy – running down Sandgate.'

As one, the crowd turned. They caught the fleeting glimpse of his coat tail as he ran into the mist that filled the street. Jago heard the shouts as he pressed on, knowing they would come after him.

The first shout of Vampyre came quickly. It echoed around him like the call of a hunter. The crowd screamed in odious delight and those protected with amulets gave chase. Their sea-boots and hobnails clattered on the stone as they rushed to seize him.

Jago did not know where to run. He wanted to stop, give himself up. They could inspect him, check the teeth in his mouth and see he was not a Vampyre. But, he knew they would not wait. He was the stranger, the outsider, the enemy in their midst, the boy from London. They would catch him and kill him, so he must not be caught.

The screams grew louder as the sound of the hunt spread from street to street. It overtook Jago as the warning spread and the calls of his pursuers ran ahead of him. People turned and looked, stared at his bloodstained face, saw his fear. Women screamed as they stepped from the curious little shops that sold vagabond clothes and ladies' gloves. Jago sprinted on, turning towards the bridge just as the gates swung shut. He could feel the whirring of the gears beneath his feet. The road juddered and shook as the swing bridge started to open. The crowd pressed on, spilling from the narrow lane onto the road. They screamed as they caught sight of him in the mist.

'That's him! Vampyre boy!' shouted one man ahead of the crowd.

Those waiting by the gates turned. A soldier made a grab for Jago and held tight to his jacket.

'I'm not a Vampyre,' Jago screamed in protest as he gripped the man and threw him to the ground with incredible force.

'Look what he did,' an old man shouted as the soldier slid across the road. 'Vampyre!'

Jago leapt the gate and ran onto the swing bridge. It opened quickly, the gap between each side widening by the second. Already the pursuers were nearly upon him. He ran on, checking the distance he would have to leap.

'I'll stop him,' Jago heard as he ran faster. There was a click of a rifle bolt and then a shot. The bullet whistled passed his head and smashed the glass of a disused lamp post.

The bridge opened wider as a fishing boat came towards it. Jago ran on as the crowd pushed open the gate to follow on.

'Got him now!' shouted a man, 'He'll never make it . . .'

Jago ran faster. He could see the expanse of water below as the bridge moved beneath his feet, and he thought of Bia and his mother as he steeled himself. With all his strength he leapt from the bridge and flew. It seemed like minutes passed in slow motion. The wind blew back the hair from his blood-stained face and the sound of the baying crowd dimmed as blood pumped through his head. Jago looked back at the crowd and saw the soldier aim another shot. The explosion ripped towards him as again the bullet missed his face. Jago realised he was falling. The edge of the bridge came closer – he knew he had to make it.

Suddenly he hit the ground. The steel lip of the bridge caught his leg as he tumbled head over heels.

'Stop him!' shouted a soldier to the guard by the work hut.

A man ran towards him with a bludgeon in his hand. Jago

couldn't escape. The blow was swift, painful and sharp. He fell to the ground clutching his knee. A fishing net was cast over him as the man hit him again.

'Leave him!' shouted a constable as he ran towards Jago, helmet in hand. 'He's to be arrested.'

'You don't arrest Vampyres, you kill them,' the man protested as he took another swing, crashing the bludgeon onto the ground near Jago's head.

'Leave him,' the constable insisted as he tore the net from Jago and pulled him to his feet. He stared at Jago, examining every inch of his face. 'This lad isn't a Vampyre, you fool. He's just a boy and he's injured.'

The constable brushed the strands of hair back from Jago's face. There was a long cut at the side of his forehead. The man tried to smile as a jeering crowd gathered.

'Leave him for us,' the soldier shouted from the other side of the river. 'He nearly killed me.'

'He's under arrest. If you want to complain, go to the courthouse,' said the constable quickly as he snapped a handcuff on Jago's wrist. 'Do what I tell you,' he whispered. 'They'll kill you, given half the chance.'

'I'm not a Vampyre,' Jago insisted as the man dragged him from the bridge. 'I want to go home, to London . . .'

'You'll have to come with me,' the officer said as he pushed his way through the gathered crowd that lunged at Jago yet seemed fearful to get too close. 'These people are superstitious. They'll only be satisfied if they hang you.'

'I've done nothing wrong,' Jago protested.

'You're from Streonshalgh Manor. The whole town is saying they saw a Vampyre and he was from that place. They don't care if they are right or wrong, they just want a body on the end of a rope.'

Jago was dragged through the street. His wrist was burning from the tight metal band that held him to the man. The crowd followed at a distance, not daring to come too close. They shouted and snarled and threw discarded fish heads that were stacked in boxes on the quayside.

'Kill him! Pull out his teeth and then we'll see if he can bite,' shouted a woman who vanished into the swirling mist.

'Keep walking . . . faster,' the officer said as he held Jago closer. 'If they want to make a move it will have to be soon. The courthouse is just down the street.'

The crowd pressed nearer. Shabby men with brown teeth and lathered faces spilled out of the doorway of the Angel Inn and stood leering in the street, beer in hand.

'I'm innocent,' Jago said as they spat at him and threw the dregs at his feet.

'They don't care – stay close – don't look at them,' the officer said as he twisted the cuff and eyed the gang of men with shaved heads and fishermen's scarves. 'Only twenty yards . . .'

'Get the lad,' one of them shouted as a hail of stinking beer glasses landed in the street. 'String him!'

'Run!' shouted the constable as he dragged Jago towards the courthouse. Jago sprinted, running as fast as he could. Two barefoot lads, just his own age, lashed out at him with fists.

'Which way?' Jago screamed as the constable stumbled, twisting the handcuff before he let go.

'Straight on, straight on,' he shouted urgently. Jago saw

348

him draw a short wooden staff from an inside pocket of his serge trousers. 'Back!' he shouted at the crowd as he hit out with the staff. 'Keep back.'

Jago could tell the man was frightened; his eyes spoke more than his words.

'Give us the lad,' the fishermen shouted as they chased on. 'Let us do what's right.'

Jago knew what they meant – he could smell it on their breath and hear it in their voices. In ten paces they were on the steps of the courthouse. It was an old building with pillars on either side of a large oak door. A blue lamp swung over the entrance and lit the fog. They ran the several steps. Jago grabbed the handle as the officer beat back the gang with his staff. Jago was frightened and out of breath. It was as if he was surrounded by a pack of wolves.

'Get inside, get inside!' the officer shouted as the mob surged forward.

The door slammed behind them. The entrance hall was icy cold. It echoed with the sound of shouting outside. Chequerboard tiles disappeared into the darkness of a long corridor with rooms off both sides. Each was labelled with a wooden plaque above the door that stuck out like a dull road sign. The constable slid two brass bolts across the door and dropped an oak beam into a slot at either side. The thick mist crept underneath, surrounding his feet like bonfire smoke.

In front of Jago was a tall oak counter topped in black leather and etched in gold. It looked as if no one had ever dared to touch it. The wood was brightly lacquered and the leather polished. To one side was a small brass bell.

'What will you do with me?' Jago asked.

'You better not be a Vampyre – not after all that I have done for you,' the constable said as he brushed the spittle from the sleeves of his black coat. 'That lot would have killed you.'

The taunts grew louder in the street. Furious voices shouted raucously. Jago could see from the officer's eyes that they were not out of danger.

'What is this place?' Jago dared ask.

'The police station,' he replied abruptly. 'There are cells below. You'll wait down there.'

'Don't I need to be put on trial or something?' Jago asked, having no idea how the law worked.

The man laughed. 'What's your name?' he asked.

Jago answered softly as he wiped the blood from his face.

'Well, Jago Harker, I am the law in this town. All the others spent the night chasing a ghost around the town – army and everyone . . . But I decide who goes or stays. '

'And there is only you against all those men outside?' Jago asked suddenly realising the drastic jeopardy of the situation. 'Who will stop them?'

The man laughed. 'Well, you might well ask . . .' He took out the keys and released the steel bracelet from Jago's wrist. 'You're not thinking of trying to escape?' Jago shook his head as tears mixed with the blood on his cheek. 'It'll be all right. They won't get you. I'll telephone the battalion. They'll come and disperse the crowd.' His words were kind and made Jago sob even more. 'Come downstairs, it'll be safe in the jail.'

He led Jago down a flight of tiled stairs. The air grew colder and was too chilled to breath. At the bottom, in a corridor lit

350

only by a meagre light bulb, was a green steel door, its shutter smeared with spilt porridge.

'This it?' asked Jago, his voice echoing around the cold vault with its white ceiling and tiled walls.

'Paradise Hotel,' the man replied sarcastically. 'Safest place in Whitby,' he shrugged.

'You going to lock me in?' Jago asked as the man pushed him inside and began to close the door.

'That's the idea,' he answered with a bemused smile. 'I could always let that lot out there have a go at you?'

Jago shook his head. He had nowhere to go and no one to turn to. In the absence of all benevolence, this shabby policeman with his frayed trousers and oversized jacket was the only kindness he knew.

'Very well,' Jago answered as the door closed with an irritating squeal.

The hatch slid open and the man looked inside. He tried to be reassuring. 'It will be all right,' he said with a cough. 'I'll go and talk to them – say I'm awaiting the doctor to examine you and prove you aren't a Vampyre.'

'I need to go – catching the train to London,' Jago said hoping his bloodstained face would sway the man.

'No trains,' he replied. 'Problem at the station.'

The man slid the hatch shut. Jago knew what he was talking about. Bradick was dead. They would have found him by now. Soon the news of Jago's capture would be around the town. Sibilia Trevellas would find out where he was. With Henson captured, Jago felt he had no hope.

He sat in the cold damp cell and listened to the sound of water lapping against the walls outside. Jago could still hear the faint shouts and taunts of the mob. They had gathered around the door and screamed for his release. He knew they would hang him as a Vampyre. In a way, it amused him. He wondered how surprised they would be to find out that it was people in their midst who were the real Vampyres. But he knew he should not be surprised that he, a stranger, should stand accused.

Jago was alone with his thoughts for several hours. He sat in his leather coat, a blanket over his feet, and watched a cockroach circle the floor in the cold light of the cell. In the hurry of his arrest, Jago had not been searched. The knife felt snug in his pocket. He pushed the blade until it snapped through the lining and he slid it into the hem of his coat so it could not be found. Jago wrapped the pyx in his handkerchief and hid it in the lining near to the dagger.

Some time later, after he had counted every tile in the cell and wondered who had put them in place, he heard footsteps. They were lighter and faster than the constable's and came down the steps to the cell quite urgently. There was a jangle of metal as a chain clanged against the door. A key turned the lock and as it opened, the loud click echoed through the room.

The door grated against the tiles. Jago sat back, pressing himself against the wall in dire expectation.

'I'm surprised you never told me that you were in the care of Mr Morgan,' the constable said as he pushed the door open until it hit the wall. 'It would have been so much simpler.'

The man stepped aside and gestured with his hand to the tall shadow behind him.

'Jago, Jago . . . We have been worried about you,' Ezra Morgan said like a snake as he stepped inside and pushed the officer out of the way. 'I have been searching the town trying to find you.'

'See,' said the constable. 'You weren't alone after all. And all that talk of going to London.'

'Don't let him take me,' Jago said. 'He's the Vampyre.'

'Vampyre?' Morgan said, his voice tainted with mirth. 'Of course I am a Vampyre – PC Crake has known that for many years.'

The constable laughed. 'Told you he was speaking rubbish,' he said. 'All yours. I'll help Rathbone get him into the car.'

'What about the people – they still want to kill me?' Jago asked.

'Gone away,' Morgan said. 'They found the Vampyres – or what they thought were the Vampyres – at the bottom of the cliff. Must have fallen when the chase was on. They were from Streonshalgh Manor. Mrs Macarty is heartbroken. She had such great expectations for them.'

'What? Griffin and Staxley?' Jago asked.

Ezra Morgan thought for a moment as he put a long finger pensively to his chin. He looked at PC Crake as if asking him to confirm the names.

'Gladling, I believe they were called – all brothers – so they were,' Crake answered.

'The Gladlings are dead?' Jago asked incredulously.

'All of them,' Morgan said. 'Chased out of the Manor by the mob and fell from the cliff. The Vampyres are now dead and peace has returned. It's amazing how easily people are placated.'

'But . . . but . . .' Jago stumbled over his words as the fate of the boys set his mind racing.

'Rathbone is waiting,' Morgan answered coldly as he pointed to the door.

Friday the Thirteenth

EZRA MORGAN NEVER SPOKE as the car dragged itself up the hill and out of the town. As always, the road to Hawks Moor was empty. Jago had seen only one car since they had left the courthouse. It had been parked across from the bridge, its engine running, fumes coming from the tail pipe. He had given particular attention to the men inside – both had worn black trilby hats with their collars pulled up. They had watched the Daimler drive by and had stared at Jago as he looked out of the window. He had wanted to shout out, let them know he was being taken against his will, but deep inside he knew it was useless. Throughout the journey Morgan had held him by the wrist so he could not move, whilst Rathbone had constantly looked back in the rear-view mirror.

Jago had tried to reason with them, and had even asked Morgan to let him go. Neither Morgan nor Rathbone had spoken. It was as if they both knew what turmoil was going on inside his head, and they were mocking him.

As the car reached the top of the hill, the fog was lifting. It filled the estuary and clung to the moorside, but at the pinnacle of the hill all was clear. Above the town, Jago could see the bright blue sky that filled the everlasting horizon. He looked up at a sky like nothing he had ever seen before. Already, in the highest part of the sky, tiny flecks of silver broke against the heavens and were instantly consumed. They flashed like momentary sparks as the meteorite cloud came closer. When the car dropped over the brow of the hill and skirted the valley towards Hawks Moor, the dark of night was already drawing in.

Ezra Morgan ruffled like an old hen. He looked at his gold watch and then without warning handed Jago a bar of chocolate wrapped in silver foil.

'I forgot I had this,' he said in a melancholy voice. 'It is quite a rare thing in these days of rationing. Perhaps you would like it? It is from Bonnets the chocolatiers.' It was as if he remembered some kind gesture from his own childhood and wanted to give Jago at least one good memory before what was to come.

Jago took the chocolate and hesitated.

'Don't worry – it's not poisoned.'

'Why did you allow Hugh to be with my mother?' Jago asked.

Morgan waited until the car had stopped on the gravel drive under the trees before speaking. 'Rathbone, I would like a few moments alone with the boy – if you would be so kind . . .'

Rathbone slid from the Daimler and shut the door. He walked under the trees and lit a cigarette.

'Trevellas said she was a brood mare – what did she mean?' Jago asked.

'She is bitter and in some ways I can understand her. It is

only when you have a child of your own that you know what it is like to think you will have to one day give him up.'

'But I will never know that, I will be dead,' Jago said.

'On the contrary, Jago. You will be very much alive. To-night you will become like us,' Morgan answered, his breath heavy with the scent of red wine.

'I think you are being replaced – that it's all over for you. Strackan wants a new Quartet. That's what Lorken told me before he died. He said that Sibilia Trevellas –'

'Ridiculous,' Morgan interrupted quickly. 'I have known Strackan for eight hundred years. He cannot clear away a generation of Vampyres just like that. We have served him well.'

'This could be your last night on earth. Think of it, Mr Morgan. The Lyrid of Saturn has never happened before. It's as if Strackan wants to start all this again.'

Morgan frowned as he looked at Jago closely. 'I should have had you come and live with me instead of Cresco,' he said with slight admiration. 'I feel I have missed so much of your life. Of course, Julius kept me informed by letter. But I should have been there. I am your grandfather.'

'And you will see me changed into another creature?' Jago said.

Morgan looked uncomfortable. 'It will be a good thing. It is what Strackan wants,' he replied.

'Are you sure it's him and not Sibilia Trevellas?' asked Jago, sensing his hesitation.

Morgan sat back into the leather of the seat and sighed. 'Am I that easy to read?' he asked as he raised a wrinkled brow.

'She said to me you asked her to kill your wife. Brought her from Edinburgh,' said Jago.

'It was not quite as she has explained. Sibilia arrived at Hawks Moor when I was away. As soon as I got back, I knew something was different. Then I saw Hugh. He was crying by the edge of the cliff and shouting that a woman had pushed my wife. Believe me, I loved her.'

'Then why have her killed?' Jago asked.

'I didn't. It was just an unravelling of time. The consequences of actions long ago. Sibilia Trevellas was my first wife. She came with us when we went to kill Strackan and the Hermit. Sibilia practised witchcraft and sorcery. She told me she could charm the Vampyre and we would be safe. What she kept secret was that he had been visiting her and that the venom was at work within. She wanted us to be just like her. My dear wife set an elaborate trap and in it consumed me and my friends.'

'Then why didn't you stay together?' asked Jago.

'When I realised I was a Vampyre just like her, my interest in Sibilia waned. She wanted to be with Strackan. It was as if he had power, and power for its own sake can only destroy. We came to an agreement. I would live my life alone and she would leave this place. Sadly, I forgot that not even the strange life of a Vampyre could rid my wife of the one demon she was born with.' Morgan reached across and took hold of his hand and stroked the soft skin. 'My wife, Sibilia, could not bare to see me happy. Not in any way. That is why I could not trust Sibilia with Hugh. I would have gladly allowed him to become a Vampyre, but I thought that she would have tried to kill him.'

'She said he will die,' Jago answered.

'And that is the reason why she has never done him harm. She wants me to see him die. To suffer with the skin disease, the blindness and then death. That is the way of those who stand in this world and the next. It will be your fate – *if* you don't allow Strackan to take your blood.'

'And what about Biatra? Why does she have to suffer?' Jago asked as Morgan appeared to grow restless.

'An accident, there are always accidents – especially where Sibilia is. Biatra – the brothers Gladling – Jack Henson and even Hugh. Sacrifices to eternal life. Nothing is ever free and wrongdoing always has a consequence,' Morgan answered impatiently. He waved to Rathbone, who stubbed out the cigarette and opened the car door. 'It's time to go inside. I take it my wife is already here?'

'There is also another guest,' Rathbone said as he pointed to a car parked at the side of the house.

By the entrance to the labyrinth was an old car. Jago knew it immediately. The broken headlamp of the blue sedan meant only one thing – Julius Cresco.

'He's here?' Morgan asked.

'Must have come whilst we were out,' Rathbone said as he led Jago to the house, followed swiftly by Morgan.

'But he was not expected,' Morgan said irksomely, as if he did not want Cresco to be there.

'Since Draigorian is dead, he has to be here,' Sibilia replied. She walked behind him, having appeared from nowhere. The woman looked at Jago and rubbed her hand around her wrist. 'I see they found you,' she said with a smile as she felt where the dagger had cut her. 'Not going to escape again?'

Jago had no time to answer. The door was opened and he was pushed inside. He looked for Hugh Morgan but the house seemed empty. The fire in the hallway burnt brightly and lit the room. Shadows reached out like dragons' tongues across the wooden floor.

Morgan walked ahead of them all. He pressed his hand against the wooden panel, then slid his fingers behind the secret door and pulled it open.

'I think we should go this way. Julius will be waiting.'

They stepped inside the room. Jago saw the painting of the Vampyre Quartet. Draigorian could clearly be seen. His face smiled down and his sad eyes glistened as if freshly painted.

'Let that be the first and the last,' Sibilia said as she pushed Jago inside. 'I think we should ask Cresco to paint another picture – this time of Jago and the others. That would bind the lad to what we are to do.' She shuddered visibly with joy; her thin face and red lips were radiant.

'There will be plenty of time for that,' Morgan replied as he crossed the small room and pressed another panel.

The wall opened. A small section of wood slid to one side. Behind the panel was an oil lamp that hung from the rock wall.

'Midnight shall soon be here,' Sibilia Trevellas said solemnly. 'I took the liberty of placing the girl in the charnel house.' Jago didn't know what she meant. Her manner was as brusque as her jet-stone eyes. She looked at him as if she read his mind. 'The charnel house is where we keep all those people we have bitten and not killed. It is a larder of blood.'

'You can be so vile, Sibilia,' Morgan said as he led down

the steps and into a passageway below the house. 'Take no notice, Jago.'

They were soon far below the house. The staircase spiralled down and down and echoed with the sound of the sea. Waves crashed on rocks far away and sucked the air back and forth.

'There is much to be done,' said Sibilia Trevellas as she opened a wooden door with three metal bars that covered a small opening. 'I think he will be fine waiting in here.'

She spoke to Morgan as if he would have to do what she said. Morgan didn't argue. He nodded as Jago stepped through the door and then picked a lamp from the wall and handed it to him.

'You will need this – don't let it go out,' Morgan said, and Jago realised these were important words. 'I will be back for you later.'

'What about my father? Does he know I am here?' Jago asked as the door was slammed in his face.

'Hugh Morgan is . . . indisposed. I doubt if he ever will be seen again,' Trevellas said happily, gloating upon the words. 'Enjoy the darkness. Things will change for you once Strackan has exchanged blood.'

Jago held the light until he could feel the hot glass begin to burn the back of his hand. Placing the lamp on the floor, he sat down and leant against the wall and stared into the black void of the cave.

Almost immediately, he could hear footsteps coming near to him.

'Jago? Is that you?' the voice said as three small shadows approached.

Jago looked up. There in the light of the lamp were the Gladlings. They held each other close and walked as one as they came closer.

'I thought you were dead?' Jago asked as they stood near to him, cold and dishevelled.

'We fell from the cliff. Mrs Macarty told the fishermen we were the Vampyres. She hid Griffin and Staxley and pushed us outside.'

'How did you survive?' he asked as Morris and Boris shivered near to the lamp in hope of warmth.

'A man found us and brought us here. There is a cave that comes from beneath the cliff all the way to this place,' Laurence said. He held out his shaking hands towards the flames. 'Said we were lucky to be alive.'

'Lucky?' Jago echoed.

'Will you get us out?' Morris Gladling asked in a sullen voice.

It was the first time Jago had heard him speak. The voice made him smile with its innocence.

'Of course, Morris,' Jago said. 'In no time at all.'

He saw the boy's face change.

'Told you he would, told you,' Morris shouted. 'Laurence said –'

'Shut it, Mo,' Laurence said. 'Jago needs to know.'

There was silence. Jago looked at them in turn as each one stared at the ground. 'What is it?' he asked, knowing something was wrong.

'It's . . . it's . . .' Morris tried to answer.

'Biatra,' Laurence said before his brother could finish. 'She's in the back of the cave. It's not good, Jago.'

362

Shielding his hand with his coat sleeve, Jago picked up the lamp. He held it above his head and pointed its light to the blackness of the cave. There, in the vast expanse of shadow land at the back of the cave, was Bia. She was chained to the wall like a dog. Around her neck was a studded metal collar with a forged ring and chain. Curled like a small child, she slept, her eyes firmly closed, her red hair jaggedly cropped above her shoulders. Jago could clearly see the blood-red mark of the moon on the side of her face.

'What have they done to her?' he asked.

'She was there when we came here,' Laurence Gladling said. 'Just like that – always the same – never moved. I even tried to talk to her but she opened her eyes and stared at me without speaking.'

Jago leant closer to her. Bia was bruised around the face as if she had been beaten. Her hair was in short strands as if it had been cut with a knife. In the nape of her neck were two more bite marks. They were dark and bruised. Each stood proud of her skin and was rimmed in blood.

'Bia . . . Bia,' Jago said as he gently rubbed her shoulder.

Bia opened her eyes slowly and looked at him as if he was nothing more than a vague reminiscence.

'Jago?' she asked, her words slurred. 'Is it you?'

He smiled. 'I'll get you out of this place, all of you,' Jago said.

'Too late,' Bia answered slowly, breathing heavily. 'Too much venom.'

'I have found a place where you can be healed. Believe me, Bia, it's not too late,' Jago said as the Gladlings clung to his leather coat.

'Just leave me here. Please, Jago. It is dangerous for you if I go with you. I . . .'

Bia opened her eyes. They were dark and bloodshot, as if they had been sucked of all life. She stared at him vacantly, her mind elsewhere, in another land.

'We'll be with you,' said Morris Gladling impatiently.

Jago caught a glimpse of the boy's neck. Under his shirt were two faint, red marks.

'Who did this?' Jago asked.

Laurence Gladling held his brother close to him. Jago could see he didn't know what to say. His hand trembled as he tried to smooth the blonde hair that curled in his fingers.

'It was a woman,' Laurence muttered, as if ashamed by what he had done. 'She took us to a room and then did this to us,' he said as he showed Jago more teeth marks.

'She needs strength. I heard her telling another man I haven't seen before,' Bia said, stirring from her sleep. 'The Lyrid of Saturn. Strackan is already here . . . somewhere.'

'When they brought you here, did you see Hugh Morgan?' Jago asked.

'He came back this morning. They were waiting for him. Rathbone held him at gunpoint. Told him he couldn't interfere,' Bia said.

Boris Gladling began to cry. He stood barefoot on the cold stone. His thin blue legs were wasted, skinny and shivering. He held up his arms to Jago as if he wanted to be held close. Jago looked at Laurence, who sighed.

'I'll sort it out for you, Boris,' Jago said as he lifted the lad in the air and held him. 'I promise it will be all right.'

Jago looked at Bia. He had made the same promise to her

and now she lay chained in the cold cave, already transformed to a Vampyre. Gladling held on tightly, his tiny fingers gripping the leather of the coat.

'Promise?' said the boy, ever hopeful.

'I'll get you out of here and find you somewhere to live. It will be good again,' Jago answered, his words fooling no one.

Jago settled the Gladlings by the door and told them not to move. He looked at the neck ring that bound Bia to the chain. In the hinge of the metal was a small pin. Quickly he unscrewed the pin and the neck brace fell open. Bia rubbed the wound. She was still dazed, her mind far away. All she could see was the beautiful face of Sibilia Trevellas – it was as if the woman was watching her from within and knew her every move.

'Don't leave me, Jago,' she whispered.

'I'm here,' he answered, suddenly aware of footsteps coming closer down the long passageway.

'The Lyrid of Saturn,' Bia said anxiously, suddenly aware of all that surrounded her. 'It's time.'

[30]

Julius Cresco

A KEY TURNED IN THE LOCK. As it did, the Glad-lings scurried like mice back into the shadows of the cave. Bia sat up and tried to focus on the shaft of light that came in through the crack of the opening door. She could see Jago standing defiantly, hands in the pockets of his leather coat. As she looked at him, an inner voice told her he had the silver dagger. Whilst Jago waited for the door to open, Bia watched him intently, wondering in which pocket the dagger was hidden.

'Jago,' said a warm voice as the door opened further. 'It is so good to see you again.'

Jago didn't answer. He stared straight ahead at the man and gripped his hands into tight fists hidden in his jacket.

'It's me – Uncle Cresco.'

Cresco looked into the cave. He was taller than Jago had remembered and looked different. The lines that cut so deeply in his face had smoothed and faded. He was broader, and his smart striped suit a change from the white vest and open shirt that was always crumpled. His skin was smooth; Cresco had shaved the stubble from his face and looked half the age that Jago remembered.

'You lied,' Jago said. 'Lied for years.'

'What was I supposed to say. That I am a Vampyre?' he asked, his voice charmed. 'You would not have believed me. What is important is how all of this will change your life.'

'You have betrayed me and my mother,' Jago snapped angrily.

'She knew, Jago,' he said before Jago could say anything else. 'She knew the consequences of what she did. I looked after you. Kept you safe – made sure all was well. Who was it who warned you of all this? But you didn't listen . . .'

'You told me stories of a faraway place that I thought wasn't real. When I came here it soon became clear that all you said was true,' Jago shouted, his words shrill and cold as the air. 'Look what they have done to my friends.' He pointed in to the darkness. 'Vampyres have stolen their lives – poisoned their blood – taken their future.'

Cresco boiled with anger. Without a word of warning he snapped his hand through the air and slapped Jago across the face.

'How dare you?' he said as Jago fell back. 'You have no understanding of what I have been through. One day they will thank me for what has been done to them. They won't die like the others. It will not be thirty days and then hell for them. This is the Lyrid of Saturn. The anniversary of what happened all those years ago in the hermit's cave. You and your friends will inherit eternal life . . .'

His words hung in the air like knives about to fall. Jago stood back from the door and thought what he could do to escape. It was then he heard a voice in his head – it was like a whisper, dull and distant, on the edge of hearing.

'He can hear you,' Bia said in his mind as she looked at them both from the back of the cave.

'Very good . . . And who are you?' Cresco asked as he shut the door of the cell behind him and pushed the lamp to one side with the toe of his brogue boot.

'That's Biatra. She's my cousin,' Jago answered for her. 'Sibilia Trevellas took her for her own.'

'So, you are the one? I have heard so much about you,' Cresco said as he leant forward to look at her.

There was something about the man that Jago knew was different. It was as if everything he had been before was just an act to fool him. He seemed sly, snake-like and untrusting. His eyes glowed mistily green as if they had been stoked like the embers of a fire.

'You know what we are thinking?' Jago asked.

'It is more that I know *how* you are thinking and feeling. It is a primeval power like that of a wolf,' Cresco said.

'All the time, in London?' Jago asked 'When we were alone. All my fears and concerns, you knew them all?'

'It saved a lot of wasted conversation,' Cresco said as he crossed the room and examined Bia more closely. 'Sibilia said that your blood was special,' he said as he pulled back the collar from her throat and smiled.

'If you touch her, I will kill you,' Jago said.

'What? After all I have done for you?' Cresco asked. 'I doubt you could muster the strength. You are not a Vampyre yet.'

'I trusted you, Cresco, loved you as my father . . . You were the only man there for me,' Jago answered as he felt the knife through the pocket of the lining of his leather coat.

'It had to be done. In the morning you will come to understand. Becoming a Vampyre alters how you see the world. What happened before doesn't matter. It is only the future that is of concern.' Cresco appeared to ignore Jago as he leant further towards Bia and stroked her neck.

'Touch her and I mean it . . .' Jago scowled as he kicked the door shut.

The thud of wood against metal made Cresco turn to him. 'Do I take it you want her for yourself?' he asked. 'She is beautiful, if somewhat scrawny.'

'She's my family,' he answered.

'I am your family – Morgan is your family – Strackan is your family. Life changes.' Cresco showed his dog-like teeth as he snarled the reply. 'What we once were is not what we always have to be. Eight hundred years ago I was a man who had nothing. I was a servant to Morgan and his wife – that's all. When Strackan took my blood, I changed. I gained respect, admiration, everything the world could give. I had power – power over life and death, and that is all that matters.' Cresco suddenly gripped Bia by the throat and lifted her from the ground until she hung in the air like a rag doll. 'Is this what you would have me do? Kill her. She means nothing to me.'

'What about love? My mother said that was important,' Jago pleaded as Bia choked in his grip.

'Love? Love? It is nothing more than a fool's errand. Meaningless and lacklustre. A decay of the heart,' he said as he squeezed harder. 'This is what it is all about. In my hands I have the choice of life – or death. A Vampyre can take the life of a Vampyre with just the snapping of the neck.'

'Leave her, Cresco. I warned you before,' Jago said.

Cresco spoke without turning his head. 'I choose, Jago. I choose . . .' He stared at Bia as she gasped for breath. Her legs shivered as she fought to breathe. To him, it was a great pleasure.

At the back of the cave in the bleak darkness, the Gladlings hid from sight. Jago could sense their fear. Morris Gladling was sobbing quietly.

Jago stepped the four paces across the room silently. It was as if his feet never touched the ground. Without a thought he took hold of Cresco's hand and pulled it from her neck. Bia fell to the floor of the cave and gasped for breath as she held her throat.

'No more!' Jago shouted as he ran to Bia.

Cresco turned. He pushed Jago from her and laughed.

'If we didn't need you so much alive I would kill you now. Fifteen years of your whining and moaning is enough for any-one to take. I can't believe it is you with whom I will serve an eternity.'

The Vampyre stepped closer and closer to Jago. But Cresco didn't finish his words – he gasped and reached out his hand as his eyes flashed about the cave. His mouth filled with blood. It stained the bright white teeth that pushed so prom-inently against his lips. His arms dropped to his side as life flowed from him. Then Cresco fell to his knees. All the time, he looked at Jago. He could not take his eyes from him. With each second it was as if he wanted to consume every memory of the boy.

Jago looked at Bia. She held the silver dagger in her hand.

'How?' he asked.

'I took it from your pocket I was going to . . . to kill,' she said as she looked at the bloodstained blade. 'I knew it was there – I saw your thoughts.'

Cresco tried to speak. He coughed blood and bent forward as if to pray.

'I loved you, Jago . . . in my own way. You were my son . . .' His voice was distant and soft, like the sound of water flowing through a brook.

'If only I could believe you,' Jago answered.

'Is it true you killed Draigorian?' Cresco panted out the words with aching breath.

'I set him free,' Jago answered.

'Remember me – when I step into your kingdom,' Cresco muttered, looking up as if he stared at someone standing before him. Then he slumped forward, face down in the dirt.

'No!' Jago shouted as he saw Bia take the knife and pull it towards herself.

Jago grabbed her hands and struggled to free the dagger from her grasp.

'Let me, Jago. It is the only way,' she pleaded. 'I need to die.'

'Never! Not like this.' Jago snatched the blade from her hands as the Gladlings gathered around him. Cresco groaned on the dirt floor, his fingers gripping the earth.

'He's alive,' Laurence Gladling said as he tugged Jago. 'Can we get out of here?'

Jago looked at Cresco. The man stared back, his eyes blood red. He was still breathing.

'I'll get you out of here. We'll go to London. I know a way,' Jago said as he lifted Bia to her feet.

371

'What about the man?' Boris Gladling asked. He prodded him with his toe to see if he moved.

'Leave him,' Jago answered as he picked up the lantern and held it above his head to light the cave.

'I don't want to go,' Bia said. 'It can't go on.'

'I know a pool that Sagacious said would heal you. I can take you there. Jack Henson knows the place – we have to find him,' Jago replied as he dragged her towards the door.

'Are you going to leave him?' she asked as with a faint hand she pointed to Cresco.

'He'll be dead soon. The knife is like a poison to a Vampyre,' Jago answered as the Gladlings followed on, holding each other's hands in a frightened train. 'It will not be long.'

'You can't leave him,' Bia protested, struggling to get her hand free.

'It's the only way. I have to find Jack Henson and get us out of this house,' he answered.

'But what of the Lyrid of Saturn?' she asked.

Jago thought her words were strange. With the keys that dangled from the lock he opened the door of the cell. He looked back at Cresco. The man looked as though he were dead, his body lying still without a sign of movement.

'Which way is the sea?' Jago asked Laurence Gladling, hoping he would be able to remember.

The boy looked back and forth along the narrow stone passageway that had been carved from the rock. 'That way,' Gladling said, jabbing the air with the point of his finger.

'Then go – take your brothers and go. When you get to Whitby, find the cottage of Jack Henson and wait for me there,' Jago urged as he pushed Laurence on.

'But what will you do?' Gladling asked quizzically.

'I'll find Henson. They must have him here somewhere. I'll take Bia with me.' Jago looked at the girl, who cowered by the open door like an owl. Gladling did not have to ask why. He too could see it in her face. The dark-rimmed eyes and blood-filled lips spoke of her hunger.

Boris Gladling stared up at Jago.

'It will be fine, Boris. I will come and find you,' Jago said.

The boy tried to smile, his lips trembling, his face etched with grief.

'Promise?' he asked, as if it was the only word he ever wanted to hear.

Jago touched his shoulder. 'Promise,' he answered, as he turned to where Bia was slumped by the door. 'We go this way,' he said to her, holding out his hand.

Bia gripped his fingers. They were warm and soft. She could feel the rapid pulse beat in the tip of each one. They spoke of a pounding heart and racing blood. She thought for a moment.

'Let me go with the Gladlings, Jago,' she said in a whisper.

'I need you with me. The Lyrid of Saturn,' Jago answered.

Bia opened her eyes wider. 'Are you going to . . .?' she asked expectantly.

'Of course – what do you think? It has to be done, but my way,' Jago said as he led her away.

Jago watched the Gladlings disappear from view. He heard their footsteps fade into the darkness of the tunnel and soon they were gone. Together, he and Bia walked up the steps and back to the hidden room. The rough wood of the pan-elled walls was lit by the tallow lamp that sooted the low ceiling above. Jago slid the catch and the door opened into the empty room.

He looked at the painting, expecting to see the face of Julius Cresco appear on the canvas. Bia pointed at the picture with her long bloodless finger as she shared the same thought.

'He's not there,' Bia said as she looked back at the door. 'He's not dead . . .'

Jago held the lamp higher and examined the painting more closely. It looked as though something had changed. It was only when he stepped back from the canvas that he saw the snake had vanished from near the woman.

'Strackan is here,' Jago said, as if something in the ether that surrounded them shuddered in his presence.

Bia gasped. 'How do you know?' she asked.

'I can sense it – taste it,' he answered as the sound of long steady footsteps echoed in the passageway below. 'It's Cresco, he's following us,' Jago said.

Opening the door that led to the hallway, they looked outside. The room was empty. The warm fire glowed brightly in the iron grate and lit the room with a soft glow. Jago realised it was now pitch black outside the house. He stepped across the room and hid in the shadows of the inglenook. He listened as the long case clock ticked the minutes.

'Outside?' Bia asked as she shut the door behind her, just as she heard the latch click behind the heavy curtains that shielded the entrance.

'You?' said Rathbone as he pushed aside the curtain and stared at Bia, who stood alone. 'You were supposed to keep your eye on Harker. Where is he?'

374

Jago pressed himself against the warm stone that edged the large fireplace.

'He's gone, that's what I've come to tell you,' Bia said.

Then the panelled door to the secret room opened and Julius Cresco staggered out.

'You bloodless dog,' he said as he gripped her tightly by the arm and then threw her against the wall. 'She tried to kill me – stabbed me with . . . with a silver dagger.'

'Leave her, Cresco,' Jago said as he stepped from his hiding place, dagger and lamp in hand.

'This, Mr Rathbone, is what betrayal looks like,' Cresco snarled as he stepped painfully towards Jago. 'It is what rudeness looks like, what ungratefulness looks like . . . To think, I nursed this lad on my knee. Lived in squalor so I could look after him and this is what thanks I get –'

'You are a self-seeking liar,' Jago answered as he stood his ground against both men. 'I was just a chattel – something useful for the future – an investment.'

'If only Strackan didn't want you, I would drink your blood and live five score years on the taste of it,' Cresco muttered. 'Get him, Rathbone. I do not want to soil my hands.'

Rathbone stepped forward. Jago looked at Bia. As the man made his move, Jago threw the oil lamp at Cresco. It smashed on the stone floor at his feet. There was a bright burning of exploding whale oil that quickly engulfed him.

'No!' Cresco screamed as he was overwhelmed in scorching flames like a tinder-dry human candle.

Rathbone didn't move. He looked on as the Vampyre burnt like a corn-doll.

Cresco staggered towards Jago. He held out his burning

fingers as he got closer and closer. 'I loved you . . .' he said, before everything he had been was subdued by the flames.

The blackened carcass slumped to the floor like a falling tree. Ash splintered over the stone flags as his body fragmented. He bones were broken, dry and charred.

'Come to me, Bia,' Jago said.

'He's not to be trusted,' Rathbone answered as he held out his hand towards her. 'We are your family. *He* is still human.'

Bia looked at Jago as he stood over the smouldering remains of Julius Cresco.

'You're a Vampyre?' Jago asked.

'Of course,' Rathbone answered as he pulled a gun from his pocket and aimed it at Jago. 'Who else would work all these hours for no pay?'

There was a sudden lurch from the shadows and a hand took hold of Jago by the collar. Jago reached in his pocket for the dagger. It was gone.

'I see that you have managed to kill another of my friends,' said Ezra Morgan as he squeezed Jago around the neck. 'You are becoming quite troublesome, quite troublesome . . .'

[31]

Deus Tantum Iudicabit

THE PASSING CLOUDS squalled bitterly to the far horizon. In a quarter of an hour the sky had cleared and the stars of the night shone down. As Jago was dragged from Hawks Moor, he could see every part of the spiralling galaxy high above him. Where the comet had been there was a dark hole in space. Jago caught a glimpse of yet another rain of meteors – they broke the atmosphere in sparkling bursts of white and blue light as the Lyrid of Saturn showered down. The shooting stars crossed the sky like hot knives cutting the velvet-black heaven.

'Like a bombardment,' Ezra Morgan said as he dragged Jago towards the centre of the labyrith, his rough hands gripping Jago's leather coat. 'I remember the night I first saw them. It is hard to believe what has gone on in my life since that time. Eight hundred years – think of it, Jago. And tonight is the start of your life.'

Jago looked back. Rathbone held Bia by her arm as if he would never let her go. She seemed not to care, her eyes staring straight ahead.

'What will you do with me?' Jago asked.

'If I had my way, Jago, I would kill you here and now. Sadly,

Strackan is insistent. You have to be alive and from now on you will live at Hawks Moor.'

Morgan gripped his coat harder and pulled him along the gravel path that twisted right and left through the verdant high hedges of the maze. Jago could feel a lump grow in his throat. His chest burnt and his hands trembled as he held back the tears.

'Where are Hugh and Jack Henson?' Jago asked.

'Locked away in the tower room, where they can't do any harm,' Morgan answered with sharp words. 'Neither is to be trusted. When your fate is sealed, what is left of the Quartet will decide their future.'

'They did nothing,' Jago insisted.

'Nothing? My own son was planning to have me killed – he confessed, after a little persuasion,' Morgan snapped. 'In league with Henson – to do away with the Quartet. He would rather die than follow Strackan. That, I cannot under-stand.'

Ezra Morgan had one thought in his mind and it was un-welcome. All he could think of was the day he had first seen his son. There, lodged in his mind, was the image of his Hugh, wrapped in a pure white blanket. In that one moment, Ezra Morgan had cause to doubt what he now did. As he gripped Jago harder, a voice repeated the words: *flesh and blood* . . .

'Answer me one thing,' Jago asked as they neared the cen-tre of the labyrinth and the bright light of flaming torches. 'Why wouldn't you let Hugh be with my mother?'

Morgan faltered in his step, as if the words had caught him off guard and bitten through his steely armour.

'She was not worthy,' he said slowly as he looked to the

shower of meteors that crashed above him. 'No woman on this earth would ever be.'

'It's time,' Rathbone intervened. He pushed Bia against the thick hedge and quickly bound her hands with a ribbon of holly leaves. 'Can't be having you hurting anyone.'

'Leave her, Rathbone. When I get free I will kill you,' Jago shouted as he struggled to break the grip of Morgan's hand.

'Holly takes away the hunger. Anyway, you will soon be one of us and all such thoughts will leave your mind. When Strackan bites, all thoughts of the old life fade. You will be a new creation,' Morgan answered eagerly as they turned a corner and the centre of the maze came into view.

Before them, like a wall of flame, were several tallow lamps. They stood on the tips of thick oak staffs high above the ground. Lumps of burning rag dropped to the shingle path that Jago could see was made up of millions of tiny shells. At the centre of the maze was a single wooden chair. Everything else had been cleared away, all except a long flat stone that lay in the earth several feet away like the covering of a tomb.

All around, Jago could see the shadowy figures of people in the lee of the high hedges. They were gathered in groups of twos and threes, their faces hidden by ornate animal masks. It like some play, a pageant of Vampyres waiting for what was to happen. He had expected there to be only Ezra Morgan and Sibilia, but coming from every passageway were more and more people. Long cloaks hid everyday clothes. Some were finely dressed, others not. Each of them wore a mask.

They crowded under the light of the tallow lamps and

circled the old oak chair with winged arms that took pride of place in the centre of the maze.

'I thought it was just four Vampyres – a Quartet?' Jago asked.

'We are more each day, some for the season of a moon and others for eternity, just like you,' Morgan said as he entered the centre of the maze and looked about at the bowing heads of all that gathered there.

As Bia pressed closer to Jago, Morgan puffed up his chest, straightened his tweed coat and began to speak. 'Such a fine gathering . . . A time that we thought would never happen. Within our land, we are people who defy time. Rulers may come and go – wars start and then cease – but the Vampyre will always be in the world . . . And, tonight, beneath the stars that break through the glass of heaven, this boy – my true-blood descendant – will become one of us. The stars demand a sacrifice – a life that will bring life – blood that shall change blood. Lord Strackan, prince of our world, shall stand amongst us and we give him our worship.'

The long slab of stone that lay before them began to move slowly. It juddered in the earth and trembled the shell path all around it. Jago looked at those near him. He could recognise Griffin and Staxley. Even though they wore wolf masks, the long cloaks that trailed on the ground and twice-turned khaki trousers gave them away. He could see them staring at him through the slits in their masks with envious eyes.

As the stone moved, the gathered crowd backed away. Rathbone left Bia standing near to Jago and went to pull the slab from the ground. It opened like an old casket with a sudden rush of air.

A gasp echoed through the high hedges as, slowly and meticulously, Strackan walked up a long flight of stone steps.

'Morgan, I see you have the boy,' Strackan said, his face hidden by the brim of his black fedora.

'He is ready,' Morgan answered as the crowded gently applauded his capture.

'Then he must be in his place,' Strackan replied as he pulled back the sleeves of his fine striped suit, clicked the heels of his pointed shoes and took a long stride from the grave.

Morgan pushed Jago into the chair.

'Don't struggle, and do what is asked. It will be over quickly. I know,' he said.

Jago felt Bia standing close to him. The crowd of Vampyres gathered around until all he could see was Strackan surrounded by a sea of mask-clad faces.

'You have cost me a great deal,' Strackan said as he took off the fedora and revealed his bark-like skin stretched across ancient bones. 'Two of the Quartet are dead – by your hand. It is as if you relish what you do.'

'I don't want to be a Vampyre,' Jago shouted belligerently.

The crowded muttered and moaned in discontent as they stepped even closer to Jago.

'It is not what you want that matters,' Strackan said. He looked to the sky just as a large meteor burned brightly above him. 'This is a moment I have waited hundreds of years to enjoy.'

Jago felt something cold being pressed secretly into his palm. Bia squeezed his shoulder. He heard her whisper something but could not understand the words.

Strackan stared at him. Bloodshot eyes glared from dark

wrinkled skin that could hardly move or even show expression. As his lips shaped to speak flakes of skin fell to the ground.

'You're dying,' Jago shouted. 'That's why you need me.'

The gathered crowd was hushed in silence. The night breeze rustled the autumn leaves under the hedges. The masked faces stared at Jago in disbelief.

'*Need* is not a word I would choose to use – not in front of all my friends,' Strackan said patiently as he reached out and touched Jago on the cheek. 'Certain blood, the blood taken from the descendant of a Vampyre, is like an old wine. What you carry in your veins is enough to refresh these weary bones and bring me youth.'

'Tell me one thing. Who were you before all this?' Jago demanded.

Strackan stepped back and looked at those around him. Each eye was upon him. They stared in silent admiration as if they looked on a god.

'I am who I am,' Strackan answered with a short breath. 'My mind cannot remember so far into the past. All I know is that *this* is my fate and *you* are my future.'

'ENOUGH!' Sibilia Trevellas shouted as she ripped off her mask and pushed Griffin out of her way. 'Take his blood, kill him! We don't need the likes of Jago Harker.' Her voice betrayed her knowledge that he was a threat.

'Patience, Sibilia,' Strackan answered as he held out a hand to stop her coming closer. 'I am waiting for the night to burn brightly. Fear brings a rush of the blood and I sense the boy is far more terrified than he would have us know.'

Jago slipped his right hand behind his back and leant

against the chair. He looked up at Ezra Morgan, who in turn glared at Sibilia, his eyes betraying the jealousy of his heart. Morgan shook his head and sighed.

Sibilia Trevellas rustled angrily in her long purple crinoline dress and leather boots. 'He tried to kill me,' she shouted as she held out her hand. 'He can never be one of us. Take this boy,' she said as she pushed Staxley towards him.

'It has to be Jago. That is why we have waited. It is him alone,' Strackan groaned.

'But you took his blood?' Sibilia said, hoping to persuade Strackan to give in to her whim.

'Jago is the one and now is the time,' Strackan said as he pointed heavenwards. High above, crossing the path of the moon, a burning meteor slashed across the atmosphere. It shook the air and the ground trembled. Sparks cascaded from the tail as the first shockwave trembled the hedges of the maze. Then it roared out to sea and, just as it reached the horizon, crashed into the water. 'There, I told you that a sign would come.'

'Then do it and do it now – we cannot wait,' Sibilia answered as she pressed Strackan to take the blood.

Jago saw Strackan swallow hard as he stepped towards him, reaching with a gnarled hand. Long brown nails curled over his dead fingertips.

Stackan saw the boy look at him. 'Once I have drunk your blood then you will see me as I really am,' he said.

'I know what you are like,' Jago answered. 'I can see it in your eyes. That's what my mother said – truth is found in the eyes.'

'And what of mine?' Strackan asked.

'You are a liar and you care for no one but yourself,' Jago answered.

The gathered crowd muttered their discontent. Jago turned. The woman near to him looked just like Mrs Macarty. Her hair trailed over the mask of a badger just like it had done over her face on the first night they had met.

Strackan stood and gloated over him. He quivered with excitement.

'I care not what you say, Jago. From tonight we shall set out from this place and day by day we shall take this world. We will be the bringers of peace and stop this war. No one will know who is in control, but Vampyres will take their places as heads of state, ministers and prime ministers. We shall be the people of power.' Strackan waved a hand through the air as if he were laying waste to all before him.

'And it starts with me?' Jago asked.

'Morgan's blood. A descendent of the first blood taken at the hermit's cave,' Sibilia interrupted, still gripping Staxley.

'Then so be it,' Jago said as he undid the collar of his shirt and offered Strackan his smooth, tender white skin.

The Vampyre salivated at the sight. His hand juddered and shook uncontrollably as he leant forward to steady himself against the chair.

'I am glad you understand,' he whispered to Jago with stenching breath.

Jago waited as Strackan came closer. He could feel the warm panting on his face like a kiss.

'Make it quick,' he said as he waited for the Vampyre to bite.

The crowd was silent. From far away came the rumbling of

the sea. Strackan leant nearer. He nervously hesitated, as he looked Jago in the eye. Then quickly he slipped his gaze to the neck as he opened his mouth.

'Do it!' Sibilia insisted, but Strackan was not listening.

In his mind he was back in the cave of Sagacious the hermit eight hundred years before. As he smelt the scent of Jago's skin he thought of every wonder in his life and what it would be again.

'Deus Tantum Iudicabit,' he said to himself, the words spoken like a prayer as the sky thundered and lightning cracked to the sea.

The wind came quickly from the moor and shook the hedges, brushing the tiny shells across the pathways of the labyrinth. The squalling gale howled from Hawks Moor to Whitby. It ripped at the trees that lined the lanes and grabbed tufts of grass from the cliffs. Seabirds swirled and fell and dived above them as if they twisted and turned within the meteors and shooting stars. In the bay below, the sea was pulled back. Rocks unseen for millennia were exposed once more. Fish as big as shovel handles were left on dry ground.

Far out to the horizon, unseen by those within the maze, the sea boiled where the comet had struck. To the north, the bells of the church rang out in calamitous applause as the wind got stronger and stronger.

'What is it?' Ezra Morgan asked.

'The Lyrid of Saturn. Do you not remember that first night?' Strackan laughed as he took hold of Jago by the shoulders to hold him tight. 'The whole of creation is angered by what we do and yet cannot stop us.'

'But I can,' Jago whispered – and suddenly he stabbed the

silver dagger into Strackan's neck, kicking him back at the same time.

Strackan gasped for breath, clutching his throat with his hands, unable to pull the dagger from within his neck. Ezra Morgan lunged for Jago just as Bia lashed out at him with her fist and Jago pushed Rathbone out of the way. Lumps of the thick hedge were being pulled from the ground by the second.

'Run, Bia! Run!' Jago shouted as he grabbed her hand and battled against the piercing gale that shook everything around them, growing ever louder.

'Stop him!' shouted Sibilia Trevellas, her voice faint against the wind, as Jago and Bia ran into the darkness of the engulfing storm.

Staxley and Griffin gave chase. Their masks were torn from them by the storm and their cloaks were discarded in the pursuit. Through the labyrinth they ran like sniffing dogs chasing their prey.

Far ahead, Jago had found the entrance to the maze. He looked down across the moonlit bay. The final shards of stardust crashed to earth. Far out to sea, a wall of water gathered speed, turning and twisting as it came closer. The shape of the coast appeared to shield the town from its impact, but still the wave crashed and roared, tumbling over rocks as it sped towards the cliff.

'There's not much time,' he shouted to Bia as they ran to the house. 'I have to find Jack Henson and my father . . .'

They were soon inside Hawks Moor. The large oak doors gave way to the wind and slammed back and forth like rags on a line. Bia ran ahead as Jago forced the doors to close and slammed the iron keeper to hold them shut. The house fell silent. All he could hear was the whistling of the wind down the chimney pots and the crackling of the fire in the grate. Taking the iron key, he turned the lock. The burnt ashes of Julius Cresco covered the stone floor.

'They're coming,' Bia shouted from an upstairs window. 'Griffin, Staxley and Trevellas.'

'Henson and my father are in the tower room – get them!' Jago shouted as he ran to the kitchen to secure the door. He crossed the hall, entered the passageway and turned into the kitchen. Across the room he could see the door. Cast by the moon, two shadows crossed the window. Jago raced as fast as he could, knowing he had to be there before them. He reached for the handle to turn the lock but the door flew open as Staxley pushed against it.

'Get out!' Jago shouted. 'This is my house.'

A wooden panel was smashed and splintered. Outside, Griffin hammered at the wood with an old axe from the woodpile.

'You have business to finish, Jago,' Staxley shouted as Jago slammed the door and pushed the bolt.

Griffin hacked and hacked with the axe. The door splintered, sending jags of wood into the air. Knowing they would soon be inside, Jago turned and ran back to the hallway. The door to the room hidden behind the panel was open and he looked inside. The face of Julius Cresco was in the painting – the first time he had seen him that way. Cresco looked not much older than Jago. He wondered how his life would have been had Cresco not cared for him like an uncle, and seemed to hear the man's soft, warm voice telling him stories.

The words in his head were suddenly interrupted.

'You shouldn't have run away,' Sibilia said as she stepped from the shadows. 'Strackan is injured. That will never be allowed to go unpunished. Vampyres from all over the world have gathered tonight and you, Jago Harker, have destroyed everything.'

'Do you think I would just let him rip out my neck and drink my blood?' he asked as he stepped from the room and kicked a brittle piece of ash towards the fire. 'You have used me all my life and I would rather die.'

'And I shall grant you your wish,' said Trevellas as she turned and took an ornamental sword from the wall. 'Nothing will give me greater pleasure . . .'

As she spoke the ground began to shudder. The sea roared louder and louder until nothing else could be heard. Hawks Moor trembled upon the rocks on which it was built. The gigantic wave broke against the cliff. Outside, the tidal wave engulfed the labyrinth. A spout of water blew high into the air and crashed to the ground, shattering the windows of the house. Shards of glass flew like jagged knives and showered down into the hallway.

Jago dived to the cover of the fireplace. Trevellas ran across the room and lifted the sword high above her head. Jago looked up – he could not escape.

'I should have done this the first time I saw you, Jago Harker. I was there when you were born. It was into my hands that you fell. I should have killed you then,' she screamed as she plunged the sword towards him.

There was a splintering of wood as the front doors were smashed from their hinges. The tidal wave rushed in and the

388

house was flooded with seawater. Before she could strike the blow, Sibilia Trevellas was engulfed in the deluge and swept from her feet. The twisted iron doorkeeper scraped across the stone floor as the doors were pushed back. The blistering wind ripped the curtains from the rails and shot them across the room as fanned flames leapt from the fire.

Then there was darkness. The wind plucked the candles from their holders as the wave killed the fire. Smoke filled the room as the water hissed.

Jago closed his eyes and gripped the stone pillar as hard as he could, holding tight for his dear life. The water beat against him as it came higher and higher. It was as if a hand of nature had reached inside Hawks Moor to rid it of all evil. The water that filled the hallway bubbled and swirled as the wave began to ebb back to the sea. It dragged from the house the ashes of Julius Cresco, which floated away amongst the broken furniture.

'Jago! Jago!' Bia shouted as she ran down the stairs. As she turned the corner of the carved stairs she saw Jago lying motionless. His hair was soaked and fell across his face, lit by the lantern carried by Jack Henson.

The harsh wind gave way to a gentle breeze. In the long shadows, amongst pools of seawater, Bia stroked Jago's face.

'Is he . . .?' Henson asked as Hugh Morgan lifted Jago from the pool.

'Breathing – but only just,' Hugh answered.

'The others?' Bia asked.

'Gone,' Henson answered as he looked to the night outside. 'Lucky the house stood against the sea. I saw the meteor strike the water. The tidal wave was higher than the cliff.'

'Trevellas . . .' Jago muttered as he opened his eyes.

'Gone. Gone for good,' replied Hugh Morgan.

'Father?' Jago asked as he looked into his eyes.

'Son,' Hugh Morgan replied as he brushed the hair from his brow.

RedEye

Shortly before Jago Harker Arrived in Whitby

IT WAS SEPTEMBER, and the night sky glowed blood red. In the east, above the far hills away from the town, gnarled fingers of cloud gripped the horizon. It had been that way since the last full moon. Every alleyway and ginnel, every yard and street glistened with sky-silver. It followed the contours of the houses like a gossamer thread, a spider's web of moonlight.

At the very height of the sky, at its darkest place, was a slither of light. Some thought it was a comet, an unexpected return of a travelling star. Others, who were wise and could remember what they had been taught when they were small children, knew differently. It had appeared before, exactly one hundred years ago on the same date and at the same time – on 3rd September 1840, at 7.30 p.m. Those now old had heard the story of its appearance time and again. Many thought it was a bad omen. An eye, cut into the fabric of heaven at the zenith of the sky. An eye, blood red and edged in gold, that could be seen even on the brightest autumn day at the time of the harvest moon.

In the churchyard, high on the clifftop above the harbour and the estuary beyond, an iron spade dug into gravelled earth. It echoed through the gathering of tombstones with each sharp cut. An old man in a black gabardine with leather-patched elbows worked on. He dug in the grave, twisting each sod of brown dirt and throwing it high above his head just as he had done every night that week. It was only when he heard the strange sound coming in from the sea that he stopped. He climbed the steps of his wooden ladder and looked out across the town. There was not a single light to be seen, not a flicker or flame or burning candle. Every window was daubed with paint, every glass covered with the blacking of curtains. Even the infrequent cars that sped across the river bridge that linked the two sides of the town had no lights. The gravedigger could hear their engines, just as he could hear the low, vibrating hum . . . hum . . . hum . . . that seemed to come from the depths of the rolling sea.

'This is what war does for you,' he said to himself as he stepped back down to his work. 'Dig a grave every night only to be filled by morning, seven this week and not a word of thanks.'

He spoke to himself and for his own benefit. It was to reassure his own mind that he was alone.

Since the coming of the scarlet star, no one who knew Whitby would enter the churchyard after dark. Only Jack Henson, the gravedigger, would venture to that place. He knew it well, too well to be frightened by idle talk. He had an understanding with the unseen whisperers that would hide behind the gravestones and watch him from their world. Henson knew their ways; he studied them and some say even talked to the unseen guests at every graveside. As the church clock chimed, he turned the spade again and again as he edged the grave and scraped the top of the coffin under his feet.

Far below and across the river, the door of the Glory Hand opened quickly. A brief bright light shone into the street. There was a shout and the pub door slammed shut. The air-raid warden nodded to the man who staggered from the ale-house and down the street. She looked at her watch and calculated the hours until dawn. Then, instinctively, the woman looked up between the old stone buildings to the sky and listened. All she could hear was the sound of the sea. With each surge of the tide the waves broke on the harbour piers as if they laughed sarcastically.

Taking the photograph from the pocket of her khaki overall, the woman pressed the button of her torch. For the shortest moment, she allowed the light to be cast across the sepia face of her husband. He was dressed in his beret and jacket, his arms folded and lips smiling.

She sighed and turned off the torch, quickly putting the portrait of Corporal Eddie Barnes, 1st Battalion of the Green Howards, back in her pocket for safekeeping. The woman looked to the door of the pub once more and then carried on her patrol. All was well. The bombing had not come this far north. London had been hit many times, but Whitby had been forgotten.

Each night she would put on her overalls, helmet and fire boots, leave her solitary house and walk the streets of the town. Like Willie Winkie, she looked for lights in windows, any break in the blackout, anything that could be seen from the sky. Not that it seemed to matter. The sky didn't darken as it used to, the red-eyed comet and harvest moon had seen to that. Now, in the half-light, she heard the clock of the town hall strike the hour before midnight.

The streets were empty and silent, nothing stirred but the wind at the eaves. Warden Barnes turned into the narrow street that led down the hill to the harbour.

On every side ran the dark alleyways that led to the backs of the shops. They were impregnable black hollows, each wide enough for a man to walk carrying a keg of beer. Barnes kept her eyes to the street ahead. Above the roofs she could see the church and the ruins of the old abbey on the far side of the river.

It was then that something far away caught her eye. A lamp moved along the high cliff path on the other side of the town. Steadily it went towards the church, yard by yard weaving through the night. The light skirted the old monk's house as it journeyed along the donkey path. Then, in a shaft of moonlight, she saw the figure that carried it. The man was tall and wrapped in a dark cloak with a fedora hat. From the great distance this was all she could make out. He was too far away for her to shout, too far to be told to extinguish the flame. She looked again and he and the light had vanished.

'Stupid,' she muttered under her breath.

Mary Barnes shivered as she suddenly became aware of something or someone close by. It was the feeling most pure in childhood – that simple understanding of when all is not well. She edged slowly back towards the window of the apothecary's shop and leant against the glass. It was instinctive, the frightened action of a woman alone.

Then she heard the sound. First it came to her as a low, rumbling growl. It was like the moaning of an injured animal, a beast woken from painful sleep. The street was empty. She looked to the entrance of the yard before her. It was murder black, dark beyond dark. There, in the midst of the blackness, were what she thought were two staring red eyes. She could not be sure or see them clearly. But for that moment they were cold, sterile and without compassion. The eyes didn't move or stir or come closer. When she looked again, they were gone.

'Stupid,' she muttered again under her breath as she took the torch from her pocket and held it like a short staff. 'You'll be believing them, Mary . . .'

She knew the stories all too well. They had been told and retold for the last week. It was the conversation in every pub and on every street corner. They were spoken quietly, as if careless talk cost lives. There had been no mention in the *Gazette*. It reported the sinking of enemy ships, which family was digging for victory and the birth of Eric Strickland's two-headed chicken. What the newspaper said nothing about was the white, bloodless body that had been found in the river. The illicit rumour was that seven more blood-drained cadavers had been discovered – one every night that week. If it were true, they were all discovered below the high cliff, near to the churchyard. Each had a fearful look upon their face and a bloody puncture wound to their neck. But that was something that Mary Barnes didn't believe or, more truthfully, didn't want to believe.

She had heard nothing. There had been no cries in the night, nor had she seen anyone. Her fire watch had kept her to the west side of the river by the railway station, goods yard and hospital. Beyond the bridge were just the old houses. The fishermen's dwellings were stacked precariously one above the other, medieval cottages that climbed the hill in a myriad of narrow ginnels to the ruined abbey.

As she walked on, she put down the sight of the red eyes in the darkened alley to the work of her imagination. She had deceived herself many times in the dark and this was just once more.

'Stupid,' she said again, to reassure herself it was not a chimerical thought. 'Seeing things . . .'

Then came the footsteps. They struck the cobbles like cloven hooves. She turned and looked. From the shadows of Pilgrim's Yard came the voice of a man.

'No bombs tonight, Mary?' he asked slowly, as if he drank his words.

'New boots, Billy?' she replied as she looked at the clean hobnailed army boots.

He smiled. 'Just like sparking clogs,' he said as he leant against the wall to steady himself. 'I'm away in a week – got the call-up and glad to be going. Sent me the boots to wear them in. Can't be tramping through France in new boots – bad for the soul.' He laughed.

The young man walked on, staggering down the hill and singing to himself pleasantly. Mary thought he was now't but a lad – to young to go to war but too stupid not to. As she watched him go, the mist rolled in from the river, brought in by the tide.

'Straight home, Billy,' she shouted after him as he disappeared into the darkness.

'Home,' echoed his reply as the houses mimicked her call.

Then she heard the sound again. This time it was different. It stood up the hairs on the back of her head and shot a shivered hand down her spine.

'Who is it?' she asked as she shone the torch to the street behind her. There came the sound of a thousand voices, whispering, crying, calling her name. It was as if the darkness covered a crowd of people all speaking at once. 'You messing with me, Billy?' she shouted.

All was quiet but for the rush of the distant waves and the swirling of the wind above her head.

Reluctantly, Mary walked slowly on. She kept close to the windows of the shops and turned with every other step to look back. She cared not for the blackout. Her torch scanned the road in front of her and was shone into the opening of every alleyway and yard as she fought the desire to run.

She knew there was an all-night café by the Fishermen's Mission. It was next to the harbour. The windows had been boarded to keep in the light. There would be people there, fishermen, dockers and those who just could not sleep for fear of the war. Most of all, there would be someone to talk to and pass another hour of darkness with, hoping the night would be swiftly gone.

Taking the steps by the side of the cinema she dropped quickly from the street. The houses loomed above her as the stairs became a dark tunnel with just a flicker of grey in the distance. It was a dark short cut, one she would never usually take, but it was quick and the dreadful night would soon be over.

Mary could smell the sweet scent of fried fish and tea. It swept around her like a mistral wind and reminded her of home before the war. Three more steps and she would be away from the steps. All she had to do was cross the flagged yard of the Mission and turn the corner.

It was then she again heard the whispering. She shone the torch back up the steps. They rose like a jagged chimney up to the road above. The grey mist swirled in the light. Mary stared. For a moment she thought she could see a face. She shrugged her shoulders and the image was gone.

'Who is it – what are you doing?' she shouted, as if she was being tormented by her own mind. There was no reply.

Mary ran as she tried to cast off the darkness. She turned the corner past the old Mission. The door to the café was cracked open. A shaft of light flooded the street. Pushing it open, she was soon inside. The argon lamp that hung from a brass hook in the middle of the room burnt brightly. The café was full of men drinking beer and eating corn-fish. Mary saw one other woman by what used to be the window. She was looking out of a small hole cut in the wood. Unlike the others, she didn't stop to look at Mary when she came inside. She just smoothed the sides of her red dress as if to push away the creases.

'Seen a ghost?' asked the man behind the counter. 'The usual?'

Mary nodded as she took off her steel helmet, tightened the chequered headscarf and rested against the bar.

'All that talk of people being killed,' she said as she sipped at the hot barley milk that steamed in the thick glass. 'Gets you thinking someone *could* be out there.'

'No proof,' replied the man, as if he had heard the words a thousand times before. 'I was talking to one of the soldiers from the factory. He said that nothing had been found and the bodies were sailors washed up in the storm.'

When the factory had opened three weeks after war was declared, the town had changed. Several old railway sheds had been taken over on the far side of the harbour. The buildings had been clad in scaffolding and black tarps so they could no longer be seen. The factory had become a place of secrets. Workers were shipped in and kept in a camp on the open ground between the river and the wood below Hagg House.

A tall steel fence capped with barbed wire had been placed all around and even the water of the estuary had been covered so that no one could see what went on. It was called the factory because of the noise of the steam generator that started every morning before it got light. It would churn for twelve hours, gushing smoke out of a hastily built chimney, and then it would stop.

The factory was guarded by soldiers. A sign on the fence said that anyone entering illegally would be shot. Some people thought it was a place for germ warfare, either that or a base for submarines. It had to be something. In the woods behind were gun emplacements covered in spidery camouflage netting.

'I heard that,' Mary said in a whisper, hoping that no one would overhear. 'Didn't believe it. The bodies were on Tate Hill Sands the night the sea began to make all that noise.'

'It's like I said last night, Mary. Switch jobs – go work on a farm or something – it's not right you being out alone at night. Even if there is a war on.'

'Not that easy. Not since the factory opened. I don't have

the security clearance. My father was Irish – Free State. Don't want people like me working in a place like that.'

'Then stay here all night. Wash up – serve drinks – make breakfast. I'll look after you,' the man said as he touched the back of her hand. 'If you hear the bombs falling run out and catch them.'

Mary laughed. He was the one man who could make her do that.

'And what would Eddie say if he found out I was washing up for you and making breakfast?' she asked.

'Better me than the Devil out there snatching children from their beds and doing away with anyone he finds in the street. You know what happened the last time the red-eyed comet appeared.'

'That was a hundred years ago,' she replied.

'And what happened then is happening now.'

Somehow he didn't seem funny any more. Mary looked to the door as she drained the milk from the glass. The café was full of noise. Men talked loudly. The woman by the window was watching her as if she was trying to listen to everything Mary was saying. The brass clock that hung on the grease-stained wall behind the counter signalled eleven-thirty.

'Have to check the bridge. I'll be back before morning,' she said as she unwillingly put the glass down on the counter and looked back at the woman in the red dress. 'Keep the water hot.'

'Same . . .' said the voice as she closed the door behind her and stepped into the cold street.

Mary glanced back at the boarded-up window. It was covered in torn war posters with frayed edges that flapped in the breeze. A fat man in a polka-dot bow tie stared grimly. He pointed his finger and demanded *Deserve Victory* – whatever that meant. She noticed a chink of light in the far corner just above his head. She looked up. From inside, the woman's eye followed her along the street as she walked towards the harbour.

When she reached the Esk River, she stood for a while holding on to the metal railings and looked down to the two gigantic piers that stretched out to sea. Floating on the incoming tide was a veneer of mist. It grew in depth and thickness as it reached the bridge. There, it swirled darkly over the peat-brown water and rose up in spirals that twisted like figures dancing along the iron stanchions. Mary set off and walked slowly into the mist that spilled across the quayside and shone blue in the moonlight. The fog filled the empty street to the height of her waist and had thickened even more by the time she had reached the bridge.

As usual, she took out her notepad and looked up to the sky as she wrote '*All Clear*'. It had been the same every night she had been a warden.

Midnight on Whitby Bridge.

Check for aircraft.

Complete pocket book.

Return to point.

As she wrote, an old Daimler coupé broke her concentration as it crawled slowly through the fog. The haar-fret covered most of the car, leaving just the windscreen eerily above the mist. Silently, the car slowed as it went by. Mary looked at the sombre chauffeur in his grey coat and hat. There was an old man in the back seat. He covered his face with his hand as they drove by. It looked deliberate, as if he didn't want to be seen. She made another note in her pocket book: 'Car on bridge – nothing else to report.'

It was then that she heard the sound of someone running. The footsteps clattered in the empty street. Coming towards her along the quayside was the woman in the red dress. With every pace, the woman looked back. It was as if she knew she was being followed. Their eyes met.

'He's there!' the woman shouted. 'I saw him in Calvert's Yard.'

'There's no one,' Mary said as the woman ran towards her through the veil of mist. 'You're alone.'

'No,' said the woman as she grasped Mary's arm. 'I saw him. I came out of the café to speak to you – but you'd gone. There is something you should know. I waited and had a ciga-rette and then I saw him. He was in the shadows looking at me. I couldn't go back. He was between me and the door.'

'Who was he?' asked Mary as she looked back along the empty street.

'Just a man. He was hunched over as if he was sick. It was his eyes – they were . . .'

Her voice was sharp. The woman in the red dress didn't finish what she was going to say. Mary was staring into the fog.

'Is that him?' she asked as she pointed through the mist.

The woman turned and looked. There, coming towards them, sauntering along the empty street, was the dark figure of a man. He kept close to the walls of the buildings along the quayside. His long black coat trailed behind him and for a moment Mary could see him sniffing the air like a dog.

'You have to know,' the woman said to Mary urgently. 'It is true about the bodies. I saw them myself. I work for the morgue. We were told to say nothing.'

'But who were they?' Mary asked quickly as the man leant against the wall by a lamp post.

'They were from the factory, all of them,' she whispered, a look of fear on her face.

'But what of the . . .' Mary didn't have time to finish. The man was running towards them with a knife in his hand. 'Run!'

Before the woman could even scream, the man was upon them. He smashed Mary to the floor with a single blow. Then he picked the woman up and threw her into the river as she kicked and screamed. Mary lashed out with the steel flash lamp, striking the man as hard as she could. She got to her feet and ran towards the police box across the bridge. The woman in the red dress was in the river screaming for help. Mary knew she had to escape. She looked back. The man was gone. She was alone. The screaming had stopped and the water was still beneath the bridge.

'EDDIE!' she shouted in fearful prayer as she gripped the door handle of the police box. It was soothing and cool in her hand but it wouldn't open. The door was jammed shut. Mary heard footsteps. They echoed along Sandside Row. She ran again, hoping to make the door of her small, meagre house on Church Street just a hundred yards away. She knew the door would be open. Mary had left it so since her husband had gone to war. It was in case he ever escaped the fighting and came back unannounced. She held the image of his face in her mind as she ran. The footsteps followed, keeping pace with hers. Mary looked back. The man was there, the tails of his long black coat billowing out like a raven's wings.

Mary ran faster, banging on the doors of houses as she went by. No one stirred. It was as if they were charmed in their sleeping. The man made no attempt to catch her. He ran at the same pace, as if he was waiting for the right place to strike or for Mary to give up the fight. His feet made no sound as he skipped across the cobbled stones.

'Biatra . . . Biatra,' Mary sobbed for her daughter as she got close to the house. She clutched the brass handle as if it were sanctuary. The man was nowhere to be seen. The street was empty. 'Biatra,' she said again.

'She can't hear you,' said a soft voice from the darkness of Arguments Yard.

'It's you?' Mary replied slowly, as if she recognised the man.

She sighed and said no more. His hand gripped her throat and dragged her to the floor as he covered her with his long black coat.

In the churchyard the wind blew and masked the screams from below.

'Should do for now,' said Jack Henson as he finished his digging and scraped the clinging earth from the spade with his boot. 'See how long it takes to fill this one.' He climbed the wooden ladder with the spade over his shoulder and stood for a moment over the empty pit. 'Not fair on you, Maria Barnes – not fair on your lass.' Henson looked above his head to the red-eyed comet. 'All this for your sake?' he asked the star in his melancholy.